ID0590842

STRANGE BEDFELLOWS

Strange Bedfellows

Herbert Burkholz

HEADLINE

First published in Great Britain in 1988 by
HEADLINE BOOK PUBLISHING PLC

British Library Cataloguing in Publication Data

Burkholz, Herbert, *1932*–
Strange bedfellows.
I. Title
813'.54[F]

ISBN 0–7472–0091–2

Typeset on 11/12 pt English Times
by Colset Pte Ltd, Singapore

Printed and bound in Great Britain by
Richard Clay Ltd, Bungay, Suffolk

HEADLINE BOOK PUBLISHING PLC
Headline House
79 Great Titchfield Street
London WIP 7FN

For
Dick Gardener
and for
Steve DiLauro

Misery acquaints a man with strange bedfellows . . .
The Tempest

ONE
Saturday

**USA and USSR in Joint Address on Disarmament
Surprise Move at UN**

United Nations, Sept. 17. The United States and the Soviet
Union announced today that the President of the United
States and General Secretary Gorbachev will jointly address
the opening session of the United Nations General Assembly
when it convenes here on Monday. The two leaders will share
the rostrum and issue a joint statement on the subject of
nuclear disarmament and arms control.

The announcement of the unprecedented dual appearance
by the President and the General Secretary was made simulta-
neously by the White House and the Kremlin this morning.
Neither the President nor Mr Gorbachev had been scheduled
to speak before the Assembly, and their joint request, which
stunned the diplomatic community here, was made only yes-
terday to General Assembly President Mario Cortenyu.
Mr Cortenyu at once announced that the request would be
honoured.

While the statement to be made by the two leaders remains a
closely guarded secret, informed observers in Washington
believe that it can signal nothing less than a major break-
through in the ongoing negotiations over nuclear disarmament
and arms control.

'Coming after the failures at Reykjavik and Vienna,' said
Sen. Richard Pauling (R), Vermont, 'there is a feeling on
Capitol Hill that this is the real thing. The missile systems,
strategic arms, the whole ball of wax. The world may well be a
different, and far better, place to live in after Monday.'

Said Sen. John Gimenski (D), Mich., 'It seems clear that

1

what we have here is a classic case of one-on-one negotiations between the two leaders, done outside the normal channels of diplomatic procedure. I'm normally not in favour of this sort of "back-channel" diplomacy, but if it works this time I'll have no complaints.'

The same air of secrecy, and of muted optimism, prevailed in Moscow today as the General Secretary and a small entourage departed for New York. Mr Gorbachev is expected to arrive here on Sunday, and proceed to the Soviet Mission to the United Nations on East Sixty-seventh Street, where he will stay until his joint appearance with the President before the General Assembly on Monday.

In London, reaction to the announcement. . . .

TWO
Sunday 11:55 AM

'Gin,' I said.

'Shit,' said the FBI.

I laid down my cards. The Bureau guy was tall, and lean, and sour. His name was Ritter, and he didn't like me. People like me made him nervous. He looked at my cards, looked at his own, and slammed them down on the table.

'Twenty-four.'

'Spades double.' I wrote down the score; it put me out on the first game. I pushed the cards toward him. 'Your deal.'

'Screw that.' He let the cards lie. He didn't like sensitives, and he didn't like losing, either. He looked out of the window. DeKalb was in the building across the street. He said, 'I wish the son of a bitch would show his face.'

'He'll come out. He has to.'

'He doesn't have to do zilch. He could stay in there all day.'

'He'll show. He has to make a move.'

'How do you know?' Ritter's voice was high and nasty. 'You got a feeling? You got an intuition?'

I let it ride. I was used to comments like that. It was exactly the sort of thing that someone like Ritter would say to a sensitive. All I said was, 'Fifty bucks says that he comes out inside an hour.'

'You're on for five. I don't make your kind of money.'

He was right about that, which was why we were playing gin rummy for peanuts. We were on a plant in the back room of a tailor shop on Columbus Avenue with a clear view of DeKalb's rooming house on Eightieth Street. We had been on the plant since early morning, it was just before noon on a September Sunday, and gin was a way to deal with the time. We were playing for peanuts, but after three hours he owed me

3

over two hundred dollars. I was cheating, of course, reading his head to see what cards he was holding. He didn't know that, but he should have. He had worked with sensitives before.

The pigeon we were waiting for, Richard DeKalb, was a colonel in the Air Force, and he had been on the run for a week. He had left his home in suburban New Jersey heading for his office in Manhattan, and he never had arrived. His office pushed the buttons, and bells began to ring. DeKalb was more than an ordinary colonel, he was a senior desk man at the Defense Intelligence Agency, the umbrella group that services all three branches of the military, and people like that are not allowed to drop out of sight. The DIA brought the FBI into it, and the Bureau turned him up in six days. The colonel could run from his suburban home, his cars, his golf club, his wife, and his teenage daughter, but not from a woman he had stashed in an apartment on the Upper East Side. Her name was Kathy Benton, and the DIA had a file on her. DeKalb showed up at her place on Saturday afternoon, and when he left there he was followed to a rooming house on West Eightieth Street near Columbus. The Bureau people could have grabbed him then, but they didn't. At that point both they and the DIA wanted to run him for a while, see where he was heading. That's when they called us in. They wanted us to pump his head.

Ritter picked up the cards, shuffled, and dealt. I looked at mine, and then went into his head to see what he was holding. A short run in hearts, a pair of nines, and nothing else. While I was in his head, I poked around. I don't usually do that. When you spend as much time as I do inside other people's heads, you learn to get what you need and get out quickly. There are fires in there that burn deep. But I stayed for a moment with Ritter, examining his hostility to me. I was strange, I was different, and I could do things that frightened him. And so he hated me. I didn't much blame him. In his shoes I might have felt the same.

'Knock with three,' said Ritter.

He had bought three cards in a row, and he picked up a few points. Even the way I play, you don't win them all. I dealt, and listened to the radio going in the front of the tailor shop.

4

The news was all Gorbachev; it had been that way for twenty-four hours. The latest was that he was *en route* to New York and would arrive at Kennedy shortly. That shot my day completely. The United Nations was my regular assignment, and where I should have been for the opening of the General Assembly. Instead, I was teamed up with a Bureau guy who hated sensitives, on a plant that was probably a waste of time.

DeKalb had surfaced on Saturday, the day before, and by Saturday night they had brought the Centre into the job. None of us at the Centre wanted any part of it. It wasn't a job for sensitives, but we were stuck with it anyway. Sammy Warsaw called us together to tell us about it. Sammy was the new boss, running the Centre now that Pop was dead, but he had been one of us once. He knew it was a rotten assignment, but he had no choice. The Agency wanted it done, and the Agency owned us. Theirs was the only organization that could afford to pick up the tab for the Centre in Virginia where all of the ace sensitives were raised from childhood and trained. It was the same with the Russian sensitives and the KGB, the British sensitives and SIS, the Israeli sensitives and Mossad. Wherever there were sensitives, and that was everywhere, the senior intelligence organization of the country owned them and ran them.

'We're going up to New York tonight,' Sammy had told us. 'You'll be on loan to the DIA, but I'll still be running you.'

There were groans in the room at the idea of working with the Defense Intelligence Agency. We were owned by the CIA and, I suppose, we had absorbed some of their prejudices about military intelligence. It was more than the usual civilian versus military conflict. The problem with working with the DIA was that the field of intelligence-gathering was not the way to the top in the military, and so the best and the brightest stayed away from it. Also, the military policy of frequent rotation meant that an officer handling intelligence this week might have been running a motor pool the week before.

'The DIA,' Sammy repeated firmly, cutting through the groans. 'DeKalb is their pigeon and you'll have to work with them, and with the Bureau. They want an Alpha tap on DeKalb. They want everything you can find in his head.'

'While he's loose?' I asked.

5

'That's right.'

'Almost impossible.'

'Tell me something I don't know.' Sammy pulled a face of disgust. His beaky nose, frizzy hair, and batwing ears made it look comical. 'As usual, they want miracles.'

They always did. Most people knew nothing at all about sensitives, and we preferred it that way. But those who did know about us . . . a selected few at the Agency, the Bureau, State, Defense, and the White House . . . had an exaggerated idea of what we could accomplish. If you listened to some of those people they'd have you believing that an ace sensitive could read minds in the Kremlin from a thousand miles away, lift a two-ton truck by sheer willpower, or think himself from Kansas City to New York in the blink of an eye. It was all nonsense, born out of ignorance. A sensitive, because of his neurological imbalance, was highly receptive to the thoughts and emotions of others. He could hear those thoughts as if they were spoken. That was all that he or she could do, and it could only be done within a range of two hundred feet at the most. That was the problem with the DeKalb job. They wanted an Alpha tap, everything in his head. If they could have put me in a room with him for half an hour, I could have pumped him dry. But they wanted him loose and unaware, and that made it almost impossible.

Sammy looked around, inviting comment. There were four of us sitting in his office: Martha, Vince, myself, and Claudia, whom we all called Snake. The Snake jumped in first.

'Sammy, who ever heard of an Alpha tap on somebody who's loose?' she asked, her voice hard and cold. 'What are we supposed to do with this pigeon? Take him to lunch and pump him while he's eating his soup? Why can't they bring him in?'

'Because they don't want to,' Sammy said patiently. 'They want him on the street for a while.'

'I can understand that part of it,' said Martha in a gentle voice. She did everything gently. As much as Snake was lean and whippy, Martha was full-bodied and soft, everyone's Earth Mother. 'So he has to stay loose, but why put us on it? We're the senior team. With this Gorbachev thing breaking, I thought that we'd all be at the UN.'

Vince stretched his legs, and yawned. His ebony skin glistened under the fluorescent lights. When he stretched, his chair creaked. He was built like an NFL linebacker. 'I was sort of looking forward to the UN myself,' he said. 'Party time. Look, Sammy, why do you need all four of us? It isn't gonna work, but say that it does. One of us is enough to do an Alpha tap.'

Sammy nodded. He looked at me. 'Ben? Anything to add?'

'Yeah, all of the above plus one thing more. You're holding out on us. What is it?'

Sammy stood up, and walked to the window. From there he could see the Centre laid out before him, surrounded by the security fence. Outside the fence was Agency country, the squat and functional buildings of the barracks and the motor pool set against the rolling Virginia countryside. On our side of the fence were the fieldstone and ivy-covered structures of the Centre: the living quarters for the aces and the instructors, the mess hall and lounge, the long, low block of the hospital and research complex, the athletic fields and swimming pools. The place looked more like a small-town college than anything else, and with good reason. The sign on the gate read *The Federal Centre for the Study of Childhood Diseases*, but that was a fiction to discourage the curious. The Centre existed for only one purpose, the training of sensitives. Right now there were about seventy kids in training, ranging in age from twelve to twenty, and there were one hundred and eleven other aces on assignment all over the world, some with diplomatic or commercial covers, others buried deep in covert operations. Sammy was responsible for all of them. It was a job he had never wanted.

Without turning from the window, he said, 'Tune in on me.'

He wanted us in his head, all of us. He wanted us to see what he was seeing, through his eyes. We went in, and saw the Centre spread out before us. He was showing us our home. It was the only true home we had ever had. Before the Centre, for all of us, there had only been madness. He showed us that, too, reminding us of how it had been in the beginning, in the year when the Centre had found us.

The Centre had found Martha Marino in a home for retarded children in Omaha. She had been there for a year. She

7

heard voices in her head that no one else could hear. When she heard the voices she went wild. She screamed for hours, she clawed her body, she soiled herself. When the Centre found her she was under constant restraint and sedation. She was twelve years old.

The Centre had found Vince Bonepart in a drug-abuse clinic in Boston. Vince also heard the voices. His parents had abandoned him when he was seven, and after that he had lived in the streets and in the odd corners of the city. He learned from his elders how to steal and how to shoot smack. The smack kept the voices quiet. When the Centre found him he had been placed in a drug-withdrawal facility, and the voices were back and filling his head with their howls. He was twelve years old.

The Centre had found Claudia Wing in a religious commune in Idaho. The members of the group worshipped snakes. They also worshipped Claudia. When Claudia heard the voices she went into a trance and made hissing noises. That, to the members of the commune, made her a part of the godhead, a higher form of snake. They kept her in a cage and fed her what the snakes ate. When the Centre found her she had not spoken a word in months, and she moved by slithering across the floor on her belly. She was twelve years old.

The Centre had found Sammy Warsaw in an expensive sanitorium north of New York City. His parents had placed him there. He was catatonic, incapable of voluntary movement. He could not speak, and his limbs remained fixed in whatever position they were placed. His eyes stared straight ahead, unblinking. He had been that way since he first heard the voices. He was twelve years old.

The Centre had found me, Ben Slade, locked in the back bedroom of a shack in Freeman Texas, just south of the Oklahoma line. The room had a bed, a chair, and a slop bucket. I was chained to the bed, and I was naked. My body was covered with old scars and fresh welts. The man I called my daddy said that the voices I heard were the tongues of the devil. He was a shade-tree mechanic and a part-time preacher, and he knew about devils. At the end of each day he whipped the devil out of me with a razor strop, and then prayed for my deliverance. When the Centre found me I could not stand or sit, and my body was a festering wound. I was twelve years old.

8

That's what we were, my generation at the Center. Other generations, before us and after, came from the same sort of background: the abused, the imprisoned, the seemingly mad. The ones who heard the voices in their heads. The Centre took us in, nurtured us, healed us, and taught us how to live with the voices. Each year a few more sensitives were found as they came to puberty, and were brought into the Centre. Not all developed into aces; some were deuces who dropped by the way. But those who stayed were bound together within each year group by ties far stronger than any family could forge. The five of us had been together since we were twelve, and now we were thirty-five. There was nothing that we did not know about each other, and we had placed our lives in each other's hands more times than we could remember. We were more than brothers and sisters. We were one.

Sammy showed us that. He was the boss now, but the bonds still held. He turned from the window, and looked at me. His voice was light and mocking. 'Do you still think I'm holding out on you, *tus*?' He used the Russian word for ace. We all used it.

'No,' I said, 'but somebody is.'

Sammy nodded.

'Delaney,' said Vince. 'Has to be.'

'That shit,' said Snake.

Sammy nodded again. Delaney was Agency, the Deputy Director for Science and Technology. He controlled our finances, our security, and our assignments. He owned us. He was not a popular person.

'The orders for the Alpha tap came directly from Delaney,' said Sammy, 'and I agree with you all. They don't make sense. DeKalb obviously hasn't been abducted, and he hasn't defected or he'd be gone by now. So why not pull him in and pump him? Delaney doesn't want it that way. He wants to run the pigeon and tap him on the run. As I said, it doesn't make sense.'

Martha said, 'So Delaney is holding out.'

Sammy nodded. 'DeKalb is hot, hotter than Delaney is willing to admit. I don't know why, but there it is. I can't turn down the assignment, all I can do is use my best people, which is why you won't be partying at the UN tomorrow. I need all

9

four of you on this. Aside from the Alpha on DeKalb, I need three Delta taps.'

'On who?'

'His wife, his daughter, and his girlfriend.'

More groans, heavy ones this time. An Alpha tap was relatively simple once you got the subject to hold still. You went into his head and took everything you could find. A Delta tap required fine tuning. You went in looking for information on someone else, a profile of personality. Sammy wanted to know what the women in DeKalb's life thought about him in terms of the classic Delta triad: personal, political, security. It was a messy job, sifting mental garbage.

'I want a deep Delta on all three of them,' said Sammy. 'I want to know how he rings their bells.' He smiled. 'Vince, you've got the wife. Paula DeKalb, age forty-three, lives in a place called Apple Valley, New Jersey.'

Vince looked pained. 'Shit, Sammy, not again.' Sammy had a theory about Vince. He was convinced that the man was unbeatable when it came to working on older women, that any woman over forty automatically melted at the sight of him and opened up in every way possible. 'God damn, it's downright degrading. Let someone else take her.'

'No way, *tus*, she's yours. Snake, you've got the daughter, name of Laura.'

'I'll trade with Vince if he wants to.'

'No trades. Martha, I want you to take the girlfriend. Her name is Kathy Benton and she's twenty-four, more than twenty years younger than DeKalb. She's been involved with him for about a year.'

'Involved?' asked Martha.

'He screws her on Tuesdays and Saturdays.'

Martha wrinkled her nose, but nodded.

Sammy looked at me. 'That leaves you, Ben. You've got the Alpha tap on DeKalb.'

'As usual. The others get a piece of cake, and I get the impossible dream.'

'Doing a Delta is no piece of cake. I'd take DeKalb myself, but I'm not operational any more. I'll be coordinating the four of you from the Manhattan house.'

'This coordinating, does it involve any manual labour,

10

Sammy? I wouldn't want you to strain yourself.'

'I think I can handle it, *tus*, and let's have a little respect for your elders.'

They all laughed, family laughter. They had been handing me that one since the days when we were kids. We were all within a year of same age, thirty-five, but Sammy was the eldest, then Snake, Vince, Martha, and me. I was the youngest by less than a month, and because of that for twenty-three years I had always been the one who got up before sunrise to milk the cows.

Which was why, on that September Sunday, I was the one sitting in the back of the tailor shop on Columbus Avenue waiting for DeKalb to show his face, and playing gin with an FBI man who was too slow to realize what I was doing to him. I looked at my watch. It was just after twelve, plenty of time for the pigeon to make a move. All I could hope for was that he would head for a restaurant, or a movie, or a park where I could get up close to him and go to work.

I went gin twice in succession, enough to put me out on the second and third games. I added up the damage. I was into Ritter for over three hundred. He looked at the scoresheet unhappily.

'I'll have to give you a cheque,' he said.

'Forget it.' I tore the paper in half, and crumpled it. 'Chalk it up to experience.'

His face froze. He said stiffly, 'What's that supposed to mean? I pay my debts.'

'Here's what if means.' I picked up the deck and dealt him five cards. 'Look at them.'

He hesitated, then picked up the cards, and looked. I went into his head. 'You're holding the queen of diamonds, the nine of clubs, two of spades, four of spades, and the four of hearts.'

He stared at me. 'You son of a bitch.'

I shrugged. Bureau people, very low on humour. He started to say something else, but I held up my hand. My eyes were on the building across the street. DeKalb stood in the doorway. He was wearing faded chinos and a light nylon windcheater. He looked up and down the street, squinting his eyes against the sun.

'He's out,' I said. 'You owe me five.'

Ritter swivelled around, looked, and then we were both on

11

our feet, moving out of the shop and onto the street. There was a Bureau car, the usual plain black Chevy, parked in front of a fire hydrant. We slipped into the back seat.

Ritter said to the driver, 'He's moving toward the avenue.'

DeKalb came up to the corner and looked around for a cab. There were plenty of them cruising down Columbus at that hour on a Sunday. He hailed one, went south a block, turned east to Central Park West, then north, then east again into the Eighty-first Street transverse through the park. We followed behind on a loose tail. Ritter handed me a five-dollar bill. He paid his debts.

'Patch me into my people,' I said.

He leaned over the front seat, pushed buttons on the dashboard, and gave me the hand mike. The speaker up front crackled.

'Sammy?' I asked.

'Yeah.' He was working out of our New York house, a brownstone on East Sixty-fourth Street. He called it coordinating; I called it loafing. 'Ben, that you?'

'Yeah, our pigeon is flying.' I described the situation. 'Any orders, coach?'

'Same as before. Get up close and tap him.'

'Right, tap a man in a moving taxi. You call that an order? I call it a fantasy.'

'Take it easy. Any idea where he's heading?'

'I figure Minneapolis. Or maybe Kansas City.'

'Be serious.'

'How the hell would I know where he's heading? You think I'm some kind of a mind reader?'

'Just stay close and move in when you can. He has to stop someplace; you'll get a crack at him.'

'Sammy, I told this to the captain of the *Titanic*, I told it to Edsel Ford, and I'm telling it to you. There's a lot of failure going around these days.'

'Give it your best shot.'

'Are you comfortable? Do you have your shoes off? I worry about you, *tus*, you work too hard.'

'Go get him, tiger.'

A crackle and a click, and he was gone. Ritter looked at me

strangely, and said, 'That is without a doubt the worst radio procedure I have ever heard.'

'You mean Roger Wilco, over and out, stuff like that?'

He nodded.

'We tried that once, but it didn't work. Everybody laughed.'

We followed DeKalb's taxi crosstown to the FDR Drive, up to the Triboro Bridge, and over to Queens on the Grand Central Parkway. The taxi left the parkway at the Flushing exit, rolled down Roosevelt Avenue, and only then did I realize where DeKalb was heading. I punched in Sammy again.

'Yeah, Ben.'

'We're outside Shea Stadium. He's going to the ballgame.'

'Who's playing?'

'The Mets and the Pirates. Gooden is pitching.'

'Now maybe you'll stop complaining about your assignments.'

THREE
Sunday 12:27 PM

'The blue pinstripe, Mikhail Sergeyvich. I assure you it is the proper choice. In fact, it is the only choice.'

'Then, by definition, it is no choice at all,' said the General Secretary of the Central Committee of the Communist Party of the Soviet Union. 'Frankly, I'm bored to tears with wearing blue, always blue. What's wrong with wearing the plaid?'

'Everything. It is entirely inappropriate for the occasion,' said his valet.

'What occasion? A few minutes in front of the television cameras. I'll be wearing the suit for less than an hour.'

'So, the General Secretary wishes to appear on American television looking like a Caucasian fruit pedlar. Very well, so be it.'

'Fruit pedlar? Anatoli, do you know how much that fabric cost in London?'

'Fruit pedlar,' Anatoli repeated firmly. 'When did you ever see the American president wearing a plaid suit at an official function?'

'He does know how to dress,' Gorbachev conceded. 'I suppose it goes with being an actor.'

'Then you'll wear the blue?'

'Don't bully me, Anatoli. I won't be bullied.'

'I am merely trying to perform my duties properly. If that is bullying, then so be it.'

Gorbachev sighed, and turned his head to look out of the cabin window. The sky was clear in all directions, and far below his Aeroflot jet . . . the Soviet equivalent of Air Force One . . . the expanse of northern Canada was an unbroken sheet of white. It could be Siberia, he thought, and turned back to his valet. The short, squat, balding Anatoli returned his gaze without flinching. Over one of his arms was draped the jacket of a blue pinstripe suit, and over the other was a jacket made of tartan cloth.

'With all respect,' said the valet, 'a prompt decision is called for. We are due in New York in less than two hours, and I must sponge and press one of these before the arrival.'

Gorbachev stroked his chin thoughtfully. 'If I wear the blue pinstripe for the arrival, then what do I wear tomorrow when I speak to the General Assembly?'

'The solid blue, of course.'

'Again, blue.'

'This cannot be helped, Mikhail Sergeyvich. Please, we have had this same discussion many times before. Try to think of your clothing the way a soldier thinks of his uniform. You have little choice in the matter.'

Gorbachev stood up abruptly. He was dressed in a maroon tracksuit and running shoes. The name *Dynamo*, Moscow's football team, was picked out in crimson letters across the back of the jersey. He began to pace up and down the cabin, which formed the rear third of the aircraft. Beyond the cabin bulkhead, in the front section, sat the General Secretary's travelling secretariat, together with various dignitaries, and representatives of *Tass, Izvestia*, and Soviet television. The rear cabin was furnished simply, but comfortably, with rust-coloured carpeting, deep chairs bolted to the deck, a sleeping section, and a long table of the conference-room style. Two of Gorbachev's close associates sat at the table watching the byplay between master and valet. One was Eduard Shevardnadze, Foreign Minister of the Soviet Union, and the other was Yegor Ligachev, chief party ideologist and number two man in the Kremlin. Gorbachev stopped his pacing, and turned to face them.

'Well, what do I have advisers for?' he asked. 'Do I hear an opinion from either of you?'

'The blue,' said Shevardnadze promptly.

'Yegor Kuzmich?'

Ligachev shrugged his bull-like shoulders. Thick strands of grey hair stuck up over his horn-rimmed glasses. He looked bored. 'What you wear is a matter of indifference to me,

Mikhail Sergeyvich. More important, may we please discuss the matter of General Shvabrin?'

'What about him?'

'He's waiting to see you.'

'Let him wait. First, your opinion, the blue or the plaid?'

Ligachev's lips tightened. 'Very well, the blue.'

'A conspiracy,' said Gorbachev. 'Yegor Kuzmich, I forgive you. After all, what could a Siberian know about style? But you, Eduard Ambrosievich, I expected better taste from a sophisticated Georgian.'

Shevardnadze laughed. The General Secretary's preoccupation with clothing was an old joke to him. Gorbachev turned to the only other man in the room, the KGB head of his personal security detail. Boris Prokoroff stood with his back against the cabin door, his face impassive.

'Well,' said Gorbachev, 'what do you think?'

Only Prokoroff's lips moved. 'With the General Secretary's permission, I think it would be improper for me to have an opinion in this matter.'

'No, no, you are entitled to your opinion, although it might be improper for you to voice it. All right, I won't force it. My God, I wish that Raisa were here. She'd tell me what to do.'

'Will someone please tell *me* what to do?' complained Anatoli. 'A decision, please.'

'The plaid,' said Gorbachev, and flung himself back in his chair. 'The plaid, and no arguments.'

Anatoli said icily, 'Indeed. And perhaps the General Secretary would care for a kerchief to tie around his neck?'

'I said no arguments. The decision is made.'

Anatoli inclined his head, and retreated to the alcove at the rear of the cabin that was his domain.

Shevardnadze said, 'A wise decision, Mikhail Sergeyvich. Truly statesmanlike.'

Gorbachev grinned at him. 'What a trimmer you are, what an *apparatchik*. You voted for the blue.'

'Did I? Then I wish to revise my vote. I wish to be historically correct.'

'What about you, Yegor Kuzmich. Do you also wish to revise?'

Ligachev shook his head shortly, tossing his shoulders like

16

an impatient bull. 'Enough, please. What about General Shvabrin? He has asked three times to see you, and now he is out there in front boiling like a pot of *borshch moskovskaia*. Will you speak with him?'

Gorbachev shook his head.

'May I remind you that it is only because of your permission that he is on this aircraft at all?'

Shevardnadze said softly, 'We agreed that there would be no military on this mission. Civilians only, that was the understanding. And then at the last minute you approved his request to come along.'

'Request,' Ligachev snorted. 'It was more like a plea.'

'It *was* a plea,' said Gorbachev, 'and I approved it. What else could I do? I've known the man since childhood. He is my oldest friend.'

'And now you refuse to see this friend?'

'It was enough that I approved his request. I do not have to see him.'

'And why do you think he wanted to come along? To go shopping at Bloomingdales?'

'No, I know what he wants. We all know that.'

'Still, you must see him,' said Shevardnadze. 'You can't ignore the man.'

'Why not?' snapped Gorbachev. 'What purpose will it serve? We know what he is going to say, and we know what our reply will be. Why bother to go through the charade?'

'Why do we go through any of these routines that are forced on us?' said Ligachev. 'Shvabrin may be your oldest friend, but he is also the personal representative of the Army Chief of Staff. You must give him the courtesy of a hearing.'

Gorbachev looked inquiringly at Shevardnadze, who nodded, and said, 'I have to agree. You should never have allowed him to attach himself to this mission, but since you have you must see him. I am afraid that this is one of those times when you must wear the blue suit, like it or not.'

Gorbachev was silent for a long moment, then said, 'I suppose I must.' He motioned to Prokoroff. 'Tell General Shvabrin that I will see him now.'

FOUR
Sunday 1:07 PM

Vince Bonepart felt distinctly uncomfortable as he parked his car in front of DeKalb's home in Apple Valley, New Jersey. He looked over the house and the street. Quiet surburbia. Neat lawns and hedges, well-paved roads, houses in a variety of architectural styles, geometrical flower beds, and discreet ornamentation. No pink flamingos in Apple Valley. The street was on the upscale side, a touch heavy for an Air Force officer with no source of income other then his pay. Vince registered the thought, then dismissed it. His job was to record, not to analyse. He looked around again, still uncomfortable and reluctant to get going.

His discomfort stemmed from two reasons. One was the uniform he was wearing. It was Air Force blue with a major's insignia, and he knew that it looked well on him, but anything to do with the military made him itchy. He had worn uniform before as part of a cover, but he had never adapted to the idea. He was the ultimate civilian. Also discomforting was the knowledge of why Sammy had picked him to tap DeKalb's wife. There was a certain amount of truth in Sammy's theory about Vince and older women; indeed there was a great amount of truth in it, but Vince preferred not to see himself that way. He knew himself as a man of delicacy and discrimination, a man capable of profound and lasting relationships, and not just a hunk who specialized in knocking over middle-aged broads. In particular, he resented being classified as that most conventional creature of his times, the black superstud. But there it was, Paula DeKalb was forty-three, and he had drawn the obvious assignment.

He grunted, half a sigh, as he levered himself out of the car, and started up the driveway to the front door. He was almost there when it opened. A woman and a girl stood framed in it. Vince's discomfort factor jumped another notch. Paula DeKalb was listed in the files as being forty-three, but she looked a decade younger with a smooth oval face, long dark hair, and a slim body cased in jeans and a jersey. The girl had to be the daughter. She was a skinny seventeen, with a sullen face.

'I'll be back when I feel like it,' she was saying.

'That's not good enough,' said her mother.

'It'll have to do.' The girl turned away and came jogging down the driveway towards the garage. She brushed past Vince.

'Laura, you come back here,' called her mother, and when she didn't get an answer, added, 'Take the Buick. I don't want you using the Porsche.' There was still no answer. The mother's face changed as Vince approached.

'Yes,' she said coolly.

'Good afternoon, I'm Major Bonepart. About your husband.'

'Another one. You're the fourth so far.'

'I've been assigned to follow up on the case. I hope I'm expected.'

'You're expected.' Her eyes met his. 'Somebody named Warsaw called to say that you'd be here.'

He went into the woman's head. She was thinking, *But he didn't say that you'd be so big, black, and beautiful.* God damn that Sammy, he thought, this is one time I keep a grip.

An engine roared. The DeKalb daughter backed a silver Porsche out of the garage and sent it spinning down the driveway.

'Christ,' said Paula DeKalb. 'You got any kids?'

'No.'

'Want to buy one cheap?'

Vince grinned, and shook his head. 'If I ever want one, I'll roll my own.'

She grinned back. 'I bet you will. Come on in.'

She turned and walked away from him. She walked with a pronounced limp. She led him into a sitting room with a bar set in one corner. She went to the bar and splashed vodka into a glass filled with ice.

'That child will drive me to drink,' she said over her shoulder. 'Not that I need much driving. That's mostly what I've been doing since Dick left.'

'Left?'

'You want to say that he disappeared? Call it whatever you like, but as far as I'm concerned he left. He skipped. He scrammed. He cut out.'

'Yes, and we have to find out why,' Vince said slowly. He did a quick scoop of her head to establish basics. She did not know that her husband had been spotted, and she did not know the name Kathy Benton.

'Why? I'll tell you why?' She tossed her head angrily. 'Look, let me give you a tip. I told it to the others and I'll tell it to you. Don't make a federal case out of Dick DeKalb. He hasn't defected and he hasn't been abducted. He's just off chasing a new piece of tail, that's all.'

'This has happened before?'

'More times than I can count.' She turned to face him, leaning back against the bar with her elbows on it.

She's practised that, thought Vince. Standing that way, you can't tell that one leg is shorter than the other. He said, 'But he's never dropped out of sight like this before.'

'No, I'll give him that much. This is the first time he's gone all the way. But he'll be back, I promise you that. Dick always comes back.' She took a sip of her drink. 'Shoot, where are my manners? What'll you have?'

'Thanks, but not while I'm working.'

'Balls.' Her grin was back. 'I've been an Air Force wife for twenty years, so don't tell me about not drinking on duty.'

'Bourbon, one rock.'

She made the drink, and held it out to him, making him come for it. He took it from her.

'Cheers,' she said. 'Here's to my wandering husband, the prick.'

FIVE

Sunday 1:34 PM

It was a good game for the first three innings if you were a Mets fan. At the end of three the Mets led the Pirates two-zero. I didn't see much of the game. I still don't know what the final score was.

During those three innings I didn't score any better than the Pirates did. DeKalb had a seat in section ten behind third base, and there was no way that I could get close to him. The stadium was packed for a Sunday afternoon game with the Mets in the heat of a pennant race, and every seat in the section was taken. The closest that Ritter and I could get was enough to keep the pigeon in sight, but not enough to tune in on him. Theoretically, he wasn't out of range, but I was bucking against the mental static put out by forty-five thousand charged up baseball fans, and the odds against picking out DeKalb's head were astronomical. So we kept him in sight, watched Gooden knock the Pirates over, and every once in a while I'd take a scan around with the faint hope of picking up something worthwhile. Which I didn't, but I picked up something else that surprised me.

There are always some fans who use portable television sets in the stands to give them a better view of the action, but there were an unusually large number of them that day, and they weren't all tuned into the game. Many were set on the network channels covering the arrival of General Secretary Gorbachev at Kennedy airport. He was due there any minute, and while they waited the commentators were filling air time with profound guesses about the disarmament proposals that he might be bringing to the United Nations. It was hard to believe. There were the Mets playing pennant-winning ball down on the field, and up in the stands a substantial portion of the

21

faithful were concerned with such weighty topics as world peace and nuclear disarmament.

It surprised me because sports fans tend to be single-minded, at least when they're watching a game. Nothing else counts at the moment, and in that they are much like gamblers. There was a time when I played a certain amount of high-stake poker, and did very well at it until the word got around that I seemed to know every card in every hand as soon as they were dealt. After that, I wasn't welcome in the big-league games, but during the years that I played with the heavy hitters I learned exactly how unimportant was the outside world. Nothing, but nothing, mattered except the cards and the chips on the table. Same with baseball fans. What's the score? How many out? Who's up next? That's all that counts. But today there was something else begging for their attention. The joint announcement scheduled for the General Assembly the next day had caught the public fancy, and within the public consciousness there was a flicker of hope that this time it might just be the real thing. It was enough of a hope to tear some die-hard Met fans away from the game on the field.

'Hey,' said Ritter, 'what's going on?'

It was the end of the third innings, the players running off the field, but Ritter's eyes were on our pigeon. The seat next to DeKalb was suddenly empty. The man who had been sitting there was edging his way out of the row. Someone else was coming in the other way. He took the empty seat. The new man was wearing a camelhair coat and cap that made him look like those old photos of Babe Ruth. It was a smooth outfit, but too heavy for a warm September afternoon. He took off the cap and fanned his face with it.

'Christ,' said Ritter, 'what the hell have we got here?'

'The first guy was a patsy, holding the seat.'

'And who's this one?'

With the cap off, the man's face was clearly visible. He was Carlo Vecchione, and he worked for Uncle John Merlo, who ran a substantial portion of the DiLuca crime family. It was then that I stopped watching the ball game.

SIX
Sunday 1:45 PM

Kathy Benton came out of her apartment building on East Sixty-eighth Street and hurried up towards Second Avenue. DeKalb's girlfriend was young and she was probably pretty, but not at that moment. Her face was puffy, her nose was red, and there were heavy smudges under her eyes. She had the look of someone who had dressed rapidly, throwing on anything handy, and there was a gap in her skirt where she had forgotten to do up the zip. She walked with her head down, dabbing at her face with a wad of tissues.

Martha sat in a Bureau car parked up the street. The driver asked, 'Do I follow?'

Martha shook her head. The girl was approaching the car, close enough to read. As she passed by, Martha went into her head. And came out almost at once. And burst into tears.

The driver stared at her. 'What's wrong?'

Martha shook her head again, unable to speak. The tears rolled from her eyes and down her cheeks uncontrolled. She had been in the woman's head for only a few seconds, but that had been enough to overwhelm her. There was a sadness within Kathy Benton, a hopelessness so profound that touching only the edges of it had reduced Martha to tears. That head . . . it was a crazy-quilt of despair with only one coherent thought running through it.

He's coming back, I know it. No matter what he said, he'll be back. People like us, what we have, it doesn't just stop. You can't turn it on and off like a tap, it goes on forever. So he's coming back, and there has to be food in the house. Things that he likes . . . shrimp, and steaks, and things like that. For when he comes back. If he . . . when he comes back.

The pathetic echo of the woman's thoughts came trailing

back along the street, and brought fresh tears to Martha's eyes. It was often that way with her. Other aces could go into a head and remain unaffected by the joys and the sorrows that they found there, but not Martha. She identified totally with every head that she tapped, riding the highs and the lows of each psyche. She was unable to stay uninvolved, and she considered it a weakness.

'Are you all right?' asked the driver.

Martha nodded. There was no way to explain what had happened, except to another ace. She dried her eyes, and opened the doors of the car. She said, 'I'll do this on foot.'

'Where's she going?'

'I'm not sure, but I'd bet on the nearest supermarket.'

It was the Food Emporium on Second Avenue and Seventieth. Martha followed Kathy into the market, grabbed a shopping cart, and stayed close behind her. She was reluctant to dip into that head again, but she knew that she had to. She braced herself and went in. Again that wave of despair, and as Kathy went from shelf to shelf, a rambling refrain that spun through her mind.

Garlicky shrimp to start with, that's what he likes. Anything hot and spicey, chillies, and curries, and jalapeño peppers with practically anything, and when he comes back he'll want something hot. He'll walk through the door and kick off his shoes, sit down and sigh, and he'll want a beer right away with some garlicky shrimp to go with it. Shrimp, lots of it, and then a steak. That's the way it'll be. As soon as he starts on the shrimp, I'll put up the steak. A sirloin if I can find a nice one, or a porterhouse. Likes a steak when he's weary, like a little boy tired after playing hard all day. Little boy look on his face, boy inside the man cutting into the meat, crusty on the outside and red at the centre. I make it just right for him, do everything right for him, and when he comes back it will all be right again. Shrimp and steak, something green, baked potato, and you-know-what for dessert. Has to be vanilla fudge, oh Lord; can that man eat ice cream, little boy again. Never got enough as a child? Don't know, don't care. Just want him back soon, and when he walks in the door I'll have the beer nice and cold, and the garlicky shrimp, and the steak, and he'll come back soon and I'll be ready. Have to be ready. Have to have everything right.

Martha followed, tuned in to the ramble, and watching as Kathy went from shelf to shelf, starting with the frozen foods. She put a two-pound bag of cleaned and shelled frozen shrimp into her cart, and stared at it doubtfully. She took another bag of shrimp, then another, and another. She hesitated, then emptied the shelf, filling the cart with eleven bags of shrimp. She found another cart and moved to the meat counter. She picked out a sirloin that she liked, and put it in the cart. Then another, and another, and another . . . all into the cart. When she had cleared off all the sirloins, she started on the tenderloins, the flank steaks, and the London Broil. She filled up the second cart with thirty-two packages of meat, and then pushed both carts over to the ice cream section. She picked up a third cart and stacked it full of vanilla fudge, all brands, forty-two quarts in all. She left the three carts in front of the ice cream case, got a fourth cart, and filled it with beer. When the fourth cart was overflowing with six-packs of Bud, she found a fifth cart and filled it with Miller. She did all this in an orderly frenzy, never pausing in her work, but never hurrying, either. Her eyes darted from shelf to shelf, from package to package, seeing nothing else. Those eyes were dull, and her face was a mask. She was deep in a tunnel of dreams. She wheeled both carts full of beer back to where she had left the other three. She lined up all five in a row, and looked down at them proudly.

There, she thought, *that should do it. Shrimp and steak, ice cream and beer. I'm ready for him, whenever he comes back. Because he will. No matter what he said, he's coming back.*

'No, he isn't,' Martha said gently. She stood in front of Kathy, the row of shopping carts between them.

Kathy's head snapped up. 'What?'

'I said he isn't coming back.'

'Who are you? I don't know you.'

'He's gone.'

'What are you talking about?'

'He said that he was going away for good, didn't he?'

Kathy's lower lip began to tremble.

'He told you to forget about him, didn't he?'

The mask of her face began to dissolve.

'That's what he said, and you'd better start believing it. He's gone, and all the steaks and beer in the world won't bring him back to you.'

Kathy closed her eyes. 'I know.'

'Then why?'

'Hoping, I guess. Pretending.'

'Shopping your way out of misery,' Martha said firmly.

Kathy opened her eyes. 'Is that what it was?'

'Certainly.' Martha pushed the shopping carts aside, breaking the barrier between them. 'You don't really need all this, do you?'

Kathy shook her head wearily. 'No, of course not. I'm all alone now. I guess I always was. I only saw him twice a week. That's alone, isn't it?'

'Very.'

'And he isn't coming back. How did you know that?'

'Do you want to talk about it?'

'Yes. I don't even know you, but I think I can talk to you.'

'You can.'

'I want to.' Kathy looked in sudden dismay at the loaded carts. 'Oh, Lord, I'll have to put all this stuff back.'

Martha took her arm firmly. 'Someone else will do it. Come on, let's go someplace where we can talk.'

SEVEN
Sunday 1:55 PM

'Do you make him?' asked Ritter, his eyes on the man in the camelhair coat.

'Carlo Vecchione,' I told him. 'He works for Uncle John Merlo.'

'Christ, the fucking mob. Just what we needed.'

Carlo Vecchione wasn't a big time wiseguy; he was far from the centre of power in the families, but he was Uncle John Merlo's only blood nephew. Uncle John was the underboss of the DiLuca family, and the Uncle gave Carlo a living, enough to keep him in Guccis, and Puccis, and camelhair coats. Carlo did some loan-sharking, and wholesaled some bookmakers, but mostly what he did was run a high-stake poker game for the Uncle. He ran the game out of his apartment on Jane Street in the Village, the entire first floor of a reconditioned brownstone. The apartment was furnished palatially, and in fact it was known to those who played in the regular Friday night game as The Palace. Friday night was for the heavy knockers, some of whom flew in from as far away as Houston, and Vegas, and Miami. Playing in the Friday night game was known as playing The Palace, and only the heaviest players sat in. The action was Texas-style Hold 'Em, and a pot of fifty thousand was not exceptional.

Back in those days, big-league poker had been my passion, and Uncle John Merlo had been my backer, putting up the money that allowed me to play at such a rarified atmosphere. In return, he took seventy-five per cent of the winnings, which I figured was fair enough. At that level I was making plenty. I was cheating, of course, reading the other players' cards from their heads, which made it less exciting, but which also made it an unbeatable lock. Uncle John didn't know why I always

27

won, nor did he care. The money was too good to care. Besides, the Uncle figured that he owed me. I had done him a favour once. The way he saw it, I had saved his life, and the obligation was as pressing to him as an unpaid marker. I never saw it that way, and I never tried to collect on the marker, but the Uncle always figured that he owed me.

That was Uncle John, but what the hell was his nephew, Carlo, doing with my pigeon on a Sunday afternoon at Shea?

'Could be a coincidence,' said Ritter, but he didn't really believe it.

'It's some kind of a meet, but don't ask me what.'

'Delivery?'

'Could be, but what?'

'That's it. Watch it, there it goes.'

It went down so smoothly that I almost missed it. Carlo waited until something happened on the field, and the crowd noise soared. His hand went inside the camelhair coat, and came out with a package the size of a cigar box. He laid it on DeKalb's lap. DeKalb ignored it. He had his hands cupped around his mouth, yelling for the Mets. Carlo stood up, and edged his way out of the row of seats. The patsy came back in and took his place. It was over in minutes. Carlo sauntered down the ramp at the back of section ten, and was gone.

'Figure a few minutes, and then the pigeon flies,' said Ritter. 'He's made his meet.'

In exactly five minutes, DeKalb stood up abruptly, and left. The package was inside his jacket. We followed.

EIGHT
Sunday 1:58 PM

Arina Zourina shifted in her seat, and then forced herself to sit still. She felt a giggle growing, and she stifled it. Her left foot began to tap, and she crossed her legs firmly. She was excited, she was elated, she was nervous. She was nineteen years old, a Russian ace sensitive, and she was on her very first trip outside the Soviet Union. She was on her way to New York, and she felt like a little girl going to the circus. Her enthusiasm was dampened only by the gnawing question of why she, of all people, had been chosen for this assignment.

Aside from crew members, there were one hundred and seven passengers seated in the front section of Gorbachev's Aeroflot jet as it sped over northern Canada. Only one, General Shvabrin, was a military man. Of the others, twenty-three were members of the General Secretary's travelling staff; eight were Foreign Ministry people responsible to Eduard Shevardnadze; six were from the office of Yegor Ligachev; twenty-seven were representatives of the Soviet communications media; eleven were civilian researchers and analysts in the overlapping fields of missile deployment and nuclear disarmament; twenty-three were members of Colonel Prokoroff's security detail; and five were translators.

Of those five translators, three were that and nothing more. The other two were ace sensitives, products of the KGB Centre at Gaczyna, southeast of Kuibyshev, the Soviet equivalent of the American Centre in Virginia. One of the aces was Arina Zourina. The other, Yuri Muzalev, was fast asleep beside her, his seat tilted back as far as it would go and an open copy of *Playboy* spread over his face to keep out the light. Arina envied him his ease. He was ten years her senior, a veteran, and an ace with a reputation for a whirlwind way of living, a cutting wit, and an abiding irreverence for all institutions. Back at the training centre she had heard dozens of Yuri Muzalev stories; he was on his way to becoming a legend, and it was consistent with that legend that he should flaunt a copy of the forbidden *Playboy* in a cabin filled with high officials. Still, it was an honour to be assigned to his team. Yuri Muzalev had been everywhere and had done everything that an ace could do. He had held diplomatic postings in Paris, and Rome, and Washington; he had been covertly operational in Afghanistan and Nicaragua; he had been seconded for a year to Special Service II of the KGB for counterintelligence work; and, of course, he was an old hand at the translation game.

Arina had been well trained at Gaczyna, and she knew that the use of sensitives as high-level translators, perched behind the ears of world leaders, was as old as the use of the sensitives themselves. She also knew that an ace performed two functions on the job, the less difficult of which was the actual task of translation. For Arina, as for any other ace, the acquisition of language was little more than a parlour trick, for she could absorb any idiom whole by tapping into someone's head. There was no need for her to study, or to memorize. An hour or two spent inside the head of a well-educated Frenchman, was enough to make an ace proficient in French, and the same procedure applied to other languages. Any ace could do it, and it was a trick that they performed casually. The far more important function that the ace performed during translation was to establish a mental block to shield his leader's thoughts from the prying of opposition aces. The block had to be absolute, and had to be maintained for as long as the two sides were in contact. It was an exercise in willpower, and one that guaranteed the ace a roaring headache at the end of every session. Arina had been through hundreds of similar training sessions at the Centre, but now she was about to experience the real thing, and again she had to ask herself why she had been chosen. She was much too young and inexperienced for such an important assignment. True, she had been placed in the upper ten per cent of all her classes at the Centre, and she had been awarded an Order of Merit in her final year, but still . . .

What nonsense, said Yuri Muzalev. He was speaking to her head-to-head, his face still covered by the copy of *Playboy. If you don't know why you were assigned to this team, then you ought to have your head examined.*

Arina started, then got herself under control. She looked around nervously, but, of course, no one else could have heard the words. There were no other aces on board.

Stop that, she said sharply. *You must not do that.*

I beg your pardon, Arina Egorovna. I should have knocked first. May I come in?

But this is not allowed. Mental communication is forbidden within two hundred metres of the General Secretary or any other member of the Politburo. It is also forbidden in the presence of field grade military officers except under conditions sanctioned by Special Service II for the purpose of . . .

Enough. God help me, I've got one straight out of the convent. Are you always so righteous?

I was trained at the Centre to follow the rules, she said primly.

And did you? You mean you never tapped an instructor's head for an answer to a quiz? You never peeked at a young boy's mind to see what he thought of you? You never broke a single one of all those silly rules at the Centre? I don't believe it.

Well . . . of course, we all did sometimes. But that was different. That was training, this is real.

Arinoushka, I assure you that the rules here are just as silly, and just as easily broken. Besides, it's so much more fun that way, isn't it?

Arina found herself wanting to giggle again, and covered her mouth with her hand. It was a habit she was trying to break. The giggle was caused not so much by what Yuri had said, but by the sight of the *Playboy* that covered his face, and the sudden thought that his nose might be poked, most improperly, into the centre of a centrefold.

No such luck, said Yuri, who had picked up the thought. *It's an advertisement for a male deodorant. Tell me, do you go for men who wear deodorants?*

I don't know, I've never met one who did.

You will in New York. They all use it there.

I doubt that I will meet many American men. Except their sensitives, of course.

A good bunch of guys.

Do you know many of them?

31

Yuri flashed her the image of two fingers pressed close together. *Sammy Warsaw and I used to be like that. He's running their Centre now, but for a while we were opposite numbers in Washington. We used to drink together every night.*

How could that be?

Oh, we couldn't actually be seen together, but there was this place in Georgetown, the Hell's Bells, where we met after work. He's be at one end of the bar, and I'd be at the other, but we talked back and forth head-to-head.

What about Ben Slade? Do you know him?

Why the interest in Slade?

I've heard the stories about him. He's the one who married one of our aces.

Yes, Nadia Petrovna. The only time that's ever happened. She was a wonderful woman.

What happened to her?

You don't know? No, you wouldn't you were too young when it happened.

Tell me.

Not now; you have a visitor.

Arina felt the light touch of fingers on her shoulder. She looked up. Colonel Prokoroff stood over her, smiling down. It was a tight smile that split his pudgy face like a knife across a pomegranate.

'How is it with you?' he asked. 'A good trip?'

'Yes, Comrade Colonel. No problems.'

'And that one?' He nodded at Yuri.

'Asleep,' she said, not knowing why she lied. 'He's been asleep since we left. I think he could sleep through a thunderstorm.'

Prokoroff nodded slowly. 'No nerves. He's a good man, one of the best. You're lucky to be on his team.'

'I know that, Comrade Colonel.'

'You could learn a lot from him on this trip.'

'Yes.'

'There's much that he can teach you, some of it valuable, and some of it . . . questionable. Do you know what I mean?'

She shook her head silently.

'He has some strange ideas, so be very careful what you

32

learn from him, Arina Egorovna. Be very careful. Now do you understand?'

'Yes, Comrade Colonel.'

'Good.'

The fingers squeezed her shoulder, and Prokoroff moved on. Arina watched as he stopped next to the seat of General Shvabrin. The colonel bent over and spoke softly into the general's ear.

Pompous ass, said Yuri. *Something's up. They want Shvabrin in the back.*

Yuri Ivanovich, what did you mean when you said . . . about why I was chosen for this team?

My dear, have you looked in the mirror recently?

Oh.

Exactly.

But . . . who?

Who chose you?

Arina hesitated. *He did.*

Prokoroff? Then there you are.

Arina, indeed, had looked in the mirror recently. She looked often, and was always pleased with what she saw. She knew herself to be a highly attractive young woman. She was, in fact, a beauty. She knew that too, although she rarely admitted it to herself. As young as she was, she already knew that beauty draws problems the way sugar draws flies.

He wouldn't dare, she said defiantly. *That would be sexual harassment.*

Indeed, it would be, and it will be. Count on it, little one, the colonel will be in your pants within a week.

He will not.

A mental shrug. *In that case you'll be on the next plane back home with a reprimand in your file. Wake up, stupid, that's the way things are done.*

Prokoroff and Shvabrin were coming back up the aisle towards the rear cabin. Prokoroff smiled at her again as they passed by.

I can't believe it, said Arina. *These things are specifically forbidden by regulations.*

Those rules of yours again. Why don't you see for yourself? Break one of those rules and take a peek.

Why not? she thought.

She opened her mind, and jumped into Prokoroff's head. She jumped out quickly, her cheeks burning. Yuri laughed. He sat up, and the magazine dropped to his lap. His face was oval, olive, and smooth. His eyes looked older than the rest of him.

Well, he said, *was I right?*

Arina did not answer. She stared straight ahead. Her mind was racing. She threw up a block to keep Yuri out of her head. He tried to come in, and bumped into it.

'Hey, why the block?' he murmured aloud.

No reply.

'You angry with me?'

She shook her head.

'Is it Prokoroff? Come on, don't let that bastard bother you. It's all part of the game.'

'It isn't that.'

'Then what?'

Again no answer. Yuri looked at her carefully, shrugged, and leaned back again in his seat. He closed his eyes.

Arina looked back at the door to the rear cabin. General Shvabrin had gone in, and Prokoroff stood guarding the entrance. He saw her staring at him, and he winked. She faced forward again. Her stomach was churning, and she felt ill. Questions bounced back and forth in her head. She clenched her fists, and stared down at them. She stayed that way for more than five minutes, then she suddenly rose and started up the aisle towards the rear cabin. Prokoroff frowned as she stopped in front of him.

'What do you want?' he said. 'You have no business here.'

'I must speak with you. Privately.'

NINE
Sunday 2:00 PM

'I know what you need,' said Harry Falk. 'You need to get high.'

'What I need is my father,' said Laura DeKalb.

'No, what you need is to get high. You'll hear something soon about your dad.'

'Six days and not a word.'

'They'll find him. They're looking for him.'

'They come every day and ask questions, but nothing happens. There was another one at the house when I left. They won't find him, Harry. He's gone.'

'Nobody just drops out of sight that way. How about it? Time to get high.'

'Thousands of people drop out of sight every day. What about all those kids who disappear?'

'I'm not talking about kids, I'm talking about an Air Force colonel. They'll find him.'

'Not if he doesn't want to be found.'

They were both seventeen, both starting their senior year in high school, and they were best friends in the best way that a boy and a girl can be friends. They spent a lot of time together, some of it in bed, and they told each other everything. They were sitting at their favourite table in the Colonial Diner on Route 202, coffee and Danish pastry in front of them. The table was their favourite because it was tucked away in a corner, where, if they kept their voices low, they could not be overheard. Their voices were low now, but Snake, sitting three tables away, had no trouble tuning into their conversation. She was into both their heads, reading it that way as she prepared to dig for a Delta tap on the girl.

'You think he doesn't want to be found?' asked Harry.

Laura nodded. She picked at the cheese Danish in front of her, cutting it into tiny squares. 'I'll tell you what I think. I think he finally had it with that bitch.'

'Come on, don't talk about your mother that way.'

'I think she finally drove him out of the house.'

'You don't know that, you're guessing.'

'And you don't know what she's like these days. You don't hear all the arguments, and the nagging. It's been that way the past two years, ever since the accident.'

'You really think he took off just to get away from your mom?'

'I think he met a woman he could love, someone who respects him, someone who can give him what she can't. I think he saw his chance, and he grabbed it.'

'You're guessing again.'

'No, when it comes to a woman, another woman always knows.'

'You're not a woman, you're seventeen. That's maybe seventy-five per cent, but definitely not a woman.'

'Thanks. I'll remind you of that the next time you get horny.'

'You know what I mean.'

'All I know is that I hate her.'

'You don't. You're just talking.'

'No, really.'

'Okay, so you hate her. You're supposed to. At your age, all girls hate their mothers.'

'What book did you get that out of?'

'It's an accepted fact. Right now you hate her, next year you'll love her again.'

'I don't think so. I don't think I ever did, really. Not the way other kids love their mothers.'

'Not to mention their fathers.'

'Don't start.'

'There's nothing unusual about it. Teenage girls compete with their mothers for their fathers' attention. It's an accepted fact.'

'And what do teenage boys do?'

'Jerk off,' Harry said promptly. 'It's a lot less trouble.'

Snake covered a smile by raising her cup to her lips. She was

36

beginning to like these kids. She could feel the pinholes in their brains where drugs and booze had already begun to pick away, but that didn't change her opinion of them. Everybody had pinholes these days. No, these two were all right, only moderately screwed up. She prepared to go deep into the girl's head for a Delta tap, but first she wanted to know more about the accident that had been mentioned. She found it lying on the surface of Laura's mind like a well-worn garment that had been temporarily tossed aside. She picked it up and examined it.

Memories of two years ago, her mother and father driving home late after a party. Dick driving, the wet road, the curve, the crash, and the months in hospital that left Paula with one leg shorter than the other. Snake turned the memory over and saw the resentment that had bloomed, the blame that Paula had laid on Dick, and the bitterness of every halting step along the way from then to now. And now he was gone, driven out of the house by a mother turned shrew. That was the way it lay in Laura's head, a well-worn garment always ready for use.

Neat and convenient, thought Snake, who had been into so many heads, and who knew all the tricks that a mind could play to satisfy itself. It was such a handy way to hate. She replaced the memory, and went deeper for her tap. She went down, and sifted mental garbage. She came up, and out. It was done in seconds, and when she was finished she knew what her report to Sammy would look like.

Delta tap subject: Laura DeKalb
Delta tap target: Richard DeKalb
Personal: Laura thinks of her father as being patient, understanding, and forbearing; an honest man whose only weakness is his inability to control his wife. She dismisses his relationships with other women as the natural products of an unhappy home and, in a sense, approves of them. She is convinced that her father has left her mother for good, and that she will never see him again.

All this should be viewed in the light of a young girl's adoration of her father, and Laura's memory is saturated with it. There are shining memories of a child's days with Daddy, always Daddy at her side, and her mother shows only as a shadow. There are trips to the seashore: Asbury Park, Cape

May, Wildwood. There are trips to the city: Bronx Zoo, the Music Hall, the circus. There are innumerable movies with Daddy in the next seat holding the bag of caramels, ice skating on frozen Sundays with the hot chocolate that Daddy bought afterwards, and there are the strongest memories of all in the stories that he told her.

He started to tell these bedtime stories to her when she was four, Daddy sitting on the edge of the bed while she curled up under the covers absorbing every word. They were no ordinary stories, no Jack and the Beanstalk, no Little Red Riding Hood for Daddy's girl. These were handcrafted tales created for Laura alone, stories of a kingdom far away in place and age, a land that Daddy said we all once knew, but had forgotten many times.

He called it the Kingdom of the Sea, an island with two castles topping the heights at either end, and in between them a green valley where all the good things grew. In the castle to the west were the people of Candore, spelled with an *e*, and they were the good guys: open, honest, and brave. In the castle to the east were the people of Luc, spelled without the *k*, who were also very brave, but sly and sneaky. And in between them in the valley lived the Tweenies, who were neither brave nor sneaky, but who were only simple farmers caught in the middle whenever the castles warred upon each other. Then the soldiers of Luc and Candore would flood into the valley, burning homes, killing and looting, and Laura's bedtime would be filled with the clang of steel on steel, and the cries of the warriors. There was Sir Giles of Candore, and Sir Rupert of Luc, and Boswirth, his evil companion. There was the Armourer, and the Falconer, and the Master of the Horse. There was Mungor, the leader of the Tweenies, and Melanie, his beautiful daughter, and all of these people created by her father were more real to Laura than most of the friends and family that she knew in the flesh. They filled her childhood, and even today her memory is layered with them. Her father told her the stories of the Kingdom of the Sea for ten years, from the time she was four until, at the age of fourteen, she decided that she was too old for such amusements.

That's where the head of this girl is now, still floating high above a far-off land that her father made for her.

Political: Laura has little real knowledge of her father's work with the DIA. Her image of him is the flyer-hero, the decorated veteran of Vietnam. Her own political development is retarded for a seventeen-year-old, and her thinking is simplistic. She has absorbed a vocabulary of cold-war rhetoric from her father, and thinks in terms of good guys and bad guys. She knows with conviction that her father is one of the good guys.

Security: This category is non-applicable. The possibility of her father's defection or disloyalty is beyond Laura's comprehension.

Summary: This is worthless, Sammy. It's what any teenage girl would think about her father. Tell Delaney that this is a bullshit operation.

TEN
Sunday 2:14 PM

If DeKalb had taken the subway I could have got close to him, but that kind of luck wasn't running. With the game less than half over, there were plenty of taxis outside Shea. DeKalb flagged one down, and we followed in the Bureau car. He went back to Manhattan using Grand Central and the Triboro again, and then down the FDR Drive. His taxi left the drive at Ninety-sixth Street, and went south on Second Avenue. There was little traffic, and he was easy to keep in sight. I punched in Sammy again.

'What now?' he asked.

'We're back in Manhattan, still following. Our boy had a meet at Shea, someone I know. A package was exchanged.'

'Who was the meet?'

'Remember the guy who used to back my play at poker?'

'The Uncle?'

'Right. His nephew was the one who passed the package.'

'Complications.'

'It's a whole new dimension. Sammy, this is stupid chasing after him. It's time to pull him in.'

'That's not my decision to make.'

'I mean it, *tus*, pull him in. Lock me in a room with him and I'll get you your Alpha. That's the only way to do it.'

'Can't be done. We just follow orders on this one.'

'It's like trying to rope an eel.'

'Can't be helped.'

'One last time. Pull him in.'

Sammy's voice sharpened. 'Why? You know something that I don't?'

I didn't. All I had was a gut feeling that we were engaged in a fruitless venture, and that while DeKalb was running loose we were open to an infinite number of screw-ups. It was a doomsday feeling, a warning tingle in the nerve ends of impending disaster. But for all of that, it was only a hunch, and I had learned not to articulate those. All they got me were funny looks.

I said, 'No, you know as much as I do.'

'Right, carry on.'

'Roger, over and out.'

'What?'

'Forget it.'

I clicked off. The gut feeling was still there, prodded by memories of Carlo Vecchione, Uncle John Merlo, and the electric excitement of those Friday night sessions at The Palace. After a while, I swore off playing major-league poker. After a while, it wasn't exciting any more, not when I could read every card at the table. And after a while, the cheating began to bother me. Not that I was taking money from widows and orphans, but still, it bothered me. In those days I played against the best-known guns in the game, people like B. B. Thayer out of Houston, Mario Villalonga, Leroy Coopersmith from Vegas, and T. L. Thuc. They were the class of the action, and then there were others like Harry Bowen. Bowen's money came from drugs. There was always a lot of drug money around the tables, but it tended to be discreet, handled by well-dressed people with quiet manners who could drop a bundle with a smile and come back for more. Not Harry Bowen. He dressed like a slob, he talked like a spouting sewer, and he bitched and moaned about every hand that he lost. Which was often, because Bowen was a truly rotten poker player. He was the type of gambler who throws it away with a shovel, and then blames his luck on the cards. He had it going against him two ways. He didn't have the brains to win right, and he didn't have the class to lose right. On top of that, he was his own best customer for coke, riding a perpetual high that robbed him of whatever card sense he once might have had. It also affected his basic judgement. On one of those nights he dropped a quarter mil in less time than it takes to tell about it, and somewhere in that watermelon seed that he used for a brain he decided that the deck wasn't right. Which was absurd on the face of it. Uncle John's game had to be straight

41

at that level of play, but Bowen was too far gone to see that. The way he saw it, the house was screwing him, and he flipped out right there at the table. It was straight John Wayne at the Golden Nugget Saloon. Bowen pulled out the old pistola and went rooty-toot-toot, and it was after that night that Uncle John Merlo decided that he owed me.

'Up ahead,' said Ritter. 'Get ready.'

His voice jarred me out of reverie. DeKalb's taxi had stopped at the corner of Second Avenue and Seventy-second Street. We pulled in half a block behind. DeKalb got out and headed west on Seventy-second. Ritter opened his door.

'On foot from here,' he said. He was out of the car. I did not move. He looked back at me. 'Come on.'

'I don't like this. I don't like any part of it.'

'Christ, what a time to get temperamental. You coming, or not?'

I slid out of the car, and we hurried down the street.

ELEVEN
Sunday 2:15 PM

. . . my back like this against the bar you can't tell. Weight on the right leg, left foot kicked up against the wood. Girlishly casual. Can't tell, good for the posture, too. Boobs out, shoulders back. Fetching. Inviting. Not that I'm selling anything.

'The trouble with you people,' Paula said aloud, 'is that you're trained to see ghosts under every bed. Red ghosts. That's all you can think of. You think that Dick either defected, or he was snatched. You can't think in human terms the way I can. I know that he's off with some new piece of ass, but for you people it has to be politics and international intrigue. And so you miss the obvious. You want me to tell you the obvious?'

'Sure, go ahead,' said Vince. Deep in a comfortable chair, he sipped at his drink, stretching it. He was still on his first, while Paula was working on her third. She had not moved from her position against the bar.

'The obvious is that Dick DeKalb doesn't have anything worth selling, and he doesn't know anything worth stealing. You think I don't know what he does? So he runs a desk at the DIA, but what does he actually know? Oh, Christ, don't look at me that way. You think the husbands don't talk? There's damn little about Dick's work that I don't know. Look, what comes over that desk of his? Soviet silo capacities, test sightings, all the space junk that has to be plotted, things like that. Routine. It isn't a hell of a lot more than a clerk's job, handling figures like that. And remember, those are Soviet figures that he handles, not ours. So what has he got to sell, or what has he got that they can steal? Their own stats, that's what. Stuff they already know. You see what I mean? But you still go looking under the beds for those red ghosts.'

43

'You underestimate your husband's job. It's a great deal more than clerical routine.'

'Major, if you really think that my husband is some sort of an international superspy, then they handed you the wrong briefcase this morning. Please, I know better. You're talking about Dick DeKalb, the laughing stock of the DIA. You've heard about that boat race, of course.'

Vince nodded. He had seen the reference in DeKalb's file to the proposed operation, a hare-brained scheme to rig one of the America's Cup yacht races so that the Australian boat would win. DeKalb had been the author of the plan, and he had fought hard for it, claiming that it could have a profound effect on US–Australian relations. He had bucked it all the way up the line to General Bruce, the DIA director, who had turned it down with the devastating comment that Colonel DeKalb had been spending too much time in the bathtub playing with his rubber duckies. The more formal comments on the plan had used such words as *ill-advised . . . overly romantic . . .* and one emphatic *juvenile*. It had never become operational.

'Did you ever hear of anything so wacky? A boat race, of all things, and he really believed in it. I mean, he thought he had come up with a major coup, and he was crushed when Brucie turned it down. Poor Dick, they practically laughed him out of the DIA. That's the kind of man you're dealing with, major, and you'd better understand that. Dick may have been a hot-jock fighter pilot once, but he is absolutely lost in the world of military intelligence. They never should have put him there. He's a field man, the boy-warrior who never grew up. You put him behind a desk and his eyes glaze over. That yacht race thing is a perfect example of how his mind works, and after that they never trusted him with anything more important than shuffling files. All right, so I'm exaggerating a little, but I know what he knows, and he doesn't know any earthshaking secrets. He knows routine crap . . .'

She went on and on. Vince nodded at the appropriate times, barely listening. Not that she was totally wrong about her husband's work. The yacht race proposal had indeed been a fiasco, and ninety per cent of DeKalb's daily work was routine, but she was way off about the other ten per cent. Colonel

DeKalb could tell the Soviets plenty about DIA procedure and analysis, enough to make him a valuable asset. As Paula rambled on, Vince tuned out her words and went back into her head.

. . . how anyone could think that Dick was a security risk. Dick the patriot, the cold warrior. The hot warrior, too, those two tours in Nam and all those lonely nights. No, this hunk of a major is barking up the wrong . . . whee, now that's a thought. Think he'd like to bark up . . .? Woof, woof, do it doggy, the way Dick used to like it, God, it seems so long ago. Not really, only two years, but it seems like a century. Everything is long ago these days, seems so long since things were right. No more woof, woof, or anything like it. Anything at all, not since. And he tells me that it's all my fault, the prick, talks to me like a text-book on sex, the changing forms of attraction as a marriage matures. Big words. Why can't he say it straight? Can't get it up for me any more, not since. Turns him off to see me limp. As if it's my fault with him driving the car pissed out of his skull. Begged him to let me drive, but no, he had to. And who winds up in the hospital? And who's walking around with one short leg? Not Dick DeKalb, that's for sure, but it's all my fault, and he says it's not the leg, the liar. The changing forms of attraction as a marriage matures. Share my fantasies, he says. Talk dirty, wear this, paint your nipples, touch me here, and all I want is him to hold me. Share his fantasies? Share mine, you son of a bitch. Fantasy of an old-fashioned fuck, take me and love me. But no, that's too simple for him, the changing forms of. So he has to find somebody else. And somebody else. And somebody else, and he's in the shit this time if he ever comes back, because they'll never believe that he was just off chasing. Never. They don't think that way. It has to be political with them, but I know better. Ah, Dick, you bastard, you really did it this time.

Vince tuned out the surface of her head, and went deep for his Delta tap. He lowered himself past the levels of her discontent, her rage, and her despair, until he was able to tap at the source of her. He sifted mental garbage, and came up. It was done in seconds, and when he was finished he knew what his report to Sammy would look like.

Delta tap subject: Paula DeKalb
Delta tap target: Richard DeKalb
Personal: The subject is still strongly attached to the target

after twenty years of marriage despite the fact that his drunken driving caused her disability. She bears no resentment, but on the other hand she is convinced that because of the accident she is no longer attractive in his eyes. They have not been sexually intimate since the accident and, indeed, the subject has had no sexual contacts at all in the past two years. She is aware of her husband's infidelities and, despite the bright exterior that she maintains, each new affair reinforces her despair.

Political: At the surface level, and for several levels deeper, the subject displays a sincere belief in her husband's patriotism and incorruptibility. Her words: *He may be a prick, but he isn't a traitor*. But buried deep in her primary level is the suspicion that if any factor could move DeKalb from a position of loyalty it would be a woman, and that this may be what has happened. The suspicion is buried so deep that she is not consciously aware of it, but *au fond*, she fears that he may have been turned by a female working for a hostile intelligence service.

Security: The risk is there, the target is vulnerable, and should be treated as such.

Summary: I don't want any more jobs like this, Sammy, I really don't. Tell Delaney that this is a bullshit operation.

Paula stretched, smiled at Vince, and said, 'I suppose you've noticed that I walk with a limp.'

'Do you? No, I didn't notice.' It was time to go.

'You're being kind. You'd have to be blind not to see it.' She swallowed the last of her drink. 'But there's something very strange about my limp. Can you guess what it is?'

'No, I can't.' He gathered himself to get up.

'You probably won't believe this, but I only limp when I'm wearing clothes. When I don't have any clothes on, I don't limp at all. Can you believe that?'

Vince smiled, and said, 'No.'

'I didn't think you would. Look.'

She took off her clothes in three rapid motions: top, bottom, and a wisp. She walked across the room to him. She was right. All he could see was the woman, not the limp. She came very close.

'I told you so,' she said.

TWELVE
Sunday 2:14 PM

Mikhail Gorbachev and Nikolai Shvabrin were sons of the Caucasus, born the same year in the District of Krasnogvardeysk where the Yegorlyk River winds its way down from the Black Mountains and onto the fertile plains. There, in the village of Privolnoye, the two boys played together, studied together, and lived through the Great Patriotic War. After the war they worked together in the grain fields as husky teenagers until the fates tugged them in different directions: Nikolai to a career in the Army, and Mikhail to the Lomonosov State University in Moscow. Since those boyhood days they both had travelled far along the corridors of power, and if one had travelled somewhat further than the other, both were entitled to the sense of satisfaction that comes with goals accomplished. Now they faced each other across the conference table in the rear cabin of the Aeroflot jet. They were alone, save for Anatoli quietly at work in his alcove; Shevardnadze and Ligachev had gone forward to give them this privacy. They stared at each other silently. Their paths did not cross very often these days, and each searched the other's face for signs of age and change.

'Will you have something to drink?' asked Gorbachev. He used the intimate *ti* of their childhood as he indicated the cluster of bottles on the table. There was mineral water, orange juice, and a single flask of Georgian wine.

'No, thank you. I'll try to be brief, but first I must ask after the health of your wife, and of Maria Panteleyvna.'

'Raisa is well, thank you, and mother . . . well, the usual aches and pains at seventy-five. And your family?'

'All well. And does your mother still make *Liulia-Kebab*?'

'Every time I manage to visit her.'

47

'Remember how she would send us hunting for the mint leaves? We had to bring back a basketful.'

'And they had to be fresh. After all, what's lamb sausage without mint? In those days I could eat a dozen at one sitting.'

'I think I still could.'

'You were always the big eater. Remember your birthday when your aunt made the *Kotmis-Satsivi*? There was supposed to be enough for six, and you ate half of it yourself.'

'Never.'

'I remember it clearly.'

'Well, perhaps,' Shvabrin conceded. 'To tell you the truth, in those days you could put *satsivi* sauce on a piece of blotting paper and I would eat it.'

Both men smiled at thoughts of simpler days, and for a moment time hung suspended. Shvabrin broke the silence, saying, 'You realize that I did not ask for this meeting to talk about chicken with walnut sauce.'

Gorbachev nodded.

'They have sent me to make a final appeal. They beg you not to sign the treaty.'

'They?'

'I am here as the representative of the General Staff, but it should be understood that I also speak for the Soviet Navy, the Rocket Troops, and the Air Force.'

'Quite a burden for a junior general to carry.'

'I assure you that I did not seek this assignment. I am acting under orders, and I am sure that you realize why I was chosen.'

'It seems obvious. You are an old friend. They think that I will listen sympathetically to you.'

'It is more than that. They also feel that I am the only one who can speak candidly to you without running any risk. Without incurring your wrath. Without any jeopardy to myself.'

Gorbachev's frown grew ominous. 'What risk? What jeopardy? Do you think that we are still living in the days of Josef Vissarionovich?'

Shvabrin's hands went up in denial. 'No, no, I'm not talking about a bullet in the head, but careers have been wrecked for what I am going to say to you.'

'Are you asking me for dispensation in advance?'

'I am asking you to understand that the men who have sent me to you are true patriots and good communists. Their only concern is the safety and stability of the Soviet Union.'

Gorbachev said drily, 'As they see it.'

'Conceded. As they see it.' Shvabrin poured some mineral water, and took a sip. 'Mikhail Sergeyvich, in order to clear the ground, I must ask some questions. May I ask them, and will you answer them?'

Gorbachev nodded slowly. 'Within reason.'

'Thank you. First then, it is my understanding that the Politburo has granted you full discretionary powers in the matter of disarmament negotiations with the Americans. Further, that this power was granted to you *carte blanche*. In other words, they gave you a blank cheque. Am I correct in this?'

'Substantially.'

'Very well. Now, despite the secrecy surrounding your intentions, the general shape of them has . . . er . . . become known to the Army Chief of Staff and his colleagues in the other services.'

'You mean that he has an informer in my secretariat. How would you like to be a field marshal?'

'I . . . I don't know what you mean.'

'Give me the name of the informer and I guarantee that you will have a baton within the year.'

Shvabrin shook his head slowly. 'You tempt me, but I know nothing of the details. Please remember that I am little more than a messenger. May I continue?'

Gorbachev said grimly, 'Go on.'

Shvabrin took another sip of water. 'From the information we have received it is our understanding that your agreement with the American President will be based on five points. May I review them?'

'Please do.'

'First, the United States and the Soviet Union will remove all medium-range missiles from European soil. The United States will maintain one hundred missiles in America, and we will maintain one hundred missiles in Soviet Asia. Am I correct on this point?'

49

Gorbachev stared into space, and drummed his fingers rapidly on the tabletop. 'Listen to me,' he said. 'I'm going to answer these questions of yours, but not because of the uniform you wear, or because we used to go fishing in the Yegorlyk together. I'm going to answer them first because I want to see what you're getting at, and second because it doesn't make a damn bit of difference anyway. In a few hours we will be landing in New York, and by tomorrow morning the whole world will know these points. So to hell with your colleagues and their questions. Yes, you are correct on that point.'

'Thank you. Second, the Soviet short-range missile strength in Europe will be reduced by two hundred and twenty-five units. Correct?'

'Yes.'

'Third, the Soviet Union will give up its demand for an immediate end to nuclear testing, and will agree to the American plan for a step-by-step reduction.'

'Correct.'

'Fourth, that the Anti-Ballistic Missile Treaty of 1972 will be extended for another ten years, which means that during that time neither the Soviet Union nor the United States will deploy missile defence systems other than the one land-based system presently allowed by treaty. Is this also correct?'

'It is. As you must know, there is nothing new in all of this. These four points were agreed to in principle when I met President Reagan at Reykjavik.'

'Quite so. But at Reykjavik there was a fifth point. Star Wars.'

'I prefer to call it the Strategic Defense Initiative, SDI. Star Wars is a foolish term invented by the American press.'

'At Reykjavik you were willing to agree to the first four points if the Americans would give up the SDI. Reagan refused, and the negotiations collapsed.'

'Totally.'

'And now you have changed your position. It is our understanding that you have withdrawn your demand on SDI. You now are willing to make the deal that Reagan wanted in Reykjavik. You have given in. Once again, I must ask if I am correct.'

'No, you are not. You are totally incorrect.'

Gorbachev stood up, and looked around the cabin. He found what he was looking for on one of the chairs. It was a half-size soccer ball meant for children. He dropped it on the floor and tapped it lightly with the toe of his running shoe, tapped it again and danced behind it, dribbling the ball across the rust-coloured carpet. He worked the ball down to the end of the cabin and back again, taking mincing little steps as he dodged imaginary defenders. He feinted left, then right, then drew back his left foot and slammed the ball on a hard, straight line into the wall of the cabin. It ricocheted off, and spun into the alcove where Anatoli was bent over an ironing board, working on a suit. The valet jumped, then put down the iron and retrieved the ball. He tucked it under the ironing board.

'Sorry,' said Gorbachev. Anatoli nodded, and went back to work.

Gorbachev sat down at the table. He folded his hands in front of him. He said, 'Let me tell you something, Nikolai Ippokratovich. I have told this to your superiors at the General Staff over and over again, so often that I am sick of hearing myself say it. But I will say it one more time for you. There is no way in the world for us to build an SDI of our own before the Americans build theirs.' Gorbachev's fist came down on the table. 'No way at all. The best minds in the Soviet Union have assured me of this. They have assured the General Staff as well, but the General Staff prefers not to listen. The General Staff believes in miracles. Well, I do not. The plain fact is that we lack the technology, particularly the computer technology, to do the job. Do you understand? It can't be done.' The fist came down again. 'If the Americans are ten years away from SDI, then we are twenty years away. If they are twenty years away, then we are forty years away. The equation is immutable . . . fixed. In this particular area of the arms race, we lost the race before it began. We were doomed to lose it. Which is why I have done what I have done.'

Gorbachev reached for a leather-bound file on the table, looked through it, and selected a single sheet of paper. He slid it across the table to Shvabrin.

'Read it,' he said. 'Point five of the treaty.'

(5) *Strategic Defense Initiative.*

The United States and the Soviet Union agree to a policy of open laboratories and open testing of the SDI. Upon ratification of this treaty, the United States will at once deliver all existing research material on SDI to the Soviet Union. At the same time, a joint research centre on SDI will be established at a neutral site in Switzerland. The centre will be administered and staffed jointly by scientists from the Soviet Union and the United States, and will constitute the only such research facility for this purpose.

The goal of this centre will be to develop a missile defence system designed to protect not only the United States, and not only the Soviet Union, but the entire world.

Shvabrin looked up. His face was pale. 'The Americans have agreed to this?'

'They have.'

'And you trust them? You believe they will do this?'

'I do.'

'Then I must say, General Secretary, that you are a trusting, naive fool.'

Gorbachev's eyes narrowed. 'I gave you dispensation in advance. You have just exhausted it.'

'Do you really think that they are going to turn over years of intensive research to us? Do you really think that they are going to cut their own throats?'

'Get out of here. Return to your seat.'

'You've stripped us of our defences, and for what? A dream that even a child would laugh at.'

Gorbachev's fist hit the table. 'Be quiet. You are walking a line close to treason.'

'Yes, I thought you might say that, but we both know better, don't we? We know who the traitor is here . . .'

Shvabrin stopped short as the door opened, and Prokoroff came into the cabin. The KGB colonel closed the door firmly behind him. His right hand hung by his side, but the hand was holding a pistol.

'What is this?' asked Gorbachev.

Prokoroff ignored him; his eyes were fixed on Shvabrin. He said, 'General, you will place both your hands on the table, and stand up very slowly. If you move rapidly, or if you reach for your pockets, I will kill you.'

Shvabrin stared, then slowly raised himself to his feet. He looked down at Gorbachev. 'I believe something was said about not living in the days of Stalin?'

Gorbachev barked, 'Prokoroff, explain.'

'Will the General Secretary please move away from the table. I have reason to believe that this man is armed.'

Gorbachev did not move. He looked quickly at his boyhood friend. 'You came into my presence armed? Is this true?'

Shvabrin's smile was plaintive, almost sweet. 'Actually, I'm not sure I would have done it. I was ready to, but now . . . I really don't know.'

Prokoroff said, 'Turn around. Hands on top of your head.'

Shvabrin leaned forward slightly so that his face was close to Gorbachev's. He said, 'I was right, you know. You really are a trusting, naive fool. You let me get within seconds of killing you, and all for an old friendship. You're soft, Mikhail Sergeyvich, too soft for the job. You're just not tough enough.'

'We'll see about that,' said Gorbachev. 'We'll see who's so tough when I watch them shoot you.'

Shvabrin smiled again, and said, 'No, not even that.' His jaws moved convulsively.

Gorbachev shouted, 'Look out, he's swallowing something.'

Prokoroff leaped. Shvabrin's face twisted, and a shudder ran through his body. He slumped forward onto the table. Gorbachev recoiled, pushing back his chair. Prokoroff grabbed the general's head, and pulled it back. The face was distorted, the eyes opened wide. Prokoroff bent over, and sniffed. He looked up.

'Dead,' he said. 'Instantaneous. Cyanide.'

THIRTEEN
Sunday 2:27 PM

The clam bar on Mulberry Street had no name. It was known only as the clam bar, and it was also known as the best in Little Italy. Part of that reputation was due to the freshness of the clams, the piquancy of the sauces, and the sensibility of the prices. The other part was due to the ownership. The clam bar on Mulberry Street was the property of Uncle John Merlo, who was the underboss of the DiLuca family. The family controlled the major action in Lower Manhattan: the loansharking and the bookmaking, the hookers along the docks, the after-hours clubs, the linen supply and garbage disposal for the restaurants, the locals of three unions, and several wholesale drug operations. Very little of illegal consequence below Fourteenth Street went untapped by Salvatore DiLuca. Uncle John Merlo was his second in command, and Uncle John's base was the clam bar on Mulberry Street.

The bar itself was dark and narrow, and on this Sunday afternoon it was empty of customers. Sunday business started late. A sign behind the bar read *Cherrystones – $3.00 a dozen*, and under the sign a fat man in a white apron worked over a pailful with a shucking knife. There were three jars of clam sauce on the bar marked *Mild*, *Hot*, and *Crazy*. A short, dark man in a pinch-waisted suit leaned against the bar and watched nervously as Uncle John paced up and down the room. The short man, Tony Spats, was Uncle John's driver, and he knew that his boss was close to losing an explosive temper.

Sunday afternoon was a sacred time to John Merlo, that part of the week devoted exclusively to his family. Childless, and a widower, that family now consisted only of his ancient mother, and his nephew, Carlo Vecchione. Every Sunday afternoon, promptly at two-fifteen, uncle and nephew would meet at the clam bar, and then walk the few blocks to the house on Elizabeth Street where Mama Merlo had lived for over forty years. There, with Mama perched comfortably on a pile of damask cushions, the three would drink cup after cup of *cappuccino*, munch *amaretti*, and review the occasions of the week just passed. Nothing of consequence was ever discussed, and no important decisions were made, but it was a ritual that pleased the old lady, and Merlo, as a dutiful son, was happy to oblige her with it. So, too, was her grandson Carlo, but on this Sunday afternoon he was unaccountably late.

Uncle John stopped his pacing long enough to shoot back the cuff of his white sharkskin jacket, and glare at a wristwatch the size of an oyster. 'Christ almighty, look at the time,' he said. 'That Carlo, where the hell is he?'

'Shoulda been here by now,' said Tony.

'I mean, how long does it take to get out to Shea, and back?'

'Uncle, he'll be here soon.'

'Mama gets nervous when I'm late. She likes that everything should be on time.'

'They get that way at her age. It's like every minute counts.'

'I don't get it. All he's gotta do is go out to Shea, drop off the package, and make it back here. How long does that take?'

'Traffic, maybe?'

'Or maybe he meets a broad out there.'

'Come on, Uncle John. At Shea?'

'At Shea, or anyplace else. That Carlo, he'd chase pussy in hell.' His nephew's womanizing was a longstanding sore point with the Uncle.

'Give him a break, it's gotta be the traffic.'

'You're too easy on him, Tony. He gives you the charm, just like he does it to everybody. He's probably charming some woman right now.'

'Uncle, did you ever take a real good look at the broads who go out to Shea? Carlo wouldn't stoop so low.'

The Uncle waved that point aside. 'Did you see what he was wearing? Camelhair in September.'

'That's just his way, he likes to look sharp.'

'I never should have sent him. Better I sent you.'

Tony made a noise of protest to reject the compliment, but

he knew very well why he hadn't been sent. A favour had been asked, and the request had come from the Don, himself, Salvatore DiLuca. The big man had asked his trusted under-boss to handle the delivery of the package, and under the circumstances the Uncle could do no less than entrust the job to family. He was Uncle John to everyone, but he had only one real nephew. It made no difference that the nephew was an empty-headed skirt-chaser. Blood was blood. Carlo had been given the job with plenty of time to make the meet, and be back for the Sunday ritual with his grandmother. Now he was late, and the Uncle was fuming.

'A simple favour for the Don, and Carlo's gotta screw it up.'

'You don't know that he screwed it up yet.'

'Then why is he late? I can't wait no more, I gotta go.'

'Give him a few more minutes.'

'I'm not gonna keep Mama waiting.' The Uncle checked his appearance in the mirror behind the bar, then whirled and pointed a finger at Tony. 'You tell him when he gets here to move his ass over to Mama's right away. I'll make some excuse for him.'

'I'll tell him.'

'And tell him that I'm plenty pissed off.'

'I'll them him that, too.'

Once the Uncle had left, Tony went behind the bar and fixed himself a plate of clams. He covered them with sauce from the *Crazy* bottle.

The fat man looked up from the bucket, and said, 'That stuff'll kill ya.'

'So I'll die happy.'

'That Carlo, he's something else.'

'Something,' Tony agreed, but without conviction. Carlo was a screw-up, but never before had he missed a Sunday afternoon with his grandmother.

FOURTEEN
Sunday 2:30 PM

Kathy Benton was part of a great American tradition, the smalltown girl who came to New York to conquer Broadway. She was nineteen years old when she left her home in Billings, Montana, convinced of her future. She knew that she was a born actress, destined to succeed. She also knew that success would not come easily, and she was prepared to travel the traditional route of rejection and grinding poverty before she reached her goal. Thus prepared, she came to Manhattan, found the traditional studio flat, made the traditional circuit of the theatrical agencies, and took the traditional job in the food service industry. The FSI, cocktail party jargon for waiting on tables.

Oh, you're in television, how interesting, I'm in the food service industry.

Four years later, at the time that she first met Dick DeKalb, Kathy had performed onstage before a paying audience exactly twice: once in a church basement in Brooklyn as Masha in *The Three Sisters*, and once in a SoHo loft in *The Glass Menagerie*. She was also, by then, a veteran of the FSI, working mostly in the cutesy-poo restaurants of the Upper East and West Sides. Her ultimate job was at Batman & Robin's on Columbus Avenue, where almost all of the other FSI waitingpersons were also waiting for their break on Broadway. The work was hard and the hours were long, but the money was decent and there was an important fringe benefit: the opportunity to perform several dozen times each night before a captive audience.

'Hi, my name is Kathy, and I'll be serving you this evening. Our specialties today are Prime Ribs of Beef at thirteen ninety-five, Fillet of Salmon grilled with pine needles at eleven fifty,

57

Vitello Tonnato at eleven dollars, and Lobster Fra Diavolo with the price according to weight. All of the main dishes come with a choice of sautéed spinach or the garden veggie mix, and either baked potato, hash browns, or french fries. For starters there is a shrimp cocktail, a gallantine of pheasant, and the soup of the day is a seafood bisque . . .'

It was the next best thing to being on stage.

The custom prevailed only in the cutesy-poo spots. The fine restaurants still treated their customers with an old-fashioned courtesy, and the cheap joints still worked from grease-stained bills of fare. But the cutesy-poos announced their food, most of which was slanted to the taste of a generation only a few years removed from Pizza Huts and Burger Kings. Moneyed now, the members of that generation had never tasted a farm-fresh egg, or a genuine rasher of bacon, or a chicken innocent of the deep freeze, and to them the cutesy-poo cuisine was the ultimate in sophisticated dining. Never mind that the sauces were sweetened to the level of a teenager's palate, that the pasta was pap, and that the quiche was first cousin to a pudding. The cutesy-poo restaurants of Manhattan flourished as an unknowing generation complacently paid for its ignorance, and patiently listened while aspiring actors practised their trade.

'Hi, my name is Kathy, and I'll be serving you this evening. Our specials today are . . .'

'What kinda bullshit is this? Look, sweetie, just bring me a menu, huh?'

It was a slow Tuesday night, a table for two men, and both more than a touch old for a place like Batman's. Mid-forties, she figured, and they had been tanking up at the bar. One was slim and sort of cute, shy looking, while the other was built like an oil furnace with ears, and a scowl stamped on his face. He was the one who wanted the menu.

'. . . our specials today are veal cacciatore at twelve-fifty, crabs Maryland at eleven ninety-five . . .'

'Hey, girl, didn't you hear what I said? I don't want the spiel, just a menu.'

Kathy frowned. Sometimes a customer would cut her off kindly, saying, 'That's all right, miss, I know what I want,' but it was rare for someone to refuse to listen. It was like hearing the catcalls of a hostile audience. She shook her head in annoyance, and noticed that the slim one was looking at her sympathetically.

'I'm sorry, sir, but there is no written menu,' she said in a controlled voice, and started over. 'Tonight we have veal cacciatore at twelve fifty, crabs Maryland at eleven ninety-five, a sirloin steak . . .'

'I don't believe this. Dick, she's gonna give me the whole routine whether I like it or not.'

'Ease up, Eddie,' said the slim one. 'She's just doing her job.'

'Balls, she's just practising her elocution on us.' Eddie leered at her. 'What comes next, Ophelia's death scene?'

'. . . either baked potato or french fries . . .'

'Will you tell me what I'm doing here?' asked Eddie, reaching for his drink. 'All I want is something to eat, and I gotta listen to a third-rate Mary Springburgen, she's gotta keep her voice in tune.'

Dick said mildly, 'Eddie, let her finish.'

'. . . shrimp cocktail, gallantine of duck . . .'

'I mean, shit, if I want to go to the theatre, I go to the theatre. I don't need amateur night with my food.'

'Put a cork in it, pal.' Dick's voice was no longer mild.

'. . . scallops escabeche . . .'

'Do we have to applaud when she's finished?'

'I said, cork it.'

'. . . and the veggies are cauliflower with hollandaise . . .'

'Veggies? Hey, Dick, we're in a veggie joint. What happens if I don't eat my veggies, babe? No dessert?'

Dick leaned across the table, and said tightly, 'Eddie, if you don't shut up I'm going to haul you out on the street and do you some damage.'

'Act serious. You and how many other shirts?'

'I mean it. You're talking like a jackass and you're being insulting.'

'Insulting? To who?' Eddie looked hurt and surprised. 'I'm the one who's being insulted. These people think I can't read a menu.' He looked up at Kathy. 'You insulted?'

She said quietly, 'Would you care to order now?'

'Maybe you better run through the routine again. I missed the part about the veggies.'

Dick held up his hand. 'Don't bother, miss, just bring us two sirloins, medium rare, home fries, and the cauliflower . . .' He hesitated.

'Anything else?' she asked.

'. . . and a banana for my monkey.' His smile was warm, and she saw that his eyes were grey.

'Hey,' Eddie protested, 'what monkey?'

'Easy, boy; back in your tree.'

It went on that way after she had served their food and while they ate, with Eddie thrusting orders at her for more butter, a fresh knife, another beer, and Dick doing his best to keep his friend quiet, blunting those thrusts with that gentle smile. Those grey eyes of his, she felt them on her as she moved around the room. There was nothing new about that, she was accustomed to the admiration of the people she served, and she was not surprised when, after dinner, Eddie left quickly while Dick went over to the bar. He spent the next hour nursing nips of Scotch and following her with those eyes. After four years in the FSI, nothing much surprised her.

Dick made his move at eleven, stopping her as she passed by the bar. 'I've been waiting around to talk to you,' he said. 'I want to apologize for the way my friend acted.'

'Acted is right. He's a very good actor.'

'I beg your pardon.' He looked puzzled.

'And so are you. I'm an actress, and believe me, I know.'

'I don't understand.'

'Sure you do. The good guy, bad guy routine, just like the cops. The bad guy is the insulting loudmouth and the good guy is the one who defends the lady in distress. You're smooth, both of you.'

She expected either embarrassment or bluster, but she got neither. He gave her the shy smile, and held up his hands in surrender. 'Zap, you've got me. We can't be that good if you spotted it.'

'Don't blame yourself, I've seen it done before. You see it all in this business. Do you always play the good guy?'

He shook his head. 'We switch back and forth. Eddie's really a very sweet person when you get to know him.'

'I'm sure he is. And what was phase two in the programme?'

He shrugged. 'About what you'd expect. An apology for my friend's boorishness, and an invitation to have a drink with me at Gallagher's in half an hour.'

'And an hour after that you'd be telling me all your troubles.'

'Probably.'

'All about the terrors of middle age, and how you'd like to go to bed with me.'

He smiled.

'About the two kids who are driving you crazy, and how you'd like to go to bed with me.'

'Only one kid.'

'About the wife who doesn't understand you, and how you'd like to go to bed with me.'

He shook his head. 'Wrong on that one.'

'No wife?'

'Oh, yes, but she understands me perfectly. She thinks that I'm a son of a bitch, and she's absolutely right.'

Time hung. Those grey eyes and that shy smile. She said softly, 'You *are* a bastard, aren't you?'

'Indeed.'

'Did you have to say that? Did you have to be honest?'

'Best policy. Never fails.'

'Most men would have lied. Why didn't you lie?'

'You coming to Gallagher's?'

'Your wife is right, you're a son of a bitch.'

'Will I see you in Gallagher's?'

'You know all the tricks, don't you. You're a truly wicked man.'

'What about Gallagher's?'

'Yes, damn it, I'll be there. You know I'll be there.'

'And you were there?' asked Martha.

'I was there,' said Kathy. 'That night, and any other night when he wanted me. Here, there, anywhere, for the past year. Whatever he wanted was all right with me. It makes a pathetic story, doesn't it?'

'Things like that happen. Sometimes all you can do is ride along with it.'

'Oh, I rode all right.' Kathy's voice was bitter. 'Not that it happened all that often. Twice a week, the most. That's all the time he could spare.'

'Bastard.'

'Yes, but then, he told me that, didn't he?'

They sat in Kathy's apartment, a large chocolate cake and coffee cups on the table between them. There were chunks missing from the cake, and they had gone through a pot of coffee while they talked. Kathy had done most of the talking, spinning out the sad, familiar tale, while Martha nodded sympathetically.

Now she said, 'It's probably a silly question, but why did you put up with it for so long?'

'What else was I going to do? I loved him. I still do.'

Martha shrugged. 'An ultimatum? His wife or you, force him to make a decision.'

Kathy laughed. It was not a pleasant sound. 'I didn't dare. I knew what the answer would be.'

'It looks like he made the decision anyway.'

'Maybe, maybe not. Maybe he just got tired. Maybe he found someone else. No, I don't really believe that. I don't know why he decided to break it up. All he said was that it was over, that it had to be over, that now it was time to end it. He seemed so sad, and so lost, but that's all he would say, and then he was gone.'

She began to cry quietly. Martha cut a slab of cake, and pushed it across the table. 'Here. Open-mouth therapy.'

Kathy smiled through the tears, but shook her head. 'You've been so kind, and I don't even understand why. A perfect stranger.'

'Far from perfect,' murmured Martha, feeling mildly guilty about her deception. During Kathy's narrative she had avoided going into the other woman's head, unwilling to have her own emotions bruised, but now it was time for the Delta tap. It could not be avoided. She braced herself for it, and plunged in. She did the job in seconds, and when she was finished she burst into tears.

'My God, what is it?' said Kathy. 'What's wrong?'

Martha shook her head vigorously, and tears flew. She managed to say, 'It's nothing, an allergy. It hits me this way sometimes.'

She ducked her head to avoid meeting Kathy's eyes. She knew what her report to Sammy would look like.

Delta tap subject: Kathy Benton
Delta tap target: Richard DeKalb
Personal: DeKalb is clearly a wormy type, but he has an absolute lock on the Benton girl. For the past year he has treated her with a casual contempt, taking everything and giving nothing, but she still thinks that the sun rises and sets in his scrawny ass. In my book he is definitely not one of the good guys, and I would be pleased to nominate him for a three-car collision on the Long Island Expressway.

Political: Despite the above, I can find nothing in Benton's head to indicate any political deviation on DeKalb's part. She knows nothing about his work, only that he is an Air Force officer with a desk job in Manhattan. He has told her nothing, and has committed no apparent breach of security. All he has done is prey on the emotions of a damn nice kid.

Security: Based on this tap, no risk, but I hope that I'm wrong. I'd sure like to slam this sleazeball.

Summary: I want either a vacation or a raise. Tell Delaney that this is a bullshit operation.

'Are you sure that you're all right?' asked Kathy.

Martha nodded, and wiped her eyes. 'It's gone. It comes and goes.'

'Can I get you anything?'

'Thanks, but I have some pills for it. All I need is some water.'

She got up from the table, and went down the hallway to the bathroom. She filled a glass with water from the tap. There were no allergy pills to take, but she popped two Tylenol for the headache that she knew would be coming soon. She looked at herself in the mirror, and frowned at the stress lines around her eyes.

'You're in the wrong line of work,' she muttered to herself. It was something that she told herself often.

As she turned away from the mirror, she heard the doorbell ring.

FIFTEEN
Sunday 2:32 PM

Mikhail Gorbachev, still in his Dynamo tracksuit, sat behind the conference table in the rear cabin of the Aeroflot jet. On the table before him, next to the bottles of mineral water and orange juice, and the single carafe of Georgian wine, was a hand grenade. It was a Red Army standard issue Model T-40. The body of General Shvabrin, covered by a sheet, lay on the floor of the cabin. Shevardnadze and Ligachev sat on either side of the General Secretary. Across the table, like a prisoner before the bar, stood Colonel Prokoroff. Two steps behind him stood his second in command, Major Mironoff, and next to Mironoff was the commander of the aircraft. Yuri and Arina, summoned from the front cabin, had placed themselves as far as possible from the table, close by the alcove where Anatoli continued to work over his ironing board. Gorbachev picked up the grenade, rolled it in his palm, and laid it down.

'A grenade,' he murmured. 'I could understand a pistol, but a grenade?'

'It would have blown out the side of the aircraft,' said Ligachev. 'It would have killed us all.'

Shevarnadze said, 'He was a brave man, he came prepared to die. He was dead if he was successful, and if his plans went wrong there was always the cyanide capsule.'

'You give him too much credit,' said Gorbachev. 'He wasn't brave, he was crazy, a fanatic. He sat there talking to me about my mother's cooking, and all the time he was planning to blow us up.'

The three men exchanged glances, the same question dominating their minds. Ligachev put it into words. 'Was he alone, or was it organized?'

Gorbachev waggled a warning finger, the same sort of gesture that a father might make about discussing certain subjects in front of the children. 'We can talk about that later,' he said, and turned to Prokoroff. 'What are the security arrangements in New York?'

Prokoroff drew himself up to answer. 'The Soviet Mission in New York is like a fortress. Once you are inside it, we can guarantee your safety.'

'And outside this fortress of yours?'

'Security is in the hands of the American FBI, and the New York Police Department. The police, in particular, are excellent at this sort of thing.'

'Let's hope that they are better at their job than you are at yours. Do you have any explanation as to how General Shvabrin managed to get this weapon on board?'

'No, General Secretary.'

'And your suspicions were aroused by this woman, the sensitive?'

'Yes, General Secretary. She came to me and told me that the general was armed, and was planning some sort of violence. You know what they can do, these sensitives. They call it tapping.'

'I see.' Gorbachev let his eyes wander to Arina, and back to Prokoroff. 'I thought that these people were forbidden to do their little tricks around me.'

'She claimed that it happened by accident.'

'And you believed her?'

Prokoroff knew that the axe was over his head, and he did the best he could. 'I did not stop to interrogate her then. My concern at that point was your safety.'

'Commendable, but somewhat late. You saved my life, you saved us all, but it never should have reached that point.'

Prokoroff stared at the bulkhead behind Gorbachev.

'In other days, not so long ago, you would have been shot on the spot for your negligence. You know that, don't you?'

Prokoroff was silent.

'But these are different days. You are relieved of your command, colonel. That is all.'

Prokoroff stiffened. He saluted, turned, and left the cabin.

Gorbachev said, 'Major Mironoff, you are now in charge of

the security detail. We have a mess here that has to be buried quietly. How do you propose to do it?'

Mironoff hesitated only long enough to gather his thoughts, then turned to the aircraft commander, and asked. 'What is your minimum turnaround time?'

'Two and one-half hours.'

'Is your backup crew fit for service?'

'Fit and ready.'

Mironoff turned back to the General Secretary. 'Immediately after refuelling, the aircraft will return to Moscow. An announcement will be made that during the flight to New York, General Shvabrin suffered a fatal heart attack, and that his body is being returned home for a state funeral. As a mark of particular respect, Colonel Prokoroff has been chosen to accompany the remains. To avoid any problems with the American health authorities who might want to examine the body, the announcement will not be made until the aircraft is on its way back to Moscow. Of course, everyone in this cabin will be sworn to secrecy.'

Gorbachev nodded, suppressing a smile. Mironoff had taken firm control, and at the same time he had swept his former superior from the scene. 'And what about the security in New York?'

'Upon arrival at the Soviet Mission, I will report to the KGB *rezident* in New York, and place myself under his orders. That is the only proper procedure.'

Another nod from Gorbachev, and another smile that never reached the surface. Mironoff was moving decisively, but not rashly. If anything went wrong in New York, it would be the *rezident* who took the heat. 'Very well, carry on.'

He nodded his dismissal to Mironoff and the aircraft commander. When they had left, he said to his two colleagues, 'Perhaps you might want to go forward and let yourselves be seen there. We want everything to appear normal.'

Shevardnadze and Ligachev looked mildly surprised, then realized that Gorbachev wanted to be alone with the two sensitives. They murmured their agreement, and went out. Once they were gone, Gorbachev smiled at Yuri, and said, 'Well, what do you think of this mess?'

'I think that you're deep in the shit, boss.'

Arina, amazed, watched as Yuri made an elaborate flourish with his right arm, laid it across his waist, and bowed so low that his head reached his knees. From that position, he said, 'Hail to thee, Tsar Mikhail the Second, secret descendent of the Romanoffs, illegitimate grandson of the sainted Anastasia, ruler of all the Russias, and various chunks of Europe and Asia as well. May I approach the throne?'

Gorbachev growled, 'Sit down, you clown.'

As Arina watched, wide-eyed, Yuri skipped over to the table, and plumped himself into one of the chairs. 'Gracious lord,' he murmured, and reached for the carafe of wine.

'Manners,' said Gorbachev.

'A thousand pardons. May I?'

'Of course.'

Yuri poured a glass for himself, sipped, and frowned. 'Mikhail Sergeyvich,' he said, 'do you realize that there are derelicts living on the streets of New York who drink better wine than this?'

'Forgive me, but I don't have your sophisticated palate. Besides, there is nothing wrong with that wine, it comes from Georgia.'

'That, may I say, would be a recommendation only to a Caucasian.' Yuri slapped his forehead. 'Amazing, here I am arguing the merits of a wine with the man who wants to close up every drinking shop in the Soviet Union.'

'Not close them up,' Gorbachev protested, 'just limit the hours. I'm not against drink, I'm against drunkenness.'

'Well, nobody is going to get drunk on your generosity.' Yuri fingered the small carafe. 'What a host, a one-litre bottle.'

'There's more in the cabinet. Look, you know that I'm no ascetic. I take a glass myself, on occasion.'

'True. Ligachev is the true ascetic. You're just a reformer.'

'Just?'

'Ascetics burn with a holy fire, they can't be touched. Reformers, on the other hand, get scratched by the cats that they're trying to feed.'

'The big cat damn near got me today. The biggest cat of all.'

Yuri tossed off his glass of wine, and poured another. 'Tell me, were you frightened?'

'Not then, it all happened too fast.' Gorbachev held out his hand to see if his fingers were steady. 'Perhaps now, a bit.'

Yuri raised an eyebrow, and offered his glass. Gorbachev shook his head. 'No, I don't need wine to steady my nerves.'

'Not like some people you could mention?'

'All of you sensitives drink too much.'

'Conceded, but with a reason. If you had to sift through all the sickening mental garbage that we handle every day, you'd do your share of drinking, too.'

'Perhaps. And does the young woman also drink that way?'

'Arina? Actually, I don't know. Arina, do you want a glass of wine?'

Both men turned to look at her. She had not moved from her position against the bulkhead. Staring at the two of them, still unbelieving, she shook her head.

'Well, at least come over here and sit down,' said Yuri. 'The General Secretary isn't going to bite you.'

Arina crossed the cabin slowly, and sank into the chair next to Yuri. She looked at him questioningly.

'The poor child is confused.' Yuri said. 'Let me explain. For reasons which I still do not quite understand, the General Secretary allows me certain liberties. My theory is that he really does have some Romanoff blood, and as Tsar Mikhail the Second he feels that his court is incomplete without a jester.'

'You're talking nonsense,' said Gorbachev, 'but it's true, you make me laugh. Not many people can do that.'

'I don't see you laughing now.'

'I'm not.' Gorbachev's face, indeed, was stern. 'I want an explanation. Why was she doing her little tricks in a forbidden area?'

Yuri asked Arina, 'Do you want to tell him, or shall I?'

Arina shook her head. 'I can't.'

'Look, she's blushing,' said Gorbachev. 'Well now, the motherland is safe if our women still can blush. What is this all about?'

'It's simple, you see what a beauty she is.' Yuri quickly outlined what had happened in the front cabin. 'She went to tap Prokoroff, but she got Shvabrin, as well.'

'And so I'm alive because of one man's lechery.' Gorbachev

shook his head in disgust. 'You see the sort of corruption I have to contend with? Moral, as well as financial. And all left over from the Brezhnev days.'

'I rather think it goes back a bit further than that,' said Yuri. 'Back to Adam and Eve, perhaps. It's the least of your worries right now, Mikhail Sergeyvich. What do you think? Was he acting alone?'

'I have no way of knowing . . . yet. Once we are in New York, once I am inside the Soviet Mission there, I will be able to establish direct contact with . . . certain parties at home. Then I will know how to act.'

'And against whom.'

'If anyone. He might have been on his own. It's possible.' Gorbachev leaned across the table, and grasped Yuri's forearm. 'Listen, my jester, the next few days are likely to be strange ones. I want you to stay close to me, as close as you can. I want you near me.'

'In my capacity as your jester, or as a sensitive?'

'Whichever seems appropriate to the moment.' He nodded to Arina. 'I say the same to you. You did me a great service today. Do me another if the occasion arises.'

'I will,' Arina said simply.

'I'm counting on it.' Gorbachev stood up. 'Go back to your seats now, and try not to look too serious. Laugh a little, jester, and make her laugh too.'

Yuri flashed him a grin as they left. Once they were gone, Gorbachev held out his right hand and stared at his fingers. At first they were steady, but then they began to tremble. Soon the entire hand was shaking. He put the hand in his mouth, and bit down hard. When he held it out again, the fingers were steady.

'It is time to dress,' said Anatoli from his alcove. 'We will be in New York shortly.'

'Thank you.'

Gorbachev stripped off his tracksuit, and took a flat, square box from a side cabinet. In the box was a lightweight, tailored bulletproof vest. He grimaced at it, then put it on and fastened it. He put a shirt on over the vest, then crossed to the valet's working area. His plaid suit, freshly pressed, hung there from a bar.

69

'What's this? Why the plaid?' he asked. 'Do you want me to look like a Caucasian fruit pedlar?'

Anatoli sighed. He reached back into the alcove, and brought out the blue pinstripe. It was also freshly pressed.

'I thought so,' he said.

SIXTEEN
Sunday 2:45 PM

Snake sat at her table in the Colonial Diner, and debated with herself about what to do next. The two kids were still huddled in the corner, speaking softly with their heads close together. There was no need for her to remain on the tap; she had what she needed for her report. But something about the two of them made her want to stay on. She liked them, wanted to know them better, and besides, her afternoon had already been ruined by Delaney's operation. She had nothing else to do, and so she tuned in on their conversation again, reading their words in their heads.

'I can't believe that your father would do something like that,' Harry was saying. 'He wouldn't just go off and leave without telling you why.'

There was a long silence, and then Laura said, 'I think maybe he wanted to. I think he tried.'

'How?'

'You know those stories that he used to tell me when I was a kid?'

'Stories?'

'Harry, I've told you a hundred times. The ones about the Kingdom of the Sea.'

'Oh, sure. What about them?'

'Well, the night before he left we had a talk. He came up to my room and we talked about things. College next year, my French grades, nothing special. We even talked about you.'

'Nothing special, huh?'

'Come on. Then he looked at me sort of funny, and he said, "It's getting kind of late. How about a bedtime story?" You know, at first I didn't know what he meant, like you didn't know just now. I mean, he hadn't told me one of those stories

71

in years, but then I remembered, the Kingdom of the Sea with all those knights, and battles, and things. Well, you know how it is when they say something like that, it makes you feel about two years old, and so I said something real bright, like, ''Oh, Daddy, really.'' Stuck my nose up in the air like the queen bitch, and said, ''Oh, Daddy, really,'' and he got sort of a sad look on his face, and when I think of that look now I could cry.'

'You're beating up on yourself,' said Harry. 'Don't do that.'

But she was down on herself, remembering that night, and from across the room Snake read the regret in her head, and the memory of her father wanting to travel back just one more time to her childhood and the Kingdom of the Sea. And she remembered that he said to her, *Listen, I think you'll like this one. It's the story of the final battle between Candore and Luc, and I call it The Siege of Candore. It's the ultimate battle, the end of the tale. I never told it to you when you were younger because I didn't think you were ready for it. But now you are, and I'd like you to hear it.*

'And you know what I said?' asked Laura now. 'You know what the queen bitch said? She said, ''I'm really pretty tired, Daddy. Maybe some other time.'' And he said, ''You sure you don't want to hear it? It's the end of the story, the end of all those stories. The Siege of Candore. You used to love those stories.'' And I said . . . listen to me, he was pleading, and I said, ''Daddy, I did love them, really I did, but that was then and this is now. Those were children's stories.'' Can you imagine saying something so stupid?'

'Sure. I might have said the same thing. It still would have been stupid, but I might have said it.'

'Don't be kind. I hate it when you're kind.'

'So what happened then?'

'Nothing much. He laughed a little, but I think he was hurt and he was covering up, and then he said, ''Sure, you're much too old for that stuff now. It was a silly idea.'' Then he kissed me on top of the head, and he left, and I never saw him again. Never.'

'Don't dramatize. It isn't never, it's a week. You'll see him.'

'Never.'

'And you think he was trying to tell you something?'

'I didn't think so then, but I think so now. I think he wanted to explain what he was doing. Not in real words, but in a story. I think he wanted to leave me something. And I wouldn't listen.'

'You don't know that, you're guessing.'

'No, I feel it.'

'Have you told this to anyone?'

'Of course not, it's just something he said. Besides, it was between him and me, and nobody else. And now he's gone. Ah, shit . . .'

'Hey, don't start crying. Please?'

'I'm all right.'

'Look, I really think that you need to get high. You want to go someplace?'

'No, when you get high, you get horny. I don't feel like that now.'

'I meant high, nothing else.'

'You got anything?'

'I got some blow.'

'How much?'

'Enough to get high.'

'Where would we go? Not my house, the bitch is there.'

'My folks are home, too. The motel?'

'I knew it. You're horny already.'

'Hey, come on. I'm just trying to help.'

She thought for a moment, then nodded. 'But I mean it; no sex. That's not what I want today.'

'I know what you want. You want warmth, affection, and understanding.'

'Right. That, and some blow.'

'Yeah, definitely.'

SEVENTEEN
Sunday 3:00 PM

DeKalb went west on Seventy-second Street, and then south on Lexington. Ritter and I followed behind. The Bureau car was out of it now, useless with no traffic on the streets. The avenue was as empty as a bowling alley. I was still hoping that the pigeon would pause someplace where I could move in and tap him, but he showed no sign of stopping. He strode rapidly down Lexington, the package still concealed beneath his nylon jacket.

We were passing Sixty-ninth Street, when I said to Ritter, 'Time to make a move.'

'Like how?'

'Get up close to him.'

'How close?'

'Close as we can.'

'We'll spook him.'

He was right. There was no crowd in which to mingle. If we came up close we'd be two sore thumbs to anyone with eyes. Still . . .

'It has to be done,' I said. 'We don't know where he's going or what he's carrying. I was hired to do a job, and it's time for me to do it.'

I picked up the pace to a jog, closing in slowly. Ritter said something under his breath, but he jogged along with me. We covered half a block that way, and then the pigeon made a move of his own. Without looking back, he started to run, pulling away from us.

'You blew it,' said Ritter. 'You spooked him.'

'No, he didn't see us. It has to be something else.'

Whatever it was, DeKalb was running flat out now. We raced after him. He pulled the package from under his jacket

74

as he ran, stripped off the wrapping, and flung it away. The paper fluttered to the street, and now there was a pistol in his hand. We were still half a block behind him when he turned up Sixty-seventh Street, heading for Park Avenue. Ritter saw the situation first.

'Oh, no,' he said. 'Oh, sweet Jesus, no.'

The sidewalks of Sixty-seventh Street were crowded with people standing in front of the Soviet Mission to the United Nations. About half of those people were cops, a cordon of blue uniforms in a protective semicircle at the front of the building. A motorcade was parked at the kerb, the five limousines that had just transported Mikhail Gorbachev and his entourage from Kennedy Airport. As we came pounding up the street in pursuit of DeKalb, a New York City police captain stepped up to the second limousine. He saluted smartly, opened the rear door, and Gorbachev stepped out.

EIGHTEEN
Sunday 3:07 PM

The dark of the bedroom was striped by bars of sunlight filtering through the blinds. Daytime darkness, the guilty kind. Vince propped himself up on an elbow, looked at the woman sleeping next to him, and was swept by the familiar post-coital sadness. Paula DeKalb slept lightly, only a doze in the wake of sex. She slept on her side with one hip thrust high in an arc. The sight of her stirred him again, and the sensation was unwelcome.

Enough, he told himself.

He drew the bedsheet up to her shoulders feeling messy in more ways than one. Messy from the sticky residue of passion, but also from the casual act he had just performed. He had done it again, just as Sammy had figured he would, and not for any particular profit. There had been no gain for there was nothing more that she could have told him. He had fucked the woman simply because, like Mount Everest, she had been there, and thus had extended by one more digit the score of Vince Bonepart, black superstud and harvester of middle-aged females. He told himself that this was one of those times when he had given more than he had taken, that he had provided Paula with a warm affirmation of her womanhood. He told himself this as he stared at her face, at peace in sleep, but he still felt messy.

Paula made a sound deep in her throat, and he went quickly, into her head. Nothing there but the crackle of dreams. She was truly asleep, and it was time to go, time to make Major Bonepart a memory.

You're a lot more than you think you are, he told her silently.

He slipped out of the bed, looked first at the pile of his

76

clothes on the floor, and then at the bathroom door, ajar. There was the need to leave, but there was also the temptation to rid himself of at least one layer of messiness. He yielded without a struggle, into the bathroom with the door closed to protect her slumber, and into the stall of frosted glass with the hot water beating down on him. He lathered and rinsed himself twice, but he felt no cleaner. He bent his head into the force of the water and let it flow over him. He stayed in the shower so long that when he came out his skin was a layer of tingle.

He dried his body, wrapped the bathsheet round his middle . . . and then he heard the psychic scream.

It was not a sound, it was a mental howl of terror that echoed in his brain. It was suddenly gone, cut short.

He stood poised, body damp, and his toes scrunched tight on the tiles of the bathroom floor. He opened his head and reached out beyond the walls of the room that surrounded him. He felt the presence of the intruder, a thrust of sour blood lust. He shivered.

Sammy, you and your bright ideas, he thought.

He flung open the door, and came out low and hard, rolling across the floor. He saw the intruder crouched over the bed . . . a slim figure . . . a ski mask. Vince rolled again, got his legs under him, and jumped. The intruder's arm went up, then down, but by then Vince was in midair. He felt the blow against his side, and then he was on top of the intruder. They went down together, Vince on top. The lithe body squirmed under him. He struck for the throat with the edge of his hand, and connected. He struck again, and again, and the body went limp.

Enough, he told himself, just as he had before. It was more than enough; the intruder was dead.

'Christ,' he muttered, 'Sammy's gonna bang my ass for this.'

He rolled off, and stood up. The bed and the bedsheet were red. Paula lay under the sheet. The intruder had used a knife, taking her first in the heart and then, without need, slashing her throat. There had been time only for that one psychic scream. Without any hope, Vince went into her head, but there was nothing. Her brain was as dead as the rest of her.

77

Vince felt along his ribs. The knife had sliced across his side, and had opened up a flap of flesh. He was bleeding freely. He took a hand towel from the bathroom, pressed it against the wound, then sank to the floor and pulled the telephone off the bedside table. He punched in Sammy's New York number, waited, and then began to speak. When he was finished, he dropped the phone and stared at the ceiling. He did not look at the body on the bed, or at the one on the floor. He leaned against the wall, and waited. After a while, he crawled to the pile of his clothing, and pulled on his trousers. He crawled back to the wall and settled down to wait again.

NINETEEN
Sunday 3:07 PM

When Kathy Benton's doorbell rang, Martha was in the bathroom at the other end of the apartment. She heard Kathy's voice, the ever-cautious New Yorker, call, 'Who is it?'

'Flowers,' someone answered from outside. 'Delivery.'

'*Flowers?*' Kathy's voice pitched up in excitement. 'Did you say flowers?'

'Demetrios Florists, lady. Got a box of roses for you.'

'Roses? Martha, did you hear that? He sent me roses.'

Martha did not answer. She opened up and reached out, searching. She got Kathy first, a jumble of excitement. *Roses, must be from Dick. But why? Making up? Coming back? Has to be something . . .*

'Just a minute,' Kathy called gaily. 'I'll be right there.'

Martha probed further, seeking beyond the apartment to the landing outside. She reached out for whoever was there, and found him. She grunted. She felt as if she had been hit in the stomach. Out there was a blood lust cased in a brain so elemental that it barely quivered. The force of that lust overwhelmed her for a moment, she gasped for air, and then she was running down the hallway with her heels slipping on the waxed parquet. She saw Kathy at the end of the hall, striding to the door with a smile on her face.

'No,' Martha yelled, 'don't open it.'

Kathy looked at her in surprise, one hand on the doorknob and the other on the lock. She hesitated, a frown forming between her eyes, and for a flick of time Martha thought that she might listen. But outside that door were the roses of her love, and they called to her. The frown disappeared, and the smile reformed. She turned her hands, and drew open the door.

The sound was as light as rain on a window, *tick, tick, tick*, and Kathy fell backward, blown by a force as strong as a gale. She went down, crumpled and still. Then there was the scurry of racing feet, and after that there was silence.

Martha threw herself flat when she saw the door open. She was on the floor by the time that Kathy crumpled. She lay without moving, without breathing, while her mind focused on what stood outside the door. She read the same elemental brain waves, flat and dull. It was like being inside the head of a rat. Or of a tiger.

She waited until she heard the scurry of racing feet, and those flat waves receded. She cast all around. There was no one near. She wanted to stay on the floor, but she knew that she had to get up. She rose unsteadily, and walked down the hall to where Kathy lay. The weapon that had killed her had been murderously efficient. There were holes in her chest and her head, and her face was disfigured. Only one eye remained, and it was open, staring blankly. Martha smoothed down the lid, and then went to look for a telephone. She found it in the bedroom, and called Sammy.

TWENTY
Sunday 3:07 PM

Snake was a vike, and what she did was called viking. Those
were the words that the aces used, and it worked like this.

Imagine walking down a city street at night with your head
wide open to the thoughts of the people all around you: people
in the street, in the cars, in the homes along the way. Now,
that's a mistake for an ace, because there's a lot of evil out
there, and even more madness. You learn at an early age to
keep your head closed up, to ward off the psychic wails that fill
the space around a sensitive. If you don't keep your guard up
those wails will howl in your head like winds in a cavern,
blowing your mind with the sloth of the slob, the greed of the
avaricious, the jealousy of the discontented, the righteousness
of the fanatic, the despair of the helpless, the flaring orange
delight of the arsonist, the crimson sword of the psychopath
. . . and pervading it all the deep, insistent pulse of sexual
passion. So you learn to keep your head closed, but on this
particular night you are open to the wails of the world,
and particularly to that pulsing sexual beat. It gets into your
head, and your blood, and your balls, and if you have any
sense you will then close up and walk away from it. But not
tonight, no common sense tonight. Instead, you single out the
source of the beat, and find it coming from two people near by
who are fucking frantically.

Who are they? Husband and wife? Illicit lovers? A casual
couple?

Where are they? In one of those houses? In a parked car?
Behind a garden hedge?

It makes no difference, their beat is in your blood, and you
enter into the head of the man, or the woman, or both of them,
and hitch a ride on their sexual express, pounding to a climax

with them. It can happen that way on a city street, or when you're lying alone in a hotel room with the world a beehive all around you, or as you walk along a country lane past a barn full of silent giggles. But wherever it happens, and whenever you do it, the name for it is viking.

Viking: the act of entering another person's head for the purpose of vicarious sexual gratification.

That was the way it was defined for us at the Centre when we were kids. Vicarious sex, anyone who did it was called a vike, and as young aces we were warned by our elders that the practice was morally repugnant, self-destructive, and childish. It was also supposed to grow hair on your palms.

Despite the prohibition, however, we all experimented with viking. Who could resist the temptation? It was a chance for the young male to enter into the head of a female and experience the other side of what it was all about, for a female to do the same with a male, a straight with a gay, and on through the various combinations of partners. Now, you might think that even one such experience would be enough to turn a teenage kid into a life-long vike, but in fact it did not work that way. Few of us continued the practice past adolescence. Our elders were right, it *was* morally repugnant to enter into someone's head at so private a moment. But there were those few who never abandoned the habit, the convinced vikes, and Snake was one of them. It was her not-so-secret vice.

Which was why she followed Harry Falk and Laura DeKalb from the Colonial Diner down Route 202 to the Glenwood Motel. She tailed the silver Porsche in her own car. A Bureau car and driver had been available to her, but she preferred to work alone, and she was glad of it now. She was sure that once Harry and Laura did their drugs there would be sex to follow. She discounted Laura's reluctance. The girl was feeling low now, but once she was high, she'd be ready.

The Glenwood Motel advertised closed-circuit X-rated films, and waterbeds. Snake parked outside for ten minutes to give the kids time to check in, then drove up the ramp to the motel office. She looked around for the Porsche, and saw it parked in front of unit twenty-two. She went inside and registered. The clerk gave her the key to room forty-eight.

82

'Is number twenty available?' she asked. 'I'd rather have that one.'

The clerk was an old man with shaky hands and liver spots. He shrugged. 'Lady, they're all the same.'

'I know, but could I have number twenty?'

'Except for the number on the door, you couldn't tell one from the other. Same furniture, everything the same.'

Snake smiled at him. 'Sure, but I'd still like number twenty.'

'So what's so special about twenty?'

Snake lowered her eyes. 'Let's just say I have fond memories of that room. Okay?'

The old man shrugged again. 'If that's what you want, that's what you get.' He took back the key and gave her the one to room twenty. 'Memories I can understand. That's all I got is memories.'

Once in the room, Snake undressed quickly, and lay down on the bed with her hands at her sides and her eyes closed. She breathed deeply several times, and then opened up her mind. As soon as she did she was launched upon a sea of sex, swamped with sensations. It was all around her, and her nose was quickly filled with the smells of flowing juices, her ears with the slap of flesh on flesh, and her mouth with the salts of bitten lips and probing tongues. The Glenwood Motel was a sexual playground, and within her range she counted five heterosexual couples humping away, three homosexual couples, one mixed bag of three, four people dozing in post-coital torpor, and a solitary man slowly masturbating in rhythm to the flicker of a television tube. For a moment, and only for a moment, she felt a reluctance to go on. There was always that moment of distaste, but it never lasted long. She brushed it aside and focused on the room next to hers. She came into the scene at the point she had predicted, Laura's reluctance fading.

Damn it, I knew this would happen, she was saying. *Come on, Harry, stop fooling around.*

Who's fooling? Not me.

I mean it.

So do I.

Uh . . . Harry . . . uh . . . please. You promised.

I lied.

You bastard.

83

Hey, you smell so sweet, and you feel so smooth. Especially here . . . right here.

Don't do that. It makes me crazy.

Me too. And here.

Yeah.

And here. And here.

Yeah, there.

Right there.

Oh, yeah.

Snake hooked into Laura's head, and shivered. Her nipples hardened when Laura's did, and her breath came quickly along with the girl's. She felt the slide of Harry's lips along the length of Laura's body, down to nestle between her legs. She felt the probe of his tongue, an electric shock.

Put it in, she thought urgently. Put it in her.

Put it in, said Laura. *Now.*

Put what in?

You bastard.

Say it.

Don't tease, not now.

Say it.

You son of a bitch. Your cock, God damn it. Put your cock in me.

Now why would I want to do that?

Harry, fuck me, please. Just fuck me.

Snake shuddered as she felt Harry's drive into the girl, felt the warmth in her belly ignite, and in that moment she switched into Harry's head to become the driver. Pushing, she felt his hardness, her hardness now. She slid with him into the sheath, and out, and then switched back to Laura's molten pool expanding. Bathed in that pool, luxuriating, then back to Harry, driving. And back to Laura. And back again. Switching over and over, back and forth, feeling each of them building to climax, and her own a bubble within her that grew and grew as she strained for it, reached for it, found herself a fingertip away from it . . .

She came, and the world exploded. Actually exploded. The explosion bulged out the wall of the room, and fractured the ceiling above her. The force of it threw her off the bed. She lay on the floor, gasping, confused, her body still bent in the final

84

convulsion of her orgasm. Plasterboard and dust rained down on her. She shook her head, and got to her feet. She ran out into the corridor. The door to room twenty-two had been blown off its hinges. The room, itself, was wrecked. What looked like two blobs of meat were stuck to the bed. The rest of Harry and Laura was scattered around the room. Other doors were open now, and heads appeared. Snake realized that she was naked. She dashed back into her room, and threw on her clothes. She ran for her car, and drove a mile down the highway before she stopped at a gas station to call Sammy.

TWENTY-ONE
Sunday 3:08 PM

DeKalb ran swiftly up East Sixty-seventh Street towards the crowd in front of the Soviet Mission. Ritter and I ran after him, but there was no chance to reach him in time. Gorbachev was out of the car, and on the sidewalk. He wore the usual blue pinstripe suit, topcoat, trilby. He passed through the cordon of police from the kerb to the Mission. The police captain who had opened the limousine door was by his side, escorting him to the entrance. Gorbachev smiled broadly. He took off his hat, and waved to the crowd.

Ritter stopped abruptly; his pistol was out. He went into firing stance, aiming up the street at DeKalb's back. He fired twice. He was low with both shots, trying for a leg shot because of the crowd. The slugs kicked off the sidewalk behind DeKalb. Ritter raised his sights, but it was too late. All we could do was watch.

DeKalb hit the wall of blue, and burst through it, the unwrapped pistol in his hand. He stood directly in front of Gorbachev. He raised his arm, and fired into the Russian's chest. Gorbachev fell back, his eyes wide with shock. The police captain standing beside him made a smooth draw, and fired. DeKalb went down.

I looked around for a telephone. Neither Gorbachev nor DeKalb were dead, but I did not know that yet.

TWENTY-TWO
Sunday 4:15 PM

Uncle John Merlo came back to the clam bar on Mulberry Street, ready to kick ass. Not just anybody's ass, only Carlo's. His nephew had never shown up, and the Sunday afternoon ritual at Mama Merlo's had been ruined by the absence of her grandson. Uncle John had done his best with excuses, but Mama had seen through them all. The truth had struck her like a slap in the face. Her darling Carlo now had better things to do with his Sunday afternoons than spend them with his devoted *nonna*. But that was life, she told her son, you get old and they throw you away. Between sighs and heavings, she had managed to drink only three cups of cappucino before retiring for her afternoon nap, sending Merlo away with reproach in her eyes at the callousness of the young.

So Uncle John was seething as he walked into the clam bar, and looked around. No Carlo. Plenty of other people in the place now, the bar and the tables were crowded, but no Carlo. He saw Tony Spats standing at the end of the bar along with Billy Haviland from the Third Precinct. Detective Bill Haviland, in for a free load. Like every other cop in the neighbourhood, Haviland knew that he could order a dozen on the half-shell, another dozen baked, a plate of *scungil'* with some crusty bread to sop up the sauce, and walk out without putting his hand in his pocket. Maybe a dollar on the bar for Fat Louis, but that's all. Fucking cops could eat you out of business.

Uncle John made his way across the room to Tony and Haviland, waving to people at the tables, touching them lightly on the shoulder as he passed, and saying, 'Hey.' He nodded to Haviland, and said to Tony in a low, tight voice, 'Where is he? Where is the son of a bitch?'

Tony's face was hard and set. 'Listen, Uncle . . .'

'Don't do it, Tony. Don't try to cover up for him.'

'Uncle, please . . .'

'Every time he screws up, he comes running to you. You think I don't know that?'

'Look, let's go in the back.'

'He thinks you'll put in the good word for him, but not this time. This time I want his ass.'

'The people, they'll hear.'

'So where is he, what happened? You shoulda seen Mama, she was ready to cry.'

'Uncle John,' said Haviland, 'it really would be better if we went in the back.'

Merlo looked at the detective closely for the first time. His face was as hard and as set as Tony's, and there was nothing on the bar in front of him. No free load for Billy Haviland, not this time.

'Jesus save us,' said Uncle John. It came out in a whisper. His knees went weak. 'Carlo?'

Haviland nodded.

'Ah, shit. No.' He started to go down.

'In the back.'

Together, Haviland and Tony got the Uncle into the back room that was his office. They sat him behind his desk. Tony poured a shot of Strega, and put it in front of him. Merlo ignored it.

'How bad?' he asked Haviland.

'The worst. I got it on the wire. I came right over to tell you myself. I didn't want you to hear it from strangers.'

'I appreciate that. Now tell me what happened.'

'They found him in his car on some side street in Flushing. He was over the wheel, just lying there. The precinct car thought he was some kind of a drunk, but he wasn't drunk.'

'What kind of a hit?'

'Single shot, back of the head.'

'Ah.'

'About the body . . .'

'Yes, I know what to do about the body. I have some experience.'

'The coroner's office . . .'

'Yes, I know.'

Haviland stood up. 'I'm sorry for your trouble, Uncle John, but I gotta go now.'

'I understand.'

'I'd hang around, but after what happened uptown they're shifting everybody around.'

'Uptown?' Uncle John didn't know what he was talking about.

'You didn't hear? Somebody shot that Russian.'

'Russian?' He still didn't know, and he didn't care.

'If there's anything else I can do . . .?'

'You did plenty already. I won't forget it.'

After the detective had left, the Uncle stared at the glass of Strega for a long moment before taking a sip from it. He shook his head. A little favour for the Don. After all, who says no to Salvatore DiLuca? Just a little favour, and how does it get to be like this? Carlo, hanging over the wheel of his car, Christ Jesus. Why? He put his head in his hands, trying to concentrate. There were many things to do, so many moves to make.

The telephone rang. It was Salvatore DiLuca. He said, 'Uncle John, I just heard. What can I say?'

'We gotta talk.'

'I'm on my way. Stay right there.'

'I gotta go tell Mama.'

'Of course you do,' said the Don. 'You go, and come back to the bar. I'll be waiting there.'

TWENTY-THREE
Sunday 4:00 PM

The house on East Sixty-fourth Street that we used for a New York base was a four-storey brownstone with a weathered façade. The top two floors were bedrooms, and the second floor was filled with a gleaming mass of communications equipment. The interior walls of the ground floor had been knocked out to make one large room. In the bad days before Sammy took over it had been called the Operations Room. Now it was known as The Saloon. Operations were still handled at the back of the room on a long table with a battery of telephones. In the front of the room was an eighteen-foot mahogany bar complete with stools, rail, and a back mirror. There were 'Wanted' posters of Old West *pistoleros* on the walls, a sepia print of Lillie Langtry, and a Rubensesque nude in faded oils. Sammy had wanted to put in spitoons, but Langley had refused the requisition.

Snake, Martha, and Vince were at the bar, deep into the booze, staring at their drinks. They were all the way down. They had made the mistake of getting involved with their subjects, and now they were paying for it. You don't get involved, but they had, and all three of them had seen folks blown away, folks they had come to care for. They looked awful. Vince's face was twisted into a knot, Martha looked as if she had been weeping, and Snake's lips moved soundlessly. Vince knocked back the bourbon in his glass, the single ice cube clicking against his teeth.

'You supposed to be doing that?' I asked. The slice in his side wasn't all that bad, but when they had patched him up at the hospital they had pumped him full of antibiotics and had told him that booze was contraindicated.

'Piss off,' he said, and reached for the bottle of Wild Turkey.

I moved over to stand behind Martha. I put my thumbs on the

90

base of her neck, and rubbed gently. That was usually enough to make her purr, but not this time. She shook her head in irritation, and said, 'Please, Ben, not now.'

I looked at Snake. She glared back at me, daring me to say something. I kept quiet.

We had all debriefed each other head to head, sharing information. I knew exactly what each of them had gone through that afternoon. They were best left alone. I went behind the bar, made myself a vodka tonic, and took it to the operational end of the room. I had an idea building that I wanted to bounce off Sammy. He was talking into one of the telephones that lined the long table. Ritter was there, too, his phone patched into the New York field office of the FBI. Delaney, our director from the Agency, was on a cleared line to Langley. It was less than an hour after the try on Gorbachev's life, and they were trying to put it all together.

So far they knew that Gorbachev was unhurt, with only a bruise under the spot where the bullet had hit his vest, and resting at the Soviet Mission.

They knew that DeKalb was barely alive in the Intensive Care Unit at New York Hospital with a bullet lodged in the base of his brain. He was unconscious, and he wasn't going to come out of it.

They knew that there was no identification yet of the killer Vince had iced, that whoever had killed Kathy Benton had used a Makarov AKMS, and that the job at the Glenwood Motel had been done with a satchel charge through the window.

They knew that no one yet had tied DeKalb to the DIA; they were keeping that one buried.

That was all they knew, and it wasn't much. Someone had gone to a lot of trouble to tie up the loose ends of DeKalb's life, wiping out the three people closest to him. What they did not know was why.

Sammy said something into the phone, and hung up. He saw the drink in my hand. He took it from me, bit off half of it, and handed back the glass. 'It's crazy out there,' he said. 'People running around in circles, shitting big green bricks. I've got aces tapping heads from Tokyo to Timbuctoo, and they're all reporting panic in the streets. It's Armageddon time.' He turned to Ritter. 'What's happening over at the Mission?'

'Surrounded by Federal marshals.'

'What about the police?'

'They're still there. The cop who shot DeKalb, a Captain Duffy, the Commissioner put him in charge at the scene. The lucky bastard, he'll be an inspector tomorrow.'

Delaney covered his phone with the palm of his hand, and said, 'The President is on the telephone right now with Gorbachev. I'll have a tape of the conversation as soon as they're finished. I'm also told that the President has put the One-Oh-One Airborne on full alert.'

'Just what we need, more panic,' Sammy said sourly. 'What's he going to do with them, invade Manhattan?'

'No need to take that tone, laddie.' Delaney wore tweed jackets with shooting patches, and ties that looked like rug samples. He used words like laddie. 'After all, we're in this together.'

'I'm in this because you talked me into a horseshit job.'

'A simple favour for a sister agency. Done all the time, you know.'

'Not by me, not any more.' He asked Ritter, 'Any word on who hit Carlo Vecchione?'

'The police are calling it a mob job.'

'What are you calling it?'

'I was there at Shea. I saw him pass the package to DeKalb. They wanted him to have an untraceable weapon. That's what I'm calling it.'

'And now he's dead, another loose end tied up.' Sammy held up two fingers an inch apart. 'Damn it, we were this close to tapping DeKalb. Now we've got nobody to go after.'

I looked away from him. I stared at a wall.

'Yeah, Ben, I know. You wanted to pull him in.'

I shrugged, and said nothing.

'That's all blood under the bridge,' said Delaney. 'You had your orders and you followed them. You had no way of knowing that it was going to turn wet.'

Sammy looked at him in disgust. 'So what do we do now, pack it in?'

Delaney's telephone rang before he could answer. He

picked it up, spoke briefly, and put it down. He said, 'The tape is ready.' He pushed a button on the console before him, and a whirring noise came from the speakers mounted on the wall. Then we heard the husky baritone of the President, Gorbachev's clear tenor speaking in Russian, and the careful accents of the translator bridging them both.

'Mr General Secretary, before anything else, how are you? I understand that you escaped without injury.'

'Thank you, Mr President, a bruise, nothing more. I was fortunate.'

'Thank God for that.'

'If you wish.'

'I wanted to call you personally to express my shock and indignation over what happened this afternoon. I wish to offer you my fullest apologies for the incident.'

'Thank you, your words are comforting, but how could something like this have happened?'

'I wish I could answer that question right now, but I can't. So far, our information is very sketchy, but I've ordered a full investigation of the matter, and you can rest assured that we'll get to the bottom of it.'

'Who is the man who did this?'

'As I said, we don't have much information yet, but he appears to be an American Air Force colonel with a history of mental instability. I promise you that as soon as we learn more, you will be the first to be informed.'

'Thank you, but I hope you realize that the entire world must be informed as well. The world is trembling, Mr President. Here at the Soviet Mission we are receiving reports from all over. There is panic and fear everywhere. You must do whatever you can to quiet that fear. As you learn the facts of this matter you must hold back nothing. You must be frank and open with the world.'

'I intend to be.'

'I hope so. And I also hope that I can count on a higher level of protection than has been afforded to me so far.'

'You can depend on it. Every effort is being made to assure your safety.'

'Please understand, I have a high regard for my life, every man does. But far more important than my life, than any single life, is what we hope to accomplish tomorrow morning at the United Nations. Let me be blunt. There must be no more such incidents. You and I, we hold in our hands the wellbeing of generations to come. We must not fail them.'

'Mr General Secretary, no one is more concerned than I am with the wellbeing of those generations. I assure you of my unswerving commitment to world peace and arms control, and I look forward to our joint appearance tomorrow.'

'Very well, I cannot ask for more than that.' The formalities completed, Gorbachev's sigh came over the speakers. 'Of course, I had heard about the dangers of the streets of New York, but I had not expected . . .' There was a muffled exchange with the translator. 'The word is mugged, yes? I had not expected to be mugged my first day here. At least I escaped with my wallet.'

The President chuckled, but it was forced. He was the one who made the jokes. 'Well, it came out all right in the end. The cavalry got there in time.'

'Cavalry?' Another exchange with the translator. 'Oh, yes, the police officer. He is to be commended.'

'He will be.'

'Very well then, until tomorrow.'

'Goodbye.'

There was the sound of receivers being replaced, and then a click as the tape stopped rolling.

'An Air Force officer with a history of mental instability,' I quoted. 'Who dreamed that one up?'

'That's what the President was told,' said Delaney. 'Actually, that was good damage control, somebody at the White House was on the stick for a change. Nothing was said about the DIA, or the killings.'

I asked, 'Does the President know about any of that?'

'Probably not. His people try to keep the tough nuts off his plate.'

'What about us?' asked Sammy. 'Where do we fit into this now?'

Delaney pursed his lips judiciously. 'Nowhere, I'm afraid. It's a question of security now, straight police work. I can't see any use for your particular talents at this stage of the game.'

'There might be,' I said. Sammy looked at me questioningly.

94

Head to head, I said, *Not in front of the children.*

Go ahead, what's on your mind?

It's going to sound odd.

I specialize in odd. Let's hear it.

What would you think of establishing a deep tap on DeKalb?

Odd? Yeah, I'd say that's odd. The man is just about dead. His brain isn't functioning.

I'm not so sure about that. His brain isn't working, not in the accepted way, but his brain isn't dead, either. There's electrical activity, so something has to be going on down there, all the way inside. Someone should be listening in.

Maybe. Just maybe.

It's worth a try.

I'd have to get approval.

Delaney's right here.

Have to go higher than that. Let me see what I can do.

Make it fast. We don't know how much longer he's got. And Sammy . . . the troops are low. A word from you would help.

No time. You've just been appointed Morale Officer.

I went back to the bar. I sat next to Snake, and leaned over so that she had to look at me. I said, 'Listen, I want to ask you a question. A very important question.'

'Don't try to be jolly,' she said. 'I'm not in the mood.'

'Come on, *tus*, I said it was important.'

'Get off my back.'

'Hey, where's the sisterly affection? Where's the warm, kind-hearted kid I used to know?'

She stared at me, her face set and grim.

'One question,' I urged.

'No.'

'Why not?'

'Because I know what you're going to ask.'

'You can't know. I'm blocked.'

'I don't have to read your head to know. I know you.'

'You couldn't possibly. Come on, I'll give you a dime if you'll answer the question.'

'Christ, what a bore you can be sometimes.'

'A quarter?'

'Just leave me alone, huh?'

'Final offer. One dollar.'

She sighed. 'You're impossible. Go ahead, ask your stupid question.'

I leaned closer. 'Tell me the truth, *guapa*. Did the earth move?'

'Damn it, I knew it. I knew you were going to say that.'

'Well, did it?'

'The whole fucking motel blew up,' she yelled. 'Of course the earth moved.'

'Then it was good for thee,' I said solemnly, 'and I am happy.'

'You bastard.'

She tried to keep her face set, but a giggle started deep within her, bubbled up, and escaped. She giggled again, and then smiled. It wasn't much of a smile, and it didn't last long, but it was there. I looked over at Martha and Vince. They, too, were smiling faintly, sadly. It was as much as I could expect.

'You bastard,' Snake repeated, this time softly.

I made another drink, and sat with them silently, my eyes on the back table. Sammy spoke earnestly to Delaney, and then Delaney got on the phone. He stayed on it for as long as it took me to finish the drink, then he hung up and waited. When the phone rang, he picked it up, listened, and then called my name.

'Slade, front and centre, laddie.'

I went back to the table. Sammy said, 'You've got your tap. The hospital will set you up inside the ICU. Get over there as quick as you can.'

'On my way.'

'Before you go,' said Delaney. 'I had to go to the DCI on this, and he saw fit to clear it with the National Security Council. He ran into a bit of a snag there. Seems that you weren't the only one with this bright idea. The Soviets thought of it, too. They've asked permission to send one of their aces.'

'Nervy bastards, aren't they?' said Sammy. 'On our own turf.'

'The DCI has agreed,' said Delaney. 'Everyone is falling over backwards to show what nice guys we are. It's a joint operation. One of their sensitives will meet you at the hospital.'

'Probably Yuri Muzalev,' said Sammy. 'That was his voice

96

doing the translating. Tell the clown I said hello.'

Delaney chose to ignore that. We weren't supposed to be on speaking terms with Soviet aces. He looked at me narrowly. 'The DIA connection and the killings, that's all reserved information. It stays in the house, understand?'

I nodded, and left.

TWENTY-FOUR
Sunday 4:15 PM

Gorbachev spoke to the President from the study of the apartment set aside for him on the third floor of the Soviet Mission to the United Nations. It was the apartment normally reserved for the use of the Foreign Secretary during his visits to New York, but for these few days it belonged to the Soviet leader. It was a large suite of rooms generously furnished in a heavy-handed style. The furnishings dated from the days when Gromyko had been Foreign Secretary, and they reflected his dull conservatism: dark wood, dark walls, dark floors, with little relief. It was a place in which to work, not relax, and the desk behind which Gorbachev sat could have been lifted from the office of any Moscow bureaucrat.

Gorbachev said goodbye to the President, and put down the telephone. He looked around the room, measuring the people there. Their eyes were on him, every one, waiting for him to say something.

Directly in front of him sat Shevardnadze and Ligachev, each displaying the calm demeanour that one would expect from a diplomat and a politician. Next to them sat the Soviet Ambassador to the United Nations, Oleg Panchenko, who showed no such cool exterior; his face was lined with concern. Behind them stood the three *GehBehs*, KGB officers of varying rank. The short one with the barrel chest and the long arms was Major General Yevgeni Zazulin, the New York *rezident* in charge of all operations in the area. Next to him was Colonel Frolov of Directorate K, in charge of the physical security of the Mission, and one step behind stood Major Mironoff of the Ninth Directorate, newly in charge of the General Secretary's bodyguard. Off in the corner and not far from the liquor cabinet, he noted, were Yuri and Arina, and

98

near them was the Mission medical officer, a worried little man overwhelmed by the responsibility suddenly thrust upon him. In the other corner, Anatoli sat quietly with his hands folded in his lap, ready to be of service.

All present and accounted for, he thought. Except for one man. The Navigator.

He closed his eyes, and leaned back in his chair. His conversation with the President had been an exercise of willpower designed to project the image of a healthy and confident man, but he was neither. What had been announced to the press as a bruise on his chest was, in fact, a badly cracked rib, and unannounced to the press was the mild concussion that he had sustained in the attack when his head had hit the pavement. The rib was like a spear in his side sending waves of pain from his shoulder to his hip, and his head felt like the inside of a slowly tolling bell. The Mission doctor had offered painkillers, but he had rejected them. He had allowed the doctor to strap his chest, but nothing more. His reasoning was that he needed his wits sharp, and that he preferred the pain to the dulling effect of narcotics. In truth, he was simply afraid to swallow anything. Not now.

With his eyes still closed, he let his mind drift. Two attempts on his life in a matter of hours, and now the Navigator was missing. It was a frightening sensation, alien to him, to know that he was a hunted man. Like a fox in the forest, he thought, or am I a lion in the jungle? He preferred the image of the lion, for he thought of himself as a fighter. He had, after all, fought his way to the top. It had been one long struggle to raise himself up from his roots in the Stavropol territory to Moscow State University, and then into the Byzantine world of Communist Party politics. A struggle for survival and a struggle for advancement, and only a fighter could have accomplished it. Only a lion, never a fox.

But now, leaning back with his eyes closed, his ribs a rack of pain, and the throbbing in his head a monstrous intrusion, he knew that in a broader sense he had never been a fighter at all. Beyond the rough and tumble of boyhood he had never been in a fist fight, had never served in the armed forces, had never been to war. Only ten years old at the time of the German invasion of the Motherland, he was the first Soviet leader whose age had prevented him from playing the role of the warrior. Not he, but his father, had gone off to that war to die in Carpathia. As General Secretary he could rattle off military statistics by the metre: orders of battle, concentrations of fire-power, first-strike capabilities; but in matters of practical application he was an innocent. With a sinking feeling, he realized that, although his life was at hazard, he was incapable of defending himself in the simplest fashion. He did not even know how to fire a pistol. Left to his own devices, he was helpless, and the concept terrified him.

'Comrade General Secretary?'

He recognized the voice of the doctor. He willed himself to open his eyes, but they stayed closed. He knew that he had to open them. Everyone in the room was watching him, waiting for him to open his eyes and take command. He tried again, but he could not do it. His eyes stayed shut.

'Comrade . . .?'

There was much to be done, but he was gripped by an enormous lassitude. So far he had performed a bare minimum of his duties. He had spoken to Raisa over an open telephone line, assuring her that he was well and using the most com-monplace terms, for he had been told that the National Secu-rity Agency in a place called Fort Meade, Maryland, would be recording every word. By a far more sophisticated means of communication, he had sent off messages to the Central Com-mittee and to Chebrikov at KGB Centre, detailing the two attempts on his life, and the apparent mystery of the missing Navigator. To the Central Committee he had made the *pro forma* request for advice and instructions. To Chebrikov, he had given instructions, not asked for them, and had requested information on the movements of certain men. So, that much had been done, and now he awaited their replies, but there was much more yet to do. There was his United Nations speech to be reviewed with Shevardnadze and Ligachev. There was the reception later in the evening for the ambassadors of the War-saw Pact nations and other socialist allies. There was . . . there was so much, and yet all he wanted to do was to stay just the way he was, cut off from the world with his eyes closed.

'General Secretary, please . . .?'

What did that idiot doctor want? His ribs were on fire, and his head was a throbbing pulp. This was all insane. First there was that lunatic Shvabrin on the aircraft, and then the crazy American firing a pistol point blank at his heart. He knew quite well why his eyes would not open. They were sealed by fear. Fear had filled him up to the brim, and if he opened his eyes that fear would come spilling out for all to see. Where was the lion in the jungle now?

'Your Imperial Majesty, may I approach the throne?'

Not the doctor this time, but the familiar voice of Yuri Muzalev. The mocking lilt was enough to dissolve the fear, if only for the moment. He opened his eyes. His vision was blurred, and he blinked rapidly. The Mission doctor stood over him. Yuri stood to one side. There was a glass of water on the desk, and a small bottle.

'Aspirin,' said the doctor. 'It will help with the headache.'

'No.' Gorbachev pushed himself back from the desk, recoiling from the sight of the bottle. The movement sent a stab of pain up his side, but he scarcely felt it.

'Please, it is only aspirin, nothing else.'

Gorbachev shook his head violently, his eyes fixed on the bottle. He knew that the fear was showing now, but he could not control it. He was ashamed, but he could not swallow the unknown. Not after all that had happened.

'Please, I assure you.' The doctor bent over him. He was an army doctor, in civilian clothing of course, and he wore the badge of the army medical corps in his lapel: a serpent entwined around a golden cup.

'Do you know what they say about a doctor in the army?' It was Yuri, pointing at the lapel badge. 'As crooked as a snake, and not a bad drinker, either. And speaking of drinking, that Georgian tiger piss that you gave me on the plane was enough to give the devil himself a headache.'

Yuri slid himself onto the edge of the desk, and let a leg dangle nonchalantly. He picked up the aspirin bottle, shook two tablets into his palm, and popped them into his mouth. He washed them down with water. He took two more tablets, and held them out to Gorbachev. In a murmur that only the General Secretary could hear, he said, 'Take them, Tsar Mikhail. This is no time to lose it.'

101

Gorbachev stared at him for a moment, then took the tablets and swallowed them with water.

'That's it,' said Yuri in the same low tone. 'Now pull up your socks. So somebody is trying to kill you, so what? When was the last time that a Romanoff died in bed?'

Gorbachev smiled faintly. 'They never did, did they? Murdered, every one of them. And what about you, jester? Do you plan to die in bed?'

'I plan to die laughing, Your Worship. In bed, or out, but definitely laughing.'

Gorbachev nodded his understanding. 'Thank you, Yuri Ivanovich. That's something to remember.'

Yuri leaned closer. 'A suggestion has been made by my colleague, Arina. I have discussed it with the *rezident*, and he gives his approval. It requires the use of a sensitive.'

'So? Why bring me into *GehBeh* matters?'

'I would have to leave here and go to the hospital where that animal is dying. You said that you wanted me close to you.'

'Can the woman do the job?'

Yuri shrugged. 'She could do it, but I could do it better.'

Gorbachev considered, then said, 'No, send the woman. I want you near by.'

'As you wish.'

Gorbachev waited while Yuri spoke briefly to Arina. He waited while she left the room. He waited while the others settled down, their eyes upon him once again.

The lion, or the fox, he thought. There is more than one kind of fighter.

'Very well, comrades, there is much to do,' he said in a firm voice. 'First of all, where is the Navigator?'

The *rezident* glanced at Colonel Frolov. Frolov drew himself up, and announced, 'Comrade General Secretary, the Navigator is not in the building. He is missing.'

Gorbachev said patiently, 'I am aware of that. I want to know where he is, not where he isn't.'

Mission security was Frolov's pigeon, but the ultimate responsibility belonged to Zazulin, the *rezident*, and he accepted it. 'The Navigator was last seen standing with the welcoming committee outside the building just before you arrived. He has not been seen since. Frankly, we have no idea where he is.'

Gorbachev looked over at Yuri, who nodded to show that he had tapped the *rezident*'s head, and that nothing was being concealed. In a mild voice, he said, 'Tsar Mikhail, would it be fair to say that the Navigator is sailing in deep waters? Would it?'

'It might, indeed.'

'On the other hand, he might have just stepped out for a drink. Speaking of which . . . do you think it's too early?'

TWENTY-FIVE
Sunday 3:15 PM

At the moment that DeKalb took his shot at the General Secretary, and Captain Duffy took his shot at DeKalb, the Navigator was standing in the back row of the welcoming committee that was gathered in front of the Mission. He was placed that far to the rear because his official position, as opposed to his actual importance, was only that of a third secretary. It was the custom in his service, the Soviet military intelligence or GRU, for high-ranking officers to assume inferior cover jobs when serving abroad. In contrast to the relative flamboyance of the KGB, in the GRU a third secretary might well hold the actual rank of major-general, which, indeed, the Navigator did.

It was only this custom that allowed him to slip away from the scene of the shooting. When the shots sounded, the group in front of the Mission reacted like a flock of startled sheep, milling about in confusion. Not the Navigator. He saw the General Secretary fall back into the arms of those behind him. He saw the police officer whirl, and fire. He saw DeKalb go down. And then, as if in the worst of his dreams, he saw the General Secretary stagger to his feet, propelled by helping hands. He saw pain in Gorbachev's eyes, and he saw shock, but he did not see what he was looking for. The Navigator had seen death many times, and he had learned to look at the eyes. He saw no death in Gorbachev's eyes, not now and not soon, and in that moment he knew that his time had run out. Unrestricted by the milling crowd, he detached himself from the rear rank and edged his way along the front of the building until he was clear of the police barriers. A quick look around told him that he was unobserved; all eyes were on the scene in the street. He walked to the corner of Park Avenue, turned uptown for one block, crossed the avenue, and continued west to Madison. He walked with a quick, athletic stride. He was a short and muscular man who was just past sixty, but who looked ten years younger. He spent an hour each morning in a weight room maintaining that appearance.

He found an empty telephone booth at the corner of Madison, and dialled the 800-toll-free number for Hertz Rentals. He looked around as he listened to the ring, and decided that he was still clean. The telephone clicked, and a voice from half a continent away said, 'Good afternoon, this is Hertz reservations, Maureen speaking.'

The Navigator said, 'Good afternoon, the following is my Hertz Number One Club card number.' He rattled off the seven-digit number without referring to the membership card in his wallet.

There was a pause while the operator punched the number into her keyboard, and then, 'Yes, Mr Wolfe, how may I help you?'

'I want to order a car. A Cadillac.'

'Yes, sir, what model Cadillac would that be? We have several.'

'Makes no difference, just so long as it's a Cadillac.'

'Yes, sir, and when would you want it?'

'Right away.'

'Immediately. And where will you be picking it up?'

'In Manhattan, the East Seventy-sixth Street garage.'

'One moment, please.' Another pause while the information was punched and read. 'Mr Wolfe, I can give you a Cadillac Seville at East Seventy-sixth Street. Would that be all right?'

'Fine, fine.'

'All right then, I'm confirming a Cadillac Seville for Mr Jacob Wolfe to be picked up immediately at East Seventy-sixth. Is there anything else I can do for you?'

'No, that's all.'

'Thank you for calling Hertz.'

When the Navigator left the booth, he did not start north toward Seventy-sixth Street, but continued across town to Fifth Avenue, where he hailed a taxi and gave an address on West Thirty-second Street. As the cab started down Fifth, he looked at his watch and estimated eleven minutes since the shooting. There was a radio in the taxi playing soft pop music. He waited for the flash. It came as they were passing Fifty-seventh Street, a break-in and stark announcement that the General Secretary had been gunned down in the streets of Manhattan. Nothing more.

'Jesus fucking Christ.' It was the driver. 'Did you hear that?'

'I heard it,' said the Navigator. He was having a hard time not looking back through the rear window.

'He said that somebody shot that Russian, what's his name?'

'Gorbachev.' The Navigator was careful to pronounce it improperly.

'Oh, man, this city is crazy, absolutely *in-sane*.' The driver turned around briefly. He was black, and bearded. 'I bet you some junkie did it.'

'I wouldn't know.'

'Gotta be. You know what percentage of crime in this city is connected with drugs?'

'No, I . . .'

'Bet on it. Only a junkie would do something like that. That's why I don't work nights, you know? They wanted me to work nights, but I said screw you, I don't need any more holes in my head. You know what I mean?'

'I know what you mean.'

He let the driver rattle on. At Thirty-second and Seventh, he paid off the taxi, found another, and gave an address on Twenty-third near First Avenue. The driver said, 'Did you hear?'

'I heard.'

'I bet you some nigger did it.'

'I wouldn't know.'

'Believe it. I mean, you know what percentage of crime . . .'

'I know.'

'Only a nigger would be dumb enough to do something like that. I mean, shoot the Russian president. How dumb can you get?'

'Really, I . . .'

'Do you think there'll be a war?'

'I couldn't say.'

'That would be something, a war. Just because of some

crazy spade. That's why I don't work nights, you know?'

'I know,' said the Navigator. He wished desperately that he could shut the driver up, and tell him to drive as rapidly as possible, but his training would not allow that. It was basic never to be memorable, not to stand out. He managed to keep himself under control. At Twenty-third Street, he changed taxis again and gave an address on West Tenth. The third driver told him that a crazy Puerto Rican had just shot some Russian up on Sixty-seventh Street, and that was why he didn't work nights any more. Once again the Navigator dug up the small change of conversation as they worked their way across town, and the radio reports began to fill in the details of the shooting.

The Navigator's order, under the cover name of Jacob Wolfe, for the immediate rental of a Cadillac Seville was routed through the Hertz computer system in routine fashion. In not so routine a fashion, triggered by the membership number on the order form, the information was duplicated and fed into a system that carried it to a terminal located in an abandoned red-brick warehouse on Marshall Street in Brooklyn. There it appeared on the screen of the Case Executive on duty, and stayed there unnoticed for more than a minute. The delay was understandable, given the circumstances.

The top-floor office of the Case Executive was sparsely furnished with a couple of desks, some battered chairs, a couch, a folding bed, and a squat refrigerator. The room was dusty, and the windows were thick with grime. The only items that gleamed were the computer terminal and the television set. Engstrom and Yadroshnikov sat in front of the set, absorbed by the news coverage of the attempted assassination. The Case Executive, who should have been watching her own monitor, stood behind them, her eyes on the screen. More than a dozen television cameras had been on the scene at Sixty-seventh Street to cover the arrival of the General Secretary, and now tapes of what had happened were being run over and over again. For the fourth time in as many minutes, Gorbachev appeared on the screen as he stepped out of the limousine. DeKalb burst through the uniformed lines, and fired; Gorbachev went down; Duffy fired, and Dekalb went down; all in the exquisite precision of slow motion. A television voice droned over the action, explaining it all once again.

'Did you see it?' asked Engstrom. 'One round in the chest, dead centre.'

'I saw it,' said Yadroshnikov. 'What about it?'

'The move was perfect. He did exactly what he was supposed to do.'

'No, he did not. He was supposed to drop the man, and he didn't.'

'That wasn't our fault. There was nothing in the scenario about wearing a vest.'

'You are talking about blame, and I am talking about results,' said the Russian. 'That target was supposed to go down, and he didn't. The vest was always a possibility. Your man should have gone for the head. If he had, this would all be over. In my service we favour the head shot.'

'It's risky, easy to miss.'

'The policeman went for the head, and he did not miss.'

'He was lucky. You go for the pump, and it's a sure thing. Normally.'

'Yes, normally, but not under these circumstances. The General Secretary could hardly wear a vest on his head, could he?'

'All right, take it easy.'

'I am totally at ease,' said Yadroshnikov, and he was. His long, thin face showed no sign of the strain that was etched under Engstrom's eyes. His voice was cold and calm. 'Actually, it makes no difference. The success rate for this attempt was never more than twenty per cent, only marginally better than the move by Shvabrin. The odds will improve after this.'

'If the Navigator stays in place.'

'No, no, I have explained that. It makes no difference if he stays, or if he runs. A different set of circumstances takes over, that's all. He will run, I am sure of it, but either way the odds will improve.'

'There he is,' said the Case Executive. 'On the screen, in the back row.'

The television tape now being shown was from a different angle, and on it the Navigator could be seen, his head between the shoulders of the men in front of him. The picture jerked as the shots were fired, but the Navigator's face stayed in focus as Gorbachev was helped back onto his feet.

'There,' said Yadroshnikov. 'Right there, he's ready to run. You can't see him now, but he's already running.'

'You're guessing. You don't know that.'

'I know the man. I served under him for two years in Vienna. As soon as he saw that the attempt had failed, he ran. I guarantee it.'

'His orders were to stay in place.'

'I am aware of that, but nevertheless, he is running. The progression depends on it. A probability factor of eighty per cent.'

'Don't throw your numbers at me, I'm not impressed,' said Engstrom, but, in fact, he was. The Russian's habit of expressing probabilities in terms of percentages was irritating, and would been insufferable had he not been right so often. 'What about DeKalb?'

'He is as good as dead; no longer a factor. Now the progression continues, and the percentages increase at each stage.'

'That's assuming that the Navigator ran.'

'He ran.' Yadroshnikov allowed himself to show mild displeasure. 'I have already said that he did. This stage of the progression was based on the assumption that the Navigator would stay in place if the attempt succeeded, and that he would run if it failed. It had to be that way.'

It was then that the Case Executive noticed the red light blinking on her console. She hurried over to read what was on the screen. She frowned. She was a member of Engstrom's team, and the Russian was an irritant to her, as well. Reluctantly, she said, 'Better take a look. The Navigator is bugging out.'

'Say again,' snapped Engstrom.

'I've got a Hertz here from the Navigator. He's running.'

Engstrom and Yadroshnikov moved to the terminal, and stared. Engstrom said, 'Could it be a mistake? Wrong code?'

She shook her head. 'He doesn't make mistakes like that. He ordered a Cadillac. That's a bug out. Anything else is a Ford.'

'What does that garage location mean?'

'Carlotta's place. He's headed there.'

Yadroshnikov said complacently, 'As predicted.'

'All right, all right, you hit it again. Do you ever make a mistake?'

'Often. More times than you can imagine. We should leave now. It is time to move into the next stage.'

'Is your man in place?'

Yadroshnikov did not bother to reply. The look he gave Engstrom said that his men were always in place. They left the warehouse then, and in minutes they were in a car heading over the Brooklyn Bridge into Manhattan.

TWENTY-SIX
Sunday 4:37 PM

In order to understand what happened between Arina and me
. . . the immediate magnetic attraction that slammed us
together . . . it should be explained that love does not come
easily to aces. Love demands illusions, and we have few of
those, if any. We lose our illusions early, and how could it be
otherwise? Cruising in and out of minds as we do, we see far
too much of the human condition, see the parts of people that
are best left unseen. We see with naked eyes, which means
without illusions, and without illusions how can there be love?

I do not mean to say that love is illusory, only that love is
nurtured by the unknown. At least, it is for normal people.
The normal man, or woman, makes his lover magnificent
by the parts of her that he is forced to invent. Day after day he
refurbishes the image of his love, supplying the grace notes
that she leaves unsung, the gestures unmade, the words
unspoken. Endowing her with the virtues of his imagination,
he sustains his love through illusions, making her worthy of
his love.

The ace is denied these illusions. If his love is a normal
woman, he sees her with a clarity that is passion's antiseptic;
and if his love should be another ace, they stand exposed to
each other down to the bones, unprotected. They see the ker-
nel of malice in every kindness, and the guile behind the softest
smile. They see dominance in submission, avarice in charity,
and they hear the edge of regret in every sigh of satisfaction.
They are, in short, the ultimate cynics, and because of this they
are often loveless.

Thus the conventional perception of the sensitive, male or
female, as the unabashed sensualist who skims the pleasures
of life, constantly shuffling partners and ready for anything

111

with anyone. There are, however, exceptions, and one of those was my love for Nadia Petrovna. Once in a rare while, two aces moved by a mutual attraction open up to each other, and the result is not a cynical smile but a gasp of wonderment. Open, vulnerable, uncaring, the two minds meet and mesh, and the need for illusion drops away. Each sees in the other a kindness without malice, and a humour without guile. They see neither dominance nor submission, avarice nor charity, and every sigh of satisfaction rings real. In that first moment they know that what they have for each other is enough for a lifetime without artifice, and the knowledge is a sudden trove of treasure. It happens rarely, but it happens, and whenever it does it is invariably accompanied by the odour of oranges.

Those oranges, they told us about them when we were kids at the Centre, just as they taught us all the other esoterica of the strange life into which we had entered. Along with the tradecraft of alpha taps and deltas, of quick reads and networking, of head-to-head communication and brain-wave analysis, they also taught us the customs of our new society. One of those customs was the accepted image of the free-swinging sensitive. Another was the possibility, the bare chance, that we might some day meet someone of our kind with whom we could lead the approximation of a normal life. Our instructors, however, did not encourage us to believe in this possibility.

'Don't look for it, and don't expect to find it,' the instructor would warn us, a critical forum of teenage kids. 'I can't quote you any figures on this, but it's almost unheard of for two aces to meet and to click that way. It simply never happens . . . okay, rarely . . . and the only reason that I'm telling you about it is that I've been instructed to. The same way I have to tell you about sexual hygiene and birth control.' There were hoots from the five of us. 'Sure, sure, you know all about it, but I'm supposed to warn you about this business of long-term relationships, so let's get rid of the giggles and get on with it.'

Pity the poor instructor. He was not that much older than we were, in his early twenties perhaps, and he was trying to explain something that he, himself, had never experienced, and probably never would. More, it was something that he

112

must have dreamed about having, against all the odds. Still, he had to go through the motions.

'So you can forget about the part of a normal life, what the books call an ongoing commitment. It isn't for you, and to tell you the truth, you won't be missing much. Because nothing lasts forever, kiddies, and I mean nothing. Take a good look some time at the older normals you know, the couples who have been together for ten, or fifteen, or twenty years. What do you see there? Do you see excitement? Vibrancy? Intimacy? Do you see lo-ooove?' He drew the word out mockingly. 'You know damn well that you don't. What you see there is habit, and a crippling dependency, and industrial-strength boredom. That's what happens in the long run, and it happens to all of them. Remember that when you start feeling sorry for yourselves. Take your pleasure wherever you find it, and learn to live within the moment. That's what you were made for, the moment, and nothing else. Believe me, of the two worlds, you've got the better one.'

It was a good pitch, but it didn't fully work. It was directed to the wrong audience. We were idealistic teenagers with romance still stamped on our souls. Deep down we knew that we wanted, needed, something more than a life of surface pleasures. Thinking back on my own training days, I remember that it was Snake, typically, who chose to pursue the point.

'But it *is* possible,' she insisted. 'You said that statistically it's possible for two sensitives to . . . you know.'

'To fall in lo-ooove? Is that what you mean?'

'That's exactly what she means,' said Martha. 'It's a word like any other word. Do you have to dump on it?'

'No, of course not. Look, I'm just trying to protect you against disappointment. Yes, it can happen, but it won't.'

'But it can?'

'Yes.'

'But when it happens . . . if it happens . . . how do you know that it's, you know, real?'

The instructor smiled faintly. 'Oranges.'

'What?'

'Oranges,' he repeated. 'Look, let me lay it out for you. Once you've finished your training and you leave the Centre, you'll find that it pays to go around with your head blocked most of the time. You'll find yourself opening up only when you're relaxing, like now, within your own peer group, or when you're actually on a job. The rest of the time you'll stay blocked, and that's where the oranges come in. From what we know, and we don't know much, whenever this situation arises with two aces, blocked or not, they both experience the strong aroma of fresh oranges.'

'You said what?'

'Oranges? Like the juice?'

'That's not real.'

'Hey, why not apples? Or peaches. I lo-ooove peaches.'

'Come on, quiet down. Look, I didn't say that they actually smell oranges, I said that they experience the feeling. It has to do with the neurological imbalance that all sensitives have. You have it, I have it. That's why we're here. Well, from the little that we know, when this . . . this *click* occurs between two aces, the combination of their imbalances creates the apparent odour of oranges. Apparent, get it?'

A chorus of, 'Yeah.'

'They're not actually smelling oranges, but something in the combined imbalances produces that effect in the olfactory bulb of the brain. I've been told that the apparent odour is quite powerful. Overwhelming, in fact.'

'You've been told? You mean you don't know? You've never smelled it yourself?'

'No,' the instructor said sadly. 'Never. And it's time that we moved on to something more constructive.'

That's the way I remember first having heard about the oranges when we all were kids at the Centre. At that age, of course, there had to be a spate of orange gags over the next few weeks, most of which took the form of one or the other of us slugging down his OJ at breakfast, clutching his throat , dropping to the floor, and screaming as he rolled over and over, 'My God, I'm in love, I'm in love.' But that stopped after a while, and the odour of oranges passed into the collection of legends that surrounded so much of our lives. And it stayed a legend, only half believed, for all of us including me, until the day that I met Nadia.

Nadia and I met, as aces will, across a crowded room, a diplomatic reception at the United Nations where we both

114

were on assignment. I for the CIA; she for the KGB. Our minds touched across that room, and there it was, the odour of oranges: sweet, pungent, and all-pervading, and we were the only ones who could smell it. We were lovers from that moment on, although not in the accepted sense. We met, but we never spoke aloud to each other, never kissed or embraced. We met only in those crowded rooms, and we were never alone. We could not come any closer than that, for it would have meant our lives. We were aces on opposite sides of the fence, under constant surveillance, and it was the ultimate irony for me to have fallen in love with a Soviet sensitive, a woman I could never hope to have. We lived that way for two years, meeting at the social and diplomatic functions to which our duties brought us. We laughed and loved together from opposite sides of those crowded rooms, and at the end of each of those evenings we went our separate ways with our meaningless companions, whispering bittersweet farewells that only we could hear, sniffing the odour of oranges that was ours alone. We had two years' worth of that sophisticated sort of misery before we kicked the beans in the fire and ran off together, thumbing our noses at both the KGB and the CIA. We got away with it up to a point. We had two more years, these paradisiacal, before they found us, and after the flurry that followed, Nadia was dead.

It is not my intention to retell that horror now, I have told it on other pages, but only to show how it was with me after Nadia was gone. I lived like a zombie for a while, supported emotionally by my brothers and sisters. I did my work, ran my life in an orderly fashion, tumbled with a few friendly women, and managed to convince myself that I had had my one good shot and that all the rest of it was downhill. I had lucked in once with love, and that was more than most aces got. I expected nothing like that in my life again, and then Arina walked into that room at New York Hospital to help with the tap on DeKalb.

TWENTY-SEVEN
Sunday 3:45 PM

The Navigator left his third taxi at the corner of West Tenth and Greenwich, and walked back uptown to a building off the corner of Perry Street. He let himself into the lobby with his key, took the elevator to the third floor, and entered apartment 3C with the same key. He closed the door behind him, and stood still, breathing softly. He felt a vague sense of danger, an undefined uneasiness. He knew the apartment well, but it seemed foreign to him now. It was totally dark when it should have been filled with light. It was cold in feeling when it should have felt warm and welcoming. It was silent when it should have echoed to the beat of salsa and reggae. That was how he knew it, and had known it over the past few months, as a happy haven, and not like this. Then he grunted as he realized how wrong he had been, and the sense of danger dropped away. The place was not completely dark, a strip of light showed under the bedroom door. Nor was it completely silent, for now he could make out a rhythmic squeaking from behind that same door. The apartment was still a happy haven, but for someone else this time.

He moved through the darkened apartment to the kitchen, and clicked on the light there. He found the bottle of Cutty Sark over the sink, and filled a glass with ice cubes from the fridge. He made no attempt at silence. He leaned against the kitchen counter and sipped his drink, waiting. After a while he heard the bedroom door open, and Carlotta's voice ask softly, 'Who's there?'

Just as softly, he said, 'Who the hell do you think is here? How many people have keys to this place?'

Silence, then a sigh, and then, 'Ah, Jake, I'm sorry. You should have called.'

116

'I couldn't, but that doesn't matter now. Get rid of him.'

'All right, just give me a minute.'

'Do it quickly; there isn't much time.'

'Time for what? Is something wrong?'

'Damn it, just do it.'

'All right, don't get excited.' He heard the bedroom door close.

Me, excited? he thought. Why should I be excited?

He thought of those old war movies on television where the captured soldier was confronted by the commandant of the prison camp, who always said in a kindly way, *For you, my friend, the war is over.*

'That's me, he told himself. For me, the war is over.'

He took his drink into the living room and sat on the couch in the darkness. He did not want his face to be seen. He heard low voices from the other side of the bedroom door, urgent voices arguing in Spanish. The arguing stopped, the door opened, and a male figure slipped out. He was in the light briefly, a muscular young man still buttoning his shirt as he hurried to the front door, and left.

I looked like that once, thought the Navigator. I still do, only older.

He leaned forward, and turned on the television. He was aware of Carlotta standing near by. He thought he could smell the heat coming off her. He did not turn his head to look at her. The scene on the screen was the exterior of the Mission, a talking head talking earnestly into a microphone.

'What's happening?' asked Carlotta.

'You don't know? No, of course you don't. You've been too busy fucking your brains out.'

'Jake, I said I was sorry. We never had that kind of arrangement, anyway.'

'What kind of arrangement?'

'Like we were married, or something. You were supposed to call first. You always called before.'

'My apologies, I've spoiled your day.'

'Stop it.'

'You can call him later and tell him to come back.'

'You don't have to talk that way.'

'I don't? All right, then, I won't. Turn on the light.'

She turned on one lamp, enough for him to see her by. She wore only a dressing gown pulled tightly around her, and she looked at him curiously. Not fearful, just curious. She was a long-legged woman in her thirties, a natural blonde, which was rare for a Nicaraguan. She was the ex-wife of a Somoçista who had fled to Miami, and after his money had run out she had fled to New York. For the past three months he had thought of her as being his. Even though he knew that she was Engstrom's creature and had been purchased for his convenience, he had assumed that she had been his alone. During those months he had never questioned that. He had believed in the sanctity of the purchase price. Now he knew better, and he also knew that no matter how often he worked out in the weight room, no matter how many miles he jogged each day, he would never again be the same as the young man who had just slipped out of the door.

For you, my friend, the war is over.

'Do you want to tell me what's going on?' asked Carlotta.

He gestured at the television screen. 'That's what's going on.'

He told her what had happened in front of the Mission. She absorbed it, and said, 'And he isn't dead?'

'They say he was wearing some kind of a vest.'

'And you? Why are you here?'

'I'm out of it. I'm finished.'

'Does Engstrom know that?'

'He does by now. I sent him a Hertz.'

'Then he'll be here soon.'

She went to the kitchen, made a drink for herself, and came back. She sat beside him on the couch. Now he could actually smell her warmth, but it did not excite him. She was just a warm woman sitting on the couch, a woman almost thirty years younger than he was. Despite the difference in their ages he once had thought that she might be the woman for him when it was all over. He had been a widower for fifteen years, and he had known many woman, but few had moved him the way this one did. She had been purchased for the purpose, but she moved him and he had thought that once he was out of it there could be a life for them together somewhere. Engstrom had promised him that life . . . money, a new identity, a new

118

face . . . but the Engstroms of the world were professional promisers. The Navigator knew. He was an Engstrom himself, and had been one for twenty-seven years. He had made his share of promises, and had actually kept some of them, but he had been around too long and could only hope that Engstrom was that rarity in their profession, a man of his word. He expected nothing from Yadroshnikov. He knew the man too well, and knew that compassion had never been a factor in his endless equations. But Engstrom was marginally different, an American who still had a touch of the innocence and naivety that went with the name. Not much, just a touch, but enough to let him believe that a new life might really be waiting for him. But not with this woman. Not now.

He felt her hand on his arm, a tentative touch, and she asked, 'How angry are you?'

'I don't have time to be angry. There is too much happening.'

'Yes, you're angry. We had no arrangement, but you're angry. You knew that you were supposed to call first, but you're angry. You knew that I was bought for you like a piece of meat on a hook, but you're angry. Very well then, you're angry. I'm sorry about that, I really am.'

His pride fought against the question, but he asked it anyway. 'Who is he?'

'A nobody, a Cuban. I could speak Spanish to him. He works in a garage on Greenwich Street.'

More pride sacrificed. 'Any others?'

'No, only Pepe, and only when I was lonely. My God, Jake, how often do I see you? Once a week? Twice?'

All pride gone now. 'You think I don't get lonely too?'

'You have your work. It's different.'

'It's different,' he conceded, 'but I still get lonely sometimes.'

'And what do you do about it? Don't you go to a woman when you get lonely?'

'Yes. You.'

'No others?'

He turned to look at her in amazement. 'Are you serious? I'm sixty-two years old. Do you think I still hang trophies on the wall?'

119

'I see,' she said softly. 'I did not think of it that way. And what will happen now?'

He flicked a finger at the television. 'You mean with that?'

'I mean with you.'

'A new life. Engstrom promised.'

'And you believe him? What about the other one?'

'Engstrom promised,' he repeated stubbornly. He did not want to think about Yadroshnikov.

'And what happens to me?'

He did not answer. She leaned against him, her head searching for his shoulder. He started to push her away, and then stopped. By his standards she had betrayed him, but he had been in the business of betrayal all his life. Over the years he had betrayed friends and family, he had betrayed conscience, he had betrayed every concept of decency, as decency had been taught to him in childhood. The way he looked at it, he had never betrayed the party or the motherland, but he knew that others would look at that differently. He and she were in the betrayal business together, and business was booming. He tried to imagine his new life without her, and he saw how bleak it would be. He let her head rest on his shoulder, let her warmth press against him, and he willed himself to be calm as he waited.

TWENTY-EIGHT
Sunday 4:40 PM

Arina hesitated in the doorway. There was a security guard with her. He said, 'This lady, she's got a pass for the area. Are you the one she's looking for?'

I had expected Yuri Muzalev. Instead, I saw a young woman of striking beauty and vitality. She was slim but full-figured and her dark hair came to her shoulders. Her skin was flawless, and the slight tilt to her eyes hinted at a trans-Caucasian heritage. Those eyes were opened wide as she stared at me. I was able to register that much before the odour of oranges filled the room.

'Mister?' It was the guard.

There was a silence around us. We both were blocked against intrusion. I looked into her eyes, and saw . . . what? Reflections of another time, or reflections only of myself? I was not sure which, but I was dead sure of the pungency that filled my nostrils. There was work to do, but I could not think about it. It was hard to believe, but there it was for the second time in my life, that odour of oranges. She smelled it, too, I was sure of that. It showed on her face, along with her confusion.

'Hey, mister.' The guard again. 'Does she stay, or no?'

'She stays.'

He left us alone. We continued to stare at each other, not moving. She said, 'My name is Arina Zourina. I have been sent to work with you.'

'Yes. I'm Ben Slade.'

She did not try to hide her confusion. 'What is this? What is happening?'

'Don't you know?'

'The odour . . .'

121

'Didn't they tell you about these things in your training? Didn't they tell you that it could happen?'

'They told us, yes, but I didn't believe . . . I thought it was only a story.'

'No, it's happening. Believe it.'

'The smell is so strong.' The confusion on her face was replaced by a grimace. 'It's making me sick to my stomach.'

'It will go away. That part of it doesn't last long.'

She nodded slowly. 'Yes, you would know, wouldn't you? This has happened to you before.'

'You know about that?'

'We know all about you in my service. Ben Slade and Nadia Petrovna, the great romance.'

'Is that what I am, a Russian folk hero?'

'Maybe not that, but the young ones talk about you, and what happened.'

'Are you one of the young ones?'

'No, I am nineteen.'

'That's young to me.'

'I don't feel very young right now.' The grimace had left her face. 'You were right, the sick feeling is gone. The odour is pleasant now.'

'For me, too.'

'We should be working.'

'Not yet. There's something we have to do first.'

'I don't understand.' The confusion was back. 'Please, this is different for me, I've never had this before. What are you talking about?'

'It's time for us to unblock to each other.'

She shook her head. 'I am not permitted to do that. Only with my own people.'

'I'm not looking to steal any military secrets.'

'But why should we . . .?'

'So that we can know each other. So that we can go further.'

'Perhaps I don't want to go further.'

'You do.'

'Perhaps I do, but perhaps I am afraid to.'

'Are you afraid of me?'

After a moment, 'No.'

'Do you think you might ever be?'

122

More quickly, 'No.'

'Then it's time for us to do it.'

'Our work,' she said faintly.

'There's nothing more important than this right now. Let me help you. I'll do it first.'

I set aside my block. It was like standing naked before her. I said, 'I'm open. Now you.' It was like asking her to undress.

She ran the tip of her tongue over her lower lip. She nodded, and then, the decision reluctantly made, she let it slip, mesh steel and gossamer slowly sliding down and over her, off her and into a pool at her feet. She stepped out of the pool, and stood revealed. She was as open and as vulnerable to me as I was to her. Tentatively, we reached out across that empty room, and touched. We touched in the way that only sensitives can, and in that moment we came to know each other.

In that moment I knew her first breath, and she knew mine. I knew the first bruise of her childhood, the first of her sighs, the first of her desires; and she knew mine. I knew the worst of her fears, and how she had fought them, winning some few battles. I knew the hopes of her youth, some buried and some budded, and I knew the change of the girl into woman. In much the same way she knew me as boy into man, and within the circle of that moment we grew up together.

And being grown, we created a vision of what it might be like for us together some day; flashing lights and shadows. Within the circle of the moment we lay together on a sun-baked beach near Rosas on a spit of land that poked out into the Mediterranean, and we drank manzanilla from a sand-crusted bottle. Dissolving eastward to a smoky tavern in Yalta, we ate the *basturma* that they roasted over white-hot coals, and I laughed as she tore at the meat with strong teeth. Another dissolve, and now we danced at night atop a narrow balustrade of stone, she in chiffon, while far below us the lights along the Corniche ran straight beside the sea. Over-lapping frames, we whirled into our lives, wandering through the souks of Marrakesh competing in search of gifts for each other, and my ordinary scarf was easily beaten by the empty jacket of the Beatles' White Album that she found in a corner of trash. Overlapping frames, whirling onward.

There was more, much more, as we went on that way within

123

the circle of the moment, image laid on image, until we finally lay before a fire in a house that was somehow our own, reading to each other from the books that were our treasures, sharing the music that had moved us always, and exchanging celluloid memories: Atlanta burning, Melanie weeping, and Anya lifting blind eyes to the rain that fell in *Baltic Spring*. We stared into the hearth that was part of our home, saw gnomelike faces in the flames, read our future in the popping embers, and by the time that the fire was low we knew each other, forte and foible, as well as if it had all been done in a lifetime, and not within the circle of that single moment. Then, and only then, knowing each other so well now, did we take the first step as the last and come into each other, loving. We soared together, we circled our world, we reached for the sun and touched it with our fingertips. We traded our souls, and we descended. We lay before the fire once again, and the sighs of satisfaction rang real. All this within the circle of that moment. It took no more than thirty seconds.

And then Arina said, 'Hello, Ben Slade. Hello, my love.'

'Arinoushka,' I said. 'Hello.'

TWENTY-NINE
Sunday 4:30 PM

The troops were deep into the booze at the saloon end of the Operations room. Alcohol hit each of them differently. It turned Snake into a swaggering *macha*, it turned Vince into a brooding introspective, it turned Martha into a fountain of tears. Actually, it only intensified what they were when they were straight, but the intensity could be awesome.

'Those three fine women,' Vince was saying. 'Wife, daughter, and sweetheart. Lovely people, all of them, and now they're gone. And for what? Will you tell me that? For what? Just blown away, *bang, bang, bang.*'

'*Bang,*' said Snake.

'What?'

'There were four. You forgot about Harry. He was a good kid. *Bang, bang, bang, bang.*'

'Quite right, four bangs it is. Ready on the quarterdeck, prepare to fire four bangs.'

'Please don't,' said Martha. 'All this banging makes my head hurt.'

'Not to mention the booze.'

'Cognac doesn't make my head hurt, not when I'm drinking it.'

'In that case.' Vince reached behind him for the bottle of Hennessy. He was standing on the service side of the bar, leaning forward, while the two women sat on the customers' side. It was a convenient arrangement allowing them all to rest their elbows on the mahogany and eyeball each other in a tight little triangle. 'Consider the salute as fired. Four bangs for four lovely people.'

'Five,' Snake observed. 'Five bangs once DeKalb kicks off.'

'No way.' Vince thumped the bottle on the bar, and Martha

winced. 'No way that that prick rates a bang in my book. He was definitely not a lovely people.'

'A prickperson?' Martha suggested.

'That's it.'

'Then he's out. Four bangs is our limit.'

They raised their glasses, and drank to that. Vince stared moodily into his drink. 'The problem with us,' he said, 'is that we abuse ourselves.'

'Self abuse,' Snake agreed. 'That's our problem.'

'Not mine,' said Martha. 'I'm above that sort of thing. I'm on a different astral plane.'

'No, no.' Vince wagged his head solemnly. 'I mean that we abuse our powers. We take our God-given gift, and we use it for contemptible purposes. Spying, prying, lying . . .'

'Viking,' Snake added.

'Deception,' said Martha. 'Treachery.'

'All of that,' Vince agreed. 'And why? I ask you, why?'

'Why, indeed?' Martha echoed vaguely.

Snake, chewing on a piece of lemon rind, said, 'Well, for one thing the money is good. In fact, the money is terrific.'

'Money.' Vince's eyes were sad. 'Is that what we are? Merceneries? Hired guns?'

'Certainly not,' said Martha.

'Then why do we do it?'

'I don't know about you guys,' said Snake, 'but I sort of dig all that spying, and prying, and the other shit you said.'

Martha shook her head primly. 'You're just saying that because you want to sound tough.'

'I don't have to sound tough, lady. I am tough.'

'Sure, you're tough,' said Vince. 'Nobody said you weren't. We're all tough when we have to be, and maybe we all enjoy just a wee touch of that self abuse . . .'

'Not me, I'm above all that.'

'. . . but just imagine how it would be if we used this God-given gift the way it should be used. For the benefit of mankind. For the sake of humanity.' He paused to take a slug of his drink, gulped, and went on. 'Can you imagine what the world would be like if every sensitive thought only beautiful thoughts? Thoughts about love, and happiness, and kindness? Think of it. We could network it, working together, every ace

126

contributing. We could exercise our full potential that way. We could weave a blanket of peace and harmony that would cover the world, a blanket that would protect the innocent, a blanket that would defend the helpless, a blanket that would . . .' He stopped, hung up on what to say next.

'A blanket that would keep everybody's tootsies warm at night,' said Martha. She burst into tears at the beauty of the thought.

'There she goes, Old Faithful,' Snake observed. 'Hey, you know what? Ben isn't drinking.'

'Why not?'

'Look around.'

Vince shaded his eyes, and looked around. 'Ben isn't here.'

'That's what I mean. What happened to Ben? What happened to our baby brother?'

'He's out on assignment,' said Sammy, who had come across the room from the Operations end. He was the only straight ace in the place, and he was beginning to feel left out. 'I sent him on a job.'

'What? Outside?' Vince looked horrified. 'How could you do that? People are getting killed out there. Fine, sweet, generous people, just like that. *Bang, bang, bang, bang, bang.*'

'Stop.' Martha covered her ears.

'So you sent Ben out on a job,' drawled the Snake. 'After all the shit that went down this afternoon, you sent him out into that jungle. You're a cold man, Sammy.'

'Yeah, that's me, all right.'

'Where's Ben now?'

'At the hospital.'

'Oh, my God,' cried Martha. 'They got Ben, too.'

'*Bang,*' Vince said dully.

Snake hopped off her barstool. She hitched up her jeans. 'Tell me who did it, Sammy. I'll freeze the bastard, I swear I will.'

'Look, I said *at* the hospital, not *in* the hospital.'

Vince sobbed. 'Good old Ben. How did they get him, Sammy?'

'I just told you, they didn't.'

'Flowers,' said Martha through tears. 'We have to send flowers.'

'Send them, hell, we'll bring them.'

'Right, everybody over to the hospital, but first we buy the flowers.'

Martha tried to climb down from her stool, then saw that she wasn't going to make it. She stayed perched on the edge, holding grimly onto the bar. 'Maybe better if we send them. How about chrysanthe-muh-mums?'

'Negative on the flowers,' said Snake. 'Save the flowers for the son of a bitch who got Ben. He's gonna need 'em.'

Vince said hopefully, 'What about a rose? One perfect rose?'

'Roses are for faggots. Why not a plant? Flowers die, but plants last.'

'But it's traditional to send flowers,' wailed Martha.

'Yeah, a plant. Maybe a cactus.'

'Sammy, what hospital?'

'New York,' Sammy said absently. He stepped around the bar to get a beer from the fridge.

'Where did they get him?' Snake wanted to know. 'How bad is it?'

'Will you people please listen to me? There is nothing wrong with Ben, understand? He's at the hospital doing a job. Now, please, lighten up, will you? Give the booze a rest and toe the line. I may need you for something later.'

'Which toe?' asked Martha.

'What?'

'Which toe did they get him in?'

'Oh, for God's sake,' Sammy yelled, exasperated. 'It's the big left toe. The doctors say that it's only a flesh wound, but he'll never dance the mazurka again.'

'Don't you say that,' Vince blubbered. 'Don't say that about my boy Ben. I know Ben. He'll be up and dancing in no time at all.'

'Bet on it,' said Snake. 'Can't keep Ben down, can they, Sammy?'

'No, of course not.' Resigned, Sammy made soothing motions with his hands. 'Don't worry about Ben, he'll be just fine.' He popped open his beer, and looked at the others over the rim of the can as he sipped at it. They were all in various stages of tears now, crying up a storm over their baby brother

128

Ben who had just had his big toe shot off in the line of duty, and who would never dance the polka again.

'Try to take it easy,' he said without much hope.

He took his beer back to the Ops table, not because anything was happening there, but because it was where he was supposed to be. Delaney was still on the phone, but Ritter was free. He drank his beer and traded horror stories with Ritter, tales of monumental screw-ups within their agencies. They each knew quite a few. The next time Sammy looked over at the bar, it was empty. Snake, Martha, and Vince were gone.

THIRTY
Sunday 4:50 PM

'Comrade General, I will now ask you to assess the political implications of the disappearance of the Navigator.'

Gorbachev kept his face immobile as he spoke, unwilling to show his pain. The aspirins had helped not at all. His head still throbbed, and the searing heat along his ribs had, if anything, increased. He kept his eyes fixed on those of the *rezident*, demanding a reply.

Major General Yevgeni Zazulin did not answer at once. He took time to form his thoughts. As the KGB *rezident* in New York, he held one of the three most important field appointments that his service offered, but he knew how tenuous his position was, and how close he was to a career catastrophe. One false step in this political minefield could, at best, send him home to a meaningless job in an obscure corner of the Soviet Union, and, at worst, could result in an enforced retirement without pension and the removal of his name from the privileged list of the *nomenklatura*. So he chose his words with care.

'Comrade General Secretary, I wish to say at the outset that until this moment we have had no reason whatsoever to suspect the Navigator's loyalty and dedication to his service. He has appeared to be in all respects a model officer. I cannot comment on his ability in his job, that is for his military superiors to evaluate, but within the limits of my brief on him I have had no cause for complaint. Until today.'

'And now?'

'Now I must tell you that I suspect the worst.'

'Defection?'

'Yes.'

'And what leads you to this conclusion?'

130

'Two points. The first is that nothing else could explain his absence from the Mission at such a critical time. The second is that we have found in the past that officers of the GRU have, statistically, displayed a stronger tendency toward defection than officers in other services such as my own, or the Foreign Ministry, or any other organization of Soviet citizens serving abroad. This is a regrettable statement to have to make about a sister service, but the facts speak for themselves. We must prepare ourselves for the probability that the Navigator has defected, and that the political consequences will be severe.'

'Thank you, Comrade General.'

Gorbachev inclined his head in acknowledgement, and regretted the action at once as pain stabbed at his temples. His face remained impassive, both to the pain and to the *rezident*'s words. He discounted the words automatically. The rivalry, antagonism, and at times outright hatred that existed between the KGB and the GRU, the Soviet Union's two major intelligence-gathering organizations, made it difficult to accept at face value a comment made by an officer of one service about an officer of the other. He, of all people, was in a position to know this. He also knew that most people, both within the Soviet Union and without, were unaware of the very existence of the GRU. The KGB was all that they knew.

The *Komitet Gosudarstvennoy Bezopasnosti*, the Committee for State Security, was the face that Soviet intelligence presented to the world. Through its First Chief Directorate, the KGB was responsible for Soviet intelligence operations abroad, which made it the equivalent of the American CIA. Through its Second Chief Directorate, it was responsible for counterintelligence within the Soviet Union, which made it the equivalent of the American FBI. Through its Eighth Chief Directorate, it monitored and deciphered foreign communications, which made it the equivalent of the American National Security Agency. And through two other Chief Directorates without American parallels, it was responsible for the troops that patrolled the borders of the Soviet Union, and for the suppression of ideological dissent. Thus the reputation of the KGB as a security monolith, all-seeing and all-powerful. The name was a legend throughout the world, and within the Soviet Union its public posture was part of its power. Indeed, a stranger in any provincial town had only to ask to be directed to the KGB, and he would be shown at once to the local headquarters. Everybody knew about the KGB, and the KGB was happy to have it that way.

In complete contrast, the *Glavnoye Razvedyvatelnoye Upravleniye*, the Chief Intelligence Directorate of the Soviet General Staff, operated in total anonymity, to the point where the average Soviet citizen, if asked to identify the organization by its initials, would be likely to shrug, and stare blankly. The letters had no particular significance, and in the Soviet Republic of Georgia the police actually issued car licence plates in the series GRU, not suspecting that the letters might have a special meaning. The GRU was the intelligence-gathering arm of the combined armed forces of the Soviet Union, and as such it operated with military efficiency. It was responsible only to the General Staff and to the Politburo, and it was as ruthless and as unforgiving as the legendary KGB. More so, perhaps, for while much of the terror inspired by the KGB was based on a public awareness of its existence, the GRU commanded respect through the secrecy and anonymity of its movements.

The rivalry between the two services dated back as far as the October Revolution, and, indeed, the officers of the GRU still referred to the KGB by its post-revolution name of the Cheka. In theory, and under Soviet law, the GRU was free of KGB interference and control, every recruit into the military organization was told this and taught that he need not account for himself to any KGB agent, but in practice the situation was quite different. The Cheka kept files on GRU officers just as it did on anyone else who crossed its path, and GRU agents serving abroad were under constant surveillance by the KGB's Third Directorate. All officers at all foreign stations were subject to this control, from the most junior all the way up to the senior officer in charge, who was traditionally known as the Navigator.

Now the KGB *rezident* in New York was saying that his opposite number, the GRU Navigator was a probable defector. Gorbachev thanked him for his opinion. He knew the figures for defections from the various services, and he knew the common motives behind such moves: money, ideology, a woman. He also knew the harshness that underlined life in the Soviet Union and made a foreign shore so attractive. Still, to abandon motherland, family, culture, the very language, in order to live among strangers? He wondered, not for the first time, how he would feel if he were under the heel, and not wearing the boot. Would he run for foreign shores? Would he abandon everything to get out from under that grinding heel? Better no heel, he thought, better no boot, but that was a long way into the future. That future . . . he caught himself slipping into a reverie, and brought himself up short. Someone had entered the room, an aide who excused himself, went directly to the *rezident*, and whispered something to him.

The *rezident* dismissed the man, and said, 'General Secretary, a communication has arrived for you. Your own key is required. Would you care to accompany me to the *referentura*?'

'Of course.'

Gorbachev stood up, grasping the arms of his chair. The effort cost him a wave of dizziness. To the others, he said, 'Comrades, you are free to go. You all have much to do. Anatoli, come with me.'

Gorbachev and the valet followed the *rezident* out of the suite of rooms and down a long corridor to an elevator which took them to the seventh floor. Opposite the elevator was an unmarked door. The *rezident* reached with his left hand to press a button hidden behind a light fitting next to the door, and in answer to his ring a buzzer sounded, freeing the door to open.

He turned to the General Secretary, and said, 'Your valet must wait here. Entry to the *referentura* is strictly limited to KGB staff . . . and yourself, of course.'

'He goes with me,' said Gorbachev.

The *rezident* inclined his head. The three men passed into a small anteroom, and then through a heavy steel door guarded by an armed KGB agent. Once past the second door they were in the heart of the *referentura*, the code and communications unit of any KGB residence. Set into one wall was a barred opening built like a bank teller's cage, and behind the bars sat the duty officer. The opposite wall was occupied by the main transmitter, and the rest of the room was divided into curtained cubicles, each containing a coding machine and a printer. The room was windowless and soundproofed. Two cipher clerks sat at the main transmitter. They looked up when the General Secretary entered the room, and then quickly averted their eyes.

The *rezident* said, 'You will require a cipher clerk.'

'No,' said Gorbachev. 'Anatoli fulfils that function.'

'Forgive me, General Secretary, but is he qualified?'

'Yes.'

The *rezident* concealed his surprise. The position of cipher clerk in any residency was highly sensitive, and required rigorous training. That the General Secretary's valet had somewhere received such training, and held such a position of trust, came as a shock. It was a piece of information that his service should have known about.

Again, the *rezident* inclined his head. 'Very well, cubicle twelve, please.'

The curtain was drawn back on number twelve, and a green light glowed at the top of the coding machine. Gorbachev lowered himself painfully into a chair, and Anatoli sat next to him. The valet pulled the curtain shut. Gorbachev took a ring of keys from his pocket, and selected a thin silver wedge. He gave it to Anatoli, who inserted it into a slot at the side of the machine. The green light went out, replaced by a yellow. Anatoli turned the key. The machine hummed, and a strip of film about six inches long emerged from a second slot beside the keyhole. Anatoli removed the film. The yellow light went out, and the green went back on. More than one message. He turned the key again, and another strip of film emerged. The yellow light went out, and the machine stayed dark. Transmission and reception completed.

Anatoli returned the key to Gorbachev, and turned in his chair to face the printer. He inserted one of the film strips into a slot, and the yellow light went on. He pressed the 'print' key, and the machine chattered softly. He removed the printout, inserted the second strip, and removed the second printout. He handed them both to Gorbachev.

The first message was from the Central Committee, and it was brief. It began with fraternal concern for his health and safety, and concluded with the suggestion that he take all precautions. Gorbachev smiled. He had expected nothing more. He read the second message.

134

FROM: Chebrikov
TO: Gensec
REF: 3718/P
Replying to your 1184/n.

(1) No unusual military activity observed within Soviet Union or Warsaw Pact allies. Single exception armoured manoeuvres by elements 87 Division, 13 Army Carpathian, but these plans longstanding.

(2) No adverse information on New York Navigator, but computer projection predicts possible defection on basis of psychological profile.

(3) Concerning whereabouts of Marshals Kulikov and Petrov. Both outside Soviet Union on inspection tours. Kulikov in Budapest, Petrov in Kabul.

(4) Chief of General Staff Akhromeyev is at his office at General Staff Headquarters. No changes in normal routine observed.

(5) No additional information on Richard DeKalb available at this time. Further information possible from Washington assets within twenty-four hours.

(6) Please advise if executive action is contemplated in cases of Kulikov, Petrov, or Akhromeyev.

ENF 428-00000

Gorbachev reread the message with a sinking feeling. He felt the fear rise up in him again. He told himself that there was nothing in the message to cause alarm. It was true that Kulikov and Petrov formed his main opposition within the National Defence Council, and that both were strongly opposed to the new arms control agreement, but what of it? It was perfectly logical for Kulikov, as Supreme Commander of Warsaw Pact forces to be in Budapest, and equally logical for Petrov to be in Kabul. As for Akhromeyev, he was a trimmer likely to steer a middle course, and not a source of danger.

And yet, that sinking feeling, coupled with the recent awareness that he was not, in the last regard, capable of defending himself. He bit his lip. A reply was needed. Chebrikov was one of his own people, a supporter of what he believed in, but the KGB mentality was pervasive. Executive action: when in doubt, destroy. He shook his head again.

He pulled the curtain, and came out of the cubicle followed by Anatoli. The *rezident* was waiting for them. Anatoli looked around, and asked, 'Where is your burn box, please?'

The *rezident* led him to a rectangular steel cabinet on a table beside the main transmitter. Anatoli deposited the two printouts and the two strips of film in the box, and closed the cover. He twisted the dial on the side of the box, and waited while the documents were incinerated.

Gorbachev said, 'Your traffic log.'

The *rezident* led him to a log book that lay on a shelf beside the teller's cage. The log was open to a blank page. Gorbachev wrote:

> FROM: Gensec
> TO: Chebrikov
> REF: Your 3718/P
> Do nothing. Repeat. Do nothing.

'Send this at once,' he said to Anatoli. 'I'm going back to my quarters.'

'You should rest now,' said the valet. 'Will you?'

Gorbachev put his hand on Anatoli's shoulder. 'I will, I promise you.'

THIRTY-ONE
Sunday 5:30 PM

Uncle John Merlo decided that, all things considered, Mama
had taken the news about Carlo quite well. Not stoically, but
well. Grief, yes, and a storm of tears, but she had not fallen
apart. Uncle John figured that at her age death was less an
ogre in the night than a constant companion, and at times it
could even be a kind old friend. That Carlo had died young
was a cause for grief, but Mama had seen so many others die,
and had grieved so often, that Carlo's death, in truth, was just
the latest black bead on the string. Also, Uncle John suspected
that, in the contrary way of old woman, she was still sore at
Carlo for missing the Sunday coffee-klatsch. Never mind that
he had been unavoidably detained. He had broken his *nonna*'s
heart, and he had been punished for it. But that was only a
suspicion.

Still, there were the proprieties to be observed. Once the
storm of tears had abated, a telephone call had been made,
and within minutes a steady stream of black-clad women
began to flow through the door of the Elizabeth Street house.
Each woman came bearing both food and comfort, and each
was prepared to sit through the night, to wail, to gossip, and to
soothe. It was a woman's world of mourning, and they quickly
eased Uncle John out of the house with instructions to do
whatever it was that men did at such times.

In truth, there was little to do until the next day when the
coroner's office would release the body. Uncle John went
back to the clam bar, which had been closed for business, Fat
Louis having eased the customers out with whispered words of
the family tragedy. Salvatore DiLuca was waiting in the back
room with the four *capos* of the family, and Tony Spats. The
Uncle saw with satisfaction that Tony had poured drinks for

137

everyone. One by one, they embraced him in the traditional manner.

'How's the Mama?' asked DiLuca. Big-bellied and black-suited, he kept a heavy hand on the Uncle's shoulder.

'She's made of steel. She'll be okay.'

'And you? How are you?'

The Uncle shrugged. 'The world's still round.'

The Don squeezed his shoulder approvingly. 'I've been telling the boys that what happened to Carlo, it's got nothing to do with the family business, so I don't want our people going around whacking people out.' He looked around. 'Understand? Nobody started any war here.'

Everyone nodded. One voice asked, 'If it wasn't business, then what?'

'Who knows? Maybe it's personal. Maybe Carlo stepped on somebody's toes. If that's what it is, we'll find out and we'll make the right moves. Right, Uncle John?'

The Uncle knew what he had to say. 'Right. I figure it's gotta be personal. Some woman, maybe. With Carlo, you could never tell. So like the Don says, nobody gets excited and nobody starts any wars. It's business as usual.'

'Business as usual,' the Don repeated. 'Now, maybe you people could take your drinks outside to the bar. I want to have a few private words with the Uncle.'

The *capos* and Tony trooped out of the room, closing the door behind them. Once they were gone, the formality between the Don and the Uncle dropped away. They had known each other since childhood. The Don settled into a large chair, the Uncle behind his desk. They stared at each other sadly.

'What a world we live in,' said the Don for openers. 'Well, Giovanni, I guess you've got some questions to ask.'

'I guess so,' the Uncle said mildly. 'You asked me for a favour, a little favour. You wanted an ice-cold gun delivered to a certain place at a certain time. Nothing to it, right? You're my Don, and I respect you, and I would never say no to you. So I give the job to my own flesh and blood, and on the way back he gets whacked. So I've got some questions to ask. Who did this thing, and why?'

'Would you believe me when I tell you that I don't know? That I really don't?'

138

After a long silence, the Uncle said, 'Sal, I know you too long and I respect you too much to call you a liar.'

'Thank you. I'll take that the way it sounds. I know that you mean it. Look, we both know how things work, don't we?'

'Like what?'

'Like the little favour I asked. We both know the score. I ask, and you do it because it isn't easy to say no to somebody like me. That's the way the game works. So don't you think I got people I can't say no to?'

'You saying that somebody else asked you for this favour?'

'That's exactly what I'm saying.'

'Who is he? I want him.'

'Forget it. Don't even think it. Look, I'll tell you this much. This gentleman who asked me the favour, he isn't in the business like you and me. He's straight, a hundred per cent legitimate. And he's big. Remember that. He's so big that Salvatore DiLuca can't say no to him. Now, is that big, or what?'

'It's big.'

'And that isn't all of it. I would bet a lot of money that this certain party, the favour wasn't for him in the first place. Like I said, he's straight arrow, so what would he want with an ice-cold piece? No, Giovanni, the way I see it, this certain party, he's also got people he can't say no to. People bigger than him. And maybe they've got people, too. And up, and up the line. You see what I mean?'

'Yeah, I see. But how far up?'

'I don't know, I don't want to know, and neither do you, my old friend. But you could make a pretty good guess if you look at the TV news tonight.'

'The Russian that got hit?'

'I think maybe yes.'

'That was the piece?'

'It figures. You see how it is? I got asked for a favour, and I passed it along to you. You got caught in the middle, that's all, and so did Carlo. He got caught in something big.'

'That guy at the ballpark. Carlo saw him.'

'That could be it.'

'So Carlo has to go because he saw him.'

'It could be that way.'

'That means that Carlo was dead all the time. He was always gonna get hit.'

'It looks that way. What's important now is that you understand. I didn't know what was going down. I would never put Carlo in a spot like that. I want you to believe that. Do you?'

'I guess I gotta believe it, Sal. I know you too long.'

'So I'm telling you, forget about finding out. Whatever this is, it's too big for me, and it's too big for you.'

'You're telling me to forget my own flesh and blood?'

'Look at it this way, Giovanni. It was an accident. Pretend that Carlo got hit by a car, or something like that. Make it easy on yourself. There's nothing you can do about it. Don't you see that?'

'I see it, but I don't like it.'

'What's to like? That's the way life is.'

The two men stood up, and embraced. The Don said, 'You'll let me know about the funeral?'

'For sure. I'll know tomorrow.'

When the Don had left, Tony Spats came back in. He looked at his boss unhappily, and said, 'You look like hell. You should go home and put your feet up for a while.'

'Not yet,' said the Uncle. He wanted very much to lie down and close his eyes, but there was one more chore to do before he could rest.

THIRTY-TWO
Sunday 4:55 PM

'The bullet is lodged in the brain just above the transverse fissure,' said the doctor. 'A certain amount of the cerebrum has been destroyed, and there has been substantial cranial damage as well. It's just a matter of time.'

'How much?' I asked.

'Hard to say. He could last for an hour, he could last for two, he might even last for a day, but he'll never regain consciousness.'

The doctor's name was Boskie. He was young and intense. He was trying to treat DeKalb like any other patient, but that wasn't easy. There were cops all over the place, two in the room with DeKalb, two parked outside the door, and more down the corridor. Boskie wasn't happy about that, and he wasn't happy about Arina and me. He had been told to give us complete cooperation, but he couldn't see why. He knew nothing about sensitives.

I asked, 'May I see the EEG?'

He frowned. The EEG was doctor stuff. He handed over the printout reluctantly. 'It won't mean anything unless you know how to read it. Just a lot of lines.'

I glanced at the graph, and showed it to Arina. She nodded. The heavy theta wave activity was the result of the brain damage, and the small, fast beta rhythms indicated physiological distress. In a sense, Boskie was right. The EEG told us nothing that we did not already know. I gave it back to him.

'I've been told to give you all the help I can,' he said. 'What else will you need?'

'Nothing,' said Arina. 'We'll be quite comfortable here.'

'In this empty room?'

'Quite.'

'But the patient is in the room next door.'

'Yes.'

'And you just want to sit here?'

'Yes,' I said. 'Alone.'

'Forgive me for being obtuse,' he said, 'but just what is it that you're going to do in here?'

'Pray?'

'Oh.' His nose wrinkled, the automatic reaction of the man of science.

'Colonel DeKalb is a deacon of the Third Assembly of the Godhead,' I explained. 'Sister Clara and I are here to pray for the peaceful transportation of his soul into the presence of the Central Person.'

'And that's all you want to do? Just pray?'

'Did you say *just*, brother? What more could we do?'

'Uh, well, you know what I mean.'

'I'm afraid I do. You don't believe, do you?'

'Well . . .'

'No, you don't. You worship in the laboratory, don't you?'

'You see . . .'

'I see it all clearly. You won't find God under a microscope, brother, and you won't find him in a test tube, either.'

'No, I suppose not . . .'

'Look into your heart, search your soul, that's where you'll find Him, brother. Leave off sifting through atoms, He isn't there. He can't be measured on your scales, or with your calipers. Seek him out with your bare hands, for that's the only way . . .'

Arina broke in. 'Brother, we have the Lord's work to do yet.'

'True, sister. Doctor, will you excuse us?'

'Uh, certainly. One thing, though. Could you keep your voices down while you're praying? After all, this *is* a hospital.'

'The Third Assembly of the Godhead prays silently, brother. It's those Second Assembly people make all the noise. Fear not, we'll be silent, and while we're at it we'll pray for your soul, too.'

'That's very kind of you, I'm sure.' He was shaking his head when he left the room.

142

Arina laughed, delighted. It was an earthy, dirty laugh. She said, 'It's going to be fun with you.'

'Ready to go to work?'

'Do you think we'll find anything?'

'It's possible. He isn't brain dead, the EEG shows that. Have you ever done a tap this deep before?'

'Now, really . . .'

'I'm not insulting your training, I know how good it is. But you haven't been operational very long, have you?'

'I've done it in training,' she admitted. 'Never in the field.'

I went over the basics with her. The various parts of the cerebrum communicate with each other through association tracts that consist of connector neurons. These tracts abound in the corpus callosum, which is that part of the brain that the specialists believe to be the seat of reasoning, learning, and memory. The specialists can only believe it, because they have no way of proving it. Sensitives don't only believe it, they know it. They've been there. So if there was any memory left in DeKalb's brain, and any function of reason, the corpus callosum was where it would be, and where we would have to look for it. I laid this out for Arina, and she nodded her understanding.

'I'm ready when you are,' she said.

'Follow me in.'

The first job was to clear away all the possible interference from the dozens of other people within our range. I brushed them aside one by one, and Arina followed behind me, sealing them off from the area. It was like clearing a space in a jungle. Once that was done, I went after DeKalb, narrowing down the field of my search until I was able to isolate the faint electro-chemical impulses still emanating from his brain. They were as fragile as light from a faraway star.

Arina?

Yes, I'm getting them.

Easy now, centre in, and bring them up to strength.

We came in closer, reaching for those impulses, and building them. It was like turning up the volume dial on a radio, but in this case the dial could snap off in our fingers. The volume rose, a hum at first that gradually grew clearer. And clearer. And raised in tone to a high-pitched whine that was clearer

143

still. The whine wavered, steadied, and raised itself again close to soundlessness. It whistled in my head, tuneless and insistent, and as I listened it turned into a stream of jumbled images, wordless and without connection. A shoe, a rose, a snowflake. An ear, a sunburst, a drop of blood. The images sped by.

Ben?

Yes, I'm getting them, too.

What do they mean?

Nothing yet. Wait.

We watched the flow of images, chaotic refuse thrown off by an organ in agony. Then, like a high-speed film slowing down, the images faltered, faded, came back again, and began to journey from chaos to coherence. Images first, and then words.

. . . nobody what goes the quest except himself I tell you Laura baby boy or girl whatever makes no never rose a snowflake crimson for a badge to wear. Blood of the rose a sacred but nobody's nose. The troubles, Laura baby, listen to your Daddy, nobody ever knows what a man goes through in the quest for manhood except the man. Giles knew, but he kept it to himself when the people reviled him, called him a fool and knave just like me, Sir Giles, for what he did, but he knew that he had acted in the only manly fashion. So he could bear the burden of the Siege of Candore. He knew that he was right, just the way I know that what I have to do is essentially right, gut right, because I have to trust the far neighbours. Which is what you have to remember after this happens, after it's all over my name, well, what the hell, what's in a name, right? Be lots of names they're calling me, and you'll have to listen to it all. Hear them all, hear your father called a murderer, fiend, assassin, and that's if I'm lucky. More likely hear me called a nut, crazy Dick DeKalb went off his rocker. Murderer, nut, and the one name you won't hear me called is a patriot, God damn their short-sighted souls. Ah, shit, my darling, so what? I've heard it all before and worse, a man before his time. But I've always done what I thought was right no matter what the pinheads said, and you'll have to get used to that, too. You'll have to remember that I did what was right, trusting far neighbours. So let them call the names, you'll know better.

144

Give you a little tip, my sweet, to carry through your life. Let them say whatever they like, so long as they don't laugh. But they will, they always do, the pinheads, the peabrains, the ones who can't see past their noses. That's all they can do is laugh at a man ahead of his time the way Brucie did, the pompous ass, when I told him about Australia. Little man laughing, can't see his nose, and I had to take it, man before his time with the laughter of fools in his ears. And not a damn thing I could do about it with Brucie wearing the stars. Little man laughing, and he didn't have a clue about what we had in Australia, and I don't mean just our bases or the treaties. It's the people, see? Those are our kind of people down there, faraway neighbours, and I tell you true that the way the world is turning these days you take damn good care of every friend you've got. I mean, it wasn't as if I was asking them to throw away the whole *enchilada*. At that point the *Stars and Stripes* had a three to zero lead, and there was no way that *Kookaburra* was going to win four straight. The Aussies were cooked, finished, *finito*, and all I was suggesting was a touch of class for a gallant ally, let them go down with a little bit of pride intact, you know what I mean? Let them be able to hold up their heads later, losing the Cup four to one instead of four zero. You have to understand Australians, their entire lives revolve around three things, sports, beer, and cunt, excuse me sweet, which doesn't make them that much different than anyone else except that down there they approach these things on a primitive level. Point is, the Aussies are lousy losers, which is what makes them such great soldiers, of course. So all I was saying was throw them one, let them take a race for the sake of the alliance, keep the animals reasonably content. Just don't rub their noses in it, four zero. Not that the alliance is going to go down the tubes because of a boat race, but you play for the points, you know what I mean? Sure you do, you wouldn't be my daughter if you didn't, but you think that Brucie saw it that way? Hell, no. He looked at me as if I just raped a nun, excuse me, just pissed all over the Constitution of the United States, the Magna Carta, and all points east. And then he began to laugh, the bastard, and just because I wanted to help out the Aussies a touch, not much, just once, and there were so many ways we could have done it. Thought maybe a few quiet words to the

145

Stars and Stripes people, you know, throw one for the flag, but we could have done it ourselves on the black. Slipped some kind of a drag on the hull, or a foul-up in the sail locker, the bluewater types would have known what to do. A dozen tricks we could have pulled, and *Kookaburra* wins one. Aussie pride goes up, we win the Cup anyway the next day, but it's not a disaster and our faraway neighbours are still our friends. Important, Laura, believe me, I've learned that much in my life. The far neighbours are the ones you can trust, the ones who speak your language, and Sir Rupert learned that although he had to find it out the hard way during the Siege of Candore, slugging it out for forty days with Giles under a scorching sun in those suits of armour that could roast you. But he learned, you see, that you trust the far neighbour, no matter what anybody thinks. You can understand him because he's the one who speaks your real language, just as Rupert came to understand Giles during that hot and dusty summer. Standoff at Candore, the two armies so evenly matched that the issue had to be decided by single combat. Sir Giles and Sir Rupert, head to head, *mano a mano* . . .

I came out of it for a break. He was telling his daughter the story that she had refused to hear, sidetracked for a while onto that cockeyed operation in Australia that had never come off. Because they had laughed him out of it, and he had never forgotten the laughter. Poor bastard. Poor murdering bastard.

I looked to see if Arina had caught it yet. He had mentioned it several times, and it stuck out a mile. If she had caught it, she wasn't showing it. I went back in.

THIRTY-THREE
Sunday 4:57 PM

Christatos hated working on Sundays. While the world rested, Christatos laboured. It was unfair, and he resented it. He had been doing it for most of his life and he should have become accustomed to it by now, but at the age of fifty-seven he still resented having to do it. Not that he worked seven days a week, Monday was his day of rest, but Monday could never be a substitute for Sunday.

Despite this resentment, Christatos knew that any New York florist who closed his shop on Sundays would soon be out of business. This had been taught to him in childhood by his father, his grandfather, and his two uncles, all of whom had been retail florists. Sunday was flower day. All sorts of people bought flowers on Sunday. Did you have a fight with your girlfriend on Saturday night? Quick, down to Christatos for her favourite flowers. Going visiting? Stop at Christatos for a house-gift plant. On your way to the cemetery? Christatos. The hospital? Christatos. There were as many reasons for buying flowers on Sunday as there were tears in the eyes of the martyrs, and Christatos was open to service those needs. Sunday was the day that made the week, but still, Christatos resented the need to work it.

On this particular Sunday, he decided to close the shop early. He normally stayed open until six on Sundays, but the news of the attempted assassination, only a few blocks away, had put a chill on the day. His well-honed sense of retailing told him that there would be little business in the remaining hours, and at four o'clock he sent his two clerks home. He himself stayed on only because of a wreath of lilies that had to be ready for a funeral the next morning. With his clerks gone, he worked on the wreath in the back of the shop, and kept an ear

cocked for the front doorbell. Christatos enjoyed making
funeral wreaths. It required the sort of old-time skill in which
he took pride. As far as he knew, the machine had not yet been
invented that could make a wreath of lilies. It took an experienced florist with strong and nimble fingers, and as he worked
on the job he wondered what he should charge for it. His usual
price for a wreath was fifty dollars, but as happened so often
in times of loss, the price had been left open by the buyer, and
he knew that he could get seventy-five. Cupidity argued with
conscience as he twisted the final wires, and stepped back to
admire the finished product. Pleased with what he saw, he
riffled through a box of black silk ribbons printed with gold
lettering, looking for one to attach to the wreath. There were
dozens of styles from which to choose, and not knowing the
family involved, he settled for the always popular, *Oh, death,
where is thy sting?* He had just attached the ribbon to the
wreath when he heard the doorbell. He hurried to the front of
the shop, and looked uneasily at the three customers who had
just come in: a tall black man, a short and wiry woman, and a
second, larger woman with an angelic face. They were clearly
drunk, unsteady on their feet, and their speech was slurred. In
a jumble of voices they explained that they were visiting a dear
friend in the hospital, and wished to bring him something
appropriate.

'Roses,' said the man. 'A whole fucking carload of roses.'

'Roses are for pansies,' said the smaller of the women. 'You
bring him roses, I want something tough and prickly. Like a
cactus.'

'What's so appropriate about that?' asked the other
woman. 'Ben isn't tough and prickly, he's warm and cuddly.'
She looked as if she were about to cry.

Christatos asked, 'You want the roses *and* the cactus?'

'Definitely,' said the man. 'I'm not bringing my buddy anything that sucks up water.'

'What are you going to put the roses in? Scotch? What
about you, Martha?'

'I don't know.' The other woman looked around the shop
aimlessly. 'Something with sentiment, not just a flower.'

'Look around,' said Christatos. 'I'll take care of your
friends first.'

148

He worked quickly, anxious to get rid of them. It was bad enough working Sundays without having to deal with a bunch of drunks. He assembled a dozen American Beauties, and after a moment of reflection chose a hedgehog cactus, a showy *Echinopsis*, for the woman. When he looked around for the other woman, she was gone from the front of the shop. He hurried to the back room, and found her there staring at the wreath of lilies.

'That's it,' she said softly, 'that's just what I want. He'll love it.'

'Um . . . madam, those are lilies.'

'I want it.'

'Your friend in the hospital, he hasn't . . . I mean, he's still alive, isn't he?'

'Of course he is. It's only a flesh wound. In the toe.'

'This terrible city,' Christatos said automatically. 'Actually, you see, that wreath is meant for a funeral.'

'Makes no difference, I want it. It's the sentiment that counts. *Oh, death, where is thy sting?* That's beautiful. Don't you think that's beautiful?'

'Oh, yes. Yes, indeed. But you see, that wreath was ordered for someone else.'

'Make 'em another one. How much is it?'

Again, conscience wrestled with cupidity. It would take an hour to make another wreath, but not for naught did Christatos labour on Sunday. 'One hundred dollars.'

'Sold.'

'Certainly, madam. Shall I wrap it for you?'

'No need, I'll wear it.'

She slipped the wreath over her head. The lilies framed her face, and the black ribbon fluttered at her bosom.

'How does it look?' she asked.

Christatos searched for a word, and came up with, 'Elegant.'

'It'll look even better on Ben. Have you ever noticed how some people can wear *anything*?'

THIRTY-FOUR
Sunday 4:58 PM

'You panicked,' said Yadroshnikov. 'You panicked, and you ran.'

'I ran,' said the Navigator, 'but there was no panic involved. I did what I had to do. I had no choice.'

'Your instructions were to stay in place.'

'The instructions were faulty in that they assumed a successful attempt. If the attempt had been successful, I would have stayed.'

'That is easy for you to say now.'

'Failure was not anticipated, which was a great weakness. Any plan that does not admit the possibility of failure is no plan at all.'

'The possibility was considered, and you were expected to stay.'

'This is hindsight, and it is pointless. The point is that I am out.'

'Yes, and if this were a sanctioned operation you would be shot for abandoning your post.'

'Why are you doing this? We both know what you are doing. Remember, I taught you how to do this.'

'I am discussing the facts, nothing more.'

'You are being abusive to a superior officer, that is what you are doing,' but as he said the words the Navigator knew that they had misfired. He was a major general and Yadroshnikov was a colonel, but in the traditions of their service operational rank meant little in the field. Nobody here was wearing any stars. The man with the power was the man in control. He appealed to Engstrom. 'Do you understand what he is doing, Charley? Perhaps it is different in your service, but with us this pointless abuse is part of the interrogation process, part

150

of the softening up. My only question is, why am I being interrogated?'

Yadroshnikov and the Navigator sat on facing chairs in Carlotta's living room. Engstrom leaned against a wall. Carlotta had been sent to the kitchen to make coffee, a transparent device since she could hear everything, and knew as much as she needed to know.

Engstrom said casually, 'Well, Jake, you *were* supposed to stay.'

'Charley, I'm surprised at you. If the attempt had been successful there would have been confusion, there would have been terror, there would have been an atmosphere of . . . of resignation. The king is dead, long live the king. That sort of thing. I could have survived in that atmosphere, I could have thrived in it. But not now. What do you think it's like up there now? The *GehBeh* will be looking for bodies to burn. I have seventy-three people working out of my *rezidentura*, Charley. Operational staff, technical-operational staff, and technical staff, seventy-three all together, and I guarantee you that not one of them will survive. They're finished, all of them, and they had nothing to do with it. They knew nothing about it, but they're finished. So what would have happened to me if I had stayed? Be fair, Charley, you know that I'm right.'

'Maybe you are,' said Engstrom, 'but when we deal with an old shoe like you we expect instructions to be followed to the letter. You see, there's something that's bothering us. You got out of there pretty quick.'

'I have already explained that. I got out when I saw that the attempt had failed.'

In a harsh voice, Yadroshnikov said, 'You got out before you could have known if he was dead or alive. We didn't know ourselves right away. But you knew. Do you see how that might bother us?'

The Navigator stared at him. 'What are you saying?'

'He's saying that you knew about the vest,' said Engstrom. 'He's saying that you knew that he was going to wear one, and that you never told us.'

'More abuse. What is the point of this?'

Yadroshnikov put his face only inches away from the Navigator's. 'You knew, you worthless piece of shit. You

151

knew about the vest, you knew he wasn't dead, and that's why you ran.'

The Navigator said tightly, 'Tell him to move, Charley. Get him away from me.'

'Lev?'

'You knew, all right.' Yadroshnikov spat in the Navigator's face.

'*Lev.*'

Yadroshnikov turned away. The Navigator sat motionless, the spittle running down one cheek, his eyes fixed on some far-off spot. He found a handkerchief, and used it. He said, 'So that's it. I worked for you, I gave you everything you asked for. I did this for the good of my country, and my service. And now we come to this.'

'Let it go,' said Engstrom. 'He shouldn't have done that, but let it go. You have to admit that your actions were, at best, suspicious.'

'I admit no such thing. Use your head, Charley, wouldn't I tell you if I knew about the vest?'

'I don't know. I stopped trying to figure out you Russians a long time ago.'

'Don't call him a Russian,' said Yadroshnikov. 'If you knew his real name you'd know that he was a Lett.'

'Really?' Engstrom sounded interested. 'I've never met any Letts.'

'You're lucky. He's a filthy Lett all right; his family is from Riga, so don't call him a Russian.'

At that point the Navigator knew that they were playing with him, and that whatever they said was not to be taken seriously. His real name was in no way Latvian, and his family had been Moscow-born for generations. So it was still the game of abuse, a game without rules, and he knew it was game he could not win.

Carlotta came in then with coffee and crockery on a tray. She set the tray down on a low table, and asked, 'Do I have to go back to the kitchen?'

Engstrom shook his head, and motioned for her to stay. She sank to the floor beside the Navigator's chair. She took his hands, looked up at him, and asked, 'Have you talked about it yet?'

'You know I haven't. You would have heard it in the kitchen.'

'Then I think you should. Now.'

'Talk about what?' asked Engstrom.

'My new life. The life that you promised me.'

'Did you promise him that?' asked Yadroshnikov. 'I don't remember any such promise.'

'You did, didn't you, Charley?'

'I did,' said Engstrom, his face a mask.

'Enough money, a new face, and a new identity, right?'

'Right.'

'And that place in Wyoming. I forget the name of the place.'

'Casper. Just north of Casper on Route 25.' Engstrom said it as if he were prompting a child.

'Yes, Casper. A roadside café that I could run by myself. Isn't that what you said?'

'That's what I said, Jake.'

'Ask him,' said Carlotta, gripping his hand.

'Ask me what?'

'Well, Charley, I've been thinking that if it isn't too much trouble could you make it someplace further south? Texas or New Mexico, maybe, down near the border. That way Carlotta could speak Spanish and we could fit in easily. What do you think?'

Yadroshnikov laughed softly. Engstrom looked from Carlotta to the Navigator, and back again. 'What's all this?'

Carlotta's chin came up proudly. The Navigator said, 'I want her with me.'

Engstrom shook his head. 'You know what she is. I bought her for you.'

'That's finished, too. All in the past. We want to be together.'

'I'm sorry, but it can't be done. It's outside the guidelines.'

The Navigator leaned forward, his hands clasped together. 'Listen, Charley, I'm an old shoe and I know about guidelines. You try to keep them, but there are times when you break them. This is one of those times. Let her come with me.'

'No, and I'm doing you a favour.'

'You owe it to me. I went all the way down the line for you.'

'No.'

'I know that you think that I'm empty, that I'm a shell, but there still are things that I could tell you. Things you don't . . .'

'He's begging,' said Yadroshnikov. 'He's actually begging.'

'He's right, you are,' said Engstrom. 'Don't embarrass yourself, Jake, it isn't going to change things. No matter what, the answer is no.'

Carlotta looked up at the Navigator, and put her hand on his arm. 'Enough. He means it. And he's right, you shouldn't embarrass yourself.'

The Navigator covered her hand with his. 'I'm sorry. I tried.'

'Yes. Thank you for that.'

'It would have been good.'

She shrugged. 'Maybe. And maybe I would have hurt you. Who knows?'

'I do. It would have been good.'

'Keep thinking that.' She leaned back so that her head rested against his knee. She closed her eyes briefly, and when she opened them she was looking at Engstrom. 'If I'm not going with him, then where am I going?'

There was the sound of a key in the front door. The door swung open, and the Navigator knew that he was dead. He had known it from the moment that Yadroshnikov had spat in his face, but he had refused to believe it. Now, staring at Carlotta's Cuban standing in the doorway with a Makarov in one hand and a black medical bag in the other, he knew it for a certainty. The past half hour had been nothing more than talk to mark time until the Cuban could come with his bag and his gun. There would be no chance now for a new identity, no chance to start over in Wyoming or anywhere else, no chance for a life without betrayal. He felt Carlotta's hand tighten on his, and he saw the fear in her face.

'Pepe,' she whispered. 'Jake, I didn't know, I swear I didn't.'

'Yes, I know that. Don't worry.' He tried to smile at Engstrom. 'I'm disappointed in you, Charley. I would have expected this from your colleague, but I thought you might be different.'

'I never claimed to be.'

'You promised me a new life.'

'I know I did. I'm sorry, but this is the closest I can come to it.'

The Cuban came into the room. He set down the medical bag, and adjusted the silencer on his weapon.

'Let her walk, Charley. You see, I'm begging again. Let her walk.'

Engstrom shook his head. 'I've changed my mind. She can go with you, after all.'

'I see.'

The Cuban came closer. The Navigator closed his eyes, and waited for it. *For you, my friend, the war is over.*

Engstrom said, 'Unless . . .'

The Navigator opened his eyes.

'You're dead, Jake. No matter what else, you've got to go. Do you understand that?'

The Navigator nodded.

'But there's a chance for the woman if you'll turn a trick for me. One last trick. What do you say?'

'If I do this, then she walks?'

'You have my word on it.'

The Navigator smiled thinly.

Engstrom smiled back. 'Yeah, I know, but I might just be playing it straight this time. You don't know, and you'll never know, but there's always that chance, isn't there?'

'Yes, there's always the chance. What do you want me to do?'

'It's very simple,' said Yadroshnikov, his voice no longer harsh. 'We want you to go back.'

THIRTY-FIVE
Sunday 5:00 PM

Daylight filtered into the General Secretary's bedroom through heavily curtained windows. Outside on Sixty-seventh Street, there was still September sunshine, but the bedroom was a cave of shadows. Gorbachev sat in a deep reclining chair, his head back and his eyes closed. From beyond the walls of his apartment he could hear the sounds of the Mission staff preparing for the evening's reception. The *rezident* had requested that the reception be cancelled. He and his security chief, Colonel Frolov, had presented cogent arguments. They had pointed out that two attempts on his life had been made in one day, and that it was not unreasonable to expect a third. They had pointed out that they could protect him within the limits of normal risk, but that there was no protection against a determined lunatic. They had conceded that the guests at the reception all would be representatives of fraternal nations, all dedicated communists, but they had pointed out that General Shvabrin had been a dedicated communist and a determined lunatic, as well. All cogent arguments, but he had rejected them. The *rezident* and the colonel were right, it would be prudent and proper to cancel the reception. The world would understand and approve, but he, himself, could not approve. How could he? If the reception had been cancelled only he would have known what little prudence had gone into making the decision, and how much abject fear. The fear was there, it had never left him, but he was determined now to keep it tamed.

He shifted in the chair to ease the pain along his ribs. The final draft of his United Nations speech lay in his lap, waiting for his approval. He knew that he should read it through, initial it, and send it off to the Press Office for distribution to

156

the news media, but that enormous lassitude was still upon him. He forced himself to open his eyes, ready to go to work, but when he did he saw in the dimness of the room the form of Yuri Muzalev sitting on the edge of his bed.

'What the devil are you doing here?' he asked.

'You told me to stay close to you.'

'I didn't tell you to sit on my shoulder like a pet monkey. How long have you been here? How did you get in?'

'About fifteen minutes, and the door was open. You didn't hear me, you were dozing.'

'I wasn't.'

'Have it your own way. How are you feeling?'

'My socks are up, if that's what you mean.' Gorbachev's eyes narrowed. 'What's that you have there?'

'Where?'

'On the floor, next to your foot.'

'Oh, that.' Yuri bent over, and came up with a bottle. 'Bourbon whiskey, an American invention. This business of being your shadow was beginning to cut into my drinking time.'

'Drinking alone? A bad sign.'

'I'm the best company that I know. Unless, of course, you'd care to join me.'

'I will, at that. See if there's an extra glass in the bathroom.'

'Are you serious? You, the great abstainer?'

'How many times do I have to tell you, I don't abstain. I drink moderately, in a civilized way. I may be the leader of a nation of drunkards, but . . .' He stopped, and sighed. 'Just get the glass, will you?'

Yuri took the bottle into the bathroom, and came back with a glass half filled with brownish liquid. 'I put some water in as well,' he explained.

'The way we do with wine for children. Thoughtful of you.'

Yuri raised his glass, and said in English, 'Here's mud in your eye!'

'Mud?'

'An American toast.'

'In the eye? I shall have to think about that.'

The two men drank in companionable silence. Gorbachev said, 'A trifle sweet, but it helps. Yes, indeed, it certainly

157

helps.' He held out his glass. 'Put a touch more on top of that. Too much water.'

Yuri cocked a comic eyebrow, but added a finger of bourbon. Gorbachev sipped, and said, 'Let me ask you a question. How do you think our *rezident* would react if I asked him to provide me with a pistol?'

Yuri, who was in the act of drinking, gagged slightly, but recovered. 'A pistol? You really have the jitters, don't you?'

'Answer the question.'

'It's a tough one. He'd probably have to find one for you. After all, you're the boss. But right after that he'd advise KGB Centre that the boss was cracking up.'

'Yes, that's the way I see it, too.'

'Look, you don't want a pistol.'

'Yes, I do.'

'But it's not your style. You're a world leader, you have armies, and tanks, and fleets at your command. A pistol would look silly on you. How about a nuclear missile? No, that's excessive, you want something in between like a rocket launcher. Sure, that's more like it, I can see you in a rocket launcher. Size forty-two, I'd say, if we let it out a bit around the shoulders. We'll order two for you, one in basic brown, and one in eggshell white for formal wear. How does that sound?'

'I'm serious, clown.'

Yuri looked at him closely. 'Yes, you are, aren't you?'

Gorbachev held out his glass again. Yuri hesitated, then gave him just a dollop, saying, 'Nation of drunkards, are we?'

'This is medicine.'

'It always is.'

There was a dreamy look on Gorbachev's face. 'That Captain Duffy, the American policeman. Where is he now?'

Yuri said slowly, 'He's established a command post in the lobby of the building. He'd be there.'

'Go and get him for me.'

'Mikhail Sergeyevich, you don't want to do that.'

'Do what? The man saved my life, and I haven't thanked him yet. Bring him here.'

* * *

Captain Edward Duffy stepped out of the Mission and onto the sidewalk. He looked up and down the street, surveying the scene with his hands clenched behind his back, his chin up and jutting. Looking at him, there could be no doubt that it was his scene. East Sixty-seventh had been cleared between Lexington and Park, and checkpoints had been established at the intersections. The cordon in front of the Mission had been extended and strengthened into tier after tier of uniformed policemen, their ranks liberally sprinkled with the jeans, jerseys, and jackets of the plainclothes cops who had been called in to beef up the forces. Duffy's eyes travelled over those ranks, looking for a familiar face. He saw more than a few, but his eyes kept moving until they came upon a face that brought a smile to his lips. The man at whom he was smiling, smiled back.

Detective First Grade Michael Costello smiled easily. He was essentially a happy man. At the age of forty-seven, that happiness was still a condition natural to him, which, for a veteran police officer, was not only rare, it was close to being perverse. Not that he was always smiling, and always happy. Right now, in fact, he was pissed off at having been called in on an off day to form part of the human wall around the Mission. The way he saw it, there were more than enough bluecoats to do the job, and there was nothing in the world that a plainclothes cop could contribute to the situation. But there he was, called in for no good reason. The bosses had panicked, he decided. This loony, DeKalb, had made them look bad, and now they had overreacted, calling out the troops in a show of strength. Costello thought it was stupid and wasteful, which was why he wasn't a boss, and never would be one. He had no such ambitions. He left that sort of thing to people like Ed Duffy.

Duffy and Costello went back a long way together, back to their rookie days. They shared the same background: Irish Catholic, Hell's Kitchen, St Francis Xavier High School. As young cops they had shared a few dangers and a great deal of boredom, and in the privacy of a patrol car at three in the morning they had shared their dreams and ambitions. But for all that, they had always been something less than close friends. There was something within Duffy that discouraged

159

such intimacy, a touch of ice that kept him removed. Still, they had known each other well, and they had gone part of the way up the ladder together. Only part of the way, because those dreams of theirs had never matched. For Costello, making Detective First had been the fulfilment of the dream, while Duffy had never stopped dreaming. Costello had stopped partway up the ladder, content, but Duffy had never stopped climbing. Over the past few years they had seen little of each other, but they were able to smile when their eyes met, and Costello wasn't surprised when Duffy crossed over to say hello.

'Long time, Mickey,' he said. 'Too long.'

'Too long,' Costello agreed, careful not to call him by name. You didn't palsy-walsy with Captain Edward Duffy in front of the troops.

Duffy looked at him thoughtfully. 'I've got to get something from my car. Walk me down to the garage.'

'I'm on duty here, Captain.'

'So am I, Mick, so am I. Come on.'

They walked to the entrance to the underground parking garage next to the Mission, down the ramp, and into a concrete cavern lined with cars bearing DPL and FC licence plates. Duffy's car was parked in the middle of the garage floor, and behind it was a row of the NYPD minibuses used to ferry in the troops during the crisis.

Duffy opened the front door of his car, and poked his driver in the shoulder. 'Go get yourself some coffee,' he said. 'It's been a long day and it's going to be a long night.'

The driver scrambled out of the car. Duffy slid under the wheel, and motioned for Costello to get in on the other side. When they were settled, he said, 'I don't need anything from the car, I just thought you could use a break. How's Margaret and the boys? Everybody well?'

'They're fine, Ed, just fine. Tommy's at St Peter's, graduates next year. Billy's at Xavier, on the track team.'

'Fast on his feet, like his old man.'

'Then, not now. How's Mary Elizabeth?'

'No complaints. Growing older like the rest of us.' Duffy took off his uniform cap, and wiped his forehead with the back of his hand. 'Jesus, what a day. I don't want another day like this one, not ever.'

'A good day for you, Eddie, a very good day. I never figured you for a Wyatt Earp.'

'Christ, I'm not, you know that. It was all instinct. I heard the shot, I turned, and I saw the gun in his hand. After that it was all a blur. I mean it, just instinct.'

'Still, it was good shooting.'

'From five feet away? My three-year-old niece could have dropped that asshole from five feet away.'

'Maybe, but you're the one who did it. Never gave him a second shot. Is he still alive?'

'From what I hear, just hanging on.'

'Any idea why he did it?'

'Who knows? We're living in a crazy world.'

'Crazy,' Costello agreed. 'They say that you're going upstairs for this one.'

'Who says?'

'You know, the word.'

Duffy shrugged. 'It could happen.'

'It will. You were in the right place at the right time. Like always.'

There was nothing for Duffy to say to that. It had been true all his life, the right place and time. They were silent for a while, and then Costello said, 'What is it, Ed? What do you want?'

'Hey, come on.'

'No, you come on. You didn't pull me out of the line just to give me a break. Tell me now, and save us some time.'

Duffy laughed. 'To tell you the truth, I pulled you out because you looked like you could use a new hat. When was the last time somebody bought you a hat?'

Costello considered the question. In the old days you said that somebody bought you a hat when he slipped you twenty bucks for doing him a favour. For twenty-five bucks you said that he bought you a Borsalino, but most of the time it was just a hat. Not for anything big. A traffic ticket, something like that, and he bought you a hat. You didn't hear the phrase used much any more. It had lost most of its meaning, mainly because twenty bucks had also lost most of its meaning. There were other words in use now, but an old-timer might still talk about buying you a hat, and now it could mean anything from

161

twenty bucks to a couple of hundred. And Ed Duffy wanted to buy him a hat.

'I don't wear hats any more,' he said carefully. 'I got out of the habit a long time ago.'

'Come on, Micky, it's me.'

'I mean it. Forget about the hat, just tell me what you want.'

'A favour.'

'Name it.'

'I want your hold-out piece. I need it. And there's still that hat.'

Quickly, too quickly, Costello said, 'That's another habit I got out of. I don't carry one any more.'

Duffy grinned. 'That'll be the day a dick goes to work without a hold-out. Don't shit me, Mickey. You'd go to work without your pants first.'

Costello didn't try to argue the point. Every plainclothes cop he knew, himself included, carried a second, illegal and unregistered, weapon in addition to his service revolver. It was a basic need.

'I don't get it,' he said. 'You want a hot piece, you know how to get one.'

'I need this one right now.'

'Sorry, can't help you.'

Duffy leaned over and put his hand on Costello's right knee. Costello froze. In an even voice, he said, 'Somebody sees you groping me like that and we're both in the shit.'

'You're not my type, sweetie.' He ran his hand down Costello's leg, then straightened up looking puzzled. His face cleared. 'You stay on the job long enough and your brain goes soft. I forgot that you're left-handed.'

He ran his hand down Costello's left leg, and stopped when he felt the holster strapped just above the ankle. He straightened up, and said, 'Let's have it, pal.'

'That sounds like an order. I thought it was a favour.'

'It's still a favour. For an old friend.'

Costello reached down, came up with the pistol, and gave it to Duffy. It was a nickel-plated .22 so small that it fitted in the palm of his hand. Duffy said, 'What did you do, take it off a hooker? It's a whore's gun.'

Costello stared at him. He didn't trust himself to speak.

162

Duffy turned the gun over in his hand, examining it. 'It sure won't stop any elephants.' He looked up. 'You're sore.'

'I'm sore.'

'What for? Like I said, it's just a favour for a friend.'

'Whatever you say, Captain.'

'Shit, don't be that way. Since when did you grow a new cherry?'

'There are ways of getting fucked. This isn't one of them.'

Duffy shook his head. He slipped the pistol under his tunic, and when his hand came out it was holding an envelope. He opened it. It was thick with hundred-dollar bills. He counted off five of them, and tossed them in Costello's lap. 'For the hat.'

He opened the door, and climbed out of the car. He stuck his head back in. 'Stay here for a while if you want to. You look like you could use the break.'

The door slammed shut. Costello fingered the new bills. Five hundred dollars for a piece of hot metal that you could buy for fifty if you knew the right place. Some hat. He tucked the money under the sun visor on the driver's side of the car, got out, and walked away quickly before he could change his mind.

THIRTY-SIX
Sunday 5:07 PM

'Only the first one is difficult to take,' said Yadroshnikov. 'After that, the others will be easy.'

'If it's that easy,' said the Navigator, 'then you do it first. Show me how easy it is.'

Yadroshnikov laughed. 'That wasn't the agreement. Are you going to take them, or not. Either way, you're dead, you know.'

They sat across from each other at Carlotta's kitchen table. The Cuban stood behind the Navigator, his pistol in his hand and the black bag empty at his feet. Spread out on the table were two dozens capsules filled with a strawberry-coloured jelly, a quart container of mineral water, and an ordinary kitchen tumbler. The capsules looked no more dangerous than so many vitamin pills. There were only the three men in the kitchen. Carlotta was locked in the bedroom, and Engstrom was with her to keep her quiet. They wanted no emotional scenes, and the Navigator was pleased to have it that way. Once he swallowed the first of the capsules he was the same as dead, and it was not something that he wanted to do in front of the woman.

He poked a capsule with the tip of his finger, and asked, 'How long do they take to work?'

'Two hours, more or less. It depends on the acidity in the stomach.'

'Not very precise.'

'No, but it will serve the purpose.'

'A home-grown product?'

'Actually, the Bulgarians developed it first. We added a few refinements, such as the strawberry flavour. I am told that the Bulgarian capsules tasted awful.'

'Is it something new? I've never heard of it.'

'It's been around for a while, but you wouldn't have known about it. As you might imagine, it isn't used very often.'

'Yes, I can see that,' said the Navigator, and realized that he was making conversation, postponing the moment. He poured a glass of water, and juggled one of the capsules in his palm. He put it back on the table. Yadroshnikov looked at him sharply.

'I'm going to do it,' said the Navigator. 'It's just that it takes a bit of . . .'

'You must realize that we have a time factor involved.'

'I know, but still, one has to work up to it.'

'I understand. Take a few minutes. There is still time to do things decently.'

The Navigator nodded his thanks. Now that it was no longer advantageous, Yadroshnikov had abandoned his abusive attitude, and had dropped into an easy collegiality. The Navigator tried to remember what he had been like in the Vienna days when Jacob Wolfe had been Captain Valeri Baykov, the top Viking in the *rezidentura*, and Lieutenant Yadroshnikov had been only one of twenty young and ambitious Borzois. Vikings and Borzois, a world apart in the intelligence game; the Vikings the superstar agents, and the Borzois the new boys who did all the routine work and provided support. Yadroshnikov had not remained a Borzoi for long, two recruitments in his first six months had made a Viking out of him, and after that they had worked together on a more equal basis. They had worked together well, the Navigator, who was not a Navigator then, supplying the experience, and a daring that was complemented by the newly made Viking's flair for organization and planning. Looking back on those days, he decided that Yadroshnikov had never been cruel in nature, only cruelly efficient with those neverending percentages of his. And having realized that, he also realized how well he had just been manipulated.

'You knew it all in advance, didn't you?' he said.

Yadroshnikov shrugged.

'You knew that I would run when the attempt failed. You knew how I would feel about the woman. You knew that I would agree to go back. You knew it all.'

'No, you are quite wrong. I knew nothing, I assumed every-thing. The percentages were right, and the progression pointed in that direction. I just let the percentages work.'

'Yes, you always did.' He looked at the capsules, and then moved his eyes away from them. 'And yet there was one factor that you did not include in your calculations.'

'Indeed? And what was that?'

'That all this manipulation might not have been necessary. That I might have been willing to do this as part of my duty.'

'Never. You are not the type for a suicide mission.'

'You don't know that. It might have happened.'

'A four per cent chance, no more.'

'Your numbers again. They'll hang you some day, those numbers. Do you really think that you can reduce every prob-lem in life to a mathematical formula?'

'It has worked for me so far.' Yadroshnikov looked at his watch, and for the first time he used the Navigator's real name. 'I said a few minutes, Valeri Demitrevich. There is no more time.'

'Of course.' The Navigator picked up a capsule. 'How strange this seems, almost natural. As if I had been born to do exactly this, and nothing else, at the end of my life.'

'Perhaps you were. Perhaps we all are. It's a strange life that we chose.'

'And yet, at the last moment, I have to ask . . . why me?'

Yadroshnikov looked surprised. 'Because it suited our pur-poses to use you. What other reason could there be?'

'None, of course. It was a foolish question.' He popped the capsule into his mouth, and followed it with water. He had a hard time swallowing it, but after a moment it went down. 'There. Done. Now, tell me the truth, what about the woman?'

'She will be all right, I'll see to that.'

'One hundred per cent?'

'Nothing in this life is one hundred per cent. I'll do my best.'

'Fair enough,' said the Navigator, and went to work on the rest of the capsules. Yadroshnikov had been right. After the first one they were easy enough to swallow.'

THIRTY-SEVEN
Sunday 5:14 PM

And it came to pass in the Kingdom of the Sea that the people of Luc laid siege to the castle of Candore, closing it off on all sides, and forbidding the entrance of foodstuffs, water, and the machinery of war. The siege was laid in the classic style with barricades erected far from the castle walls, and parallel trenches pushed forward by use of gabion and fascine. Catapults were brought into play hurling stones, and spears, and arrows; and sappers were sent out at night to mine beneath the castle walls. Within the fortress the people of Candore readied themselves for a lengthy siege. Food and water were carefully conserved, the armourers worked far into the nights, and the one old man who still knew the formula for the making of the Greek fire was put to work mixing the sulphur and naphtha and quicklime. Three times the soldiers of Luc approached the walls under the cover of their mantelets, and three times they were repulsed by the hail of metal and fire that came down on them from the towers. The siege was laid in the month of May, and by the new moon of June it was clear to both sides that they were evenly matched, and that the siege could be resolved only by a battle of champions. Then it was that the rules of single combat were agreed upon, and made known to all the people.

That Sir Giles and Sir Rupert would fight in the traditional style, on horse and with lances at first. And if a lance be lost, then with the mace. And if the mace be lost, then with the broadsword. And if the sword be lost, then with the knife. That the combat would last from sunup to noon, from that time at dawn when a black thread could be distinguished from a white, until the time when the sun would pass directly over the crenellated towers of Candore. That the combat would

167

continue each morning, day after day, until a victor was determined by the death of a champion, by his inability to fight on, or by a surrender; and to the victor would go all spoils of war, cattle and crops, chattels and women. After decades of contention the matter would finally be settled, Candore over Luc, or Luc over Candore.

Thus the terms were agreed upon, and the contest commenced.

The first day of combat was hot and dry, a day of dust and metallic sunshine. Long before dawn the battlements of Candore were filled with townsfolk eager to witness the spectacle on which their fate depended, and similarly the people of Luc were massed behind the lines of siege. At the moment of daybreak the two champions came forth onto the meadows below the western wall of the castle, each mounted on a white Arabian, each cased in armour of blackened steel, and only by the crimson plume of Rupert and the white plume of Giles could one be distinguished from the other. Two dark knights, they came trotting from opposite ends of the meadow, lances raised in salute, the horses stepping high, the early sun reflected in points upon their steel, and Laura baby, in that moment they were grand. Easy now to smile at their eggshell armour, their wooden lances, their Damascus blades. They were the warriors of their times, and in the end it may yet come down to that for us as well, the two best men on an open plain. In that flick of time those two were what every man would wish to be at least once in his life, and along the crowded castle walls, and along the lines of siege below, there wasn't a man, cavalier or coward, who did not know that and feel in some way lessened by his absence from the field. For that fleeting moment, Rupert and Giles were that which shines for all of us, and then, in response to a tocsin only they could hear, a signal only they could see, they couched their lances, kicked their horses into a gallop, and came flying across the grass at each other.

I know, I go slowly. Dear child of the tube, accustomed to drama that unfolds itself within the attention span of *Classic Comics*, you want to get on with the action. You want to know what it's all about, keeping a grown young lady up past her bedtime with a tale meant for children, and I can tell you this,

168

my lamb. It may be for kids, but it's a story about men and what the best of men must do in order to preserve the essence of themselves. Their honour, if I may use that weary old word, so much abused these days. And practically forgotten. Men like Brucie no longer know the meaning, if indeed the general ever did. For if he knew that much, he also would have known that you don't humiliate your friends and allies, that the faraway neighbours are the best you'll ever have, and that honour demands their consideration. But the Brucies of the world can only laugh at the concept. They're very good at laughing, they are, and wouldn't I just love to see Bruce all armoured up and at risk on the plains before Candore. How do you think he would fare, my sweet, in single combat? Yes, our turn to laugh. But not too much, because the Bruces of the world simply do not understand the ties that bind those few of us who still see clearly. He never would have understood what Rupert did in the fortieth day when the war came down to the knife. Which was why we could not trust him, you see, could never let him be a part of it despite his rank. If he could not dig what Rupert did, then his dreams could never encompass what we must do now, and yes, I know, I go slowly.

On that first morning of combat both lances snapped in the initial charge, unseating both riders, and sending their horses galloping madly across the meadow, into the fens, and down the long valley that led to the land of the Tweenies. Those horses never carried a knight again. The Tweenies took them for uses of their own, which, I fear, were not equestrian. The Tweenies, the inevitable sufferers in the wars between Candore and Luc, were not a noble people accustomed to riding about on steeds. Low, brutish, built close to the ground and far from heaven, the Tweenies laboured for a living in their fields and on the offshore waters. Those two Arabians, kin to what one day would be the Darley, were nothing more than meat for the pot in Tweenietown. Not much per Tweenie, but a welcome change from turnips and eels.

Horses gone, and lanceless, the two knights then set upon each other, first with the mace and then with the broadsword, battling through the morning, and it should be noted here that on that very first day both Rupert and Giles decided that the mace wasn't much of a weapon for individual combat. Too cumbersome, more suited to massed charges, the maces were rarely used after that first day, and often were discarded early on. No, once the lances snapped in the first charge, as they almost always did, it was sword to sword, steel on clanging steel. Throughout the morning the two knights fought on the meadow, in the fens, along the bank of the river that ran to the sea, and into the forest thickness. They hacked, they parried, they swung their steel in murderous arcs; and sparks flew bright enough to be seen in sunshine. All this while the people of Luc and Candore urged their favourites on, cheering or groaning at each palpable hit. At the stroke of noon, and the tolling bell of Candore tower, the combat ceased. The two champions fell back from each other, raised their swords in salute, and, battered but still sound, made their way back to their respective lines. Equally matched in physical frame, in martial skill, and in blind determination, they had fought to a draw.

That first day of combat set the pattern for the thirty-nine days to follow, save that from then on young men were posted near the edges of the meadow to contain any runaway horses, and the pots of the Tweenies went fleshless. But the style of the combat was settled: the furious charge, the splintered lances, the abandoned maces, and then the clash with broadswords through the morning haze and heat until the stroke of noon.

There were variations on the theme. There were days when the weather was bad and the elements clashed along with the knights: lightning bolts, sheets of rain, and skies so dark that the moment of noon could only be guessed at. There were days when the passion of the battle grew so strong that the knights fought on beyond the midday, and were separated only by the shouted reminder that they were staining their honour with such conduct. There was the day when Rupert was unhorsed, but Giles remained mounted, and the champion of Luc spent the morning with his back against a stone wall, defending himself against thundering charges, and there was the day when Giles fought half the morning waist deep in the river, while Rupert hacked at him from the shore.

There were those variations, and more, but the theme remained constant: hours of combat that ended each day without a winner. Every day at noon the knights retired, one to his

170

castle and the other to his tent, to be bathed, rubbed with oil, and dressed in soft linen. The rest of the day was spent in repose, and in the evening each retired to an empty bed, for both had sworn to be without women until the issue should be decided. It was the regimen of chivalry, much to be admired, although I must say that the part about the women intrigues me not, because you know your Daddy, sweetheart, and a life without the ladies is no life at all. Still, I suppose that when the cause is right certain sacrifices have to be made, and both Rupert and Giles made them all through those thirty-nine days of slogging battle, and it wasn't until the fortieth day that the combat became a war to the knife. Ever wonder about that phrase, baby? War to the knife, contention made so desperate that it all comes down to a sliver of steel in the hand of an exhausted man who refuses to quit. That's the way it was on the fortieth day, and there is one version of the story in which Rupert disarms Giles, and another that has it the other way around. I prefer the first. I see it more easily that way, the champion of Luc in one mighty, but lucky, swing, catching his opponent's sword behind the guard and sending it flying. Away. Up in the air. Wheeling against the sky and catching sunlight. Spinning down to earth again, and hitting the ground a dozen yards away. Too far, and all hope gone with it.

The force of the blow threw Giles to the ground, and he lay there defenceless except for the knife he now drew. Flat on his back, wearied and half crazed by the heat, still he drew that sliver of steel and was ready to fight on. It was a hopeless case and both sides knew it as groans rose up from the walls of Candore, and cheers from the tents of Luc. Leisurely, almost lazily, Rupert extended his arm and sword so that the end of his weapon, unpointed but sharp enough, rested against the fallen man's throat. That throat was protected only by the thin gorget between helmet and shoulders, the weakest link in the armoured chain, and in that position one push would easily pierce both steel and flesh.

'Surrender,' said Rupert. 'Give it up.'

Weakly, awkwardly, Giles raised his arm and threw his knife. It bounced harmlessly off Rupert's armour.

'Surrender,' Rupert said again, his voice ringing hollow in his helmet.

'No,' said Giles, 'not now, and not ever.' He raised his visor to stare his death directly in the face.

The moment hung in time, and in the silence of that moment there were flies in the field that droned, birds that called, and the river that sang as it rushed to the sea; and as that moment hangs, let me tell you, my sweet, that what happened next should not be read as a sign of affection, or respect, or that male bonding horseshit that our culture has recently foisted upon us.

Affection? The two men despised each other, always had, and nothing had happened in the past forty days to dilute that hatred.

Respect? A grudging respect, perhaps, for skill at arms, but none at all, one for the other, as a man and noble.

Male bonding? Each would sooner have kissed a snake full on the lips than have thrown his arm around the other's shoulder.

No, what happened in that moment was Rupert's dawning realization that in the whole of the world the only man who thought exactly the same way he did, who valued exactly the same standards, and who worshipped at the exact same altar, was the man who lay beneath his sword.

Giles of Candore, the far neighbour.

And with that realization, Rupert turned and stalked to where the other sword had fallen. He took it in his left hand and waited while Giles, dazed and confused, struggled to his feet. Rupert tossed the sword; it fell in front of Giles.

'Pick it up, you son of a whore,' said Rupert. 'We'll keep on fighting. I don't want it to end.'

DeKalb had been dying slowly for hours, and now he died quickly. He had told his story, had finally gotten it out, and if someone had suggested to me that the faint spark of his life had been fanned for a while by his need to tell the tale, I would not have argued much. Not that I knew. Despite all the time that I spend inside heads, I don't kid myself about the metaphysics of what goes on there. I simply don't know, and don't pretend to. But in this one case, as a guess, yes. He had had to tell that story, had told it, and with the story done, he died. Suddenly, there was nothing.

Arina looked at me, and I nodded. We both sat back. I reached for the cigarettes I no longer smoked, patted an empty pocket, and folded my hands together. Arina reached into her handbag, found a pack, and lit up.

I said, 'This is a no-smoking area.'

'I have diplomatic immunity.' The strain of the tap showed on her face. 'Well, what now?'

I stood up, pulled her to her feet, and kissed her. 'I'll tell you exactly what. Two drinks, a light meal, and the next twelve hours in bed.'

She smiled, and shook her head.

'All right, we'll skip the preliminaries. There must be an empty bed somewhere in this hospital.'

I felt her fingers at the back of my neck, her cheek against mine, and then she pushed me away gently. 'Ben, be serious, we have work to do.'

'That's what I had in mind.'

'Soon, but not now.'

She sank back into her chair. I sat opposite her, and took her hand. 'All right, let's work. What did you get out of all of that?'

'The far neighbours.'

'So you got that. I wasn't sure that you had.'

'How could I miss it? He mentioned it a dozen times.'

The expression had started in the Soviet diplomatic service, dating from the days when the Foreign Ministry in Moscow was located close to Lubyanka and the KGB. The GRU, then as now, had its Centre further out at Khodinka. Thus, to the diplomats, the KGB was known as the near neighbour, and the GRU as the far neighbour. In 1973 the Foreign Ministry was moved to Somolenskaya-Sennaya 32/34, reversing the distances between it and the two intelligence agencies, but the old terms continued to be used.

'The far neighbours, the GRU,' said Arina. 'I caught it, all right, but I don't understand what it was doing in that silly, adolescent story.'

'It was the only way he could say it. He had been trained to repress his connection with the GRU. He couldn't put it into words, not even in the privacy of his mind. He could only call them the far neighbours.'

173

'Are you saying that this man was an agent of our GRU?'

'I think it goes a lot deeper than that. I'm not sure how deep. I'll have a better idea once you tell me what you've been holding back from me.'

'Holding back? I've held back nothing. We opened ourselves to each other.'

She leaned forward and pressed my hand, her lips a perfect circle of concern. She was such an adorable little liar. I didn't know whether to kiss her again, or to slap her.

'We opened up,' I said, 'but you left one tiny block in place. I think it's time that you told me what you were blocking.'

She took her hand away. She was silent for a long moment. She said slowly, 'Very well, I concede the point. Certain matters of security must always be reserved. Actually, people such as ourselves, sensitives on opposite sides, can never be completely open with each other.'

'You're wrong. It can be done, but it takes a load of confidence and trust to do it. If you're ready to show me that trust, then I'm ready to do the same.'

'It goes against all my training.'

'I know, but if you and I are going to have anything together it has to be done. And if it will make you feel better, I held back something, too.'

'Ben.'

I grinned. She was shocked that I could have been as devious as she was. 'It's time to open up, Arina. Shall I make it easier for you? Shall I go first?'

She nodded.

'DeKalb was no ordinary Air Force colonel. He was a serving officer in the Defense Intelligence Agency.'

'Your GRU.'

'Roughly.'

'This fact was concealed. The President did not mention it to the General Secretary.'

'The fact was concealed,' I agreed, 'and I was sworn to help conceal it. I've just broken my word to my people, and I think that it's time for you to do the same.'

'I can't, not this way.' She switched over to head-to-head. *Easier this way. On the aircraft coming over there was an*

*attempt on the General Secretary's life. The man who tried it is
dead.*

Who was he?

Major General Shvabrin.

General Staff?

Yes.

So there it was, the DIA and the GRU, the warriors. Natural
enemies, and natural allies. DeKalb had said it. Like Rupert
and Giles, they could fight each other to the knife, but
they thought exactly the same way, valued exactly the same
standards, and worshipped at exactly the same altar.

Arina said aloud, 'The treaty.'

'Yes. They can't allow it. It would take away most of their
toys. They want your boss dead.'

She looked at me sadly, and said, 'This must be reported
at once.'

'Yes, to both sides. But be careful how you do it.'

'I know. I'm only young, Ben, not stupid.'

There are times when you cannot come clean with the
normals. Arina knew that already; you learn it early in
the game. You cannot tell normals the unvarnished truth about
what you do, because it would scare them silly. For, despite
what they say, those who know us, fear us. Every sensitive is
aware of that fear, and understands it. That some stranger
might be capable of invading the final privacy, the vault of
close-kept hopes, desires, dreams . . . yes, we understand that
fear. And so there are times when you don't go into details
when reporting a tap, times when you don't say anything at all
about what really went down. I knew that if I were to tell
Delaney the tale of Rupert and Giles, he would blow it away
with laughter. And I knew that if I were to tell him that I had
perched on the edge of a dying man's life and had stolen the
ultimate dream, that laughter would turn to disgust. So I
would not tell him that. There were other ways of doing it.

'Report to Yuri,' I said. 'Let him tell Zazulin.'

'Yes. And you?'

'Sammy will handle it for me. He's done it before.'

Sammy would spin Delaney a story of unmatched beta
waves, echoing theta patterns, and similar technical nonsense,
but leading to the inescapable conclusion that the GRU and

the DIA were involved in a joint operation to assassinate the General Secretary. Yuri would use the same approach with Zazulin. It was the only way to deal with normals, and the Siege of Candore would never be mentioned. Explaining away the secrets we had swapped would be somewhat dicier, but Sammy and Yuri could handle that, too. They knew, as we did, that what sensitives do for each other is sensitive business, and has nothing to do with the normal world. All that the normals are entitled to know are the results.

It was time to move, time to do what had to be done, but I allowed us one delay, a moment long enough for me to hold Arina close. And then there was another delay as the door burst open and three drunks stumbled into the room. Martha wore a wreath of lilies around her neck. Snake had a wicked-looking cactus balanced on one shoulder. Vince carried a sheaf of red roses crooked in his elbow like a bridesmaid. They were all badly damaged by the booze. They stopped short when they saw Arina and me with our arms around each other.

Vince recovered first. He said, 'Hey, man, what are you doing walking around? In your condition you ought to be in bed.'

'I know that,' I said. 'Don't tell me, tell her.'

THIRTY-EIGHT
Sunday 5:55 PM

Having consoled his mother on the loss of her grandson, and
having come to an understanding with his Don, Uncle John
Merlo then had Tony drive him to Carlo's apartment on Jane
Street. Once inside The Palace, home of major-league poker
in New York, he made his way through the empty outer
rooms, past the grandly furnished bedrooms, and down a
corridor to the card room with its oak-panelled walls and
seven-sided poker table. He pressed a button set into the wall,
and a panel slid back to show the front of a safe. He twirled the
knob, swung open the door, and took out a stack of black
notebooks bound together with heavy rubber bands. These
were Carlo's records of the poker operation . . . the weekly
gross, the expenses, the coded names of the heavy players with
their credit ratings and their limits . . . and with Carlo gone a
new place had to be found for them. He handed the books to
Tony, who slipped them into a leather case.

He was ready to leave then, but Tony said, 'Sit down for a
minute, rest yourself. You want I should make you a drink?'

The Uncle shook his head, but sank gratefully into a chair at
the card table. He was feeling it now, the loss, the grief,
and the frustrated rage that came from knowing that for one
of the few times in his life he was absolutely powerless. There
was nothing he could do, nothing. Some faceless monster had
reached out casually to destroy a member of his family, and
there would be no revenge, no compensation, no satisfaction.
It was a new sensation, this frustrated rage, and he knew that
he would carry it with him for the rest of his life. It was a form
of dishonour.

The Uncle sighed, sank back in his chair, and said, 'Maybe a
little soda water.'

Tony went behind a tiny bar, and came back with a fizzing glass. He set it down on the table, and cleared his throat nervously. 'Uncle John, is it okay if I ask you a question?'

'What is it?'

'This operation here, the poker, The Palace . . . what's gonna happen to it?'

The Uncle looked up with something close to amusement in his eyes. 'You got ideas, Tony? He isn't even cold yet, and you got ideas?'

'I don't mean no disrespect. Carlo was a friend of mine. But somebody's gotta take over, right?'

'And you want a shot at it.'

'All I'm saying is, when you get to think it over, think of me. Okay?'

'It's not your line of work.'

'I could do it,' Tony said stubbornly. 'I been watching Carlo for years. I know what it takes.'

'It's up to the Don, Tony. You know that. I just run it for him.'

'I'm just asking that you keep me in mind. That's all.'

'I'll do that,' said the Uncle, but he knew that Tony didn't have a chance. He was loyal, give him that. Also, he was tough and he was smart, but it was street-tough and street-smart. Tony was a soldier, and he'd never be anything more than that. Carlo, with all of his weaknesses, had been the perfect front for an inside operation: smooth, easy-going, a good mixer, able to handle both the winners and the losers. Actually, at that point the Uncle had no idea what was going to happen to the operation. Without Carlo it might be better to close it down, or farm it out, or turn The Palace into an after-hours joint. It just wouldn't be the same without Carlo.

It takes a certain type, thought the Uncle. Not easy to find.

And then, as he had occasionally over the years, he thought of Ben Slade. That kind of guy, cool and easy at the table, everything under control. And thought of the night when that slob Harry Bowen pulled a gun at the table, and the Uncle saw the end of it all staring out at him. Out of that little black hole. Crazy slob comes up shooting, and looking back at it later, it seemed as if Slade had started to move even before the pistol showed. Sitting across the table from Bowen, and lunging.

178

Like he knew it was going to happen, thought the Uncle. One second he's sitting there looking at his cards, and the next second he's flying across the table scattering cards and chips, reaching for Bowen's hand.

That hand came up with the pistol pointed straight at Uncle John, the hole at the end of it a tunnel of dreams, and the Uncle could only stare. Fixed and unable to move, not even hearing the little slob's high-pitched and raving voice. Fixed, and staring at the end of time as Slade slid, reached, and grabbed.

I never heard the shots, thought the Uncle, but I know that he got off two. We took the slugs out of the ceiling the next morning.

Out of the ceiling, not out of the Uncle. Slade's hand reached, grabbed, and twisted. Bowen fired twice, and then the rest of them were all over him. Took away the piece, kicked his ass out into the night, and told him never to come back. Carlo wanted to break his arms, but what good would that do? Word gets around. And through it all, there was Slade, back in his seat and stacking his chips, cool as you want and ready to play.

I owe him, thought the Uncle. I've owed him for a long time. I told him that, but he never tried to collect. And then, after a while, he never came around any more.

'Whatever happened to Slade?' he asked in a tired, old man's voice.

Tony said, 'Who?'

'Slade. The player who used to win all the time, the one I backed his play. Smooth as silk, won me a bundle.'

'When was this?'

'Couple of years ago.'

'I don't remember any Slade.'

And you want to run things, thought the Uncle. He stood up, and felt the movement in every one of his bones. 'Let's go.'

'Home?'

It was time to go home, and to rest, but home hadn't meant much since the death of his wife. He told Tony to take him back to the clam bar.

THIRTY-NINE
Sunday 6:30 PM

Less filling, said Sammy Warsaw.
  Yuri shot back, *Tastes great.*
  Less filling!
  Tastes great!
  LESS FILLING!
  TASTES GREAT!
  The *ad hoc* committee sat in the anteroom of the quarters of
the General Secretary. The Americans occupied one side of the
conference table, the Soviets the other, and the abuse that
bounced back and forth between them made the meeting
sound like a beer commercial. The committee was a jumbled
affair composed of those people already on the scene and
thus available. Both governments would have preferred a
more formal arrangement, and, indeed, the group was so
oddly mixed that, given the diplomatic realities, it could not
have been convened the day before. Now, in a state of emergency, it was assembled for the single purpose of preserving
the life of the leader of the Soviet Union.
  Gorbachev sat at the head of the table, slumped in his chair.
To his left sat Mironoff, the head of his personal security
detail, then Frolov, the KGB officer for Mission security,
Zazulin, the KGB *rezident*, and Ambassador Panchenko.
Across the table from them sat Delaney, representing the CIA,
Anthony Chavez from the FBI, Captain Duffy of the NYPD,
Harold Islington from the Secret Service, and Walter Bradley
from the State Department.
  Sammy and I sat behind the Americans; Arina and Yuri
behind the Soviets. Officially, the four of us were there as
translators, but as Bradley spoke idiomatic Russian, and most
of the other side had abandoned their pretence of not speaking

180

English, there was little for us to do along those lines. We were actually there to guarantee the confidentiality of the meeting. The rule was no peeking, and Sammy and I were blocking for the Americans, while Yuri and Arina shielded the thoughts of the Soviet group. It was the sort of job that each of us could do with half a head, leaving us plenty of room for our own conversations.

This was my first close-up view of Gorbachev. Until then I had known him as nothing more than a two-dimensional figure on television, and as the subject of the sort of speculation that runs wild around an outfit like mine. I had thought of him only in terms of the headlines about his policy of *glasnost*, his reforms of the Soviet bureaucracy, his push towards arms control, his gentle nudging of the Soviet Union towards a more civilized society; and, I suppose, like so many others in the Western world, I had allowed myself the faintest flicker of hope that in him might be found the means with which to end the decades of confrontation between the two superpowers.

Just the faintest flicker, for the cynical nature of the sensitive would not allow me any real enthusiasm. I did not expect to see socialism crumble in the Soviet Union. I did not expect to see free elections, or a free press, or an open society as we know it. Whatever else Gorbachev was doing, he was not trying to subvert the principles of Marx and Lenin, he was not trying to convert his country into a market-system capitalist democracy, he was not giving up the fight. He was out to prove the superiority of his system by making it more competitive, and his ambition was efficiency, not reform. Lord Carrington, the NATO Secretary General, put it best when he said, 'Mr Gorbachev is neither a revolutionary nor a counter-revolutionary. He is a Communist leader and he is a Russian. It would be a mistake to forget either point.' I wasn't forgetting.

Thus my distrust of the motives of the man, but still, as the meeting wore on, I found myself drawn to him. Not because of his position of power; that held no glamour for me. I had seen enough of the leaders of the world up close to be shorn of illusions about them. It was the man who intrigued me, not the office he held. He was weary, in pain, and his life was on the line, but as he sat slouched in his chair listening to the arguments that raged around him, he bore himself with a dogged sort of dignity that I had to admire. Put simply, I found myself liking him. In the hours to come that feeling would deepen into something close to affection, but I must point out that at no time did I ever trust him. Not only because of what he represented, but because I could never trust any normal, no matter who he was.

I was not alone in this. From childhood on, I had been trained never to trust a normal person, and to some degree every ace I knew felt the same way. No matter how likeable, no matter how understanding a normal man or woman might seem to be, I could not wholly trust anything that he said to me. Two reasons why. First, no matter how much he denied it, in his heart he was afraid of me, and a frightened man could not be trusted. Second, no matter how understanding he might seem to be, he understood nothing about me. How could he? He was locked outside the world of sensitives, wrapped in ignorance, and an ignorant man could not be trusted. So we all learned early on that you could never wholly trust a normal, not even the best of them, and certainly not the people who ran us, who were anything but the best. We learned to trust aces only . . . any ace. That was as far as trust extended. Everyone else was suspect.

The meeting rattled along, and the point of contention between the two sides was where the Soviet leader would spend the night. Panchenko, the ambassador, was saying, 'You understand that it would be unthinkable for the General Secretary to leave the Mission at this point.'

Bradley, the man from State, said smoothly, 'Not unthinkable at all. What is unthinkable is that he should stay here tonight. It's obvious that you have no way of guaranteeing his safety inside the Mission.'

'I dispute that statement. It is false and provocative.'

'Then let me put it this way. How many of your GRU people are unaccounted for?'

His face a mask, Panchenko said, 'There are no GRU officers attached to this Mission.'

'Mister Ambassador, I thought we had got beyond that point.'

Panchenko started to say something, but Gorbachev raised

a hand wearily, and said, 'Mister Bradley, it is clear that we are facing a highly organized plot to kill me. So far there have been two attempts, one by an officer of our GRU, and one by an officer of your DIA. This does not mean, however, that every member of the GRU is involved, nor every member of the DIA. In fact, I find such a possibility beyond belief.' He turned to his ambassador. 'On the other hand, Panchenko, this is no time for diplomatic subterfuge. Answer his question.'

Panchenko said grudgingly, 'There are several . . . operatives . . . still unaccounted for.'

'How many is several?' asked Bradley. 'Five? Twenty?'

'Several.'

'And every one of them is a potential assassin.'

'Another provocative statement. How many potential assassins are waiting out there in the streets of New York?'

'No one is suggesting that the General Secretary sleep in the streets. The New York Police Department has a secure place available for him. Captain Duffy would be in charge of the operation. Duffy, would you give them the details?'

The captain stood up. He made an impressive appearance, and he knew it. He cleared his throat, and looked around the table. 'The Police Department maintains several safe houses in various parts of the city. We propose to transport the General Secretary to one of them . . .'

Gorbachev interrupted by turning to Yuri, and asking. 'What is a safe house?'

'*Yavotchnaya Kvartiva.*'

'Ah.'

Mironoff asked, 'And where is this safe house you propose to use?'

Duffy smiled easily. 'I'll be glad to tell you the location once this proposal is approved. The move will be made in an armoured van manned by a picked squad of police officers. At this very minute the van and the men are on standby in the basement garage of this building. The move can be made at any time, and in total secrecy.'

'Very efficient.' Mironoff covered the words with a sneer. 'Total security? You intend to drive this van out of the building and onto the street under the eyes of a mob of people and half the television cameras in the city, and you call that total secrecy?'

Duffy shook his head. 'The mob, as you call it, and the television cameras are in front of the Mission on Sixty-seventh Street. There is a secondary exit from the garage that runs through to Sixty-eighth Street. There are no cameras there, no mob, and we'll make sure that it stays that way. We'll be going out the back.'

Mironoff looked at Panchenko. 'Is there such an exit?'

'We had it closed off for security purposes, but I suppose it could be reopened.'

Duffy said complacently, 'It already has been.'

Panchenko jumped up. 'You had no right to do that. That is a breach of the diplomatic status of the Mission, and I must protest most vigorously.'

Duffy leaned forward, his hands on the table. 'Mister Ambassador, I'm not a diplomat, I'm just a cop with a job to do. My job is to guard the General Secretary through the night, and deliver him to the United Nations General Assembly by eleven o'clock tomorrow morning, and I intend to do that job, no matter how many diplomatic toes I have to step on.' He looked around the table defiantly.

'Bravo,' said Mironoff. 'I appreciate your position, Captain, because I, too, am a cop in a way, and my job is the same as yours. So listen to this. What you are suggesting is impossible under the circumstances. Believe me, this is not pride talking, this is common sense. The General Secretary will be perfectly safe here, and here is where he will stay.'

'You're not a cop,' said Duffy. 'Not what I call a cop. What you are is a fool.' He sat down.

In the silence that followed, Delaney said, 'There's a factor that seems to have been overlooked. What about the Navigator?'

His question hit a wall of blank looks on the Soviet side of the table.

Delaney shook his head in irritation. 'Gentlemen, please, I thought that we were being candid with each other. We know that your GRU *rezident*, the Navigator, is one Jacob Wolfe, and we know that Wolfe is the cover name for Major General Valeri Baykov. We also know that he went missing immediately following the assassination attempt. Considering the evidence that we have so far, do you really think that you can guarantee the safety of the General Secretary while this man is loose in the city?'

The Soviets exchanged looks, and it was Panchenko who answered. 'You obviously have been given incorrect information. I have never heard of this Navigator, as you call him. We do have a Jacob Wolfe attached to the Mission, but he is a third secretary, nothing more, and he has no connection with any intelligence service.'

'Bullshit,' said Delaney. 'We're not going to get anywhere unless you stop covering up for the people who are trying to kill your own man.'

'Mister Delaney, you are being insulting.'

'And you are being less than truthful.'

'You call me a liar?'

'I do, indeed, and I ask you again, where is the Navigator?'

'There is no such person.'

'You're not only a liar, you're doing it badly.'

'You may not talk to me in such a manner.'

'I'll say it again. You're lying in your teeth.'

'This is an impossible situation.'

'I agree.'

'Provocative.'

'Intolerable.'

Less filling.

Tastes great.

Less filling!

Tastes great!

LESS FILLING!

TASTES GREAT!

What a bunch of birdbrains, said Sammy. *A plague on both their houses.*

I'm starving, said Yuri. *Do they still serve goose on Sundays at Emilio's?*

Indeed.

Then that's what I want when we break. With dumplings and a bottle of Johannisberger. Ben, how about you and Arina? Coming along?

It was Ben and Arina now. We had known each other for less than two hours now, but our names were coupled. No need for announcements. Both Sammy and Yuri had caught

the odour of oranges that clung to us, and now it was Ben and Arina. I looked at her across the conference table, and asked.
Are you hungry?

Starved. You?

Starved, but not for food.

Please, don't look at me that way.

That was all that we could do at the moment, look at each other as the argument at the table continued. There were things that we wanted to say to each other, thoughts to be nestled side by side, and most pressing of all there was the need to find ourselves a place of privacy for the night; but with Sammy and Yuri tuned in we kept all that to ourselves. With our eyes locked and boring deep, we let the other two do the talking. Yuri wanted to know about Snake, Vince, and Martha.

What happened to the rest of your troops?

Sammy said disgustedly, *You mean my three drunks? I threw them out of the game.*

Where are they?

Downstairs, in the garage, sleeping it off. I stashed them in the company car. Told them I didn't want to see them again until they sobered up.

How bad were they?

Revolting.

Yuri laughed silently. *Since when did you sign the pledge?*

Not the same thing. Did you ever see me bombed when I was working?

Is that a serious question?

Okay, maybe once in a while, but I could always function, right?

That was enough to set the two of them off on a round of reminiscence about the days a few years back when they both had been stationed in Washington. They made it sound like an unending party as they called up names from the past. After a while Sammy sighed and said, *It's all new faces now. The old aces are gone.*

What about Pat Whaley?

Back in London.

Fominski?

I heard he's operational in Angola. Remember Corvazzio?

He's running the training centre outside Milan.

Better than working for a living. Whatever happened to Sepp . . . what's his name? The guy who could drink all the beer.

You mean the West German? Sepp Kruger?

That's the one. How's he doing?

Sammy hesitated. *He isn't doing anything. He took a bath.*

You're kidding.

No, he's dead. Mokrie dela, *wet stuff.*

Shit. How?

So he didn't know about Sepp. The Germans had put a lid on it, but some of the aces were guessing. Bonn had put him on detached service and had set him up in Rome as a financial consultant. It was a neat scam, half fortune-telling and half market analysis. All he had to do was pull a tap on the client, find out what the sucker wanted to hear, and feed it back to him. The fees he charged were wickedly high, but the best part of the operation was the incidental intelligence that he collected while he was tapping the mark. He was dealing with high rollers only, people of power in the political and financial worlds. And not just Italians. Within a year he had an international list of clients, and the reports that he was sending back to Bonn were all on the A level. The Germans had an intelligence gold mine working, until he turned up dead in an alley.

What happened? asked Yuri. *Who did it?*

Nobody knows, said Sammy.

I got into it then. *Sammy, you know damn well what happened.*

That's only a guess.

He found out too much about somebody, more than he was supposed to. Couldn't be anything else. So he got wet.

Yuri asked, *What about his protection? Didn't he have any security?*

A mental shrug from Sammy. *The guess is that whatever it was that he uncovered, it was about one of his own people. His security was a little lax that night.*

Christ, his own . . .?

That's what the guess is.

Bastards.

187

Sure, Sammy agreed, *but it was a high-risk game, and Sepp made mistake number one. He trusted somebody.*

Yuri was shaken. He was silent, and then he laughed shortly. *What an incredible business this is.*

The beer commercial at the conference table raged on, but there was never any doubt as to its outcome. Our side truly believed that we could offer Gorbachev better protection outside the Mission, and he listened carefully to the arguments presented. He paid particular attention when Duffy spoke, for the cop had saved his life, but in the end he made the only decision possible for him.

'I appreciate your position,' he told the Americans. 'You have only my wellbeing in mind.' He smiled slightly. 'Not, perhaps, because you love me so much, but because you know how important it is that I appear before the United Nations with the President tomorrow morning. In any event, I thank you for your concern, but I will spend the night here at the Mission. I have every confidence that the security officers here will provide for me properly, and this implies no lack of confidence in the New York police. I have good reason to know how effective they can be, but here is where I will stay. Technically speaking, when I am here I am on the soil of the Soviet Union, and that is the place for me to be. However, in order to spread the risk to the leadership, Comrade Shevardnadze has been instructed to go at once to our enclave in Riverdale, and Comrade Ligachev has left for the compound at Glen Cove. Will their safety be assured?'

'Consider it done,' said Duffy.

'Then there is nothing further to be discussed, and this meeting may be adjourned.'

And not a minute too soon, said Yuri. *Make it two bottles of Johannisberger, and an extra order of dumplings.*

Meet you at Emilio's in half an hour, said Sammy.

I asked Arina, *Are we going?*

She hesitated. I was hoping that she would say no, that she would say the hell with dinner, let's find a place where we can be alone. I waited, but before she could answer, all of our plans for the evening were changed. The chief cipher clerk of the Mission slipped into the room, and whispered something in Frolov's ear. Frolov grunted. He stood up, and came around to the back of Gorbachev. He bent over, and repeated the whisper to the General Secretary. Gorbachev whispered something back. Frolov shook his head. They whispered sharply to each other in obvious disagreement. I saw Yuri and Arina stiffen. They were picking it up out of Frolov's head, but I was blocked from there. Gorbachev said something final to Frolov, and turned to face the Americans.

'There is something that you should know,' he said. 'Jacob Wolfe, the man you call the Navigator, has returned to the Mission.'

FORTY
Sunday 6:45 PM

'*Swing low,*' sang Vince. '*Sweet chariot. Comin' for to carry me home.*'

'Her eyes are squinty,' said Snake, 'and her nose is too long.'

'It isn't,' Martha protested. 'It's a lovely nose. She has perfect features.'

Snake shrugged. 'That's the way you see it. I don't.'

'You never do. According to you, nobody is ever good enough for Ben.'

'*Swing low, sweet chariot . . .*'

'That isn't true.'

'Sure it is. You've always been that way about Ben's girls.'

'*Ah looked over Jordan, and what did Ah see . . .*'

'Knock it off,' said Snake.

'*Comin' for to carry me home . . .*'

'I said knock it off.'

'Let him sing,' said Martha. 'It makes him feel better.'

Vince's voice filled the company car, and echoed off the walls of the underground garage. The car was Sammy's pride, a stretch limousine with all the gadgets. There was a two-way radio, a mobile telephone, an arms chest, a well-stocked bar, and the gag bag, a collection of wigs, moustaches, and all the other paraphernalia of disguise. Only the bar was locked, and Sammy held the keys.

All three of them had been into the gag bag. Vince, wearing a woman's wig of silky, jet-black hair, lay across the back seat with his roses cradled in his arms. Martha, with a blob of red putty stuck onto the end of her nose, sat sprawled on a jump seat, the wreath of lilies around her neck. Snake sat behind the wheel, Daliesque moustaches drooping from her upper lip. Apart from looking silly, they all looked badly wasted. They

190

were coming down off the high that had sustained them so far, easing the descent with nips from the bottle of cognac in Martha's tote bag. Sammy had told them to sleep it off, but sleep was far away.

'Everybody,' said Vince. 'Let's everybody sing. *A band of angels comin' after me . . .*'

The two women ignored him, still thinking about Arina. They both had seen their baby brother Ben with the Russian girl, and had caught the scent of oranges on them. Martha, predictably, had been thrilled, but not Snake. Snake didn't think much of romance for aces. Sex, yes; romance, no. Romance was sticky and counterproductive, a form of weakness, and she was sad to see one of her own caught in the trap.

'It won't last,' she said, more in hope than conviction. 'He'll screw her a couple of times, and that'll be the end of it.'

Martha smiled, and shook her head. 'How can you say that? You smelled those oranges.'

Snake, lying fiercely, said, 'I didn't. And besides, I don't believe in that crap. It's just a myth. I've never smelled anything like that in my life, not ever.'

'No, and you never will.'

'What's that supposed to mean?'

'Comin' for to carry me home . . .'

'For Christ's sake,' Snake exploded, 'if you have to sing, sing something cheerful.'

'What can I tell you?' said Vince. 'Sammy's mad, and I'm sad. Threw us out of the ballgame, that's what he did.'

'Sammy's acting like an asshole.'

'He's the boss now, he's the man. He never used to be that way. Trouble with Sammy, he's forgotten what it's like to be one of the little people.'

Snake snorted. 'Little, my ass. Who's little?'

'We are.'

'Screw that. Speak for yourself.'

Vince raised his head to look. 'You figure you're one of the big people now?'

'Big enough to kick your butt.'

'Oh, my.'

'Any place, any time.'

'Oh, my, indeed.'

191

Martha reached for her tote bag, and said quickly, 'Have a drink.'

'Don't mind if I do.' Vince took a slug from the bottle, and passed it over to Snake.

'*L'chaim*.' Snake took her share, and held the bottle up to the light. 'Running low. Time to resupply.'

'Sammy said to ease off,' Martha pointed out.

'Screw Sammy. Vince is right. He never should have benched us.' She shifted the cactus on her lap. 'Come on, *tus*, sing something cheerful.'

'Don't know anything cheerful. I'm down, way down. I saw a good woman die today, I gave up a pint or two of my own, and where am I? Out of the game. Rejected. Useless.'

'Bombed,' Martha noted.

'Not nearly enough. *Sometimes Ah feel like a motherless child . . .*'

'God damn it, Vince.'

'*A long way-ay from home . . .*'

Vince's gentle baritone floated out of the car and across the cavern of the underground garage. It easily reached the far wall one hundred and twenty feet away where an armoured Police Department van was parked, the vehicle assigned to transport the General Secretary to a safe house if the need should arise. The crew of the van, a squad of six men, lounged in the rear, waiting for orders. They heard the singing and one by one, caught up by the music, they began to hum along.

FORTY-ONE
Sunday 6:30 PM

They took Carlotta to the Marshall Street warehouse. The Cuban came with them. They put her in a small room near the Duty Office, and left the Cuban with her. Yadroshnikov told the Cuban to keep his hands off the woman. He said it firmly. The Cuban pulled a face, but he nodded.

'He isn't happy,' said Engstrom as they headed for the Duty Office. 'He's been banging her for months, and you tell him to keep his hands off.'

'It isn't sex with him any more. He'll abuse her if he can.'

'That bothers you?'

'I made a promise. I said I'd look after her.'

Engstrom looked surprised, but said nothing. They went into the Duty Office. The Case Executive had the big screen fired up and operational. It covered half of one wall. It was a grid pattern that overlaid a map of Manhattan, and parts of Brooklyn and Queens. The Marshall Street warehouse was represented by an illuminated square, as was the Soviet Mission. The only other lights on the grid were two blips within the Mission square, and a third blip near by. The third blip moved slowly towards the square. The Case Executive followed the light with a long, rubber-tipped pointer.

'He's almost there,' she said as they came into the room. They settled into chairs and watched as the third blip crossed the illuminated border. Now all three blips were grouped within the square. The Case Executive announced, 'He's in.'

'How long do you figure?' asked Engstrom.

Yadroshnikov said, 'His blip will disappear within minutes.'

'So soon?'

The Russian shook his head impatiently. 'You misunderstand. At this moment he is being taken to an interrogation

193

room. The first thing they will do is strip him and search him. It will take them only minutes to find the transponder strapped to his ankle, and to remove it. Once removed, it will cease to function, and the blip will disappear from the screen.'

'You're sure of this?'

'In this area the procedures of the KGB are essentially the same as those of my organization. His body will be examined thoroughly, fingers in every cavity. Aside from the transponder, they will find nothing. He will then be injected with a low-level dose of sodium pentathol, not so much for its value as a so-called truth serum, but to induce a state of euphoria. Then the questioning will begin.'

Both men fell silent, staring at the screen. Veterans of hundreds of interrogations, they had a good idea of how this one would go. There would be nothing physical at first, only calm questions asked by apparently reasonable men. Mironoff, as chief of Gorbachev's personal security, would most likely be in charge, dealing with the Navigator on a professional level, one intelligence officer to another. It would be soft, easy, *Come on, old friend, let's talk candidly, let's get to the bottom of this mess. You were a good man once, with an outstanding record, but clearly something has changed your life. Why not tell us about it now, get it off your conscience?* And the Navigator would respond in kind, agreeing to answer every question openly, admitting his guilt. Asked to play the role of a man overcome by remorse, he would play it all the way, presenting the portrait of a patriot and a communist who has been led astray.

'He will give them everything,' said Yadroshnikov. 'Everything he knows, and then some. He will give them dates, connections, and names. All the names, a sack full of names, even your name and mine. He will empty the sack.'

Engstrom grinned.

'All the names except one. There is one that he will hold back, a name so highly placed that it can only be told . . . whispered . . . into the ear of the General Secretary himself. That one name, so high in the leadership . . . yes, only to Gorbachev. He will insist on that.'

'What if Mironoff says no?'

'He might, but I doubt it. Look at it from his point of view.

194

The Navigator is helpless and naked in front of him, clearly unarmed and posing no threat. To beat that one name out of him would take hours, and time is precious now. No, the odds say that he will agree. He will call for Gorbachev. Seven chances out of ten, he will do it.'

'And Gorbachev?'

'A different story entirely. Ten out of ten. How could he say no?'

'No contact on the third transponder,' said the Case Executive. She used her pointer. There were only two blips of light within the Soviet Mission.

'They have found it,' said Yadroshnikov. 'Now the questioning begins.'

FORTY-TWO
Sunday 6:47 PM

When Gorbachev entered the interrogation room, the first person he saw was Mironoff, who was in shirtsleeves. The second person he saw was the Navigator, who was naked. Both sights were mildly shocking to the General Secretary. Without jacket or tie, and with his sleeves rolled up, Mironoff's cannonball belly strained his shirt, and a ridge of fat glistened at the back of his neck. Without the mask of his clothing, he looked the quintessential inquisitor: brutal, porcine, unfeeling. The Navigator, on the other hand, looked ridiculous. He stood against the far wall of the room, bright lights on his face, and his hands cupped over his crotch. Gorbachev thought fleetingly of the difference between men and women in such a situation. A woman, caught nude against her wishes, would try to protect her modesty by throwing one arm across her breasts, and the other down to cover her delta. The position, although vulnerable, was also graceful and appealing. A man, however, looked nothing better than awkward with his shoulders hunched forward and his hands at his genitals. In fact, he looked silly.

Gorbachev glanced around. Apart from Mironoff and the Navigator, there were four others in the room: Frolov, Zazulin, and two more *GehBehs*, the muscular sort. He looked again at the Navigator. On second impression, the man did not look silly at all. Although naked and defenceless, he bore himself well. Not with dignity, for no man could be dignified under such circumstances, but there was a calmness about him, and an air of peace.

He knows that he has to die, thought Gorbachev, and he is already dead.

The General Secretary knew the traditions of the GRU, and

knew about the crematorium at the place they called the Aquarium. There was only one way for a GRU officer to leave the service: through the chimney. A state funeral and honourable cremation for those who did their duty, and for traitors a trip down the conveyor belt to the maw of the furnace, alive and screaming. The Navigator would escape the furnace, no time for that now, but he would surely die some other way. The man knew it, and, already dead, he was past hope, past anger, past passion. Thus, the air of serenity that surrounded him.

Enviable, in a way, thought Gorbachev. If we could all achieve that state of mind without the certainty of death to prompt it.

He looked a third time at the Navigator. This time their eyes met and held. The Navigator smiled faintly, and Gorbachev found himself responding with a nod to the man who had plotted to kill him.

And you have something to tell me, he thought. For my ears only. What dirty little secret do you have for me?

The smile faded from the Navigator's face, replaced again by that air of serenity. Gorbachev turned to Mironoff. 'He insists on speaking to me?'

'Under the circumstances, we thought it would save time if . . .'

'I understand. What do you have from him so far?'

Mironoff said with satisfaction, 'He's spilling his guts. I never had to touch him, not even a love tap. He confirms what we already suspected, that it was a conspiracy involving elements of the GRU and elements of the DIA. He confirms his own role in the attempt outside the Mission. He's given us names, dates, places of . . .'

Gorbachev interrupted. 'Where does it end? That's what I want to know.'

'He says that it's over. The operation is over, a failure. According to him, it was a two-step attack, and both of them misfired. A fiasco, he calls it.'

'Do you believe him?'

'It is not my job to believe or disbelieve, but it's hard to see why he would lie.'

'And the information he has for me?'

'A name. That's all he would say.'

197

Gorbachev walked across the room and stood in front of the Navigator. The man was not bound; he leaned against the wall. Close up, the angular lines of his face, and his deep-set eyes, were noticeable. Also noticeable was the strong smell of sweat coming off the naked body.

The sweat of fear, Gorbachev decided. But those eyes. Burning.

'You asked for me,' he said. 'I am here. What do you want to tell me?'

Again the faint smile. 'Is that the only question you wish to ask me?'

Gorbachev realized that there was another. 'No. Why did you come back?'

'Yes, that's important, isn't it? Why did I come back to certain death? Possible torture? Why?'

'You must have had a powerful reason. A change of heart, perhaps.'

'Change of heart? Well, yes and no. A change in my convictions, no. I tell you this frankly, Mikhail Sergeyvich, with death staring me in the face, I think that your plan for collaboration with the Americans on the SDI will be a military disaster for the motherland. We will never be full partners in such a collaboration. We will be tricked, deceived, and manipulated, and in the end we will be defenceless. They will have everything, and we will have nothing. As a military man, I tell you that it means the end of the balance of power.'

'Yes, I've heard that all before, and it doesn't impress me. Still, what was the change of heart?'

'Do you think I might have a cigarette?'

Gorbachev motioned with a finger. One of the muscle men produced a cigarette and a light. The Navigator drew in smoke gratefully. 'The change? We failed, and when we failed, I ran. The change came when I realized that . . . did I use the word "deceived" before? Tricked? Manipulated? When I realized that . . . look, understand this. It was supposed to be a military operation. The American military had their objectives, and we had ours. But it was supposed to be a military movement, mounted and executed by military men for a military purpose. It was not intended as a means of promoting the personal ambitions of a civilian politician.'

'What are you saying?'

The Navigator's voice rose. 'I am saying that we tried, and we failed, and many of us will die for that failure. Perhaps that's as it should be, we risked everything and we lost. But there is one man who will lose nothing. The one who tricked and deceived us. The one who manipulated the military for his own purposes. There's your change of heart, Mikhail Sergeyvich. I came back when I finally realized how badly we had been used. I came back because I'll be damned if I'll let a civilian walk away from this and leave a lot of fine soldiers to die. Not for the motherland, not for the honour of the military, but simply because he wanted your job. The bastard has to get his, and that's why I'm here.'

'His name. Now.'

'Who else could it be? Chebrikov.'

There was a deep silence in the room.

'Yes, Chebrikov.' The Navigator was smiling again. 'The Director of your precious KGB. He wants your job, comrade. He wants it badly, and he'll get it unless you get him first.'

The men in the room stood like statues. Mironoff was the first to move. He stepped forward, smashed his fist into the Navigator's face, and knocked him down. He said, 'You stinking piece of garbage.'

'No more of that,' Gorbachev said mildly. He waited while the Navigator got to his feet. 'You're lying, of course.'

The Navigator shook his head. There was blood on his lips. 'Dead men don't lie.'

Gorbachev stared into his eyes, searching for a sign, then turned abruptly and went back to where Frolov and Zazulin stood. 'Well?' he asked them.

Frolov said, 'He's lying.'

'Without question,' said Zazulin.

Gorbachev considered their words, knowing that those words were dictated by their loyalty to Chebrikov and to the KGB. He, too, felt that the Navigator was lying, but what if the man were telling the truth? Chebrikov was in Moscow, and he was in New York, far removed from the seat of his power. If the Navigator was not lying, then he had left the thief in charge of the chickens. He had to know the truth, the real truth, at once.

'I understand your loyalty to your Director,' he said, 'but you have a greater loyalty to the state. At the moment, I embody the state. Do you understand that?'

Frolov and Zazulin nodded dumbly.

'Now listen to me carefully. If Chebrikov is involved, he is a dead man, and so is any KGB officer who tries to protect him. Is that clear?'

They nodded again.

'Now, I have to know what this man is up to, and quickly. How long will it take to get the actual truth out of him?'

'The truth?' Frolov stared at him blankly. He was accustomed to securing confessions, admissions of guilt in which the truth was a minor factor. 'A determined man can hold out for hours, even days.'

'We don't have hours of days. What about sodium pentathol?'

'He has a small amount in his system now,' Zazulin noted. 'To increase the dosage, give it time to take effect, resume the interrogation . . . two hours, at least.'

'Not good enough. I have to know now. Frolov, go to the conference room and tell Yuri Muzalev that I want him here. The woman, as well.'

Frolov nodded. 'Yes, I dislike using those people, but they can get you what you want.'

'And the two Americans. I want all four of them in here quickly.'

'The Americans?' Frolov made a protest of the words.

'All of them. I must be sure.'

FORTY-THREE
Sunday 6:52 PM

The return of the Navigator put the conference on hold. First the KGB people left for the interrogation, and then Gorbachev was called into it. That left Panchenko and one aide as the only Russian officials in the room, along with the American contingent, and the four sensitives. Only Delaney knew who and what we really were; to the others we were only translators. There was nothing for any of us to do but wait for the results of the questioning, and the formality of the meeting broke down. The Americans, understandably, clustered around Arina, flies at the jampot. Duffy, the cop, didn't waste any time. He made a quick move on her, asking if she would join him when we broke for dinner. She smiled at him, pretending to consider the invitation.

Stop playing games, I told her.

Who's playing? He's really quite presentable, and he's a hero. He saved the General Secretary's life.

He's married, he lives in Great Neck, and he has two point five children.

Where is Great Neck?

The suburbs. For the kiddies.

How do you know all that? Did you tap him?

Didn't have to. All police captains are married, have two point five children, and live in places like Great Neck.

She turned up the voltage on her smile, and said to Duffy, 'You must be very proud to be the father of two point five children.'

Duffy looked confused. 'Two point . . . what?'

'I thought that was the current statistic for police captains.'

'Is it? Well, I guess I'm the guy who drags down the average. No children. No wife either, for that matter.'

'Then why do you live in the suburbs?'

201

'Who says that I do? I have a very comfortable apartment right here in Manhattan.'

Arina shot me a look of triumph. *You see, you should have tapped him.*

Watch it. He's about to offer to show you that apartment.

Oh dear, are you going to be possessive?

Very.

Good.

Duffy pressed. 'What about dinner?'

Delaney, who had been listening, said, 'Exactly, what about dinner? The way things are going, I doubt that we'll get the chance later on.'

He wasn't talking about Duffy's move on Arina. All of us were thinking about food by then. It was still early in the evening, but most of us had skipped lunch. It was time to get something to eat, but given the circumstances no one, except Delaney, would have suggested the idea. That's the way he was. With a vision of himself that was something less than real, he saw himself as a man of action. He was a bumbler, a bureaucrat, and a pencil pusher, but in his own eyes he was the take-charge kind of guy who rises to every occasion. While others dithered, Delaney acted. That was how he thought of himself, and now, as the rest of us suffered the hunger pangs silently, he took charge. He went over to Panchenko and asked if the Soviet Mission could provide us with sandwiches and coffee.

'Nothing fancy,' he said. 'Just something to keep the wolf away.'

The ambassador looked puzzled. 'Wolf? Coffee?'

'And sandwiches. Anything you have in the house.'

Yuri chuckled, but only the three of us could hear him. *Very nikulturni, asking your host for food. That's quite a boy you've got there, Sammy.*

He's a horse's ass, Sammy agreed, *but he'll get us something to eat.*

Not a chance, you'll never see a crumb.

You don't know Delaney.

I know Panchenko. They don't come any tighter.

Panchenko finally realized what Delaney was getting at, and his confusion turned to embarrassment. 'I'm sorry . . . are people . . . is anybody hungry?'

202

The Americans looked at each other, not knowing which way to go. Delaney boomed out jovially, 'Of course they're hungry, they're just being polite. Really, Mister Ambassador, tell your people not to go to any trouble. Just some simple sandwiches.'

Panchenko's embarrassment deepened. 'My apologies, I hope this will not sound inhospitable, but with the reception here tonight the kitchen will be very busy and . . . you see, it would be most difficult . . .'

Told you, said Yuri.

Panchenko's voice trailed off. What he meant was he was afraid to risk trotting out whatever odds and ends there might have been in the Mission kitchen. Russians, as individuals, rank with the most generous of hosts. Enter as a guest into the meanest home, and out comes the vodka, the pickled cucumbers, the black bread that is the very earth of Mother Russia, and perhaps some *beliashi* or *vatrushki.* But the Soviets run their overseas establishments on a tight budget. There is plenty up front for the official receptions and formal dinners, but behind the scenes the cupboard is often quite bare. Delaney knew nothing of this, but he was a man of action, ready to take charge.

'No problem,' he said. 'There's a deli around the corner on Lexington. We can sent out for sandwiches.'

'No.' Panchenko's voice was a squeak. 'No, you must not . . .'

'Quite all right, Mister Ambassador, no trouble at all.'

'No, no, impossible.' Panchenko was horrified. He was staring at a diplomatic disgrace.

'Easiest thing in the world,' Delaney told him. He produced paper and pencil. 'All right, folks, who wants what?'

The FBI ordered ham on rye; the Secret Service wanted corned beef on a seeded roll, easy on the mustard; the State Department opted for turkey on whole wheat; and Delaney, scribbling, decided to have the same.

'Mister Ambassador,' he asked, 'how about you?'

Panchenko shook his head furiously. He whispered into the ear of his aide. The young man left the room on the run.

'Duffy?'

The cop looked at Arina, shook his head in mock resignation, and said, 'There goes our dinner date. I'll have the same as the FBI. What about you, young miss?'

Arina hesitated. Panchenko was glaring at her, daring her to compound the insult. Yuri cut in, and said, 'While she's making up her mind, I'll have a double cheeseburger, an order of fries, and a six-pack of Bud.'

Panchenko looked at him with loathing. In icy tones, he said, 'There will be no need for the sending out, gentlemen. Refreshments will be served shortly.'

Yuri's face lit up. *He actually did it.*

Did what? Yuri was into Panchenko's head, and I wasn't.

He sent his flunkey to bring in food from the reception room. Delaney shamed him into it.

Sammy laughed. *Delaney wins again. He has the manners of a jackal, but he gets results.*

The aide returned within minutes, followed by two men in mess jackets carrying trays. They laid out platters on the conference table, the aide fussing over them. There was nothing Russian about the food, it was the standard spread that you see on the diplomatic circuit: canapés, cold shrimp, slices of ham, stuffed crab claws; plenty of everything. Panchenko, once he got moving, went all the way. The Americans stampeded to the table, grabbing plates. Duffy was one of the first, gallantry forgotten. The four of us fell in behind them to wait our turn. The door swung open, and slammed against the wall. Frolov stood in the doorway.

'Muzalev and Zourina,' he called. 'Comrade Gorbachev wants you at once.' He stabbed a finger at Sammy, and at me. 'You also, both of you. Quickly.'

We looked at our empty plates. We put them down, and ran.

FORTY-FOUR
Sunday 7:00 PM

Martha's bottle of cognac went dry. Vince shook the last few drops out of it, and handed it to Snake, empty.

'Swine,' she said calmly. 'What do we do now? Sunday in New York, can't buy a bottle.'

Martha said, 'What's the problem?' She tapped the top of the bar between the back seat and the jump seats. It was solid oak with sliding doors.

'It's locked,' Vince pointed out. 'Two padlocks, one with a key and one with a combination. Of which we have neither.'

'I have opened a few locks in my time, and so have you.'

'That would make Sammy very unhappy.'

Martha put a finger to her chin. She was trying to look thoughtful. 'There would have to be a reason why we did it, a good reason.'

'A cover story.'

'Like an emergency.'

'Snakebite?'

'Watch it,' said Snake.

'Got a better one?'

'Sure. We were surrounded by Soviet agents who forced us to open the bar and drink up all the cognac.'

'Why would they want to do that?' Martha asked.

'Obvious. They were trying to get us drunk.'

'The bastards. Trying to compromise us.'

'Right. Loosen our tongues, steal our secrets.'

'Maybe even seduce us.'

'You think so?'

'It's your fantasy. Go with it.'

'None of this,' said Vince, 'is putting any brandy in my belly. Who's gonna open it?'

'Need some tools.' Martha pressed two studs set into the back of the front seat, and the panel of the arms chest slid open to show a rack of pistols, automatic weapons, and electronic devices. She ran her finger along the gleaming metal, and chose a flat probe with what looked like a stethoscope attached to it. She gave it to Vince.

'Start on the tumbler job. I'll play with the combination.'

'Play how?'

'All of Sammy's combinations are variations of the sequence eleven, twenty-one, forty-five. November twenty-first, nineteen forty-five.'

'What's that?'

'Goldie Hawn's birthday.'

'Truth?'

'Believe it.'

'How long have you known?'

Martha shook her head, smiling. They bent over the locks.

FORTY-FIVE
Sunday 7:35 PM

The room in which the interrogation was being held was down the corridor from the conference room. The walls were the usual dark brown, the carpet was thick, and there were shelves of books. A massive desk occupied one end of the room, flanked by two heavy armchairs. The Navigator stood against the far wall, with Mironoff and Zazulin close by. There were doors at each end of the room. As soon as we came in, Mironoff ordered the two KGB muscles to leave.

Gorbachev stood in front of the desk. He addressed himself to Yuri, explaining what he wanted. 'Very briefly, this man has implicated Chebrikov. I need not tell you what that means. I must know at once if he is lying. Can you do that for me?'

'Of course,' said Yuri. His face was set. No joking now. 'Do you want us all to do this?'

'All of you in turn. I must have confirmation.'

Yuri said, 'Arina?'

The tradition in their service was the same as ours. In that sort of tap, where confirmation was required, the most junior always went first to avoid being influenced by the opinions of the seniors. Yuri touched her lightly on the arm. 'No need for anything deep. In and out.'

She looked at the Navigator, then looked away. She went in, and came out. She turned to Gorbachev, and said flatly, 'He's lying.'

We did it by nationalities. Yuri went next, in and out. 'He's lying. Chebrikov is not involved.'

It was my turn next, since I was junior to Sammy. I went in and checked for the lie. It was there, glaring, a total fabrication. 'No truth to it at all,' I said, but I stayed inside the Navigator's head a moment longer. There was something about him that bothered me. At his level in the GRU he had to know who we were and what we could do. Thus, he also must have known that we were blowing his story to pieces, but he did not appear upset by that. No anger, no distress, no chagrin showed on his face, nor did it show in his mind. He was totally at ease, and that bothered me.

Sammy did his tap, and reported, 'He's lying, all right. Ben, you still in there?'

'Wait one,' I said.

There was something in that head, something difficult to define. It was a feeling, not a fact, rising up in his mind like a wave on a far-off horizon, faint, but building. It built as I watched it, first a pencil-thin line on a dead calm sea that moved along the water towards the shore. Then, in that moment, it doubled in size and doubled again, growing into the bulk of a tidal wave that raced across the sea, reached up to blot out the sun as it grew, the roar of it rushing towards me, growing and growing, the curl of the wave directly overhead now, high as a tower and trembling, about to crash and crush us all . . .

Get in here, I shouted.

They jumped in. They saw it, too. We all moved at once.

Arina and I turned toward each other instinctively, but I moved faster than she did. I leaped, and knocked her to the floor, rolling over with her until we lay behind the desk.

Yuri made the same move at Gorbachev, pushing him to the floor behind an armchair.

Sammy turned, and flung himself at the desk. He fell short, and lay with his hands over his head.

Mironoff, Frolov, and Zazulin, knowing nothing, were caught standing and out in the open when the Navigator exploded.

The force of the explosion shook the room, and bulged the walls. The floor heaved up beneath me. The roar was deafening. It went on and on, longer than it could have. The room tipped over, and someone screamed. Arina lay in my arms, eyes wide. We lay that way for a lifetime. The screaming stopped, cut short, and then the roaring stopped as well. The room tipped back, and it was over.

Ben? Arina's fingers gripped my arm.

All right. You?
Yes.

I got to my knees, and looked around. The Navigator was gone; there were pieces all over. The room was red. Even the air was red with a slowly settling mist. There was the stink of explosives mixed with the stink of a man turned inside out. Arina raised herself up to look. She gagged once, then got control.

Sammy lay a few feet from me with his left leg twisted at an angle. Yuri and Gorbachev were still behind the chair. They looked intact. I called, 'Sammy?'

'Something wrong with my leg, but nothing else.'

'Yuri?'

'No damage.'

'What about your boss?'

He hesitated. 'All right, I think. Just stunned.'

I stood up. Frolov and Zazulin were clearly dead, their bodies shredded by the blast. Mironoff was up and moving, but his shoulder was a mess. There were noises from outside the room. People were pounding at the front door. The explosion had jammed the door, and they could not open it.

Arina was at my side. She said, 'What was it?'

I was guessing. 'He was loaded. The son of a bitch was loaded, and he stood there and let it happen.'

Sammy was up. He was having trouble standing. I tried to check him over, but he pushed me away, and said, 'See how he is.'

I knelt next to Gorbachev. Yuri had pulled him into a sitting position. His eyes were dull, and his hands were shaking. I helped him to his feet. He looked around at the carnage in the room.

'God help us,' he said. His voice wavered. 'God help us.'

I asked, 'Are you all right? Can you walk?'

He did not answer. He closed his eyes.

He's okay, Yuri said. *He just had to get it together.*

He looks like he's out of it.

No, I know him. He's all right.

I moved on to Mironoff. He was covered with blood, and only some of it was his own. His left shoulder was open and raw, but he was functioning. He looked around the room wildly, searching for an enemy. I put my hand on his arm, and he whirled on me. I could see his teeth.

'Easy,' I said. 'He's alive.'

He saw that Gorbachev was standing. He stumbled over to him. The pounding on the door continued. Sammy said, 'See if you can get it open.'

I tried, but it was jammed shut. I backed off, and kicked the wood just below the handle. It held. I kicked it again, and then tugged. It swung open. They came pouring in, the Americans from the conference room, plus Panchenko and his Russians. They stared at the bodies, and at Gorbachev, so oddly still and with a dreamy look in his eyes. They weren't shouting any more.

Duffy took it all in. He said to me, 'He was loaded, wasn't he? They loaded him up and sent him back.'

'Looks that way.'

'Jesus, Mary, and Joseph, what a mess.'

They all crowded around Gorbachev, but he just stood there. I doubt if he even saw them in that moment. Yuri tried to keep the people off him, but they wanted to get close, to touch, to be sure that he was still in one piece. Duffy looked at the scene with a scowl on his face. He went over to Delaney, and spoke urgently into his ear. Delaney nodded. He climbed onto a chair. He was ready to take charge.

'Listen, you people, we need some order here. I want somebody to send for a doctor, and I want the rest of you to back off. Will you do that, please? Now, I want you to clear the room. Everybody out. What we have here at the moment is a police matter, and Captain Duffy is in charge. He wants the room cleared so that we can get some order established. So, please, everybody out.'

It wasn't easy, but he got them moving, herding them out the door. Only Duffy stayed behind. Delaney paused at the door. 'I'll send in the doctor as soon as he gets here.'

'You do that,' Duffy said absently. He waited until Delaney had left, then went to the door, and locked it. He strode across the room to face Mironoff.

'You son of a bitch,' he said. 'You miserable son of a bitch.'

FORTY-SIX
Sunday 7:40 PM

Yadroshnikov looked at his watch. It had a sweep second-hand. He was counting minutes. He looked up at the screen with the grid of the city on it. There were still two blips of light within the square that represented the Soviet Mission. He looked at his watch again, and muttered something under his breath.

He asked Engstrom, 'What figure would you give for the outside time limit?'

'We're past it.'

'So . . . failure.'

'That stuff always works. Always.'

'I'm not disputing that. I'm sure it went off, but somehow the target survived the blast.'

'If he was in the room.'

'He was,' Yadroshnikov said testily. 'Ten out of ten he was there.'

'But it failed. What are your numbers for the next phase?'

There was an edge of sarcasm in Engstrom's voice that Yadroshnikov ignored. Instead of replying, he asked, 'Are there any spirits here?'

It took Engstrom a moment to realize what he meant. 'There's a bottle in my bottom drawer. Help yourself.'

Yadroshnikov found the American vodka, and some paper cups. He poured two drinks, and looked at the Case Executive standing at the grid. She shook her head. He gave one of the cups to Engstrom, and raised his own.

'To the Navigator,' he said. 'He was a good man once, and he did his job.' He swallowed the drink whole.

211

Engstrom took only a slip of his. He looked amused. 'I didn't expect such sentiment from you.'

Yadroshnikov shrugged. 'I wanted the drink anyway.'

He settled back, his eyes again on the screen.

FORTY-SEVEN
Sunday 7:42 PM

'You miserable son of a bitch,' said Duffy. His face was only inches away from Mironoff's. 'I begged you to get him out of here, but you wouldn't, would you? No, you pig-headed bastard, you had to do it your way.'

Mironoff shook his head. 'It was . . . it was . . .'

'I can see what it was, God damn it.'

'There was no way of knowing . . .'

'There was every way, you stupid shit. They had to come after him here, anyone could see that. Anyone but you.'

'It was a risk that had to be taken.'

'Well, you took it, all right, and look what it got you. Take a look around.'

Mironoff did not want to look. He opened his mouth to say something, then shut it. He shook his head again. Duffy had him whipped.

'All right, you fucked it up. Will you use your head now? We have to get him out of here. Can't you see that?'

'But the General Secretary himself has said . . .'

'I know what he said. He was wrong, and so were you. Now, do we move him, or not?'

Mironoff was totally defeated. 'Yes, it is clear now. He cannot stay here.'

Duffy pushed him aside. He did it roughly. He said to Gorbachev, 'Your Excellency, we have to move you, and we have to do it now, quickly. Are you ready to travel?'

Gorbachev's eyes were open now, and his gaze was clear. He was back in business again as he appraised the policeman who had saved his life. His voice was firm. 'Captain Duffy, are you absolutely certain that this move must be made?'

'I am, sir.'

'It is highly unconventional.'

'I'm afraid that I cannot let that be a consideration.'

'Yes, I can see that. What are your logistics?'

'We leave here right now, just the way we are. That back door leads to the stairs. Three flights down is the garage. I have an armoured van waiting, and a crew of men. We'll go out the back way, and I'll have you in a safe place within half an hour.'

Gorbachev thought for a moment. He said to Yuri, 'What do you think? Any advice?'

Yuri looked surprised. 'Advice from the jester? Hardly my place.'

'Modesty from the jester? I'm making it your place. What do you think?'

'I think you should go. It is the logical move to make.'

'Modesty, and logic as well? I'm impressed. Major Mironoff?'

Mironoff said stiffly, 'In agreement.'

'You weren't before.'

'Recent events have changed my opinion.'

'Yes, and mine. Very well, captain, we will make the move. But your people out there, and mine. They must be advised.'

'Negative, sir,' Duffy said tightly. 'I'm responsible for your life, and I'm not trusting anyone any more. Not my people, and not your people. Please think carefully, sir. After what's happened so far, can you truly say that there's any one of them that you can trust totally. Remember, I said totally.'

'No. I have to say . . . no, you are right. Nobody.'

'I thought not. They'll be advised when we reach a safe location.' Duffy looked at the four of us. 'You people are coming along, too. You're all witnesses to a suicide, a couple of murders, an attempted murder, and God knows what else. I want you where I can lay my hands on you.'

We exchanged glances. It was no problem for Yuri; he was committed to going wherever Gorbachev went. It was no problem for Arina, either; it was her job, too. It was certainly no problem for me; I wasn't letting her out of my sight. But Sammy didn't like it. He said, 'I work for Delaney. I'll have to tell him where I'm going.'

'Negative again. I'm not risking any leaks. You can notify Delaney once we get there.'

Sammy nodded reluctantly.

Duffy said, 'Right, let's get going. Somebody check that door.'

I went to the rear door, opened it, and looked out. The corridor was empty. Directly across was the entrance to the stairway. I motioned to Duffy, and he brought the others up. Yuri, Gorbachev, and Duffy went first. Then Mironoff and Sammy. I grabbed Arina's hand, and we followed, clattering down the stairs.

FORTY-EIGHT
Sunday 7:45 PM

Vince, Snake, and Martha felt the explosion that rocked the interrogation room on the third floor. They felt it only as a tremor, they did not hear it, but it was enough to bring their heads up.

'Something?' asked Vince. His wig was on crooked, and he straightened it.

'Thunder,' Martha suggested.

'The subway?' The Lexington Avenue line was close by.

'Maybe somebody dropped a bottle,' said Snake. 'Get back to work.'

Vince and Martha bent over the bar. It took Vince three and a half minutes, using the probe, to get the first lock open. It took Martha twenty seconds longer, using the permutations of Goldie Hawn's birth date, to open the second lock. With both locks removed, the doors of the bar slid open. The interior was empty, save for a six-pack of Diet Coke, and a note in Sammy's scrawl.

Suffer, you slobs.

Vince crumpled the note, and dropped it into an ashtray. He leaned back, and said mournfully, 'That's why they pay him the big bucks. That's why he's the man.'

'I could make a run,' Snake suggested. 'I know a guy, has a bar on Lex. He'd spring for a jug.'

No comment from the others. They knew, and Snake knew, too, that nobody was going anywhere. Sammy had said to sit tight, and, no matter what else they might do, they would sit. Martha popped open a Coke, held it up to eye level, and stared at it.

'You gonna drink that?' asked Vince. 'You gonna put that in your mouth and swallow it?'

'I'll try anything that says diet on it.'

'Diet booze?'

'I wish.'

'How long do you think we'll be here?'

'You got something better to do?'

'Anything but this.'

'Forget it, we're not going anyplace. We'll never get out of here, we're doomed. Years from now, they'll find our bones.'

'Our dry bones.'

'Hold it,' said Snake. Her head was up again.

'Hold what?' asked Vince. 'I don't have anything to hold except an empty glass.'

'Quiet.'

'What is it?'

Snake did not answer at first. She was tuned into something, and bearing down hard on it. Then, 'Something coming.'

'What?'

'Can't tell yet.'

'Where?'

'Those stairs. Wait for it.'

They did not have long to wait. The door to the stairwell swung open, and people came pouring through: Duffy, Mironoff, Gorbachev, and then the four aces. They came out onto the garage floor walking rapidly, two of them hustling Gorbachev along, and Sammy in the rear dragging his leg. They did not look in the direction of the car.

'What is it?' asked Martha. 'What's happening?'

Vince said, 'Bugging out, looks like.'

'But why?'

'Easy way to find out,' said Snake. The group was well within range.

'Regulations?'

'Shove 'em. I'm going in.'

They all went in together. They tapped every head in sight.

Vince said, 'Oh dear, there is so much evil in this world.'

Martha smiled. 'I think we're back in the ballgame.'

Snake, in the driver's seat, said nothing. She started the car, and eased it forward.

FORTY-NINE
Sunday 7:47 PM

We were halfway to the police van when the company car came roaring across the garage floor, weaving in and out of the support columns. It screeched to a stop between us and the van. Snake was driving. Vince jumped out of the back. He had on a wig that was tilted over one eye.

He said, 'Sammy, baby, tell me the truth. Does it make me look like Diana Ross?'

Sammy looked murderous. 'I told you people to sit tight and sober up. Get out of the way, we're in a hurry.'

'Not yet, we've got something to talk about.'

'What is the delay?' asked Gorbachev.

'We're wasting time,' said Duffy. He tore his eyes away from Vince's wig, and peered into the car. Martha grinned at him, the putty on her nose gleaming like a glassy cherry. Snake wiggled her ears, and her curly moustaches quivered. 'Are these your people?'

'Yeah, they're mine.'

'And they call me a clown,' Yuri muttered.

'Get rid of them,' ordered Duffy.

'Vince, I'll talk to you about this later.'

'We'd better talk now, might not be any later. You going for a ride with the police people? Nice safe house? Everything tight, cops all around you?'

'What about it? What the hell are you trying to say?'

Sammy, dear. It was Martha from inside the car. *What Vince is trying to say . . . well, have you bothered to tap the gentleman in the blue suit and the brass buttons?*

Silence for a moment, and then Sammy said, *No, I haven't. Ben?*

No.

Yuri? Arina?

How could we? asked Yuri. *You had him blocked.*

Sammy sighed. *So we did. Let's do it now.*

The four of us went in together. We opened Duffy up, and took a good look. Sammy said, *Shit.* Nobody disagreed.

Do you know what stupid feels like? Stupid is when you finally see what was there all the time. Stupid is genius in retrospect. Duffy, the hero cop who killed DeKalb. Duffy, the plant who killed DeKalb to wipe the trail clean. Duffy, the backup man in case things went wrong. Duffy, whose safe house was a slaughterhouse.

'Come on, what are we waiting for?' asked Duffy. He didn't know what was happening, but his antennae were fine-tuned. His suspicion showed in his eyes. They darted back and forth. 'Let's go. Now.'

Gorbachev started forward. Arina said quietly, 'Comrade General Secretary, you cannot go with this man. He is the enemy, one of the people who have been trying to kill you.'

Duffy's face stayed set and still. 'You've made a mistake, miss. I'm a New York City police officer, and I'm trying to do my job. Don't get in my way.'

'What is this?' asked Gorbachev. 'What is she saying?'

'She's right,' said Yuri. 'He's one of them.'

Duffy said, 'I'm warning you, too, mister. You are God damn close to obstructing justice.'

Martha, from the car, said, *Do you want me to take him?* She had an Uzi from the arms chest resting in the open window where Duffy could not see it.

No, I want him alive, said Sammy. *I want his head.*

Gorbachev moved closer to Mironoff. To Yuri, he said angrily, 'And you just found this out now?'

'Not their fault,' Sammy explained. 'We were blocking them. Part of our job.'

'And you agree?'

'Yes, sir, both of us,' I said. 'He's DIA. Hired, probably, but they own his gun.'

Duffy said in wonder, 'Who the hell are you people? You're supposed to be translators.' His pistol came out, appearing smoothly in his hand.

Sammy said, 'Put it down. It's over, you're blown.'

219

Duffy shook his head. 'So this is the way it goes. I told them that the fancy crap never works. It always comes down to something like this.'

It was a speech, and it cost him. He should have shot first, and made his speech later. It gave Mironoff time to make a move. He did what he was trained to do, he jumped in front of Gorbachev as Duffy fired. He took the first bullet in his chest, but he stayed up long enough to take the second one, too. Duffy never got off a third. Martha poked the Uzi through the rear window, and blew him down. The noise echoed through the cavernous garage. Heads appeared at the rear door of the police van. Duffy's crew.

'Get back in there,' called Martha. She stitched a line in the wall above their heads. They popped back into the van, and slammed the door shut.

Martha got out of the car. She was still wearing the wreath of lilies. She knelt beside Duffy, and checked him. She lifted the wreath from around her neck, and placed it on his chest. She looked at Sammy, and shrugged.

Sammy said, 'I wanted him alive.'

'Right. Next time, do it yourself.' She got back into the car looking sulky.

Gorbachev also knelt, but next to Mironoff. He stared at him helplessly, then looked around. 'Please, I don't know how to . . . is he . . .?'

'He's gone,' Yuri said. He helped Gorbachev to his feet.

'Yes. Well. He served the Soviet Union.' It's what some of them say instead of crossing themselves. 'So. So much for the American police and their safe houses.'

He turned, and started toward the staircase. Sammy grabbed him, and turned him around again, saying, 'Where the hell do you think you're going?'

'Back to the Mission, of course.'

'You can't.'

'What choice do I have? I have no place else to go now.'

'What Duffy said before still holds. You have nobody up there you can be sure of.'

'If you go back up there,' I said, 'the odds are you won't make it through the night.'

Arina said, 'Please, you must face the facts. You have no

220

one left whom you can trust, except . . .' She left the words unsaid.

Gorbachev said them, 'Except Yuri and you? Is that what you mean?'

'And these others. It is difficult to explain, but it is something we all share. You can think of them as you think of us.'

'Perhaps. But there is nothing that any of you can do for me.'

'I think there is,' she said.

Yuri said, 'So do I.'

Together, they sent the question out to Sammy and me, to Snake, and Vince, and Martha. We saw what they had in mind, and none of us liked it. But like it or not, it was staring at us. We were the only ones he could count on to keep him safe through the night. One by one, the answers came back.

Sammy: *It's the only way.*

Martha: *I'll play.*

Vince: *Me too, but not on Diet Coke.*

Snake: *Do we get overtime?*

I'm in, I said.

Thank you, Ben, said Arina. *Thank you all.*

Yuri put it into words. 'Mister General Secretary, we all think it would be best if you came with us now.'

'With you? But where?'

He didn't know; it wasn't his town. He laid it on me. 'Ben? Where?'

I didn't answer. I didn't know, either, not yet. I watched as Gorbachev struggled with the concept. I didn't have to tap him to know what he was thinking. He had reached a point in life where certain assumptions were carved in stone, and one of those was that the state existed to preserve those in power. Armies, navies, masses of guards and policemen all had served this purpose for him, and it was difficult to accept the idea that this apparatus was no longer available. He was alone, stripped bare, and we were all he had.

Martha called out, 'Whatever we do, let's do it fast. The people in that van are getting itchy.'

Still struggling, Gorbachev said, 'This is an impossible situation . . . outrageous, really . . . a distinguished guest . . . the President would never allow . . .'

221

'The President can't sit up all night with a gun in his lap,' I told him. 'Who can you go to now? The army? The FBI? The police? That's the police lying there on the floor. We don't know who's involved, or how many.'

'But where would you take me?'

I still didn't know. 'You'll have to trust us on that.'

Vince said, 'You people are pissing away an awful lot of time.'

'Where?' Gorbachev insisted.

That question again, the one I could not answer. And then I did not have to. An alarm went off, a series of high-pitched beeps followed by the clang of a bell. Someone had discovered us missing, or someone had heard the shots. Whichever it was, someone had thrown a switch.

'That's it,' I said. 'Either you trust us all the way, or you don't. You get paid to make decisions. Make one now.'

He made it. Moving quickly, he climbed into the back seat of the car. Vince jumped in on the other side, and Yuri piled in after. Arina slid onto the jump seat next to Martha. I got in the front with Snake. That left Sammy standing alone.

'What about you?' I asked.

'Somebody has to clean up the mess and take the heat. I'll buy you as much time as I can. You know what you have to do?'

'Keep him out, keep him alive, and get him to the UN by eleven tomorrow.'

'What else?'

'Trust nobody.'

'Right, you're on your own. Don't try to get in touch with me, and don't try for help from any of the agencies, theirs or ours. Trust absolutely nobody. Where are you taking him?'

I knew by then, but I shook my head.

He grinned. 'Right. Get moving.'

FIFTY
Sunday 7:58 PM

Yadroshnikov left the duty office, and went down the hall to
Carlotta's room. She was standing by the window, looking out.
There was nothing to see out of that window, except the blank
wall of another warehouse. The Cuban lay on the unmade cot,
his hands behind his head.

Carlotta turned when Yadroshnikov came in. She looked at
his face intently, and her own face crumpled. She said, 'He's
dead, isn't he?'

'Yes.'

She went to a chair, and sat with her knees pressed together
and her hands clasped in her lap. 'Did he suffer?'

'No. I can assure you of that.' He said nothing about the
waiting for a certain death to come. 'He felt nothing.'

'Thank God for that.'

'He served the Soviet Union.'

'Please. Don't say dirty things like that.'

'As you wish.'

'And now . . . what happens to me?'

'I promised him that I would take care of you. That was part
of the deal we made.'

She looked at him in wonder. 'He died for that?'

'No, he would have died anyway. This way, he died my way.'

'Does that mean I am safe?'

'When this operation is over, I will send you somewhere.
Yes, safe.'

'May I ask . . . when will it be over?'

'By the morning. You must be patient until then.' He did not
say that she was safe only if the operation succeeded, because he
considered the chance of failure to be one in a thousand. 'Try to
sleep. It will help.'

'How can I sleep if that animal lies on the bed?'

Yadroshnikov said to the Cuban, 'Get up. Let her use the bed. And remember what I said. Keep away from her.'

The Cuban grunted as he rolled off the bed, and stood up. *'Ya estoy animál. Antes estuve tu tigre.'*

'You were never that good. A pussycat, maybe.' She went to the bed, and lay on her side, pulling down her skirt.

The Case Executive came to the door, knocked once, and came in. 'There has been a news bulletin on the radio.' She looked at him questioningly.

'Go ahead.'

'The authorities have announced that due to the assassination attempt this afternoon, the reception at the Mission tonight has been cancelled, and the General Secretary has been removed to a secret location for his own protection.'

'Duffy. Excellent. Is there movement on the grid?'

'Yes, as expected. There was also a report of an explosion inside the Mission, but that has been explained as a kitchen accident.'

'Yes, they would.'

He went back to the Duty Office, and joined Engstrom in front of the grid. The two blips of light had left the Soviet Mission, and were slowly moving down Park Avenue. Yadroshnikov settled into his chair to watch. The Case Executive pressed a button that lit up a square on the corner of East Thirtieth Street and Second Avenue, Duffy's destination. The blips travelled south along Park, past Fiftieth Street, Forty-sixth, and through the overpass at Grand Central Station. Yadroshnikov leaned forward in his seat as the lights passed Thirty-fourth Street, Thirty-second, Thirty-first. He realized that he was holding his breath. He waited for the blips to turn east on Thirtieth towards the lighted square. They hesitated at the corner . . . and then continued down Park Avenue South. Twenty-ninth, Twenty-eighth, Twenty-seventh . . .

Yadroshnikov let out his breath as the blips passed the corner of Twentieth Street. 'That's not Duffy.'

'Obviously,' said Engstrom. 'But who is it?'

They watched as the blips continued south.

FIFTY-ONE
Sunday 7:58 PM

We rolled out of the garage slowly. There was no need to burn any rubber. Sammy had said that he would handle the heat, and we knew that he could. For a while. For now, we were just another black stretch limousine cruising the streets of Manhattan. The city was filled with them.

Snake started us east on Sixty-eighth Street, and asked, 'Where to?'

Nobody answered. I let it stay that way for a couple of beats, waiting for someone to take charge. When no one did, I said, 'First get us out of the neighbourhood. Then, cut over to Park and head south.'

'How far south?'

'In a minute.' I switched over. *Listen, all of you. We have to establish something here. Who's running the job?*

The question had to be asked. In our service, and the Soviet service, and any other service that used aces, the sensitive side of the operation was loosely organized. Everyone knew that you couldn't run aces the way you ran normals. So the discipline was laughable, and the attitudes irreverent, but there was one formality that always applied: the seniority within the peer group. That was the way we were raised at the Centre, with respect for the year group ahead of us, and a chain of command within our own year. Thus, before Sammy stepped up to run everything, he ran our group simply because he was the eldest by a couple of months. As a system, it was nonsensical, but that's the way it was. So the question had to be asked. If this were to be a joint operation, then Yuri, who was senior to all of us, was the one to run it. If not, then Snake, now our senior, was the one to run our side of it, while Yuri ran theirs. Either way, the decision had to be made.

I twisted around in my seat, and looked back at Gorbachev. The windows of the car were tinted for privacy, but he could see out of them, and he was peering at the fronts of the well-kept brownstones that lined the streets. Flashes of light illuminated his face, and the wine-coloured birthmark on his scalp showed clearly. He had come away without a hat to pull down, or a coat to turn up, and there were few faces in the world more famous than his.

'Mister General Secretary, would you keep your face away from the window, please?'

'Yes, of course.'

I was finished waiting. I said, *Well, who's running it?*

I can't do it, said Yuri. *I'm off my turf. It has to be someone else.*

That left it up to Snake. She was a natural leader who commanded easily, but she said, *I'll pass. I think it's yours, Ben.*

So do I, said Vince, who was next in line. *This slice in my side hurts like hell and I can't even think straight. It's all yours, kid.*

Agreed, said Martha, who avoided command whenever she could.

Arina was out of it, but I asked anyway. *Arina?*

You.

That's it, then?

There was a murmur of assent. I said to Snake, *We want Mulberry Street, between Hester and Grand.*

She shot me a quick look. *Little Italy?*

Right.

She shrugged. *Aye, aye, admiral.*

And it's time to cut the comedy. Let's get rid of the funny faces.

Ben Slade takes command, said Vince. He pulled off the Diana Ross wig, collected Martha's putty nose and Snake's moustaches, and dropped them into the gag bag. *Done.*

Don't put the bag away. 'Mister General Secretary?'

Gorbachev started. We had been in silent communication, and the sound of my voice surprised him. 'Yes?'

'It's obvious that we're going to have to do something about your appearance.'

His face showed his distaste. 'A disguise?'

'I'm afraid so.'

'Melodrama.'

'May I suggest that you count up the number of people who have died so far, and then tell me how melodramatic that is?'

'Well said,' he grunted. 'What did you have in mind?'

'Martha?'

She cocked her head, and looked at Gorbachev critically. 'It's the birthmark, of course, and those pixie lines around his mouth. He'll need a wig and a moustache.'

'Good Lord,' was Gorbachev's reaction.

'Can you do it right now?' I asked.

'Sure.' She took the gag bag from Vince. 'Mister General Secretary, would you . . .'

Gorbachev held up his hand. 'A suggestion, please. From now on, for the sake of security we speak only in English, and no more General Secretary, or Your Excellency, or Mr Gorbachev.'

'Right,' said Martha. 'What shall we call you?'

'Yuri, what is the diminutive of my name in English?'

'Mikhail? Michael. Mike.'

'Very well, will you all please call me Mike.'

'No problem. Iron Mike, it is.'

'Iron Mike? Yuri, an unfamiliar expression. What does it mean?'

Yuri worked to suppress a laugh. 'Actually, it could be translated as "Man of Steel".'

'Stalin?'

'You said it, I didn't.' Yuri couldn't hold it. He burst out laughing.

Gorbachev wasn't amused. 'I think that Mike will do nicely. Just Mike, nothing else.'

Martha said, 'All right, Mike, lean towards me and tilt your head. Like this. Right.' She went to work on him.

I turned to the front again. We were rolling down Park, in the Forties. There was a question on all of their minds. My people weren't about to ask it. I was running the job, and that was enough for them. It wasn't enough for Arina. She put it into words.

227

'Would you mind telling us what is on Mulberry Street between Hester and Grand?'

'Don't mind at all. It's the best clam bar in Manhattan.'

'Clams?'

'Raw, baked, stuffed, any way you like them.'

She waited for me to say more. When I didn't, she asked, 'Is that all you are going to tell us?'

'That's it. For the moment.'

'I see,' she said. Maybe she did, but she wasn't happy about it.

FIFTY-TWO
Sunday 8:10 PM

Yadroshnikov and Engstrom watched in fascination as the two blips on the grid continued their steady progress down Park Avenue South, and onto Lafayette Street.

'An assumption must be made,' said Yadroshnikov. 'Since it is clear that Duffy is not in control of that vehicle, we must assume that control rests with someone unfriendly to us.'

Engstrom said heavily, 'Yeah, I'd say that's a valid assumption. I'd fucking well say that.'

Yadroshnikov ignored the sarcastic tone. 'What assets do we have in the area?'

For a reply, the Case Executive slipped on a headset, and punched a button on her console. Three yellow triangles appeared on the grid, one in uptown Manhattan, one in midtown, and one in the area of the West Side docks.

Yadroshnikov asked, 'Who is in the downtown car?'

'Two of ours, and one of yours,' said the Case Executive. 'Do you want them in?'

'Not yet.' Yadroshnikov watched as the double blips turned east on Canal, north onto Mulberry Street, and then stopped. He looked at the clock on the wall, and counted off a full minute. The blips remained stationary. He nodded to the Case Executive. 'Bring them in. We will direct them from here.'

The Case Executive pushed another button, and spoke softly into the microphone of her headset.

FIFTY-THREE
Sunday 8:23 PM

The clam bar was dark. I banged heavily on the door, and banged again. I waited. The door opened a crack, and I saw a slice of Fat Louis' face.

'We're closed,' he said.

'I can see that,' I told him. 'I want to see the Uncle.'

'Uncle who?'

'Stop the crap, Louis. You know my face. A couple of years, but you know it.'

'Go away; this is a house of mourning.'

'This is a house of clams, and the Uncle's in the back room where he always is. I want to see him.'

'Come back tomorrow.'

'Tell him I'm here. Tell him the poker player wants to see him.'

'We got more poker players than we got clams. Which one are you?'

'You know who I am. Take a good look.'

The one eye that I could see blinked rapidly. The door closed. I waited. I looked back at the car parked at the kerb. Snake had the front window down, and I could see her face. I had told them all to tune on me. I turned back when the door opened again, this time all the way.

'He's in the back,' said Louis.

'Like I said.'

I went through the darkened front room. Tony Spats leaned against the bar. He moved in front of me, and patted me up and down. He moved aside.

'George Raft,' I said.

'He don't live here any more.'

The Uncle was behind his desk in the back room, a single

230

shaded light swinging over his head. He looked old and weary. He didn't smile when he saw me, but he motioned to a chair.

'Long time,' he said. 'How you been? I was thinking about you today.'

'I heard about Carlo. I'm sorry for your trouble.'

'It's a terrible thing, a young man like that.'

'Do you know . . .?' I let the rest of it hang.

He spread his hands. 'These days, who knows anything? The way the young people do things, it's a different world.'

'Different,' I agreed.

'Is that why you came by? Because of Carlo?'

'Only partly. I guess you can figure the other part.'

'Only one reason for you to come here, unless you want some clams.'

'No clams, Uncle.'

'Then I guess it's collection time.'

'You always said that you owed me.'

'I did. And I do. What's the payoff?'

'Nothing big. It's The Palace, I figure it's got to be empty tonight. No game, and no Carlo. I want to stay there tonight. I'll be gone in the morning.'

'That's all?'

'And you keep quiet about it. Strictly between us. After that, we're even.'

'Let me get this straight. You want to use Carlo's place tonight, and you want me to keep quiet about it. That's the whole shmear?'

I nodded.

'Just you, or you got some friends?'

'Does it make any difference?'

'Maybe not. You and me, we made a lot of money together. You still play cards?'

'Nothing big.'

'You were the best I ever saw. I always wondered why you never came around any more.'

'Too much excitement. Bad for the blood pressure.'

'Yeah, sure.' He grinned without mirth. 'I never even saw you sweat. You know, you were the best, but I never figured you for a pro. I always figured that you had something else going, but I never knew what.'

231

I let that one ride. He looked at the ceiling, and the swinging light. After a while, he said, 'My nephew gets whacked today for no goddamn good reason, and tonight a guy comes by who I haven't seen for years, and he wants to use his apartment. Is that supposed to be a coincidence?'

'Maybe.'

'And maybe not. And maybe I'm beginning to figure out what line of work you're really in.'

'Don't let your imagination run. I'm not in any special line of work.'

'Yeah, and I never ate a clam in my life.'

'What about it, Uncle? You paying off?'

He didn't answer. He was weighing it up. I went into his head, and watched the balances shifting. He made his decision. He reached in his pocket, and tossed a key on the table.

'The Uncle always pays off,' he said. 'This time it's a pleasure.'

'Thanks.' I picked up the key.

'There's food, and the bar is full. Take what you want.'

'I will. Thanks again.' I stood up to go. 'About the other part. Strictly between us, right?'

'Don't worry, I'm quiet like a clam.' He laughed to himself.

I was almost to the door, when he said, 'One other thing. I always wondered. When you were playing for me, was it straight?'

'Of course not. Nobody can win that way straight. I had a gaff.'

'I thought so. You want to tell me what it was?'

I shook my head. 'You wouldn't believe it, Uncle. Really, you wouldn't.'

FIFTY-FOUR
Sunday 8:34 PM

We drove from the clam bar through the streets now dark to
the house on Jane Street. Iron Mike kept his face close to the
window, peering out. He could do that now; Martha had
transformed him. He had a head of slick black hair that hid the
livid birthmark, and a moustache that obscured the shape of
his lips. The transformation was effective, but it did nothing
to enhance his appearance. He looked like a portly lecher
fighting middle age, but he did not look like Mikhail
Gorbachev. He had not yet seen himself in a mirror.

'This place that we are going to,' he said. 'Will there be food
there?'

'Hungry?'

'Very.'

Martha fished in her tote bag, and came up with a Hershey
bar. She gave it to Mike. 'This should do you for a while.'

'Thank you.' He unwrapped the chocolate, and looked
around. 'Please, would anyone else care for . . .?'

'All yours,' I told him.

He bit into it gratefully. 'Almonds. Good.'

It was a quiet trip to Jane Street, peaceful save that Arina
was unhappy. I could feel the waves of it coming off her. Like
the others, she had been tuned in on me at the clam bar, and
she had heard the deal I had made with the Uncle. She didn't
like it, and she told me so. She did it silently. She didn't want
to upset Iron Mike.

I know that you're running this, she said, *and I know that
I'm junior, but I have to say this.*

Fire away, I told her.

I don't like this arrangement of yours.

I can see that.

233

The security is full of holes.

You have a point.

And the concept is dangerous.

You have another.

This Uncle John, his nephew was the one who delivered the weapon to DeKalb, no?

Quite right.

So he must be involved at some level.

Has to be.

You don't seem concerned about it. You are placing the General Secretary in an exposed position.

Can't be helped. Certain risks have to be taken.

This isn't an acceptable risk, it's an invitation to disaster.

You mean you don't trust the Uncle?

I'd trust a rattlesnake first.

That's unkind. The Uncle is really a sweet old guy. You don't know him the way I do.

I don't want to know him. She appealed to Yuri. *Aren't you going to say something? Or do you trust that sweet old gangster, too?*

Yuri said mildly, *Ben is running it.*

I know that, but . . . I mean, why don't we just check into the Waldorf-Astoria and tell the whole world where we are?

Don't exaggerate.

I'm not. She was angry now. *Secrecy and mobility, that's all we have going for us, and we're giving both away. If we stay at this place, we'll be locked into a single position, and as for trusting that criminal with a heart of gold . . .*

She stopped when she realized that Yuri was laughing. The others were laughing, as well. Most of the laughter was kindly. Only Snake's had an edge to it.

Arina said stiffly, *Have I said something funny?*

Hilarious, said Snake. *Just relax, and let Ben run it.*

Martha was kinder. She said, *Don't turn around, but if you could look out the back you'd see that a car had been following us ever since we left the clam bar.*

Oh, Arina said faintly. *Who . . .?*

As a guess, a guy named Tony Spats, I said. *He works for the Uncle.*

FIFTY-FIVE
Sunday 8:45 PM

'I counted seven of them in a stretch limo,' said Tony. 'They went straight to Carlo's place.'

'Did they all go inside?' asked the Uncle.

'Uh-huh. They parked the car down the street near the corner.'

'Did you get a good look at them?'

'Hey, I couldn't get so close.'

'Tell me.'

'Well, there was three women. And Slade. And one of the other guys was a *melanzane*.'

'That's five. What about the other two?'

'Just guys, you know? A young guy, and a guy who's not so young.'

'Fifties? Sixties?'

'Uncle, please.'

'Thin? Not so thin?'

'Definitely not thin. Sort of stocky.'

'That's all? Nothing else special about him?'

'Nothing.'

'Thank you, Tony.'

'Look, I'm sorry I couldn't get closer.'

'No, no, you did good. Now wait outside.'

When Tony had gone, the Uncle sat for a stretch of minutes, considering his options. He firmly believed that a man who did not honour his obligations was something less than a man. But a man had many obligations. He was obliged to his family, to his village, to his personal honour and, in the case of the Uncle, he was obliged above all to his Don. It was inevitable that on occasion these obligations would come into conflict. It had happened before, and it was happening now. He had

235

satisfied one obligation, in part, and now he had to satisfy another. He really had no options to consider. What he had to do now had been woven into the fabric of his life from boyhood onward. He reached for the telephone, and dialled the private number of Don Salvatore DiLuca.

FIFTY-SIX
Sunday 8:45 PM

The refrigerator and the bar were in the card room of The Palace. Snake made straight for the bar, and a bottle of cognac. Vince dumped the weapons we had brought from the car onto the card table. Iron Mike looked in the fridge, and found a loaf of bread and a package of sliced ham. He took them out, and began slapping sandwiches together.

'Make it quick,' I told him. 'I want us out of here in fifteen minutes.'

I never had had any doubts that the Uncle would drop the dime on us. I was counting on him doing just that. What I needed was diversion and a holding action. The Palace was the diversion, and the hold was the team that would stay behind. My people and Yuri had figured that out for themselves, but Arina was young and she was new at it. I laid it out for her.

'I figure that they'll hit us here in about an hour. It should take that long for the Uncle's word to go up the line. By that time, most of us will be gone. Whoever stays behind will buy us some time.'

'How many stay?' she asked.

'Two. Vince and Martha.'

Vince rumbled out a deep sigh. 'Volunteered again. I need a drink.'

Snake said, 'Hold it, Ben, I want a piece of this. Me instead of Martha.'

'I didn't ask for any votes, and I don't want to hear that shit. Vince and Martha stay.'

Yuri said carefully, 'You realize that I would volunteer, but my first duty is to stay close to Mike.'

'That's understood, and don't feel badly about it. This isn't a suicide mission. The holding team holds for a while, and then gets out the same way we do.'

'Which way is that?' asked Mike. He handed me a sandwich. 'We can't go out the front, we were seen to come in.' He had grasped the basics of the diversion quickly.

'Up the stairs and over the roof. The roofs of these brownstones all run together. We come down through the house on the corner where the car is parked.'

'I hope you have nothing athletic in mind. Not at my age.'

'Nothing you can't handle.' I took a bite of the sandwich. 'No mayonnaise?'

Mike made a face. 'Is that an American custom?'

'It's a personal custom.'

'The bread tastes like paste, the ham tastes like plastic, and you want mayonnaise on top of that?'

'Look at it this way. It might help.'

'I never thought of that. I'll try it.'

'Don't bother, we don't have time. Martha, Vince, talk to you a minute?'

Martha was at the card table going over the equipment. Vince had brought in a pair of Armalites, a dozen clips, a rack of four T-40 grenades, and a stainless steel jemmy. She picked up one of the Armalites. She was accustomed to the Uzi, and she checked the weapon out. Then she saw the grenades. She held one up, and said, 'Vince, what the hell are these for?'

'Thought they might come in handy.'

'We can't use these things, there are *people* living here. You want to blow down the neighbourhood?'

'Better to have too much than too little.'

'She's right,' I said. 'We're not running a war here. Let me have those things.' I stuffed two of the grenades in my pockets, and gave the other two to Yuri.

I took Vince and Martha aside. I blocked out the rest of the group so I could talk to them privately. *Look, I meant what I said before about a suicide mission. I don't want any Alamo here. You hold for as long as you can, and then you go out over the roof. Is that clear?*

We'll be good, Martha promised. *Where do we go after that?*

Anywhere but home. Find a place to hole up for the night,

and check in with Sammy in the morning. I repeated what Sammy had told me. *Remember, you trust nobody, our side or theirs.*

You want to tell us where you're going?

I want to, tus, *but I'm not going to.*

Nor should he, said Martha. She grinned impishly. *But I know where I'd go if I wanted to hide a world-famous Russian for the night.*

She gave it to me. I kept my head straight and showed nothing, but even that was enough to tell her how close she was. Her grin turned to a warm smile. She squeezed my arm. *You always were the bright one.* And then, out of nowhere, *She's a fine girl, Ben. I like her.*

Amen, said Vince.

Snake doesn't.

Don't worry about that. Snake doesn't like anybody very much. Except you.

It was getting sloppy, too much like a final farewell, and I didn't want them thinking that way. *Just remember what I said. No Alamo.* I looked at my watch. *Better get set up. You have plenty of time, but . . .*

Ben. It was Arina.

Then Snake. *Ben.*

Those two caught it first, then Yuri grunted. *Outside. In the street.*

I've got it, said Snake.

I reached for it, and found it. We stood frozen, straining. Even Mike. He didn't know what was happening, but he knew that something was wrong. A sandwich halfway to his mouth, he whispered, 'What is it?'

Arina made a quieting motion. Mike put down the sandwich. He stood stiffly, his face white.

Three heads out on the street, intruders, and they all had the minds of hunters after prey. I went to the window, and peeked around the shade. Three men in front of the building, and a car at the kerb that had not been there before.

I turned to the others. *It can't be. It's too soon.*

Snake said, *I make it two Americans and one Russian.*

But it can't. I refused to believe it. The Uncle could never have got the word out that quickly.

Ben, it is, said Martha. *It can't be anything else.*

Yuri said, *Your timing was off. What now?*

Move out, said Vince. He was at the card table, Martha beside him. They had the Armalites, and the extra clips. *Get going. Now.*

I tapped those three heads one more time. I didn't want to believe it, but I had to. It was all there, laid out in their minds. They wanted us dead. Two of them were off the street now, and into the building. I had screwed it up, but there was no time to think of that.

'All right, we move.' I said it aloud for Mike.

'What is happening?' he asked.

'Our guests are early. Let's go. Yuri and Arina, then Mike, then Snake and me. Vince and Martha, hold them until we get clear.'

'I'm staying,' said Snake.

'You're not. Move.'

I grabbed the jemmy from the table, and got them started toward the rear door and the stairs. Yuri and Arina pulled Mike along. Snake followed. I was the last one out. I turned to look back. Martha was flat on the floor, her weapon pointed at the door. Vince caught my look, and winked. I tried to wink back, but it didn't work. I turned, and ran after the others.

FIFTY-SEVEN
Sunday 9:02 PM

The city-map grid on the wall was static, the double blips of light on Jane Street poised directly over the glowing triangle that represented the assault team's car. The Case Executive stood beside the grid, headset on, her eyes fixed on the points of light. She spoke softly into the headset, waited, and spoke again.

'Anything?' asked Yadroshnikov.

'Assault under way,' she said. 'Two men in the house, one man in the car.'

'Excellent. Advise him to keep communications open at all times.'

'What odds now?' asked Engstrom. He stood up, stretched, and went to the coffee machine against the wall.

'How can there be odds on this? It is a spontaneous operation, not part of the original projection.'

Engstrom turned the knob of the coffee urn. Nothing happened. 'I thought you had odds for everything.'

'Under the proper circumstances, yes.'

'But not now?' He tapped the side of the urn. It was empty.

Yadroshnikov pursed his lips in annoyance. 'If you insist. Since we have the element of surprise here. I'd say eight out of ten.'

'What way?'

'Our way, of course. This should be the end of it right here.'

Engstrom grunted. He said, 'Hey sweets, this machine is out of coffee.'

The Case Executive gave him a level look. 'Are you talking to me?'

'Who else would I call sweets? Would you get a fresh brew going?'

'No.'

'How's that?'

'There are three things that I don't do on the job, Mister Engstrom. I don't do coffee, I don't do windows, and I don't give head. The filters are in that box under the table.'

FIFTY-EIGHT
Sunday 9:00 PM

'. . . continuing our special coverage of the events surrounding the attempted assassination of Soviet leader Mikhail
Gorbachev. So far it has been a day of rumour and speculation, with few hard facts emerging. One undeniable fact is that
a shot was fired at the General Secretary this afternoon as he
emerged from his limousine in front of the Soviet Mission here
in Manhattan. Another undeniable fact is the death of the
would-be assassin, who was gunned down on the street by a
quick-on-the-draw New York City police officer. But beyond
those facts lie the rumours and the speculations that have
raised more questions than they have answered.

'Question. Was there a previous attempt on the life of the
General Secretary while he was still aboard the aircraft that
brought him to New York?

'Question. Where is Major General Nikolai Shvabrin, a
high-ranking member of the Red Army General Staff, who is
known to have departed from Moscow with the Gorbachev
party, but who never got off the plane?

'Question. What was the real cause of the explosion that
was heard to come from within the Soviet Mission this afternoon? It was originally explained as a kitchen mishap, but the
rumours now say that it caused the death of several high-level
members of the Mission staff.

'Question. What has happened to Captain Edward Duffy,
the hero cop who saved Gorbachev's life? The latest rumours
say that he was killed while defending the Soviet leader against
yet another assassination attempt.

'But the most pressing question of all concerns the present
whereabouts and safety of Mikhail Gorbachev, himself. Both
the White House and the Kremlin have issued statements

243

expressing total confidence in the operation that has been mounted to safeguard the General Secretary's life. According to the Secret Service and the New York City Police Department, he has been taken from the Soviet Mission to an undisclosed hiding place, where he will remain secluded until his appearance before the United Nations General Assembly at eleven tomorrow morning. At that time he is expected, along with the President, to announce a comprehensive agreement on nuclear disarmament and arms control. To discuss that agreement, we have in the studio Dr Oleg Churanov, a specialist in Soviet disarmament policy, who defected to the United States in 1977. Dr Churanov, welcome.'

'A pleasure to be here.'

'Dr Churanov, we've seen today at least one attempt on the life of the Soviet leader, and rumours have it that there have been others. In your opinion, what would the effect have been on the disarmament agreement if that attempt had been successful?'

'Peter, in considering such a question one first must be aware of the differences in the political systems of the United States and the Soviet Union. Consider what would happen if the situation were reversed. If the President had been assassinated today it would have had little or no effect on the agreement. The Vice-President would have taken over and he would have carried out the intentions of the Administration. In the Soviet Union, however, there is no such clear-cut succession to the leadership. Gorbachev rules through a coalition of political forces within the Politburo, and he has no designated successor. Indeed, his coalition is a shaky one, with most of his opposition coming from those who favour a return to a more repressive form of government. This opposition, in general, is opposed to any treaties of accommodation with the West, and it would be my guess that if Gorbachev had been killed today the result would have been political chaos within the Kremlin.'

'Are you saying that the agreement would not have gone through?'

'I am saying that it would have been highly questionable. At the very best, the announcement of the agreement would have been postponed in order to allow for a realignment of forces in the Politburo. What might happen after that is anyone's guess.

The so-called Number Two man in the Kremlin, Yegor Ligachev, is one of Gorbachev's creations and must be considered loyal, but he is no mere clone of the General Secretary. Ligachev has ideas of his own, and they are not nearly so liberal as Gorbachev's. In addition, there is no guarantee that Ligachev would take over under such circumstances. In the confusion following an assassination it is entirely possible that a realignment of forces would bring the old guard back into power, and that might effectvely spell the death of any disarmament treaty for a decade to come. There is no way of saying for certain, but if the General Secretary had been killed today, there probably would have been no announcement of an agreement tomorrow.'

'What if there were to be another assassination attempt? A successful one?'

'It is my understanding that he has been secluded in a safe . . .'

'Yes, but speaking hypothetically, if there were another attempt, and it succeeded . . .?'

'Then, as I said, there would be chaos.'

'And no agreement?'

'Absolutely not. For the reasons I have stated.'

'Churanov, that snake,' said Ligachev. 'Turn it off.'

Obediently, Ambassador Panchenko pressed the remote control button, and the television screen went blank. The television had been set up at the far end of the conference room where the *ad hoc* committee at the Soviet Mission still sat. The committee had been reduced in number by those who had been killed, and increased again by the speedy return of Ligachev and Shevardnadze from the Soviet enclaves at Riverdale and Glen Cove. All the Americans had stayed in place, and it was understood that they would sit through the night with their Soviet counterparts. The only other man in the room was Gorbachev's valet, Anatoli, whose presence the others tolerated.

'Snake,' Ligachev repeated. 'How can such a man live with himself?'

'The hell with that.' Bradley, the State man, leaned forward intently. 'Is he right? Would there be chaos?'

Ligachev glanced at Shevardnadze, who shrugged. 'I would

have to say yes. The balances are delicate, and nobody knows how they would shift in such a situation. Nobody, not even me. The agreement would be in definite jeopardy.'

'It all hangs on a thread,' said Shevardnadze. 'It all hangs on one man's life.' He fixed his eyes on Sammy Warsaw. 'If we were in Moscow, I would have you shot.'

Chavez, the FBI man, said, 'I'd shoot him myself if I thought I could get away with it.'

'Shooting is too good for him,' said Bradley.

'All this talk about shooting gives me an appetite,' said Sammy. He poked through the remains of the meal still laid out on the table. He found a stuffed crab claw, and bit into it. He made a face. 'Anatoli?'

The valet looked up. 'Sir?'

'If these people are going to shoot me I want a hot meal first.'

'There's nothing funny about this,' said Delaney. 'What you did was dangerous and irresponsible.'

Sammy, still chewing, nodded his agreement. 'Right, and it was also the only possible move I could have made under the circumstances.'

'The only possible move,' said Chavez, contempt in his voice. 'You entrusted the safety of the General Secretary to a bunch of circus freaks, and you call that your only possible move?'

'Circus freaks? I'll remember that. The next time that the FBI asks us for help is when I'll remember that.'

'You can take your help and shove it. You people are a convenience, nothing more. We can live without you.'

'You may have to.' Sammy stood up. 'Those circus freaks are my brothers and my sisters, and they were the only ones I could trust with the job. Everyone else was suspect, Americans as well as Russians. I used the best I had, and I'd do it again if I had to.'

'I can accept that,' said Ligachev. 'Conditionally, but I can accept it. What I cannot accept is your refusal to tell us where your people have taken the General Secretary.'

'You've asked me that question six times so far, and each time I've given you the same answer. I don't know where they took him. I didn't want to know, and so I didn't ask.'

'Six times, yes. I didn't believe you the first six times, and I don't believe you now. If I had you on my home ground you would tell me the truth very quickly.'

'I've already told you the truth.'

'And then, of course, I would shoot you.'

Sammy shook his head in disgust. 'No wonder you're the Number Two man. With those brains you'll never be number one. Ligachev, I'll guarantee you this much. Those circus freaks of mine will deliver your boy to the UN tomorrow morning, on time and in one piece. If they don't, *then* you can take me out and shoot me.'

Sammy stalked out of the room. He did a good job of it, slamming the door behind him, and at once felt very foolish. He had forgotten where he was, and he had no place to go. He leaned against the corridor wall, and closed his eyes. He was not nearly as confident as he had sounded inside. Circus freaks. In a way, Chavez was close to the truth. They were freaks, all right, good for tapping and prying, but not truly geared for this sort of work. He was weary, through to the bones, and he needed a place to lie down and rest. A little sleep, a little slumber, a little folding of the hands. He heard the door to the conference room open, then close.

'Sir? Please.'

Sammy stiffened, and opened his eyes. It was Anatoli. Gorbachev's valet wore a worried face, and his hands were clenched at his chest.

'What is it?'

'Sir, I could not help to hear what you said inside about the General Secretary, about where he is . . .'

'I don't know where he is, Anatoli.'

'Yes, I heard that, but . . .'

'Christ, you too? I'm telling you, I don't know.'

The valet's hands fluttered. 'Please, I understand, I believe what you say. But you see, he has gone off without a hat or a coat, just the clothes on his back, and it will be cold tonight. He is not accustomed to taking care of himself, not for years. I am the one, always, who has to worry about these things, and now, who knows? These people he is with, will they make sure that he is warm?'

247

'Don't worry, they'll tuck him into bed with a glass of hot milk and a cookie.'

'You laugh at me.'

Contrite, Sammy said, 'I'm sorry, I shouldn't have said that. Really, don't worry, they'll take good care of him.'

'And you really think that they will bring him to the United Nations tomorrow . . . how did you say? On time and in one piece?'

'You can bet on it.'

A look of concern crossed Anatoli's face. 'But his clothing, he will be wearing the same suit all this time. All crushed and wrinkled. He cannot appear before the General Assembly that way.'

I don't care if he gets there wearing gym shoes and a jock strap, thought Sammy, but he put his hand on Anatoli's shoulder. 'Look, I'll tell you what we'll do. We'll go to his suite now and pack a bag for him. Suit, shirt, tie, underwear, the works. Tomorrow morning you'll be waiting for him at the UN with everything he needs. How does that sound?'

'And you say that he will be there? That I should bet on it?'

'Everything you've got, including the rent money. Look, once we get this bag packed, is there someplace where I can lie down for a while?'

'Of course. You may use his bed. He won't be sleeping there tonight.'

FIFTY-NINE
Sunday 9:05 PM

I turned my back on Martha and Vince, and followed the others up the stairs. I still couldn't believe it. There hadn't been time. The word was a beat in my head as I ran. Time, time, there hadn't been time, but there they were, three of them down below, and we were running. But still, there hadn't been time.

Those five flights of stairs were the hardest part of it for Iron Mike. It wasn't easy for any of us, except for Snake who was always in shape, but it was roughest on Mike. By the time we reached the roof he was red, and blowing, and soaked with sweat. He almost went down on the last set of stairs, but Arina tugged and Yuri pushed, and he came out onto the roof with the rest of us. It was dark now, but I could see the way his ribs were heaving. He looked like a foundering horse.

'You said,' he gasped, 'nothing athletic.'

'I lied. Let's go.' We had eight roofs to cross, and then down to the street where the car was parked.

'Wait.'

'Can't. Move it out.'

Snake took the lead. It was easier for Mike on the flat, the footing was firm and smooth, and we moved him along. The buildings were divided by waist-high walls that the rest of us could vault, but they were too much for Mike. He threw himself at each of them, rolling over the top to the other side where he fell to his knees, picked himself up, and kept on going. He wasn't a foundering horse any more. He wasn't any kind of a horse. He was a short and stubby bull, graceless and determined.

We ran, we stumbled, we jumped and ran again, and as we ran we listened for sounds from below. There was nothing.

249

Straining forward, we reached back for the sound of gunfire, but the night was still. Neighbourhood noises rose up from the streets, traffic and kids, but nothing more. We ran, and jumped the last of the walls between the buildings, Mike rolling over with an awkward lunge, and then we were there. Stairwell door of the corner house, padlocked against intruders. Snake slipped the jemmy behind the hasp, and twisted. The door popped open. The others poured through, but I waited, listening. Nothing. I followed, pounding down the stairs.

We came out onto the street; the car was parked at the corner. We stood beside it, looking back up the street at The Palace. The ground-floor windows were dark, and the air was silent. Seconds passed, no more than that. We were poised for flight, but held in place by a binding thread. I snapped the thread.

'Snake drives, me in front,' I said. 'You three in the back.'

Pop-pop-pop-pop-pop. We heard it then. *Pop-pop-pop*.

An innocuous sound, it could have been firecrackers, or bottles breaking. It did not stir up the street. There were some strolling couples, and some kids on the steps. A few heads turned, but nobody jumped, or screamed.

'In,' I said. 'Move out.'

The three Russians piled into the back. Snake did not move. Her eyes were on The Palace, and she had the hard, tough look on her face. I knew that I could not stop her, but I tried.

'Snake, get in.'

'Can't do it, Ben.'

'I need you.'

'They need me more.'

'We don't have time to debate this. Get in.'

She leaned over, and kissed my cheek. She did that about once every five years.

'Snake.'

'Sorry, but I can't. You know that I can't.'

She started back to The Palace, running. I slid behind the wheel, and watched her in the rear-view mirror. I started up, and pulled away from the kerb. When I looked in the mirror again, she was gone.

SIXTY
Sunday 9:11 PM

Engstrom fussed with the coffee machine. He made a bad job of it. He wasted several filters before he could get one in straight, and then he upended the coffee sack and emptied it onto the table. He flung the sack away, and said to the Case Executive, 'Look, I can't get this right. Will you give me a hand?'

'I told you before,' she said coldly. 'There are three things that I don't do on the job.'

'Yeah, I know, but I'm not looking for sex, and as far as I'm concerned the windows can stay dirty. Just the coffee, okay?'

The Case Executive muttered something about brain-damaged males. She stripped off her headset, and handed it to Engstrom. 'Here, take the board.'

Engstrom put on the headset, and watched admiringly as she went to work on the machine. 'I appreciate this, I really do.'

'Sure, sure.' She slammed in the filter, filled it with ground coffee, and adjusted the water level. She flipped a switch, and a red light glowed on the urn. It took her no time at all. She went back to the grid.

'Terrific,' said Engstrom. 'When can you start on the windows?'

She held out her hand. 'Just give me those phones.'

Engstrom put his hands to his ears, and then stopped. He stiffened to attention.

'What is it?' asked Yadroshnikov.

'Backup reports gunfire in the building.'

'Very well,' Yadroshnikov said calmly.

'He requests permission to investigate.'

251

'Negative. Instruct him to stay with the car and keep the loop open.'

Engstrom spoke into the headset. He looked up. 'Backup repeats request.'

'Negative.'

'Negative,' Engstrom repeated into the headset. 'No, definitely not. No, you're in no position to judge that. Stay put.'

'What now?'

'He says there was no surprise. He says they were waiting for them. He still wants to go in.'

'Who the hell does he think he is?'

'He says that . . .'

'I don't give a damn what he says. Who is he, one of mine or one of yours? If he's mine, I'll crucify the bastard. Tell him I said . . .' Yadroshnikov stopped at the look on Engstrom's face. 'What now?'

Engstrom said with wonder, 'He cut me off.'

'He what?'

Engstrom clicked a button on the set. 'No response. It's dead.'

'Give me that.' Yadroshnikov reached for the phones.

'No, really, it's dead. He cut it without a sign-off.'

'The fool, he can't . . .'

'Action on the board,' said the Case Executive.

Both men wheeled to stare at the grid. The two blips of light were in motion. They moved slowly as far as the river, and then turned south. The triangle of the assault car remained motionless. The blips picked up speed, heading downtown.

'Sweet fucking Jesus,' Engstrom whispered.

Yadroshnikov grabbed the headset, and put it on. He spoke into it urgently, first in Russian, then in English.

'Anything?'

'Nothing.' He ripped off the headset, and threw it on the floor.

The Case Executive picked it up, and slipped it on. 'What's happening?'

'Quiet. Something has gone wrong. Very wrong.'

'Yadroshnikov went back to his chair, and sat down. He closed his eyes. He clenched his jaws, and his hands gripped the arms of the chair as he fought for control. The blips continued to move south along the river. The triangle stayed where it was.

Yadroshnikov opened his eyes. He said calmly, 'We must re-evaluate. Continue calling the assault car. It was a diversion, and it worked.' Softly, as if speaking to himself, he said, 'Who is in that car? Who is running it?'

'Someone who doesn't know the odds,' said Engstrom.

Yadroshnikov waved that one aside. 'It is a postponement, nothing more. We can track them for as long as those lights stay on the board. Keep after the assault team.'

'Nothing there,' said the Case Executive.

As she spoke the double blip reached the southern tip of Manhattan, and disappeared. It was as if a switch had been thrown. They were gone.

'That's impossible,' said Engstrom.

Yadroshnikov asked, 'What is at that point? A tunnel, perhaps?'

'The Brooklyn-Battery Tunnel,' said the Case Executive.

'I thought as much. They are in the tunnel. A transponder cannot penetrate that much water. It is necessary only to wait.'

They waited, three pairs of eyes fixed on the grid. After twelve minutes of waiting, the double blip appeared on the Brooklyn side of the tunnel, and moved smoothly onto Prospect Expressway, and then onto Ocean Parkway, heading for Brighton Beach.

SIXTY-ONE
Sunday 9:35 PM

'What city is this?' asked Mike, looking out the window at the broad expanse of Ocean Parkway, the neat streets and the carefully tended buildings, a synagogue on every block and respectability a presence in the air.

'We're still in New York,' I told him. 'The borough of Brooklyn, celebrated in song and story, home of the Botanic Garden, the Brooklyn Museum, the Academy of Music, and more churches than you can shake a bagel at.'

'Ah, Brooklyn, yes. Also once the home of the Brooklyn Dodgers.'

'You know about baseball, Mike?'

'Of course I do. We invented it.'

'Fighting words, pardner.'

'No, it is true. Your baseball is derived from the Russian game of *lapta*. It was brought to California many years ago by the Russian *émigrés* who settled there. There have been several articles on this subject in *Izvestia*.'

'I know about those articles. Just like years ago you were claiming that Russians invented everything from the airplane to penicillin.'

I checked his face in the rear-view mirror. He looked serious and concerned. He said, 'Well, yes . . . that. You must understand that in those days we were younger, and cruder, and less sure of ourselves. Extravagant claims were made to bolster the national ego. This is no longer necessary. Under socialism we have transformed ourselves into a superpower. Now our achievements speak for themselves.'

'Including the invention of baseball?'

'Oh, yes, that is a well-known fact.'

'Well known to whom?'

'To everybody,' said Yuri. 'Even your President refers to our evil umpires.'

He got his laugh, but not from me. I had no laughter in me.

Arina asked, *Ben, not funny?*

Yes, funny. Sorry.

Ease up. You can't blame yourself for what happened.

I'm all right.

You're not, you're leaking guilt all over this car. Block it out, there's nothing you can do about it now.

She's right, said Yuri. *Your people knew what they were doing. Martha and Vince volunteered to stay, and Snake made her own decision.*

They're back there, and . . .

Block it.

Ben, you have to.

I had to, and I did. Reluctantly, but I did it. It was a trick of the mind, nothing more, and mind tricks came easily. I had been taught to do it years before at the Centre. I blocked out the sight of Martha lying on the floor of The Palace, her Armalite pointed at the door. I blocked out Vince's wink. I blocked out the mirror image of Snake jogging back up Jane Street. I blocked that all out, but there was one thought that I could not block.

Time. There hadn't been time for the Uncle's word to get up the line. No possible way, so how . . .?

Block that, too, said Yuri. *You made a mistake, that's all. You're human. Block it.*

I'm human, all right, and I make plenty of mistakes, but not that time. It just isn't possible.

Ben, block it, please. There's nothing you can do about it now.

There was one thing I could do about it, and I did it. I turned off Ocean Parkway and went looking for a gas station. I found one open on Coney Island Avenue. I pulled in past the pumps, and parked near the rest rooms. I jumped out, and opened the back door.

'Pit stop,' I said. 'Anybody have to use the facilities?'

All three looked at me, puzzled. All three shook their heads.

'Suit yourselves. Mike, come with me, please.'

'But . . . it is not necessary.'

255

'Please, just do as I ask. Yuri, I want a few minutes alone with Mike. Make sure that no one comes into the men's room.'

Still puzzled, Yuri nodded. Mike climbed out of the car reluctantly. I got the key from the attendant, and we went into the men's room. It was empty, and it wasn't bad for a gas station, relatively clean and smelling of a strong disinfectant. I told Mike what I wanted him to do. He looked shocked at first, but then he thought about it for a long minute.

'You have a good reason for this?' he asked slowly. 'This is not a caprice.'

'It's a hunch. It may be a bad one, but I have to play it.'

'Very well, I have trusted you so far.'

He took off his jacket, and gave it to me. He went into the toilet stall, and closed the door. He took off his trousers, his shirt, and his tie, and handed them to me over the door. He did the same with his undershirt and shorts. He took off his shoes, and passed them under the door.

'This floor is dirty,' he said. 'May I keep my stockings?'

'No, I have to have everything.'

He took off his socks, and threw them out.

I asked, 'Are you totally naked now?'

'Totally, and quite uncomfortable.'

'I'll do this as quickly as I can.'

I went over every inch of his jacket and trousers, running my fingers inside the cuffs and behind the collar and lapels. I did the same with his shirt, his tie, his underwear, and his socks. I checked the insides of his shoes, looked for marks on the soles, and tried twisting the heels. I found nothing. I gave everything back to him, and told him to get dressed. When he was ready, he came out of the stall and went to the mirror to adjust his tie.

He shrugged himself into his jacket. 'Did you find what you were looking for?'

'No.'

'Do you know what you were looking for?'

'In a general way. I was hoping . . . never mind, it doesn't matter now.'

He wasn't a sensitive, but he was sensitive enough to read the tone of my voice. 'You are feeling badly about your friends, yes?'

'I don't understand how it happened.'

He put his hand on my shoulder. 'Since you call me Mike, I will call you Ben. Listen to me, Ben. Every day of the week I make decisions that affect the lives of millions of people. I am not always right in those decisions, but I do the best that I can, and then I move on to the next decision. I know that you are doing the best that you can for me. Your friends knew that, too.'

I nodded. I didn't want to say anything. We went outside to the car, and Mike got into the back with the others. Arina looked at me anxiously. Yuri said, 'Do you want to tell us what this was all about?'

'He had an idea,' said Mike. 'It did not work out. There is nothing more to say.'

But there was one thing more, a question that had to be asked. Standing at the back door of the limousine, I leaned into the interior, and said, 'Mike, in the last few weeks, before you left the Soviet Union, did you need any medical attention? Did you see a doctor?'

'No. What are you getting at?'

'The same old hunch. Forget it.' I opened the front door.

'No, no doctors, only my dentist. About two weeks ago.'

I closed the front door. 'Dentist? For what?'

'A new bridge, a temporary one. The permanent bridge will be ready when I return to Moscow. Why are you smiling?'

'Would you take out the bridge, please?'

'I'm not supposed to. The dentist said to leave it in at all times.'

'I know,' I said gently, 'but I have to see it. Can you get it out easily?'

'I suppose so, but he specifically said . . .'

'Please.'

He hooked a finger inside his mouth, and worked at it. After a moment, it came free. It was a three-tooth bridge, wet and gleaming. He looked around for something on which to wipe it.

'That's all right.'

I took it from him. It looked in no way unusual. I dropped it on the gritty cement, and stamped on it with the heel of my shoe. Arina gasped. Yuri murmured something. Mike watched silently. I picked up the crushed bridge. All three of the teeth were cracked. The first two were normal enough. The third held a silvery pellet with fine wires that were anchored into the metalwork of the bridge. I held it up for the others to see.

'What is it?' asked Mike.

'A transponder,' said Yuri, his eyes bright. 'A bloody great transponder.'

'What does it do?'

'It emits a radio signal,' Arina explained. 'A powerful signal to a central location.'

'Inside my mouth?' Mike put his hand to his jaw.

'They set you up way in advance,' I told him. 'These people laid out this operation like a chess game. If the attempt on the aircraft missed, and if the attempt by DeKalb missed, and if everything else went wrong for them, they would still be able to find you wherever you ran.'

'My dentist.'

'They got to him. They have long arms.'

'Not as long as mine,' he said grimly, 'once this is over.'

Arina said, 'Is that how they got to the house so quickly?'

'I'm sure of it.'

'How did you know?'

'I didn't, but it was the only way it could have happened.'

'Is that thing still working?' asked Mike.

'I doubt it, but we'll make sure.'

I dropped the bridgework on the ground again, and stamped on it. This time I ground it into powder. 'That's it. They can trace us this far, but no farther. We're off the leash.'

I got behind the wheel. Without saying anything, Arina switched from the back to the front, sliding in next to me. She moved close, snuggling happily. I pulled out of the gas station, and made my way back to Ocean Parkway. Yuri leaned forward, and said, 'Under the circumstances, don't you think that a drink is called for?'

'A drink, and a meal, and a bed for the night,' I agreed. 'And all the wine you can drink. Georgian wine.'

'Georgian?' He sounded horrified. 'Why Georgian?'

'Because that's all they serve where we're going.'

SIXTY-TWO
Sunday 9:16 PM

Snake jogged up Jane Street towards The Palace. Her first concern was the car that was parked in front of the house. If the intruders were working by the book, there had to be a backup man there. She started casting as she approached the car. She found him quickly.

Look, I'm telling you, I think I'd better go in.

Pause.

That's just it, there was no surprise.

Pause.

No, I'm sure of it. The bastards were waiting for us.

Snake cut out into the street, and came up to the car on the driver's side. There was a man behind the wheel, and he was speaking into a microphone. The windows of the car were up and she could not hear his voice, but she could hear him in her own way.

I'm the man on the spot and it's my call to make . . .

Snake tapped on the window. Still talking, the man looked up at her. He was thin and young, with a caved-in face. His eyes flicked away, dismissing her. She tried the door handle. It was locked, and she knew that the others would be, too. She tapped on the window again. When the man looked up this time she made a twirling motion with her finger, inviting him to open the window. He mouthed the words, *Fuck off.* She grinned at him. Her hand went under her shirt and came out with a K-bar combat knife. She held it up for him to see.

'Open up,' she said. She said it loudly, and some of the strollers on the street turned to look at her.

The thin man did not move, but she saw his thumb click off the microphone switch. He sat staring at her. She bent over and slashed the left front tyre of the car, digging deep and

259

gouging. Air hissed, and the tyre began to collapse. She looked up. The thin man had not moved. She went around to the other side and slashed the right front tyre. The car began to settle at the nose. That was enough for the thin man. He unlocked the kerbside door, and came out onto the street. He was taller than she had thought, and he towered over her.

'You stupid cunt,' he said tightly, 'what the hell do you think you're doing?'

'Trying to get your attention.' She smiled sweetly. She let her right hand, the one holding the K-bar, hang loosely by her side. There were people staring now. 'I thought you might like some company.'

'Company? Jesus, look at those tyres.'

'You mean you don't want company?'

'You, you scrawny bitch? Is that what you mean?'

'Not me. Inside. Let's go inside and keep your friends company. Your friends and mine.' She raised her hand slightly, and let him see the knife again.

It registered then. Until now she had been nothing more than a street pest, but now he knew. She saw his eyes widen. She tapped his head, and she knew that he was going to go for it. It was tucked on his hip in a spring holster. She knew his move before he made it. As his hand started back, she brought the K-bar up and slammed it into the notch below his ribs, reaching for the heart. His eyes bulged, and his mouth popped open. She twisted. The light went out of his eyes, and he went down.

A woman on the street screamed. Snake ignored her. She got her knife out of the body, turned, and ran into the house.

SIXTY-THREE
Sunday 9:21 PM

The Case Executive was still trying to raise the assault car on Jane Street when one of the two blips on the grid went out.

'Action on the board,' she said, but the two men had also seen it.

'Which one?' asked Engstrom.

Without hesitation, Yadroshnikov said, 'It has to be the tooth. It could not be the other.'

'Could it be an accident? Mechanical failure?'

'Not likely.'

'Then they have discovered it.'

'They. I would like to know who *they* are.' Yadroshnikov sounded almost wistful. 'I would like that very much.'

'Anything on Jane Street?'

'Nothing at all from the backup,' said the Case Executive. 'Damn that man, he knows that he's not allowed to keep his key closed for more than sixty seconds. Either he disobeyed orders and went into the building, or he's been taken out. Either way, his team is out of touch.'

'And useless to us,' said Yadroshnikov, his eyes on the grid. 'We have movement.'

All three watched as the single blip went into motion, leaving Coney Island Avenue, and turning south on Ocean Parkway.

'What other assets are available?' asked Engstrom.

The Case Executive punched up the grid. There were two other triangles positioned in upper Manhattan.

'Too far away,' Engstrom said disgustedly. 'Christ, what a fuck-up.'

'Not at all,' said the Case Executive. 'Would you two gentlemen like to hear my analysis, or would you prefer that I make some more coffee?'

261

Yadroshnikov looked amused. 'By all means, let's hear it.'

'The discovery of the first transponder is not a calamity. The possibility was anticipated, which is why there were two. The discovery of the first one is bound to induce a sense of false security. Whoever is running the opposition now thinks that he is free of surveillance. Do you agree?'

'So far,' said Yadroshnikov. 'Please continue.'

'Two questions now arise. What is the destination of the opposition, and what must be done to complete the operation? As for the destination, that now appears obvious.'

'The hell it does,' said Engstrom.

The Case Executive ignored him. She was directing her words only to Yadroshnikov now. 'Where would you go to hide an apple? To a bank vault? Under a mattress? No, you would hide an apple in an orchard, among all the other apples. By the same reasoning, where would you go to hide a world-famous Russian?'

'Brighton Beach.'

'Exactly. Also known as Little Odessa, the largest community of Russian *émigrés* in the United States. It lies at the end of Ocean Parkway, and that has to be where they are going.'

'Again, I agree,' said Yadroshnikov. 'The possibility had occurred to me.'

The Case Executive said politely, 'I'm sure it did.'

'And the second question? How must the operation be completed?'

'I believe you know the answer to that one, as well. We have no further assets in the area. It is time for you two gentlemen to get off your butts and go to work.'

SIXTY-FOUR
Sunday 9:23 PM

Vince lay on the floor of the kitchen of The Palace in the dark. He lay on his belly, propped on his elbows, the Armalite cradled in his arms. He lay that way because he could not move his legs. He lay in a pool of blood. He was hoping that most of the blood was Martha's, because he figured that Martha was dead by now, and so it wouldn't matter to her.

Martha lay about six feet away, sprawled face up. She had taken the first burst of fire, and after that she had not moved. He had tried to tap her head, but had heard nothing, and so he figured she was dead. He figured that he was dead, too; not yet, but soon. There had been two of them on the break-in, with a third one waiting outside. He had killed one when they burst through the door, the one who had shot Martha. The second one had got him in the legs, and then there had been silence. It was a silence of waiting. It was one on one now, but that didn't make the odds even. The intruder was untouched, Vince was pinned, and there was always the third man out on the street. So Vince knew that he was finished, but before that happened he wanted one more scalp. It wasn't much to ask for. Just that, and then he could rest.

The intruder waited just beyond the doorway to the kitchen, out in the hall. Vince had tapped his head, and knew who he was, a full commander in Naval Intelligence. Vince thought of him as The Sailor, a black-shoe swabbie who had wandered into the world of dirty tricks, and there had found his place in life. It happened that way sometimes. A man goes along from childhood on thinking of himself as a civilized gent, and then someone hands him a weapon and a licence for murder. Not the stand-up killing of open warfare, but back-alley murder with all of its secret delights, and the civilized gent tastes blood. And learns to like it, then love it, then live for the taste of it. That was The Sailor out in the hallway, waiting for another taste of blood.

Vince waited with him; it was The Sailor's move to make. He reached out and tapped, looking for a sign that the man was ready to commit himself. But The Sailor had a huge supply of patience. He had been told to kill Gorbachev and everyone with him. He had been told that it would be an easy op. He had been told that he would have the advantage of surprise. But it hadn't worked out that way. There had been no surprise, he had no idea where his quarry was, and one of his partners was dead. Other men would have backed away, but The Sailor had a taste for the wet stuff, and he was willing to wait for his kill. He was waiting now for a sound, a scrape or a sigh, to point the way to his prey. So far, Vince had given him nothing, lying silently in his blood with his pain blocked out. Now, he decided, it was time to give The Sailor what he wanted.

He reached around him, his fingers skimming silently over the floor, searching. He came up with a piece of china, half of a dish that had been shattered by gunfire. He tossed it in a high arc toward the other side of the room. It hit the wall there and shattered, breaking the silence.

Inside The Sailor's head, Vince felt him stiffen, then relax, and he caught the one word, *Bullshit*. The Sailor did not move, he did not fire at the sound, he did not reveal his position. He continued to wait.

That's it then, thought Vince. He's good, and he's cold, and he's willing to wait. He'll wait out there all night if he has to, and by that time I'll be meat.

He was losing blood badly; the pool around him was larger, and it wasn't all Martha's. He had lost some earlier in the day, was losing it now, and he knew that he could not lose much more and stay alive. Already his head was thick and woozy, and he felt his thoughts slipping into foolishness. He decided that it wasn't such a bad thing to die. It was worse for the ones who stayed behind, and he wondered how it would be for the others with him gone, and Martha gone, and only the three of them left. They had been a team for so long, but it had happened before to other teams, and the survivors had . . .

survived. That's the way it would be with his people. Sammy was the boss man now, and he had other interests to help him survive. Ben had his new woman, yeah, the smell of those oranges, and she'd help him to survive. And Snake? Snake was family, Snake was team, but Snake was also the one who slid off into the woods every once in a while just to be by herself. Snake was the ace of loners, and she of them all would be able to survive a busted team. Not because she was so tough, but because she was so sweet. She played it so tough, but underneath it was all so sweet.

I'm touched, said a voice in his head. *Am I supposed to break down and cry?*

For a moment he thought it was his woozy head, and then he knew. He grinned in the darkness. *You can cry in your own time, not mine,* he told her. *Where are you?*

In the hallway, behind your villain. Where's the other one?

Out.

Martha?

Out.

She bent, and then she was tough again. *What kind of shape are you in?*

Minor bruises and contusions. What about the one on the street?

He's out, too.

In the street? You looking to collect a crowd?

I had no choice. Do you want to argue about it now?

Maybe later. Right now we have to take care of The Sailor.

Who?

The villain in front of you.

Who does it, you or me

Uh . . . would you mind? You've got the position, and besides, I'm a little stiff in the joints right now.

She did it quickly and efficiently. One moment The Sailor was crouched in the hall, all senses alert, and the next moment he was dead, the K-bar buried in him. She turned on the light. She saw the demolished kitchen, the bodies, and the pool of blood, and she did not even try to be tough.

'My God,' she said. 'Oh, Vinnie, my God.'

She knelt beside him, and saw the way he was. She cradled his head in her arms, and murmured, 'Minor bruises and contusions. Oh Vinnie, oh baby, a little stiff in the joints, that's what you said.'

She did what she could to staunch the flow of blood, and went over to Martha. She felt for a pulse, put an ear to her chest, and peered into her eyes.

'Don't,' said Vince. 'She's gone.'

'She isn't. She's damn close to it, but she's still there.'

'She can't be. I tapped her head, and there was nothing.'

'She's alive,' Snake said flatly. 'I don't know how much longer, but she is.'

'She went to the telephone. She had it in her hand, when Vince stopped her. He said, 'You can't. Sammy gave it to Ben, and Ben gave it to us. No contact, not with anyone.'

'That doesn't mean anything now. If I don't, Martha is dead, and you are, too.'

'Those were the orders.'

'My hero,' she said with a touch of her old sneer. 'You'd rather bleed to death than disobey orders. Since when did orders mean that much in this outfit?'

She dialled 911, said the right words, and then she came back to sit by Vince and wait for the sound of the sirens.

SIXTY-FIVE
Sunday 10:12 PM

The *zakuska* table was a groaning board. Set on linen of alpine whiteness were dishes of pickled mushrooms and cucumbers, stuffed cabbage and grape leaves, kidneys in a Madeira sauce, and stacks of *blini*. There were mounds of beluga, grated onion and eggs, wedges of smoked sturgeon and eel, slabs of herring and pâté. There was a mountain of black bread, a tub of butter, heaps of *pirozhki,* and bowls of sour cream and yoghurt sprinkled with cinnamon. There were carafes of wine and a forest of vodka bottles. It was a first-rate Russian *zakuska*.

'But no salmon,' said Yuri.

'You wouldn't want the salmon,' said the waiter. 'It wasn't good today. Moshe wouldn't buy it.'

'But what is a *zakuska* without smoked salmon?'

'There isn't enough on the table?'

Yuri said petulantly, 'I like a touch of salmon when I'm drinking.'

'Believe me, this salmon you wouldn't touch.' The waiter leaned forward and whispered, as if imparting a state secret, 'It was very dry.'

'But surely you could find a little piece . . .?'

The waiter drew back. 'Absolutely not. Moshe Birnbaum serves nothing but the best. Remember, this isn't an ordinary restaurant, it's a bordello. We have our standards to maintain.'

The *zakuska* table had been set up in the sitting room of a two-bedroom suite on the second floor of Moshe Birnbaum's Bath House. The name of the place was misleading. Moshe provided both wet steam and dry heat, birch twigs and lavender water, but he also provided women, wine, and superior food. Moshe Birnbaum ran the premier cathouse in Brighton Beach.

Twenty years before, Brighton Beach had been no different from any of the other seaside areas that lined the shores of Brooklyn and Queens. Like Coney Island, Rockaway, Manhattan Beach, and the others, it had been a community of small middle-class homes made special by the bracing sea air and the wide boardwalk that provided a promenade beside the sands. Apart from the sea, it had been a thoroughly ordinary place, and thoroughly American.

Brighton Beach now was still thoroughly American, but with a different accent. Of the 200,000 Soviet Jews who had emigrated to the United States since the mid-1970s, about half had settled in Brighton Beach, and the atmosphere was thoroughly Russian. The Primorski Restaurant served the Georgian cuisine that was popular in Moscow, the White Acacia Supermarket sold seven varieties of caviar in bulk, the newspaper of choice was *Novoye Russkoye Slovo,* and the political arguments that raged at the Boardwalk Men's Club took place in Russian or Yiddish. A town within the city, Brighton Beach offered homesick *émigrés* all the comforts of home, and one of those comforts was Moshe Birnbaum's Bath House.

Moshe was a friend, or as much of a friend as anyone in that line of work could be. He had done favours for my outfit, and we had done favours for him. That made him the sort of friend I needed at the moment, and there had been no difficulty in securing the second-floor suite for the night. No difficulty, and no questions, either. It was cash up front, and the vodka was on the house. At the prices that Moshe charged, he could afford to be generous with the vodka.

The only problem had been Mike's appearance. Not that there was anything wrong with it; Martha had done her job well, and with his licked-down hair and pencil-line moustache he bore only a passing resemblance to a world-famous statesman. But Mike didn't know that, and he was nervous. Like anyone new to disguise, he fussed with himself constantly, touching a finger to his hair or his upper lip to reassure himself that everything was in place. I told him to keep his hands in his pockets, if he couldn't control them.

268

'You're only calling attention to yourself that way,' I had said. 'Stop worrying; you look like a travelling rug salesman from Odessa.'

I made two other rules, these for all of us. We would speak only in Russian, and we would assume that the rooms were bugged. I had no reason to believe that they were, but it was the sort of thing that Moshe might do in the hopes of turning up a nugget or two.

'Relax, and keep the conversation light,' I had told them. 'We're off the hook now, all we have to do is get through the night. We'll have something to eat, turn in early, and make our appointment on time tomorrow.'

By something to eat I had meant a bowl of soup, or a sandwich, but the others had vetoed that idea. They wanted a proper meal in the Russian manner, which called for a *zakuska* table as an appetizer. They crowded around the table, munching happily. Yuri forgave the absence of the smoked salmon, and poured vodka for Mike, himself, and me, while Arina took a glass of wine with her to inspect the bedrooms. The waiter stood by, ready to take the order for the main part of the meal. He was an old man with bad feet, and a bad temper, and he waited impatiently.

Finally, he said, 'Don't bother telling me what you want, I know already. Everybody orders our *shashlyk*. It's the best.'

'*Shashlyk* for me,' said Mike, and I nodded. From a bedroom, Arina called, 'Me, too.'

'And you, gentleman?' The waiter looked warily at Yuri. 'The *shashlyk*?'

'I don't think so.' Yuri stroked his chin in thought. 'It's fish that I'm thinking of.'

'No salmon,' warned the waiter.

'Yes, yes, I know. Actually, I was thinking of *osetrina po Russki*. Do you think I could have that?'

'You could have it, but I don't suggest it. The sturgeon wasn't so good today, either. Take my advice, take the *shashlyk*.'

'I don't want lamb, I want seafood.'

'So how about a lobster?'

Yuri's face showed his surprise. 'A lobster? Here?'

'Why not? You think Moshe Birnbaum keeps a kosher kitchen?'

'Well, I thought . . .'

'Don't be ridiculous, you could have a whole roast pig if you ordered it in advance. Besides, what difference does it make to you? You're not a Jew.'

'You've convinced me. I'll have the lobster.'

'Take two, they're small.'

'You've convinced me again.'

The waiter looked around. 'Anything else?'

'One thing,' said Mike. 'How did you know that he isn't a Jew?'

'How? Mister, I've been a Jew all my life. I shouldn't know one when I see one?'

'But how did you know?'

'I just know, that's all. He isn't a Jew.' He stabbed a finger at me. 'He isn't either, and the woman, too. You and me, we're the only Jews in this room.'

'I see,' Mike said solemnly. 'You are very observant.'

'In this job you have to be.'

'Tell me, where are you from?'

'Fourth Street, corner Neptune.'

'I mean in the homeland.'

'Fourth Street, corner Neptune,' the waiter insisted. 'That's my homeland.'

'Have you been there long?'

'Long?' The waiter cackled. 'I was an old man when I came to Brighton Beach, and I'm an older man now. That's how long.'

'And before that? What did you do in the Soviet Union?'

'What does any Jew do in the Soviet Union. I waited.'

'For what?'

'To get out, of course. You ask a lot of questions.'

'I'm sorry, I don't mean to be offensive. Yes, I ask a lot of questions, it's my nature. I don't mean anything by it.'

'I see. I get it now, you're a greenhorn.' He said the last word in English.

Mike looked puzzled. Yuri explained, 'It means a person new to the country.'

'That's it, isn't it?' asked the waiter. 'You just got out, yourself. Right?'

Mike nodded slowly. 'Right. I just got out.'

'I thought so. Let me tell you something, Mister Greenhorn, let me give you some advice. Don't ask so many questions, not right away. Some people might not understand.'

'I see.'

'Like asking people where they come from, and what they did in the homeland.'

'Yes.'

'For myself, I don't care. I'm an old man, it means nothing to me. You want to know? In those days I lived in Kiev. I was an optometrist.'

'An eye doctor. An important job.'

'Not an eye doctor, an optometrist. There's a difference, but yes, an important job.'

'And now you work in a bordello.'

'That's right, Mister Greenhorn, and I'll tell you something else. If I had to clean the toilets in this bordello, I'd still be better off than I was in Kiev. You're new here. You'll learn.'

'But still, a man of your education, why can't you work at what you were trained for?'

The waiter cackled again. He held up his hands, and ticked off the points on his fingers. 'First, the language, my English is rotten. Second, the licence, I'd have to go back to school. Third, my age, an old man doesn't learn so easily. Fourth . . .' He shrugged. 'I could give you a dozen reasons.'

'But must you work in a bordello?'

'I'm not ashamed of the work I do.' The waiter's voice turned nasty. 'At least I just work here. I don't bring a young girl here to share with my friends. Three men and one girl. Disgraceful.'

There was a shocked silence, and then Arina said from the doorway, 'It isn't that way at all. You must not say such things.'

She crossed the room quickly, and put her hand on the waiter's arm. 'You don't understand, this is a wedding party. My husband and I were married today.'

'Your husband?'

Arina reached for my arm, and tugged me over. 'This is my husband.'

The waiter scowled. 'Your husband makes a wedding party in a brothel?'

271

Ben, you'd better take it from here.

Thanks. I told the waiter, 'You see, it was a secret marriage.'

'Ah-hah?'

'Her parents, they objected.'

'Ah-hah?'

'They tried to stop us.'

'Ah-*hah*,' said the waiter, this time with enthusiasm. He took over. 'And so you had to go to City Hall to get married.'

'It was the only way.'

'On the sly, so to speak.'

'Totally.'

'And these two gentlemen, they were your witnesses.'

'Exactly.'

'And you had to take your bride someplace where her parents would never think of looking for her.'

'You've got it.'

'And so you brought her to Moshe's Bath House.'

'It was all I could think of.'

'It was a stroke of genius.' The waiter clapped me on the back. 'Young man, I owe you an apology.' He made a quick bow to Arina. 'Lady, my apologies.'

'It's all right.' She patted his arm. 'A misunderstanding, that's all.'

'If there is anything I can do . . .?'

'If you would just bring us our dinner, please. It's been such a long day, and I'm tired.'

'Of course, of course.' He looked at his pad. 'That's three *shashlyk,* and a double order of the lobster.'

'Forget the lobster,' said Yuri. 'I'll have the *shashlyk,* too.'

'I thought you would. Everybody orders the *shashlyk*.' The waiter scurried out, closing the door behind him.

There was laughter in the air, but no one laughed. We did not dare. We stared at each other, stifling smiles. Finally, Mike said to Arina, 'This romance of yours, it was rather sudden, wasn't it?'

'Very.' She gave him an impish look. 'I hope you don't mind.'

'Why should I?'

'Because I meant it. This is our wedding night. One of those bedrooms is for us. The other is for you and Yuri.'

Mike frowned, and shook his head. He chose his words carefully, aware of the possibility of bugs. 'I'm an old-fashioned man, Arinoushka. You know that.'

'I know that, and I respect it.' She, too, had to be careful. 'But you see, I love him. I really do. And he loves me.'

'Love at first sight?'

'Something like that, but different. It's something that can happen to people like Ben and me.'

'Something that I wouldn't understand, no doubt.'

'No, you wouldn't. You would have to be one of us.'

Mike asked Yuri, 'Do you understand?'

'I sure do, boss, but I wouldn't try to explain it to you.'

'I see.' To Arina, 'And now you want my blessing on this?'

'That's one way of putting it,' she said. 'I don't want to offend you. In a way, I'm as old-fashioned as you are.'

He looked at her for a long moment. 'Perhaps there is such a thing as being too old-fashioned. Raisa says I am.' He raised his glass. 'Yes, of course, You have my blessing. As the only Jew in the room, what else can I say exept *mazel-tov*?'

SIXTY-SIX
Sunday 9:50 PM

They took the Cuban with them. He sat in the back of the car, and dozed. Engstrom drove, and Yadroshnikov handled the radio, keeping the loop open with the Case Executive at the Marshall Street warehouse. She directed them down Ocean Parkway, past Coney Island Hospital, past Trump Village, and ordered a left turn onto Brighton Beach Avenue. Engstrom wheeled the car in under the tracks of the elevated line. Even at this hour of a Sunday night, the avenue was alive. Store fronts were lit, shoppers and strollers filled the sidewalks, and the D train rumbled overhead. There was roadway construction on the north side of the avenue, huge holes torn out of the pavement, and the traffic was condensed into one lane. They crawled between the pillars, and stopped behind a truck that was unloading crates. The Cuban came out of his doze, and looked out at the store windows with their signs in Russian, and at places like the Moscow Nights Disco, the Byelorussian Restaurant, and the Black Sea Book Store, all with their names presented in Cyrillic characters. Voices drifted from the sidewalk, and he heard a strange tongue.

'Hey, what is this place?' he asked.

'Brighton Beach,' said Engstrom.

'What's all these people?'

'Russians.'

Yadroshnikov pursed his lips. 'Don't call them Russians. They're Jews.'

'Russian Jews.'

'Perhaps, but don't call them Russians.'

'Whatever you say.'

The truck in front of them moved, and they lurched forward.

274

SIXTY-SEVEN
Sunday 11:46 PM

Arina had chosen the smaller of the two bedrooms for us, and we made of it a tent in the desert, pretending that we were far away from the troubles and fears that lay on the other side of the door. We placed a desert between ourselves and those fears, and designed in our minds a damask tent that sloped from floor to peak, billowed in the desert breeze, and opened a flap to the stars. We spread our pillows on the sand, bathed ourselves in water of roses, and sipped the wine that we had brought from the other, troubled, land. Outside our tent there were goats that nibbled oasis grass, and the bells round their necks tinkled softly. Fires burned somewhere in the night, and the smell of burning fat was mixed with the stink of the camels. We had no need to burn incense; we were still engulfed in orange. Sweet and pungent, familiar and rare, it spiced the sands of our desert.

Within our tent it seemed as if we had waited a lifetime, although it was only hours. We reached for each other, to see, and to touch, and to taste. Whispers of cloth, and my heart rose up at the sight of her sleek softness, filled my throat and threatened my breath. She smiled at the look on my face, content with herself and with me, and she reached to touch me. A finger to her cheek, to her ear, to her eye, at first just the tingle of skin on skin, and then the touch turned fierce. Fingers at the back of my neck, at the base of my spine, and we were locked, pressing hard on soft, sliding down to lie upon the sand. We tasted each other, nibbling at fruits, but as I reached for warmth she shifted, and drew back.

What is it? I asked. *What's wrong?*

A sadness, she said. *Don't you feel it?*

Something in the air that came creeping, and I felt it then. It

275

was a bitter sadness, nothing sweet about it, the sadness of the doomed beyond aid, the damned beyond redemption, and it chilled my bones. It was the sadness of the whipped and the beaten, of the jails and the *gulags,* of the torture cells and the rubber rooms. It was the sadness of a past that screamed to be recalled, the sadness of hope abandoned.

I feel it now, but where is it coming from?

A soul in hell, she said simply, and burst into tears. They came and went quickly. She clung to me, wet cheek on my shoulder. *I'm sorry. Such sadness.*

Russian tears, salt for the sea. Do you really believe that? Souls in hell?

I'm Russian.

Is that an answer?

It frightens me. For us. What will happen to us when this is over?

Don't think of that now.

Will we be happy?

Yes.

Will we be together?

Yes.

You don't know that.

No, I don't.

Will we be enemies? You on one side of the fence, and me on the other?

I don't know that, either.

You must know, she insisted. *You had this once before. What happened then?*

I don't want to talk about that now.

You must.

Nadia and I ran away together, we had to, but the world was different then.

Not so very different. It's still a crazy world, murderers giggling in the night.

We've made another world. I showed her again the tent and the desert we had created. *Won't this do for now?*

For now, yes, but . . .

I stopped her words. *For now.*

For now, she agreed, and came back to me.

We came together, we did what lovers do, and it was very

276

bad. Nothing worked well, not for her, not for me. The mechanics of it were there. We heaved, we sighed, we peaked; but it was meat on meat. The sadness had withered our loins. After it was over, we lay staring at the ceiling, stretched out on a rented bed in a whore house in Brooklyn, the tent and the desert faded and gone. Even the smell of the oranges had changed, no longer fresh, but bitter.

It's still there, she said.

Yes.

It poisoned us.

Perhaps.

It did. But who would have such sadness here?

Brighton Beach. Silent screams in the night.

That world out there, it never lets go.

Never. We'll have to fight it every day. Has this changed anything for you?

Nothing, she said fiercely. *Nothing.*

Once this is over . . .

Yes. It will be better, I know it will.

We rested in the dark, the sadness still clinging, and after a while we slept.

SIXTY-EIGHT
Monday 12:20 AM

Mike and Yuri sat up late, drinking brandy. They sat in deep armchairs, facing each other, the bottle between them. They sat silently, each with his own thoughts. The night had turned quiet, the sounds of the city subdued, and at times each imagined that he could hear the whisper of the surf on the beach beneath their window.

Mike stared into his glass, and said, 'We should get some sleep.'

'We should,' Yuri agreed, 'but strangely enough I don't feel sleepy.'

'Adrenaline.'

'No, I don't feel pumped up, either. Just pleasantly weary. I could sit here all night and sip this delightful cognac.'

'You amaze me. How much of that stuff do you drink every day?'

'Oh, I get enough. Just enough to blot out the day.'

'You drink to forget?'

'Why else does a Russian drink?' Yuri reached for the bottle, and topped off his glass.

Mike made a face. 'Drink, the Russian disease.'

'No, the Russian symptom. the Russian disease is melancholy.'

'Yes, I see it in your eyes.'

'Sorry, didn't know that it showed. A jester isn't allowed to be melancholic. I'll get my cap and bells.'

'Quiet; you don't have to entertain me.'

'But I do, that's my function in your life. Shall I tell you a story?'

'No.'

'I insist. It's about a lawyer in Leningrad who saves up his

278

money to buy a car. He goes to the proper office, fills out all the forms, and plunks down his rubles. The clerk examines the application, and says, "Right, everything in order. You can take delivery of your car exactly ten years from today." "Morning or afternoon?" says the lawyer. "What difference does it make?" asks the clerk, and the lawyer says, "Because the plumber is coming in the morning." '

Mike said sourly, 'I've heard it before. I hear them all.'

'Not funny?'

'Oh, it's funny, all right. It's so funny that a couple of years ago you could have been shot for telling it.'

'I'm not sure which is worse for a jester, getting shot for telling a joke, or having the joke fall flat. You're right, we should get some sleep.'

'A touch more.' Mike poured an inch into his glass. 'What a day. If you had told me this morning that I would be spending the night in a bordello in Brooklyn, USA . . . what would I have said, I wonder?'

'I know exactly what you would have said. Don't tell Raisa.'

'That's just about as funny as the last one.'

'So shoot me.'

There was a knock at the door. Both men started. Mike whispered, 'What do we do?'

'Wait.' Yuri went to the door, and stood there silently. He reached out to the other side, and tapped. He smiled.

Mike, watching his face, asked, 'Who is it?'

'The entertainment committee.'

Yuri swung the door open. The woman who stood there was in her mid-twenties, with curly black hair that framed a heart-shaped face. She wore skin-tight electric-blue shorts, and an orange blouse tied up under her breasts. She breezed into the room, looked around curiously, and said, 'Hello, my name is Rose. I heard you were having a party up here, and I decided to see if you needed any help in the wine, women, and song department.'

She was speaking Yiddish. Yuri interrupted. 'Speak Russian.'

She wrinkled her nose, but she switched languages. 'It looks like you have plenty of wine, but I don't see any other women, and I don't hear any singing, so I guess I'm in the right place.'

Mike, puzzled, asked, 'What do you want?'

'Well, honey, it isn't what I want that matters, it's what *you* want, right? You just tell me what I can do for you, either one, or any way you want it.'

'Want what?' asked Mike, and then it hit him. 'Yuri, is she . . .?'

'In the flesh,' said Yuri, delighted with the situation.

'Get rid of her.'

'Why so quick?' Rose gave them each a pretty pout. 'Aren't you going to offer a girl a glass of wine, at least?'

'Of course we are,' Yuri said gaily. He rushed to the table. As he passed by Mike, he whispered, 'Don't be so stiff, you'll make her suspicious.'

He poured a glass of wine from the carafe, and gave it to the girl. She raised the glass in thanks, and sank into a chair. She took a sip, and said, 'Delicious.'

'Do you really think so?' asked Yuri in his most superior voice. 'I found it rather fruity, but then I've never been partial to Georgian wines.'

'Actually, it's from California,' said the girl. 'Moshe puts it in carafes and says it's from Georgia. Makes the customers happy, reminds them of home.'

Mike snorted in glee. 'My expert. My connoisseur.'

Yuri tried to appear unruffled. 'At least the vodka is Russian.'

Rose nodded, sipping. 'It certainly is. Moshe makes it himself in the cellar.'

'Fascinating.' Mike leaned forward. It was his turn to enjoy the situation. 'This Moshe sounds like quite a fellow.'

'Oh, he's all right. He knows how to do things the American way.'

'And what way is that?'

'Are you the greenhorn? Jacob, the waiter, said that one of you just got out.'

'That's me.'

'Well, you'll learn. In America, everything is advertising. It doesn't make any difference what something is, it's what you call it. Like Moshe with the wine. You can take a piece of dog shit, wrap it up fancy, and sell it for candy. That's America.'

'The land of opportunity,' Mike said drily.

'That's it.' Unaware of any irony, she said, 'You can sell anything here.'

'I believe it. And you're happy in America?'

'I'm alive, and I'm free. That's enough for me.'

'Do you think I'll be happy, too?'

'Of course you will, once you learn the ropes. There's no place like America.'

'Have you ever thought of going back?'

'To the Soviet Union? Do you think I'm crazy?'

Yuri put in smoothly, 'But I read that some people have gone back. There was a group of fifty from here in Brighton Beach.'

'Sure, and they're probably dead by now, or in a camp. Those idiots believed all the propaganda about *glasnost*.'

'You don't?'

'It's the same old tune, just different words. Nothing changes.'

Mike said carefully, 'You don't think that Gorbachev can make a difference?'

'Please, talk sense. Even if he means what he says, they'd never let him get away with it.'

'They?'

'The KGB, the military, the politicians. Never. Believe me, nothing is going to change.'

'But just suppose,' said Mike, pressing, 'just imagine in your mind. If he could really do it, if he could really open things up, if he could really do away with the more repressive aspects of the state apparatus . . .'

'My, such big words.'

'You don't seem to be a stupid woman, You know what I mean. If he could reorganize the Soviet Union into a socialist state without repression . . .'

'A dream.'

'I said if . . . only if. If he could do that . . . then would you go back?'

She thought for a moment. 'No.'

'Why not?'

'I like it here. I'm free.'

'Free to do what? To buy things in the stores? Pretty

281

clothes, a television set, a washing machine? A piece of dog shit wrapped up like a candy bar? Is that your America?'

'What are you getting so excited for? You just got out. You should be happy to be here.'

'I'm not excited, I'm just asking a hypothetical question . . .'

'More big words.' She stood up, walked over to Mike, and put her hand on his arm. He tried to draw back, but she held him. 'Look, you don't know how it is. After a while you'll see. It isn't something I can explain, you have to see it for yourself. It isn't just the things you can buy in the shops. This is a wonderful country.'

Mike said softly, 'What about the motherland? If things were better at home, would you still give up the motherland?'

'I gave it up a long time ago. I can't even remember what it was like. I'm an American now.'

'So you say, but I wonder. I don't know where you come from, and I don't want to know, but I can see that you're not from the city. You're a village girl, right?'

She nodded. 'What about it?'

'Are you going to tell me that you don't remember the birds that used to wake you every morning in the summer? The way they sang in the yard outside the house?'

'What are you getting at? There are birds all over the world.'

'Not Russian birds. And what about your tree?'

Her eyes narrowed. 'What tree?'

'Your special tree. Birch, wasn't it? With branches you could climb?'

'What do you know about my tree?'

'And when it was in leaf you could go all the way to the top and make a secret place there, a place where you could hide away from the world. You mean you don't remember that?'

She stared at him.

'How about the old woman who first taught you how to knit? Have you forgotten her?'

Rose murmured, 'Tanta Leah.'

'Have you forgotten the big meadow where the rabbits used to run? Or that fuzzy dog who always had fleas? Or the smell of fresh bread baking?'

'How do you know . . .?'

282

'Have you forgotten how the very earth of Mother Russia smells? Have you forgotten what it's like to lie on the ground with your nose pressed into a furrow that the plough just made, breathing deep? Have you forgotten the bitter smell of a Russian winter, like a piece of cold iron held under your nose? Have you forgotten how your heart jumped when the snows began to melt, and the signs of spring broke through? Go ahead, tell me you've forgotten all that, and I'll call you a liar.'

Rose's eyes were wet. She whispered, 'You devil, who are you?'

'Just a greenhorn who remembers his homeland. It's not so easy to forget.'

'No, it isn't,' she admitted. 'I spent a lot of time trying to forget things like that, and now you've brought them all back.'

'They were always there. You can never forget the motherland.'

In a tight little voice, she said, 'Fuck the motherland.'

'You don't mean that.'

'I do, and I'll say it again. Fuck the motherland, and fuck Mother Russia.' In a sudden change of mood, she tossed her head, and her eyes flashed. She pressed her breasts against his arm. 'And speaking of fucking, who wants to be first?'

'Is that all you can say?'

'You almost had me with that motherland shit. Come on, let's do it. It's party time.'

Mike shook his head. He disengaged himself, and moved away. Rose turned to Yuri. 'How about you?'

Yuri smiled broadly, but he, too, shook his head. He took out his wallet, and found two fifty-dollar bills. He pressed them into her hand. 'We're both very tired. No offence, you're a lovely girl. This is for your time.'

'Well, thanks. You're sure?'

'Positive.'

'Much appreciated, very sporting of you.' She looked at Mike. His back was to her. 'Your friend has some funny ideas for a Jew. Tell him to take it easy. He has a whole new world to get used to.'

'I'll tell him,' Yuri promised. He saw her out. Mike turned

round at the sound of the door closing. He wore a sad smile.

'Good try,' said Yuri. 'How did you know about the tree, and the dog, and the old woman?'

'There's always a tree, and a dog, and an old woman. If she had been a city girl, it would have been a certain street, and a lost kitten, and a teacher in school.'

Yuri laughed. 'What a fraud you are. You would have made a remarkable priest.'

'I'll take that as a compliment. For that matter, so would you.'

'Not me, I lack the conviction. I'm only a jester.'

'You haven't been much of a jester tonight, just a few bad jokes, and you certainly haven't lived up to your reputation.'

'I'm sorry, I'm drinking as fast as I can.'

'Not that, I meant with the ladies. You found her attractive, no?'

'Very tasty.'

'I thought you would eat her up alive. I didn't expect you to turn her down.'

'Why the surprise? You turned her down, too.'

'That's different. I'm a happily married man. I would never do anything to hurt Raisa.'

'Ah, you're talking about love.'

'Of course.'

'And has it never occurred to you that a jester could be in love?'

'No, it never has. I never thought . . .'

'This reputation of mine, you shouldn't pay too much attention to it. The drinking, yes, and the jokes, but the business with the ladies stopped a while ago. When I met Anya.'

'Anya. I see. This is the woman you love?'

'More than anything else in the world.'

'Do I know her? Should I?'

'No. She is a simple person.'

'And you never said a word. Why, Yuri?'

'She wanted it that way. As I said, she is a simple person.'

'And why tell me now?'

'Perhaps it was that woman. I was attracted and I was tempted, but you see, just like you and Raisa, I would never do anything to hurt Anya.'

'She lives in Moscow?'

Yuri hesitated. 'Yes.'

'I must meet her. I must know more about this woman who turned my jester into a man of honour.'

'Hardly that.'

'Still, I must meet her.'

'You will. Some day.' Yuri looked at his glass. It was still half full, but he set it on the table. 'And now it's really time for us to get some sleep.'

'Each to a cold bed.'

'Men of honour.'

SIXTY-NINE
Sunday 11:16 PM

The voice of the Case Executive came over the radio. 'Turn right at the next intersection.'

'Roger.'

'Right again.'

'Roger.'

'Procede slowly, about fifty feet . . . another fifty . . . hold it . . . there.'

'Holding.'

Following the Case Executive's instructions, the car turned off Brighton Beach Avenue heading for the beach, turned again, and came to a stop in front of Moshe's Bath House. The street was dark and deserted, with only a dim light over Moshe's front door.

Yadroshnikov said into the mike, 'Case, we are holding at your last fix. Can you give us a fix from here?'

'Negative, car. I have you on an overlap with target. That's your final fix. You're there.'

Yadroshnikov swore softly. On the grid back at the Marshall Street warehouse, the triangle that represented their car and the blip from the transponder were overlapped, which meant that the target was somewhere inside Moshe's Bath House. But that was all that the grid could tell them. It could not be tuned any finer, and could not pinpoint the exact location of the target within the building.

The radio crackled. 'Car, do you read? You're on final fix.'

'Ah, roger, Case. Please hold.'

Engstrom spat out of the window. 'What do we do now, go knocking on doors?'

'They're in there. They, whoever they are. Either we go in and get them, or we flush them out.'

'We go in there, and we start a war. Not acceptable.'

'I agree. They must come to us.'

Yadroshnikov got out of the car and checked the street. It was empty. He surveyed the building. It was about fifty feet wide, and three storeys high. On one side of it was a one-storey shoe-repair shop; on the other side was an empty lot. The rear of the building appeared to abut on the boardwalk.

'Pepe.'

The Cuban got out of the car. Yadroshnikov spoke to him briefly. The Cuban nodded, and moved across the street, blending into the darkness. He disappeared into the empty lot. He was gone for ten minutes. During that time Yadroshnikov keyed his mike every sixty seconds to let Marshall Street know that the loop was open. When the Cuban returned, he got into the back of the car, and reported.

'There's a back door in the building that leads out under the boardwalk. It's locked. Nothing else back there, no fence, nothing. You go out of the building, under the boardwalk, and onto the beach.'

Yadroshnikov asked, 'At that point, is there any way of getting up to the boardwalk from the beach?'

'Right there? No, you gotta go down to the next corner and up the ramp.'

'Is there cover under the boardwalk?'

'How?'

Yadroshnikov said patiently, 'If I position you there, will you be able to keep the back door under observation without being seen?'

'No problem. It's dark under there, like the bottom of the well.'

'Did you check the shoemaker's shop?'

'Like you thought. Made outta wood.'

'You're sure? Not brick or stone?'

'I know wood.'

Yadroshnikov asked Engstrom, 'How much gas can you siphon out of the tank?'

'Maybe ten gallons.'

'More than enough. You see what we must do?'

'Yeah, I see it. I don't like it.'

287

'You are concerned about innocent lives?'

Engstrom stared at him coldly. 'I'm concerned about the attention it will draw.'

'Do you see a workable alternative?'

'No.'

'Then we have no choice. We must burn them out.'

SEVENTY
Monday 3:17 AM

When we were kids at the Centre, they took us out camping when the weather was fine, hiking the trails up Blue Boar Mountain to a hogback ridge where we camped for the night. We went in year groups with one instructor along as a guide. Most of the time the guide was a broken-down ace named Riordan. He wasn't much good for anything else, but he knew the trails, knew how to pitch an efficient camp, and knew how to handle kids. He had one other asset as a guide; he owned what seemed to be an unlimited supply of ghost stories. At night, once camp was made, he would cook up a discouraging stew of sardines and potatoes over an open fire, and while we ate he would spin out his tales to take our minds off the awful food. The stories were blood-chilling in the best of campfire traditions, and they scared the socks off all of us except Snake, who thought they were silly. They were scary enough for me, and for many years later, whenever I sniffed the aroma of pine smoke I was forced to think of sardine stew and ghost stories.

I came up out of sleep with the smell of woodsmoke in my nose and the taste of sardines on the back of my tongue, and in the moment of waking I thought I was trapped in the web of one of Riordan's terrible tales. There was smoke all around me, but it wasn't the pungent pine of those childhood campfires. It was heavy, oily smoke with the stink of the ages in it, and after one good whiff, I knew that it wasn't part of any dream.

'Ben?' Arina was up, and half out of bed. 'Ben, it's a fire.'

There was fire roaring someplace below us, and now I could hear the crackle of burning wood, and muffled voices calling out. 'Grab what you can, and move out quick.' I said.

We came into the sitting room tugging on clothing as Yuri

and Mike came out of the other bedroom. There was less smoke in the sitting room, but coils of it were curling in under the door from the corridor. Mike was fully dressed, right down to his tie; he looked as if he had slept in his clothes. Yuri looked pale, but he had his head on.

In a petulant whine, he said to me, 'Now look what you've done. I told you to tip the waiter, but no, you wouldn't listen.'

Mike said, 'It's a fire, yes? A bad one.'

'It sure as hell ain't no fish-fry.'

'A coincidence, you think?'

I hadn't thought it out that far. I was foggy with sleep, and part of me was still nodding over that long-ago campfire. All I could think of was getting out quickly. The place was built like a matchbox. Arina went to the door, and eased it open. A wall of black smoke rolled in, choking us, but there were no flames yet, and no great heat. The crackling sound was louder, and so were the voices, but all that came from the floor below. I put my head out into the corridor, coughing. Visibility zero; a tunnel of smoke.

'Ben.' It was Yuri. 'The window?'

'Too much of a drop, we'll have to use the stairs. You first, then Mike, then Arina, then me. Single file holding hands, and keep your heads low.'

Yuri led us out into the corridor, and down the stairs. He did it blind, but he did it. I kept Arina's hand firmly in mine. The stairwell was boiling with smoke, and the walls were hot to the touch. Patches of dull red showed in the blackness, hot spots about to break through. We were gasping and tearing when we came out into the lobby of the building. It was packed with people. The fire had broken through the west wall, pushing them ahead of it. They were jammed up at the doorway to the street, fighting to get out, and there was lots of shouting in Russian. A beam crashed behind us, and a sheet of flame shot out of the wall. A woman screamed, and the crowd surged forward. The jam at the doors broke, the doors went down, and people poured out into the street.

The surge of the crowd bore us along like chips in a stream. I had to fight to stay on my feet. I kept one arm around Arina and one eye on Mike, struggling beside me. My head was clear now, no more campfires, and I was open wide. I was getting it all from the people around me: the fear of fire, the panic, the animal push for survival, the urge to trample a neighbour in the race for safety . . . and then something else.

Something frighteningly familiar. It came not from the crowd of panicky people around me. It came from outside, from the street.

Arina. Yuri. Something outside. Check it.

Arina was pressed against me. She looked up, puzzled. Yuri's head snapped around to stare at me. Mike struggled on, unaware. I dug in my heels, and pushed against the people behind me. They pushed back. I struck out, elbows and fists, to clear a path. I dragged Arina with me to the side of the lobby. Yuri followed, pushing Mike ahead of him. We stood flat against the wall, and let the tide flow by us.

'What are you doing?' said Mike. 'We must get out.'

'Not yet.' *Arina, got it?*

She gave a mental sigh. *Yes, they are outside. They are waiting for us.*

Yuri?

I make it two of them. Waiting in the street.

'What is it?' asked Mike. 'Why are we standing here?'

'We can't go out,' I told him. 'They've found us again. They're waiting out there.'

He understood at once. 'So it wasn't a coincidence. Still, we can't stay here.'

The crash of another beam on the other side of the lobby punctuated his point. I could hear the sound of sirens over the roar of the flames, the first of the fire engines on the way. It was move or die, and I was unarmed. In the race from the room, I had left my weapon behind. Arina, too, was empty.

Yuri, are you holding anything?

Nothing except those grenades.

The two T-40s I had given him a thousand years ago back at The Palace. Heavy duty stuff, but they were useless to us now.

Mike pulled at my arm. 'Ben, we must move.'

'Not this way. Out the back.'

I pushed my way into the crowd. We had to work against the flow, but most of the people were out by now, and we broke through the last of them. We raced across the rear of the lobby, the wall on our left shooting flames, and the wall on our right leaking smoke. Through a service door and down a smoky corridor with me leading the way, and the others close behind. There were flames in the hallway, curling down from the ceiling and exposing the beams.

There was so much smoke that I stumbled into the rear exit before I saw it. The door was made of wood, hot wood, and it was locked. There was fire over my head, and a smouldering beam that hung by a crazy angle. I kicked the door under the knob, but it held. I kicked it again, and the wood gave. The door swung open into cool darkness, and the smells of sand and sea.

And something else. Out there.

I took an instinctive step backward, and as I did the beam above my head gave way. It fell across my shoulders, knocking me to the floor, and as I went down I heard the stutter of gunfire and the thud of the rounds hitting wood above my head. I tried to move, but I was pinned by the beam as I lay on my side.

'Stay back,' I called. 'There's another one out there.'

More gunfire, and more thuds in the wall above me. I was covered by a curtain of smoke, and the shooter was shooting blind. I felt a tug at my ankles; Arina was trying to drag me back. I reached out to tap the shooter. One man, with orders to kill anyone who came out the back door.

Yuri, can you get at him?

I can't even see him. If I just pitch a grenade out there I could blow us all to hell.

I heaved up desperately, and the beam moved, but not enough. A breeze blew in from the sea, shredding the curtain of smoke, and I saw him then. He was crouched under the boardwalk about twenty feet away. He saw me at the same time, and saw that I was helpless. He straightened up, and the muzzle of his weapon swung towards me.

Yuri.

But before Yuri could move, Mike stepped out of the doorway with a pistol in his hand. It was a tiny gun; it looked like a toy. The shooter never saw him. Mike raised his arm, and fired. It sounded like a poodle barking. He fired three times. The shooter went down, his face in the sand. He did not move.

'Get this thing off me,' I said.

Mike and Yuri rolled the beam away, while Arina ran to check the shooter. He was dead. I stood up, and pain shot through my shoulders. Mike handed the pistol to me.

'You take it,' he said. 'These things make me nervous.'

'You did a good job with it. I'm in your debt.'

His face brightened. 'I've been in yours for hours. Take it, please. I wanted to see if I could use it, and I did, but it really isn't my style.'

Yuri said nervously, 'We'd better get moving. Those two out front . . .'

I nestled the pistol in my palm. 'Which way would you suggest?'

'Up the beach. Anyplace away from here.'

'Why bother?'

'We can't just stand here.'

'Why not? Running won't do us any good. Not now.'

Arina, her face anxious, said, 'What do you mean?'

I threw back my shoulders, and the pain stabbed again. Arina and Yuri stood side by side, staring at me. 'One of you knows what I mean.'

'I don't,' said Mike. 'What are you talking about?'

'There's a second transponder,' I told him. 'There has to be. That's how they found us again. The way things are now, they'll find us wherever we go.'

SEVENTY-ONE
Monday 3:30 AM

Engstrom huddled in a doorway across the street from
Moshe's Bath House. The handset was under his arm, and the
microphone in his hand. Yadroshnikov stood in front of him,
shielding him from sight. The Bath House was engulfed in
flames, and the street in front of it was filled with the fugitives
from the fire, the neighbourhood curious, and the firemen
from the first engine company on the scene, who were trying
to clear the area.

Yadroshnikov's eyes darted over the crowd, flicking from
face to face. He did not expect to see Gorbachev, he expected a
disguise, but he was looking for one key face that would home
him in on his target. He saw nothing that pleased him.

'They can't still be inside,' he murmured to himself. 'Or if
they are, they're dead.' That thought, too, was less than pleas-
ing. He wanted a confirmed kill, and now.

He heard a crackle on the earphones of the handset behind
him. Engstrom said, 'This is Mobile One.'

Yadroshnikov leaned back to catch the sound of the
Case Executive's voice. 'Mobile One, I have movement on
the grid.'

'Say again.'

'I have movement. They're out of the building.'

'Impossible.' Yadroshnikov whirled around. Engstrom's
eyes stared into his. 'What direction?'

'What direction, Case?'

'I have a slight southerly movement, just enough to register
on the grid. That would place them on the beach, or under the
boardwalk in back of the building.'

'That fucking Cuban.'

Yadroshnikov grabbed the microphone from Engstrom's

hand. 'Case, tell me this. Are they moving now, or are they stationary?'

'Stationary, Mobile One.'

'Very well. We're going in after them, and we will travel with the handset. We will be on an open key, and you will guide us to them. Report any movement on the grid at once. Understood?'

'Roger, Mobile One. Guiding you in.'

Yadroshnikov handed the microphone to Engstrom, who slipped the strap of the handset over his shoulder. The two men walked briskly away from the burning building, controlling the urge to run. Only when they reached the corner, and turned into the side street, did they begin to run towards the beach.

SEVENTY-TWO
Monday 3:32 AM

There were clouds across the moonless sky, swatches of dark
on darkness. A phosphorescent line of surf broke on the
beach, hissed, and retreated. The sand beneath the boardwalk
glowed with colours borrowed from the fire. Arina looked at
me reproachfully; dark, unhappy eyes. Yuri wore a mocking
smile.

'Are you sure of this?' asked Mike.

'It has to be,' I told him. 'I know you're not carrying it, I
checked you, and I know it isn't me. It has to be one of them.'

'But can't you tell which one? I thought you could do that
. . . see into them.'

'Not if they don't want me to. They're aces, Mike, the same
as I am. Either one of them could block me out and I wouldn't
even know it.'

'We must do something quickly.'

'It's up to them.' I kept the pistol in sight. 'Does anyone
want to make it easy for the rest of us?'

'I'm disappointed in you,' said Yuri. 'You're way off base
on this. Whatever made you think that an ace would do such a
thing?'

'I've never confused aces with saints. Arina?'

She said slowly, 'I shall say only this. It is not me, and I do
not believe it is Yuri. There must be another explanation.'

'I might also point out,' said Yuri, 'that standing here like
this is remarkably stupid. We should be moving.'

'He's right,' said Mike. 'Ben, are you really sure of this?'

'Yes.'

'Then it seems to me that there is only one thing to do.'

I nodded. I knew what was coming.

'You must kill them both. Right now.'

296

'Bravo.' Yuri burst into laughter. 'The last of the Romanoffs has spoken. That's a truly imperial edict: off with their heads, the innocent along with the guilty.'

'It's one way of doing it,' I said. 'Probably the only way.'

'You're not serious.'

'You're wrong. I am.'

I levelled the pistol at Arina. Her lips parted. She said, 'Ben, no . . .' But that was all she would give me. She pressed her lips together, and glared at me.

A blast of heat shot out of the rear of the Bath House. There were noises like the rumblings in the belly of a giant. The building was collapsing in on itself.

The mocking smile faded from Yuri's lips. There was still a smile, but a weary one. He said, 'Are you really going to do this?'

'I have a job to do, and nothing is going to stop me from doing it. Nothing.'

'I believe you.' The smile was completely gone now. 'Put the pistol away. It would be senseless to use it on Arina, she knows nothing about the second transponder. It would be equally senseless to use it on me. Even if you killed me, you wouldn't kill the transponder. It would continue to send out its signal.'

'Where is it?'

'Buried inside me, deep inside. You'd have to cut me open to get at it.'

'Inside?'

'They did the surgery two months ago. Would you care to see my scar? It's quite artistic.'

'Why?' The single word from Mike was like a bullet.

'Quite simple, really. They have my woman.'

'Anya?'

'Anya. They have had her for three months. Somewhere. I've never known where. My instructions were to stay close to you, never leave your side. That's all I was told, that's all I had to do. The business on the plane, and at the Mission . . . I knew nothing about that. I was just a piece of insurance. All I had to do was stay close to you. If I did that, then Anya was safe. If not, she was dead.'

'You could have come to me.'

'No, Your Imperial Majesty, I could not. There are certain things that even the Czar of all the Russias cannot do. She would have been gone at the first move I made.'

'Still . . .'

'No, there was nothing I could do but what I did. Need I say that I did it with a heavy heart? With revulsion? With the knowledge that I was betraying the man I most admired in all the world? Need I say that?'

'Say what you wish.' Mike's voice was gruff. 'You chose her over me.'

'I did, God help me.'

I felt the sadness coming off him then, the same sadness I had felt before. The sadness of the doomed, the damned beyond redemption. The sadness of the whipped and the beaten. Arina had called it the sadness of a soul in hell. She had been right. I was looking at him.

'Kill him,' said Mike.

'No,' said Arina. 'That accomplishes nothing now.'

'Kill him anyway. I want him dead.'

'That imperial voice, it's getting to be a bore,' said Yuri. His own voice was light again. 'Isn't it interesting how some people simply cannot handle rejection.'

'Ben, I'm telling you to kill him. Are you going to do it?'

I did not move. I was into Yuri's head, probing.

'No, he is not,' said Yuri. 'He knows it isn't necessary. He knows what has to happen next.'

I probed deeply. Yuri knew that I was there. He opened himself up to me. He left nothing blocked.

'You do know, Ben, don't you?'

I had it all. 'Yes.'

'I thought you would. You see, Czar Mikhail, I'm going to take a little stroll up the beach, all by myself. And nobody is going to try to stop me. Isn't that right, Ben?'

'That's exactly right.'

He leaned over, kissed Arina on the cheek, and said simply, 'Arinoushka.'

He winked at me. That wink, the same as the one that Vince had given. 'I'm sorry, Ben. I had no choice.'

'I'm sorry, too. About Anya.'

'Yes. I've probably been kidding myself about that. The

298

odds are she's dead by now.'

Mike asked, 'Are you really going to let him walk away?'

I did not answer.

'Your Majesty, your jester asks permission to leave the royal presence.'

Mike looked right through him.

'But before I go, did I ever tell you the one about the manager of the tractor factory and the female reporter from *Izvestia*?'

'Several times.'

'How sad. When a jester starts to repeat himself, it's time to leave the stage. Get yourself somebody else, Mike. It's a young man's game.'

He turned, and walked away. By the time he reached the open beach he was jogging, and then he was running flat out. The darkness covered him.

Arina moved close to me. 'What do we do now?'

'Nothing. We wait.'

'Did you really think that it could have been me?'

'No, but it was the only way that I could open him up.'

It was only a small lie.

SEVENTY-THREE
Monday 3:58 AM

'What odds now?' said Engstrom.

Yadroshnikov did not answer. The two men trotted along the hard-packed sand at the water's edge. They ran silently, and the only sound of their passing was the *slap, slap, slap,* of the handset and transponder case as it swung against Engstrom's hip. They surveyed the beach as they ran, seeking out detail, but there was little to see. The beach was dark and empty, except for the stretch in front of the burning Bath House. They passed by the Bath House without pausing. According to the Case Executive, their target was long gone from there.

The handset crackled. 'Mobile One?'

'Mobile One,' said Engstrom.

'I have a target fix about one hundred yards ahead of you, moving rapidly.'

'Copy.'

'Pick it up,' said Yadroshnikov. He was panting. He was older than Engstrom, and not in the best of shape, but he pulled ahead by several yards. His anger gave him speed. Against all odds, his carefully crafted operation was in pieces, close to failure, and he knew that only quick and decisive action here on the beach could save it.

'What odds now?' Engstrom said it again.

Yadroshnikov grunted, but again he did not answer. Once the job was finished, he would have to settle with Engstrom. In the planning stage of the operation it had been assumed that there would be friction between Soviet and American intelligence officers working toward a common goal, and he considered it a tribute to his organizational skill that such friction had been kept to a minimum. He had expected crudeness from the Americans, and insensitivity, but he had not expected this blatant disrespect shown to a veteran officer, who was also in command. Yes, there was a settlement due once the world was restored to the *status quo ante,* and a man's enemies were once again clearly defined.

'Mobile One?'

'Mobile One,' said Engstrom, and Yadroshnikov noted with satisfaction that he, too, was short of breath.

'Target fix at fifty yards.'

'Copy.'

'Centre of the beach.'

'Copy.'

The two men angled across the beach, giving up the firm surface near the water's edge to slog through loose sand. Yadroshnikov felt the difference at once as his already weary legs turned numb with the effort. He forced himself to ignore his legs as he scanned the beach for a sign of the target. Fifty yards was not that far, even in darkness, and he should have been able to see . . .

'Mobile One, target stationary.'

'Say again.'

'Target stationary. No movement.'

Yadroshnikov felt a surge of elation. He forgot his irritation with Engstrom, and flashed him a grin. Both men slowed their pace to a walk, moving warily, weapons ready. Ten yards. Thirty. Fifty. They stopped.

There was nothing. The beach was empty for as far as they could see into the darkness.

Engstrom spoke softly into the microphone. 'Case, give me a fix.'

'You're on target, Mobile One. Dead on.'

'Can't be, there's nothing here. Nobody.'

'That's not what the grid says.'

Yadroshnikov moved close to Engstrom, and spoke into the microphone. 'Listen to me, you must be reading the grid wrong. I'm telling you that there is no one here.'

The Case Executive's voice was clipped and cool. 'Mobile One, I can only tell you what the grid tells me. The blip and the triangle coincide. I have you on an overlap with the target.'

'You've made some stupid mistake.'

'I don't make mistakes, Mobile One, and neither does the grid. You should know that. You designed it.'

'Impossible,' muttered Yadroshnikov. He handed the microphone back to Engstrom. Their faces were inches apart. 'People don't disappear like that. Into thin air.'

Engstrom said softly, 'What odds now, you red son of a bitch?'

Yuri rose up from the beach in a burst of sand that showered over them. He threw his arms around them both, and hugged them close. He had a grenade in each hand, and he popped the pins free as the two men struggled in his arms.

'Comrades,' he said joyfully, 'I've been waiting for you. Have you ever heard the one about the Leningrad lawyer who wanted to buy a car . . .'

The explosion was a white star in the night.

SEVENTY-FOUR
Monday 4:10 AM

The Case Executive did not hear the sound of the grenades exploding. She heard Yuri's final words over the open mike, and then her headset went dead. At the same time the blip on the grid and the triangle beside it both disappeared. She sat for a long while staring at the grid, then stripped off the head-phones. She folded her hands, and bowed her head over them. She was not praying. She had been on the job for twenty hours without a break, and the muscles in her neck were like aching bands of steel. She closed her eyes, pressed her palms together, and willed the ache to go away. She felt the pressure push up from her palms to her shoulders, and after a while she was able to raise her head without pain.

She looked again at the grid, half expecting a resurrection of the symbols there, but the board remained dark. Procedure now called for her to wait at least thirty minutes for com-munications to be restored by landline, but she knew that there would be no telephone call. She had heard Yuri's words, and she knew what they meant. The operation was over, a failure. Still, she was a product of her training, and she waited the thirty minutes. While she waited, she thought of what she was going to do next. She was thirty-eight years old, a major in the US Army, and her career was now over. That was the price of failure, and she accepted it. She was a patriot, not a mercenary, and she had gone into the operation con-vinced that the joint American–Soviet Star Wars Project meant disaster for her country, and that the best way to avoid that disaster was to destroy Mikhail Gorbachev. Now the operation was a failure, but she was still convinced that its objectives had been both honourable and desirable. The President himself, in another context, once had said that the only causes worth fighting for were lost causes, and she believed in that within limits.

She had no regrets, despite the price she would have to pay. In the world in which she lived, failure begat contempt, and there would be no mercy shown to those who had failed in a rogue operation. They would be hunted down, and eliminated. The Case Executive did not intend to wait for the sound of the hunter's horn. She had a bank account in a clean name that even Engstrom had not known about, and all the ID to go with it. She had a car that was registered in that same impeccable name, a packed bag, and a new life waiting. Dedicated to success, she had anticipated failure, and had prepared for it. She had no sympathy for those who had not.

At the end of the thirty-minute waiting period, she made two telephone calls, one to a number in Atlanta, and the other to a number in San Diego. In each case she said only one word before breaking the connection, thus fulfilling two long-standing obligations to old friends in the service. She had one further obligation to the operation, and she fulfilled that one by inserting a key in a slot below the grid, and turning it three times to the left. A light above the grid began to blink, indicating that the self-destruct system had been activated. She had fifteen minutes in which to get out. After that the Operations Room, as such, would no longer exist.

She took one final look around the room, slung her handbag over her shoulder, and went down the hall to Carlotta's room. She unlocked the door, and slipped in quietly. Carlotta was asleep on the cot, her face relaxed in repose. The Case Executive lowered herself gingerly to the edge of the cot, reluctant to disturb her. Despite that caution, Carlotta stirred in her sleep, and a lock of her hair fell over one eye. The Case Executive brushed it back gently. She sat and watched the sleeping woman. What she had to do next had not been covered in any of the many contingency plans, but her years of experience made it both obvious and necessary. She took her pistol from her bag, and let it rest on her knee. Carlotta stirred again, again that lock of hair fell forward, and again she brushed it back gently. She let her fingers rest on the woman's cheek. She shook her head, and put the pistol back in her bag. She touched Carlotta's shoulder.

Carlotta opened her eyes. They widened when they saw the Case Executive looking down at her. 'What is it?' she asked. 'What's happening?'

'Nothing is happening. Everything is all right. It's over.'

'Over? He's dead?'

'No, it didn't work out that way, but it doesn't matter now. It's still over.'

Carlotta's face showed her fear. She knew what failure meant to her. The Case Executive touched her cheek again, this time cupping it in her palm.

'Don't worry,' she said. 'Nothing is going to happen to you.'

'The Russian . . .?'

'He's dead. Engstrom, too. I told you, it's over.'

'And me?'

The Case Executive let her fingers drift down the side of Carlotta's neck to her shoulder, to her wrist, to her fingers. She laced those fingers with her own. 'That place that you were going to go to with Jake . . . do you still want to go there?'

'Jake is dead.'

'I know that. Do you want to go?'

'To Wyoming.' She said the words childlike. 'Outside Casper on Route Twenty-five, a roadside café we could run by ourselves. A new name and a new life.'

'That's it.' The Case Executive unlaced her fingers. She ran her hand lightly over Carlotta's breasts, then let it rest on her belly. She kneaded the flesh there gently. 'Well, do you?'

'With you?'

'With me.'

Carlotta smiled. She moved herself under the Case Executive's hand. It wasn't quite a wiggle. 'Oh, yes,' she said. 'Oh, yes.'

SEVENTY-FIVE
Monday 9:15 AM

We spent the rest of the dark hours huddled in the car, and when the sun came up we drove in to Manhattan. Arina sat in the front with me, and Mike rode in the back. It was a silent trip.

There was sadness in the front seat, some of it for Yuri, and some of it for ourselves. I had pointed a pistol at the woman I loved, my finger hard on the trigger. Would I have pulled it, or had it been only a ploy? I was not sure, I would never know, and despite what I had told her, Arina would never know, either. Yuri had saved us from finding out, but we would have to live with the unanswered question. The odour of oranges was faint on a faraway breeze.

There was sadness in the rear seat, too, but more than that, there was anger. The world that Mike lived in did not allow for divided loyalties. Someone was either for you, or against you; to be smothered in a bear hug of affection, or crushed in a bear hug of rage. The rage was on him now, the affection forgotten, and if he could have put back together the pieces of Yuri's torn body, it would only have been to tear them apart again.

We drove into Manhattan through the tunnel, and I stopped outside a coffee shop on Whitehall Street. Arina got us breakfast there, and we ate it parked near City Hall. It was the kind of autumn morning in New York that they use for making movies: crisp, and clear, and full of promise. The streets were crowded with men and women on their way to work, and the air had not yet been laced with the poisons of the day. Manhattan in the morning is an amiable fraud, still fresh from the night and apparently unspoiled. It doesn't last long. Well before noon the ugly old whore shows her face again, but for a

306

few hours on one of those brisk autumnal mornings, Manhattan makes all of those movies seem real.

I drove up First Avenue, and cruised past the United Nations. It looked as if every cop in New York was there. I had no plan for getting Mike inside, but I didn't need one. Sammy was standing at the gate with the uniformed security people, watching the traffic on the avenue flow by. I hailed him as I passed.

Sammy, over here.

Yeah, I see you. Hey, the car is filthy. What did you do, drive it through a sewer?

Sorry, Dad, I'll wash it on my next day off. Where do you want the delivery?

Hang a left on Forty-ninth, and wait for me there.

I double parked off the corner of Forty-ninth and First. Sammy came trotting down the street along with Islington and Bradley, and half a dozen bodies that looked like Secret Service. Bradley brushed by me, and got into the back of the car with Mike. Islington started throwing questions at me, but I ignored him.

Welcome home, said Sammy. *Who's in the car?*

The big man and Arina. Yuri . . .

We know about Yuri. His body was found, along with some others. Want to tell me about it?

Later. What about the troops?

Snake is okay. Vince is pretty banged up, but he's in stable condition. He hesitated. *Martha was in surgery for five hours. She's just hanging on.*

She'll make it.

Keep saying it.

I was aware that Islington was still throwing words at me, words that refused to register. *What's he saying?*

He's in charge now, his outfit will take it from here. They've made arrangements to move the man in quietly. The Soviet delegation is waiting there.

How come the Secret Service? Last night the word was to trust nobody.

It's over. The opposition had an Op Room set up in a warehouse in Brooklyn, and they blew it a couple of hours ago. Self-destruct, but enough was left to figure it out. It has to be over.

Could be just another move.

No, it's finished. He saw the look of reluctance on my face. *You don't want to let go, do you?*

It's got to be a habit, looking after him.

Break the habit. You're too old to raise hamsters.

I slid into the back seat of the car. Arina stared at me sadly from the front, a cat with the eyes of an owl. Bradley was talking to Mike in Russian. The President would be pleased to know that the General Secretary had survived his ordeal. The President was in transit from Washington, and would arrive shortly. The President would meet with the General Secretary for a few minutes before their joint appearance. The President would join the General Secretary for lunch, to be followed by a press conference and then . . .

Mike's eyes met mine. He said, 'Mister Bradley, perhaps it would be better if we continued this conversation inside. For the moment, would you leave us?'

Bradley didn't like it, but he climbed out and stood on the sidewalk. Mike said, 'Well, Ben?'

'Other people will be taking over now, people you can trust. I came to say goodbye.'

'I see. I'm glad you did. It was quite a night. After such an experience I should like to think of you as my friend.'

Friend? It was then that I felt that touch of affection for him, but it was an affection tempered by reality. Despite what we had been through together, there was no basis for friendship. As a dedicated Communist, he firmly believed that socialism was the future, and that the future was his. I did not believe that for a moment. With all the talk of *glasnost* and restructuring, he was still the leader of a repressive, totalitarian society, one I could never condone. To me, it was a society without a future, for if age did not wither it, then *glasnost* would. Friends, no, but still there was that touch of affection.

'Quite a night,' I repeated. 'One that I won't forget.'

'Nor will I. I am in your debt.'

'You said that once before, and I told you that we were even.'

'No, the debt is mine, but it's one I can never repay.'

'You might be able to.'

'Repay you? How?'

'When we were kids they used to tell us that you can't fight City Hall and you can't change the way the world works. But maybe you can. Change the world for me, Mike; you and the President. Maybe just a little, but change it.'

'You're asking a lot.'

'I know.'

'I'll try.'

I shook his hand. 'Goodbye, Mister General Secretary.'

'Not Mike any more? No, I suppose not. Goodbye, Mister Slade.'

I turned to face Arina. 'Are you coming with me?'

'I want to,' she said softly, 'but I'm afraid to. I'm not sure that I know you any more.'

'Do you trust me?'

'That's it. I can't be sure.'

'Do you love me?'

'Yes, but what good is love without the trust? You would have killed me if you had to.'

'No, you don't know that.'

'I don't know anything right now.'

Gorbachev said gruffly, 'Stop talking like a child. The man had a job to do, and he did it properly. The pistol was a sham, a device, and nothing more.'

'With all respect, I am not talking like a child. You were the one who gave the order. Kill them both, you said. Was that also a sham and a device?'

'It was. We had roles to play, and we played them.'

'I wish I could believe that.'

'I command that you do.'

'Command?'

'Listen, Arinoushka, I am older than you, and wiser than you, and I am also Czar of all the Russias, the last of the Romanoffs . . .' His voice broke, but he hung on. 'The last of the Romanoffs, and I will not have doubt and suspicion in my court. The man loves you. He would kill for you, and he would die for you, and there aren't many men like that. So, go with him. I command it, and you disobey me at your peril. You have permission to leave the imperial presence.' He flicked his fingers at her in a sign of dismissal. 'Go, for God's sake. I have enough to worry about without you.'

She sat very still for a space of heartbeats, then said quietly, 'Yes, Your Majesty.'

She stepped out of the car, and I joined her. She took my hand. I nodded to Sammy, and we walked away down Forty-ninth Street, away from the United Nations, and away from the night behind us.

'Where are we going?' she asked.

'Home.'

'Where is that?'

'I don't know.'

'Then we'll have to make one.'

'Yes, in an orange grove.'

'That sounds like fun,' she said, and it was.